Lynn,
May truth be ~
love never grow old!
Enjoy!
Rochelle Rawson

John,

May truth be with you.

You have free will.

Enjoy.

[signature]

Truth Trippers

Rochelle Ransom

The characters and events in this book are ficticious. Any similarity to real persons, living or dead, is coincidental and not intended by the author.

Copyright © 2020 by Rochelle Ransom. All Rights Reserved. No part of this book may be used or reproduced in any manner without written permission of the publisher.

pREADtend Publishing, LLC
Gloucester, MA 23062

Present Day

LIZZY

What do squeezy cheese and silly string have in common with the truth? Lodan and I had no idea until we packed our pantries, pilfered our savings, and snuck into the night seeking answers. Turns out they all have a "no return" policy. Once they're liberated, there's no going back. But I believe it helps to check the rearview and remember why we loaded our hearts and hope into a Honda that would never come home.

One

LIZZY

LAKETOWN, NY
OCTOBER 16, 2015

I knew Lodan was different the first time I saw him. I'd climbed out my window and onto the knotty bicep of an old tree I called Colonel Maple. Height is necessary when conducting a perspective check. As I hung in the breeze, my hair reaching for the ground, blood filling my brain, knees locked, arms spread, and eyes closed, I heard the sound of a mouse-sized motor. I opened my eyes to locate this prospective pillager. Through the window of the neighboring house a guy around my age who, based on his position, had to be sitting on the floor, held plastic controllers in each hand—one red and one blue. He had a blond brush cut, and from behind his glasses, his eyes and head tracked something moving around the room. I watched him, and what I assumed was the owner of the mouse motor I heard. As I watched, I saw his face slowly transform from serious to curious to triumphant. From my perspective his upside-down mouth slid from a relaxed straight line down to an inverted U. His goofy enthusiasm for his task at hand was contagious. I had a giant grin on my face, too. His smile made me smile. I hadn't had a reason since we'd moved here two days ago. In fact, I hadn't smiled in almost a week. I refused out of principle. My dad had once again transplanted us from one small town to another. Granted this time it wasn't entirely his choice, but still. I'm getting ahead of myself. The real point is Lodan made me smile when nothing and nobody else could.

"What are you doing?" I yelled.

"Testing," he responded without looking up.

"It looks like an A," I said.

"Not yet."

"Really? What would you do for an A? Cheer? Yell? Fist-pump the air?"

"What's a fist-pump?" He bent out of my view, then reappeared, still focused on his testing.

"You make a fist, shoot it up into the air above your head, then bring it back down. You know, like Tiger Woods."

"Oh." He moved out of my line of sight again so I pulled myself up into the tree. I wobbled slightly as my head adjusted to the new latitude. I closed my eyes for a beat, until I felt my equilibrium normalize. When I opened them I could see him bent over an elaborate track, making adjustments.

"What are you making?" I asked.

"A replica of Desperado. It's a roller coaster in Nevada."

"As in 'Desperado . . . why don't you come to your senses . . .'" I couldn't help but sing the chorus from the song my dad had played a gazillion times. And for the first time he looked up at me and I could see his eyes were a unique, almost translucent green.

"You know that song?" He looked perplexed.

"In all its uplifting glory." I locked my dangling legs at the ankles.

"I don't think the coaster is named after the song but it happens to unite two of my favorite things: The Eagles and an engineering marvel." He adjusted a few of his tracks.

"My dad loves The Eagles, too." I picked at a loose piece of bark.

"Has he ever seen them perform?" He placed a small car on the track.

"Once," I said and he snapped his head back up to meet my gaze, pushing his glasses into place with one finger between his eyes.

"Really? Where? When?" His face again transitioned from awe to smile. And again my face defied my mood.

"I don't know. You could ask him. He'll be home in a few hours probably."

"You're new here." He stated rather than asked.

"Yes. Two-day resident."

"I'm Lodan."

"Hmm. Lodan, huh?"

"Yes."

"Maybe."

"Maybe what?"

"Can you stand closer to your window so I can see you better?" I asked.

"Why?"

"To see if you really are a Lodan."

He moved to the window, lifted the screen, ducked under it, placed his hands on the sill, and leaned out a little. His brows formed a deep V behind his glasses.

"Maybe Sebastian would be better?" I ran my eyes from his broad shoulders down his skinny arms and torso.

"Sebastian?" he echoed.

"No. Bartholomew." But as soon as I heard it out loud I knew it still wasn't right. "Zachariah?" I tilted my head, studied his hands. Long, slim fingers. With the exception of his shoulders, he had long and slim everything, even his nose.

"Alessandro?"

He cocked his head at me, but remained silent as I ran through the possibilities. Nothing fit. I sighed.

"Nope. You're lucky. Your mom got it right." I swatted away a curious fly. "Lodan it is."

"Yes, like I said. Lodan." He single-finger pushed his glasses tight to his face again.

"Yeah, well, you'd be surprised how rare it is to actually receive the right name at birth. Is Lodan your real name?"

"As far as I know."

"Like the one on your birth certificate? Or is it like a middle name they use as your first?"

"I don't know. Never checked."

"Hmm. Take me, for instance. My mom and dad fought over my name. She wanted to name me Paisley. He wanted to name me Henley after—"

"Don Henley."

"Exactly. When they couldn't agree, my mom told the nurse to pick."

"Bold. And? Did she get it right?"

"Do I look like a Lois?"

I watched his face as he looked me over, half expecting him to blush or at least squirm a little. His scientific disinterest brought unexpected heat to my cheeks and I shifted my gaze to the frayed edge of my cut-offs.

"I can't be sure. I've never met you before and I've never met a Lois so I don't really have any baseline to make the call."

"Fair enough. I've never met a Lois either, but I am positive I am not her."

"So, who are you then?"

"Lizzy. Lizzy Lane." I resisted the urge to extend a hand given the geographic impossibility of him accepting it.

"Like short for Elizabeth?" Lodan's thumbs methodically tapped the air above his remotes, itching for their return to testing.

"No, like just Lizzy."

"Oh." He shrugged and returned to his track. I watched for a bit, debating whether I should torture myself with another social media check, when an unusual sheep-like laugh interrupted my pity party.

"I just got it! No wonder you go by Lizzy," Lodan yelled.

"What?"

"Your parents named you Lois Lane?" His eyes tracked the coaster again.

"Yeah, so?"

"You don't know who she is?"

"No?"

He appeared at the window again. "She's Superman's girlfriend. You've never read any Superman stuff?"

"No, I guess I haven't."

"Lois Lane." He shook his head. "Vintage." And then he disappeared again. I decided to Google "Lois Lane" or maybe that's the lie I told myself as I climbed back through my window and grabbed my phone.

LODAN

LAKETOWN, NY
OCTOBER 16, 2015

I didn't really think much about Lizzy after our first meeting, other than to tell my mom Lois Lane had moved in next door. Of course, she laughed, too. She'd taken me to every Superman movie I'd seen. Most of my attention at the time was focused on the countdown.

"Fifty-two more days, Mom." I stuck a grape tomato in my mouth.

"Yes, you told me this morning." I watched as she squished her fork down onto her mashed potato volcano, forcing the butter lava to ooze in all directions.

"Did you find my birth certificate yet?" I grabbed the milk and poured another glass.

"I haven't had a chance to look. Sorry."

"And you're sure it didn't burn in the fire, too. Right?"

"No, I'm not sure. I said I *hope* it didn't burn in the fire. I can't remember."

"I can look if you don't have time."

"I don't even know where to tell you to start." She stood up to get the salt off the counter. "So you met the new neighbors?"

"Sort of." I couldn't figure out why she always changed the subject when I brought up getting my driver's license. She knew I'd been saving for a car since I turned ten. I watched her add even more salt to her potatoes. I thought they were already too salty.

"And? Is there a Clark Kent living with this Lois Lane?" She tried to catch my eye but I refused to let her off that easily.

"Just her dad. I don't know his name." I shrugged.

"Look, I'm sorry about the birth certificate. I swear I will look this weekend, okay?"

"That's what you said last week."

"I know but then Violet got sick and I had to cover her shifts. She came back today, so it shouldn't be a problem. Okay?" She reached out and put her hand on my arm.

"Okay," I agreed.

"So is Lois Lane still in school?"

"Probably. She looks around my age." I scooped some potatoes into my mouth.

"Have you seen her before—on the bus?"

I shrugged. "Not sure. This is day two for her. Her dad's a big Eagles fan. He saw them live."

"That's cool. What brought them to Laketown?"

"Who knows?" I finished the last of my meatloaf and leaned back in my chair.

"Four on the floor, please, Lodan."

I sighed and complied.

"How is your coaster coming?"

"Fine." I didn't feel like talking to her anymore. That happened more frequently as of late.

"Can I be excused?" I stood.

My mom dropped her fork. "I'm not even halfway done."

"Sorry. I guess I was hungry."

Her shoulders fell. "It's fine." She studied the butter forming a lava moat around her meatloaf.

I felt a flash of guilt. "I'll come back and help clean up." I rinsed my dishes, put them in the dishwasher, and ran up to my room.

I gingerly crossed my bedroom, strategically stepping where my long feet wouldn't cause a service disruption in any of the tracks traversing my floor. I'd just sat down at my desk and pulled up Google when I heard my name.

"Looodan!" The voice sang my name like my mother used to when I'd wander off as a child. I stepped over a portion of Desperado and looked out my open window.

"Hey." Lizzy stood below my window, squinting into the setting sun.

"Hey," I responded.

"You wanna see something cool?"

I glanced back at my computer screen. I wanted to research how to get a copy of my birth certificate. "What is it?"

"You have to come see for yourself."

I noticed Lizzy had on large forest-green rubber boots that swallowed her feet and legs, ending an inch below where her cut-off denim shorts began. Over that she wore a men's flannel shirt that covered her from neck to thigh. The image conjured a memory of my mom's furious face when she'd caught me using her rain boots for train tunnels. I'd severed the foot from the leg section.

"Come on. Hurry down here!" Lizzy headed toward my front door.

"Wait there!" I yelled louder than I meant, before I hopscotched through my track minefield, took the stairs three at a time, and opened and closed the door behind me.

Lizzy didn't look any less like a child playing dress-up when I stood looking down at her for the first time on the same level. She could have stood comfortably under my armpit.

"You stand pretty high off the ground for a guy whose name begins with 'Lo.'" She looked up at me. She had freckles.

"And you appear to have trouble selecting properly sized attire. How old did you say you are?"

Lizzy smiled and I noticed one front tooth protruded a hint past its counterparts like a standout book on a library shelf. "I didn't, but I'm seventeen. You?"

"Sixteen in December," I said.

"Is it always this warm here in October?" She turned and headed toward the patch of woods behind our houses. She took extra-large and wide steps to accommodate the boots.

"It depends. But don't get used to it. They are predicting the first freeze by the end of next week."

I followed her into the woods, the smell of moss and pine reminding me of afternoons spent collecting sticks and tiny branches to add to my earliest versions of my miniature towns. She moved slowly, her boots making an echo unique to small feet burdened by oversized rubber boots. The frogs and crickets insistently announced dusk.

We walked about a quarter of a mile before she stopped by a big fallen tree. She squatted down and pointed.

"Look," she whispered.

I followed her finger to a burrow, sheltered within the crook of the fallen tree's trunk. A large limb reached skyward at an angle to form a protective roof. A tear-shaped patch of grey and pink was nestled within a collection of leaves, paper scraps, and grass.

"Lodan, meet Kono. Kono, this is Lodan."

"Kono?" I asked.

"Yes. It's a Mandinka name that means abandoned." Lizzy took a step closer.

"Mouse?" I asked.

"Rabbit," she said.

"Strange that there's only one." I studied the body for signs of movement.

"It's been abandoned," Lizzy whispered.

"Are you sure it's still alive?"

Lizzy punched my arm. "It has to be."

"Are you sure its mom isn't here somewhere? Or more babies?" I scanned the length of the big dead tree and the surrounding area.

"See those little crossed sticks next to it?"

"Yes." I easily made out the mini cross.

"I put them there this morning to see if the mom would be back. They haven't moved."

"Have you touched it?" I asked.

"Not yet. I didn't want the mom to reject it because of my scent."

"Maybe she left because it's sick. It's nature's way," I said softly.

"It's not my way," Lizzy said. "I'm going to take care of Kono until he's strong enough to live free." She reached for the bunny.

I put my hand on her arm. "Wait. Don't touch it."

She pulled her arm back and looked up at me.

"Just in case." I said. "I'll be right back. But don't touch it, Okay?"

"What are you going to get?" she asked.

"Gloves, for one. Hold on."

I retraced our steps, then jogged to our garage. I found a pair of gardening gloves my mom used to wear before I started taking care of the lawn. I shoved them in the back pocket of my jeans. I grabbed a snow shovel, rescued a slightly cracked plastic tub from the recycling barrel, and carried them back to Lizzy.

"A shovel?" she asked.

"Just watch." I pushed the shovel into the soft ground in front of the nest and made a shallow scoop until the nest, baby rabbit, and a bit of the ground beneath rested on the shovel. Lizzy watched in silence, her hands clasped tightly in front of her mouth as I carefully transferred the bundle from the shovel to the bottom of the clear bin. Then we both knelt over it to look for signs of life.

"Here." I handed her the gloves.

Lizzy slipped them on, reached in, and gently touched its back with a gloved finger. The little bundle moved, but only slightly. I sighed with relief.

"I knew you were a fighter, Kono," Lizzy whispered. We headed out of the woods before we were in complete darkness. Lizzy carried the bin and I carried the shovel.

"We need to look up what to feed it," I said.

"Already did. The problem is the stuff won't arrive until tomorrow. I paid extra for overnight delivery, but when does UPS or FedEx deliver here?"

"Usually not until the afternoon, I think. We don't order much online."

"Me neither. I snuck my dad's emergency credit card and used it on Amazon."

"How much was it?"

"Well, if I got everything they suggested it would have been over fifty dollars. My dad would have freaked. So hopefully it will be okay if I only use Kitten Milk Replacement Powder. It was only fifteen dollars with shipping and a special feeding kit."

"Fifteen should be forgivable," I said.

"And impending death is an emergency." She followed me into my garage still carrying the bin.

"But what and how did you plan to feed it until then?" I asked, returning the shovel to its home.

"I'm open to ideas. Do you know a vet?" she asked.

"Sort of," I admitted.

"Maybe the vet could do something until we get the stuff." Lizzy set the bin on the work shelf in our garage.

"But that could be a lot more than fifteen bucks."

"Couldn't your friend do you a favor?" When Lizzy looked up at me with her vulnerable round blue eyes, I felt compelled to help her.

"He's not exactly my friend. He has a thing for my mom." I shifted back and forth on my feet.

"Even better." Lizzy's smile filled her face. "We can have your mom ask him!" And without an invitation she headed toward the door into the house.

"Wait!" I grabbed her arm again.

"What?" Lizzy pulled off the gloves.

"It's just that my mom prefers to avoid him," I explained.

"But surely if it's an emergency." Lizzy tossed the gloves on the counter and again disarmed me with the vulnerable toddler stare.

"Okay, we can see," I agreed and opened the door for her. She followed me to the kitchen where we found my mom washing dishes.

"Hi, Mrs. . . . oh, I never got your last name." She looked at me.

"Dawson." My mom turned off the water and grabbed a towel. "But you can call me Heather." She extended her hand.

"Heather, hmm." Lizzy tilted her head while she shook my mom's hand. "Maybe . . ."

I cleared my throat. "This is Lizzy. She found an abandoned baby rabbit and was hoping we knew a vet that could help."

"Oh, poor thing." I watched as my mom's thought processes played across her face. Her empathy slipping to the realization of what we were asking. "Oh, you mean Dr. Payne."

"The vet's name is Dr. Payne?" Lizzy looked horrified.

"I know. It threw us at first, too. But he saved a wild cat I accidently hit a few months ago." My mom shot me a loaded look. I knew she didn't want to ask for his help again after thwarting his advances.

"So he is good with saving wild animals." Lizzy gave my mom full-force vulnerable toddler stare.

My mom bit her upper lip. She relented. "He gave me his personal cell. It would be in my purse if I didn't toss it." She headed to the entryway to search.

"Dr. Payne? And Lodan Dawson?" Lizzy whispered. "Was Dawson your dad's last name or your mom's maiden name?"

"Maiden name, I guess. Why?" I heard my mom rummaging through her large, messy purse. She shoved everything into her purse from loose change and receipts to abandoned clothing articles. Annually, on her birthday, she'd purchase a new one, clean out the old, and toss it. She said it was her way of reflecting on the past year: receipts, movie ticket stubs, grocery lists, all marking moments lived.

"Don't you agree?" Lizzy asked.

"With what?" I must have missed what she said.

"Your name. Dawson doesn't work well with Lodan." She had taken over for my mom, her hands buried in soapy water, scrubbing the potato pot; the flannel sleeves rolled to her elbows, creating a ridiculously large cuff.

"Got it!" my mother yelled triumphantly. I couldn't believe Lizzy had convinced her to contact Dr. Payne so easily. She should ask her for my birth certificate.

My mom called, and in spite of it being a Friday night, Dr. Payne agreed to meet us at his office in an hour to see what he could do. We finished cleaning the kitchen, my mother and Lizzy comfortably comparing animal rescue stories like they'd known one another forever. I hadn't seen my mom smile and laugh like that in a while.

Dr. Payne met us at his office. He had to give Kono an insanely small IV to get him rehydrated. He said it would be touch and go for a couple days and promised he'd take care of him until our food came in. He also gave us probiotics that we'd eventually need to give him as well.

He graciously offered his services free of charge and invited all of us to go kayaking at his house on the lake the following day. Before my mom could protest, Lizzy accepted for the group.

When we got back in the car I expected my mom to admit she had no intention of kayaking, but Lizzy dominated the conversation.

"Jason Payne. I like him and turns out his name is perfect. Jason means healing. So he is healing pain. Ha. I dated a Jason in Arizona. Turns out he should have been Damien or Chucky."

"He didn't hurt you?" my mom asked.

Lizzy shrugged. "We moved straight outta there. It was fine." She cleared her throat. "So, Jason Payne. Why don't you like him, Mrs. Dawson?"

My mom blushed. "Lodan and I make a pretty good team. We've never needed anyone else." She reached over and patted my leg.

"Yeah, my dad's pretty okay, too, but he still has girlfriends. I think you should give Jason a try. He's kinda cute in a Charlie Brown sort of way."

I pictured Dr. Payne's big, round, bald head and large, easy smile. He seemed fit for his age, which I guessed to be in his forties but other than that he did resemble Charlie Brown.

"Are we really going to kayak with him tomorrow?" I looked at my mom's profile as she drove.

"Well, we can hardly not show now that he has Kono for collateral." My mom shrugged. I silently marveled at the power of Lizzy. In a matter of hours, she had distracted me from my license mission, rescued Kono, helped clean our kitchen, and convinced my mom (who as far as I can tell has not been on a single date since my birth), to spend the day with a potential suitor. Lois Lane she was not, but a case could be made for Diana Prince. (You may want to Google that if you're not familiar.)

#

LODAN

LAKETOWN, NY
OCTOBER 17, 2015

Saturday morning began foggy and chilly. But by the time the three of us had arrived at Dr. Payne's cottage, the sun had reclaimed the sky. Dr. Payne had taken Kono home with him and showed us that he'd successfully survived the night. He'd transferred him into a more appropriate aquarium-style container with a small heat source. After Lizzy confirmed Kono's wellness, we left him to sleep in Dr. Payne's mudroom.

"Wow!" Lizzy marveled. "This is by far the most beautiful dart landing my dad has pegged. Look at all those leaf colors and then their reflection in the lake. It's like a cornucopia of color. That's what they should call this. Lake Cornucopia."

"Your dad decides where to move by throwing a dart?" I asked.

"And I can assure you, his aim has been erratic and predominantly poor." Lizzy tilted her head and continued to focus on the view. We were standing on Dr. Payne's dock as he found each of us an appropriately sized life vest.

"Why do you have so many sizes?" Lizzy finally turned back to the group. "Do you have kids?"

"Two nieces and a nephew. They're all grown now, but my sister used to come spend a few weeks with me in the summer. Sometimes they still do, but it's less of a priority now that the kids are spread out. My sister spends her holidays visiting the kids." Dr. Payne put the first two-person kayak in the water.

"You two want to get in first? Then I can help your mother."

"Sure!" Lizzy carefully climbed into the backseat while Dr. Payne held it steady. I climbed into the front seat where there was more room for my legs. As soon as we were settled he gave us a shove, sending us adrift. I caught sight of my mom's panicked face at the realization that we'd abandoned her with the doctor.

"Hey, once we get used to this, we should race!" Lizzy yelled back to them.

The doctor tipped his head back and laughed. "Sure!" He had a kind, full-bodied laugh. The type of laugh I imagined sounded fatherly. Though who was I to judge?

My mom and I weren't very sporty. She still ran a few mornings a week, but I'd never been much of an athlete. However, kayaking made sense to me; it applied Newton's third law. Lizzy and I manually made the oars our propellers. As we pushed the water with our oars, we sliced across the water's surface. We fell into a comfortable quiet rhythm, only the paddles' displacement of water making a sound. Breathing the fresh autumn air, I took in the varied size, shape, and color of the cottages lining the lake. This perspective offered a stark contrast to the quieter, lifeless, even neglected sides of the houses I usually passed on the road. The lakeside revealed a picturesque, active life: large picture windows, expansive decks and docks for entertaining friends and maximizing the view. Collections of motorized and man-powered water toys all presented a more appealing reflection of the owners' affection toward their homes. We passed children jumping in leaves, men fishing, families sharing breakfast, girls basking in the unseasonably warm sun, and a few guys I recognized from school, Jet Skiing.

"You guys sure you've never done this before?" Dr. Payne and my mom glided up next to us. "You're doing really well."

"Thanks," we both said. I stole a glance and caught my mom smiling. We all rested our paddles on the kayaks and floated side by side.

"I thought we'd follow the perimeter to Minnie's and then stop for lunch if it works for you guys?" Dr. Payne pointed across at the popular lakeside beer and burger spot.

"Then we can race back to your dock," Lizzy suggested.

Dr. Payne laughed. "Yes, then we can race back."

We put our paddles back in the water and began again. Lizzy and I paddled in a comfortable silence. I guess we both got lost in our own thoughts and the hypnotizing rhythm of the paddles. My mother and Dr. Payne fell behind and we pulled up to Minnie's before they'd rounded the final corner. The lakeside shack's exterior sported layers of brightly colored paint from years of seasonal repainting. Inside, a bar surrounded the small kitchen area. A flat top grill and a fryer monopolized the far wall. The two cooks had only a small counter space behind them for food prep and plating. The wooden structure had three large openings to enable the bar patrons to enjoy the lake view and breeze as they consumed their food and drink.

"Now to get out without falling in." Lizzy held tight to the side of one of the boat slips. "Do you think I should get out first or you?" She set her paddle on the dock with her free hand.

"Why don't you get out while I hold it and then you can—" I started to say.

"Here, take my hand." Ryan Braun stood above us on the dock, his tight T-shirt accentuating his muscled, tan torso. Sunglasses hid his eyes as he held his hand out toward Lizzy.

"Dawson, hold it steady for her."

I did as he asked, a little surprised he knew my name. I mean we'd been in the same class since kindergarten, but he rarely talked to me.

He helped Lizzy onto the dock, then turned to me.

"Here, I got it if you want to hop out." He squatted to hold the kayak while I climbed onto the dock then bent to haul it out of the water. Lizzy grabbed the other end to help before I even registered what they were doing. I felt myself flush that a girl had helped before I did.

"Thanks," Lizzy and I said in unison, then shared a smile.

"Ryan Braun." He stuck out his hand.

Lizzy shook it. "Lizzy Lane. And it appears your last name is quite fitting, but I'll have to see about the Ryan part." She patted him on the bare chest and I almost laughed out loud at Ryan's puzzled expression.

"She has a thing for nomenclature," I explained, but Ryan's brow furrowed deeper in response.

"I haven't seen you around before, Lizzy. Are you like Lodan's cousin or something?"

"More like secret lover," Lizzy whispered, lifting her eyebrows suggestively at Ryan. Both our jaws dropped and Ryan's bulging eyes gave me a once-over, probably trying to access if my body were capable of this feat.

"I'm just messing." Lizzy laughed, playfully pulling me to her in a side-hug. "We're friends. I only moved here three days ago with my dad."

Ryan nodded; relief flooded his face as if things were right with the world again.

"Hey, wanna give your mom a hand?" We all turned toward Dr. Payne's voice as he and my mom slid up to a different slip farther down the dock.

"Sure." I ran over to help, leaving Lizzy with Ryan.

***

My mom ran into one of her nurse friends from work so the three adults ate together at one table while Ryan joined Lizzy and me at another. I couldn't help but wonder at the fact that Ryan, who had never uttered more than a full sentence to me before now, was sharing a plate of nachos with us. Not to mention I'd never seen him without his posse.

"Are you going to school at Laketown High or one of the private schools?" Ryan asked Lizzy as he popped a cheesy, jalapeño'd chip in his mouth.

"Oh, I homeschool. It's this special program we found for families who travel with their kids. It makes it easier for my dad to drag me around the country when he tires of his latest hometown."

"Oh, that's cool. So do you get to sleep in every day and watch TV and stuff?"

Lizzy twisted her lips to the side and tilted her head, "I guess I could, but I like to get up with my dad for breakfast because that's when we catch up. And we don't own a TV anymore; a few towns ago my dad dated this woman who was really into kickboxing. One morning she smashed her foot into our TV while doing one of those fitness DVDs. She felt awful about it, but we decided we didn't really need one. One less utility to turn off and on when we move." She shrugged and reached for a chip.

"That must suck having to move all the time." Ryan leaned back in his chair.

Lizzy shrugged. "There are pros and cons."

"What's good about it?" Ryan asked.

"I get to meet new people. If I piss someone off, chances are I won't have to avoid them for long. Different places give me different perspectives on the same things. Like if you hang from a tree in Colorado, it looks, smells, and even feels way different than hanging from a tree here."

Ryan furrowed his brows again, clearly not getting her point. An awkward silence followed until I sucked in the last bit of my pop, making that loud, empty sucking sound.

"Do you play any sports?" Ryan tipped his chair back, moving him closer to Lizzy.

"I've taken gymnastics a few places, played half a season of soccer in fourth grade, did the backstroke for a swim team one summer in Arizona, and subjected myself to a season of football cheerleading in eighth grade. My neighbor's crush played on a club team and of all our strategies to win his affection, it had the best shot at a favorable outcome."

"And, did it work? Did she get his attention?" Ryan asked.

"Yes and no. The second game in, he slammed into our crowd-inciting pyramid, while receiving a pass. He broke her arm in two places with his helmet."

"Ouch." Ryan rubbed at his bicep. "Surely he took her out to apologize if nothing else."

"Nope. Turned out he already had a girlfriend. She was the team kicker. All Jenny got were two pins in her arm and her crush's black Sharpie apology on her cast."

"What a bummer," Ryan said. He tried to pay for our meals, but Dr. Payne had already settled our tab. Ryan's family owned a lot of stuff in our town. He'd been born with the proverbial silver spoon in his mouth. He didn't run around bragging about it. It was one of those small-town facts like Dr. Hart's husband had been to prison, don't stand downwind of Hettie the can collector, and never order the popcorn at the Little League concessions if Jared Pimpkin is working because he has horrible spring allergies and refuses to cover his sneezes.

"So what about you, Lizzy? Do you have a boyfriend?" Ryan asked.

Lizzy squinted into the sun behind Ryan. "That, Von, is an excellent question."

Again, Ryan furrowed his brow and tilted his head in confusion. "Ryan. I'm Ryan."

"I know that's what your parents named you, but after talking to you, I think they were wrong. I think you're a Von. And I hope you don't mind if I call you that." Lizzy stared him straight in the eyes, awaiting his response.

Ryan pondered her question a moment, then glanced at me. I gave him no help. He shrugged. "I guess."

"Great. So, as I was saying, excellent question. I don't usually allow myself to get too attached to guys I'm attracted to, because it's emotionally draining to say goodbye. However, we stayed a little longer in New Mexico, thirteen days short of a year, and I fell in love with Mateo."

"But that's hundreds of miles away. You aren't going to stay together, are you?" Ryan looked incredulous.

"Actually it's one thousand, nine hundred, and forty-seven miles away. And why wouldn't I stay with the man I love simply because we are separated geographically?" Lizzy shot him a dirty look.

Ryan didn't have a good answer for that and I wasn't about to say anything to her scowling face.

"I mean there are cell phones and Skype and we even agreed to write snail mail letters."

"Sorry, I didn't mean anything by it," Ryan said. "I'm sure if you talk all the time it'll be fine."

Lizzy bit her upper lip, nodded, and then said, "No, you might be right."

Ryan and I shared an *are all girls this insane* look and then looked back at her.

"You see, the truth is, I haven't heard from him since we got here. We exchanged a few texts during the drive here. Then nothing. I've tried texting. He's never set up his voice mail so I can't leave one. He's gone silent."

Ryan and I shifted in our seats. Lizzy rested her chin in her hand. I didn't like to see her cheerful face distressed. She didn't look like Lizzy without a smile on her face or the sparkly light in her eyes.

"Maybe he's been sick," Ryan suggested and I nodded.

"Maybe." She didn't look convinced.

"Or maybe something bad happened to someone in his family and he had to travel to a funeral or something," I offered.

"Where there's no WiFi or cell service?" She cast her eyes sideways at me and raised one corner of her mouth in a doubtful grimace.

"It's only been three days. Maybe he lost or broke his phone or his parents cut him off as punishment for something." Ryan sat back in his seat, smugly smiling at his own brilliance.

Lizzy perked up a little at this suggestion and I wished I'd thought of a reason that gave her hope.

Then just as quickly her face fell. "Two days ago he deleted all of his social media accounts, too. That's kinda strange."

"Actually, that could support Ryan's theory of parental intervention. Maybe he got cut off digitally for some reason. Are his parents strict?" I asked.

Lizzy twisted her mouth to the right as she pondered my suggestion. "His dad is."

"Well, there you go." Ryan held up his hands as if to say *case closed*.

"I mean we spent like every waking second together the last nine and a half months, he wouldn't just forget I exist, right?"

"No way," Ryan said and I shook my head. Lizzy wasn't the kind of person you forgot in three days.

"Hey Ryan," Olivia Miles yelled from her parents' pontoon boat as her dad tied them to the dock. She and a few other members of Ryan's usual posse stepped off the boat and headed toward us just as my mom appeared at our table.

"Ready to race?" my mom asked, surprising me. I narrowed my eyes at her. Her flushed face and shiny eyes caught me off guard. I looked back at their table and saw they'd all had a few beers with their lunch. My mom rarely drank. This explained her altered state.

"Absolutely!" Lizzy stood, her usual smile betraying the sadness we'd seen moments before.

Ryan and I stood as well. Dr. Payne was down by the dock putting our kayak back in the water.

"Thanks for lunch, Mrs. Dawson. I didn't know you were dating Dr. Payne. That's cool." Ryan didn't wait for a response. My mom stood, her mouth ajar. Ryan turned quickly to Lizzy. "Nice to meet you, Lizzy. If that boyfriend doesn't come to his senses, we should hang out." He headed to meet his crew but did throw me a "See ya, Dawson," over his shoulder.

As we loaded into our kayaks I overheard Olivia ask Ryan about Lizzy. He called her "a cool new chick." Olivia squished up her face, clearly not happy with his answer.

The race back was not much of a contest. Lizzy set the pace and I did not want to disappoint her. We smoked them, getting back to Dr. Payne's dock at least five minutes before them.

We waited, perched on the edge of his dock, my toes and her feet in the water, watching their progress. Lizzy's unusual silence prompted me to break my own.

"Do you think he'll let you take Kono home, today?"

"Me? Don't you mean us? You make up half her parent base now. Don't go abandoning her like her mother." I turned to find her looking at me with a teasing smile. She nudged my shoulder with hers. "I'm only half joking. But I couldn't have saved him without your help so I do think we should consider co-parenting him." And when Lizzy turned her full smile on me, I looked straight into her hypnotic, calming eyes. It dawned on me I'd never paid much attention to people's eye color before. Hers were translucent: barely blue and I also realized that when she looked at me like that, she could probably talk me into most anything.

Four

LIZZY

LAKETOWN, NY
OCTOBER 18, 2015

I watched as my alarm clock changed from 3:18 to 3:19. I'd never had trouble sleeping before this move. I felt certain I must have missed something Mateo said or something I did that could explain his silence. He still had not responded to any of my attempts to reach him. I didn't feel like I could call his mom and wasn't sure if his dad was still deployed or not. Sebby, Mateo's brother, was too young to have his own phone. I cursed myself for my systematic deletion protocol. During the drive between moves I made a practice of deleting all contacts from the town we'd left. I should have kept Fawn's or Raj's contacts. I'd tried to get Fawn to re-follow me on social media but she hadn't responded either. Also my fault. We'd had a falling out about my leaving. She couldn't understand why I would ever delete contacts. I found it helped me to move on and prepare for the next town. I always warned people ahead of time. Often they got angry or continued to try and reach me. But I'd learned at a young age that once I moved away, there wasn't much point to keeping contact because chances were I'd never see those people again. When people don't see you on a regular basis, they stop thinking about you as often. Without the daily contact, I'd feel the distance grow between us. Eventually, the other people stopped returning my texts or calls or responding on social media. It never worked out. To protect myself from the repetitive pain of losing friends, I let them know up front that our friendship could only last as long as I lived in the same place they did. Most people didn't get it until I left. I believe there is a time and place in our lives for everyone. I've helped as many people and animals as I could while present, but then our time and mission had ended and I moved on to whatever was next. Of course, with Mateo I broke all my rules.

Five

LIZZY

TRUTH OR CONSEQUENCES, NM
OCTOBER 11, 2014

I must have finally fallen asleep because my alarm woke me up, a harsh reminder that I had SAT testing that morning. Coffee and the desire to make my dad proud fueled me through the test. I knew he'd scored close to perfect, providing me a motivating challenge.

After the test, I'd wandered out to the playground behind the elementary school where I'd taken the exam. Due to a defunct air conditioner, the test had been held in the elementary gymnasium instead of the high school. My dad wouldn't be by to grab me for another half hour, but I didn't mind. I leaned back against the heat of the slide, enjoying the sensation. After a morning deciphering analogies and balancing equations in the overchilled tundra of a gym, the hot sun on my bare arms and legs felt like heaven. In fact, I'd closed my eyes so I could turn my face directly in its burning path.

"Excuse me, miss, but Aspire needs the slide."

I sat up and turned to look at a young boy with a big mop of curly hair, pale brown eyes, and a dirt-smeared face and shirt, holding a brown and gray turtle the size of a cereal bowl. His green shirt had a cartoon illustration of a turtle shell wrapped in a brown belt with the initials for the Teenage Mutant Ninja Turtles on it. I heard a car door close and looked up to see a small line of cars picking up kids presumably after a camp or activity at the school.

"Hello?" The boy stood waiting for me to move, a few steps from the top so that his arms were stretched flat against the top of the slide, holding the turtle at the peak of its impending ride.

"Are you sure that's a good idea?"

The boy furrowed his brow and shrugged his shoulders. "I do it all the time. It's fine. They always stop at the end. Never had one fall off."

"Hmm, well, I think I'll stand here at the end, just in case." I cleared the way for Aspire, but stayed within catching distance.

The boy shook his head and released the turtle. We both watched as it slid down the slide, head buried deep inside his protective shell, and I imagined its most memorable days in the desert flashing before its eyes. As predicted, the turtle slowed to a halt an inch from the slide's edge.

"Sebby!" We both looked around to find who was yelling. "Sebastian!" This time a hint of annoyance slipped into the yell.

"By the slide." The boy waved his hand and I followed his gaze to the edge of the parking lot where a tall guy with dark hair stood by a well-worn silver pickup truck. When he caught sight of Sebby, he closed the door to the truck and headed in our direction.

"Did you like that, Aspire?" Sebby held the turtle shell up to his eyes, peering into the head hole like a pair of binoculars. My phone rang and I looked at the screen. My dad.

"Hey," I answered and watched the silver truck guy approach us with purpose. He had a military cut, stood well over six feet, and looked like he probably knew his way around a weight room. I listened as my dad explained he'd be another half hour, forty-five minutes. I assured him I'd be fine and we disconnected.

"Your shoe's untied, Seb." Silver truck guy looked young for a father.

"Can you hold Aspire?" Sebby held the turtle out to silver truck guy.

He held his hands up and took a step back. "I'm not touching that bacteria-carrying hermit helmet."

I laughed out loud that this tank of a guy backed down from a turtle.

"I can hold him." I reached out for the turtle. They both turned and looked me up and down. Sebby twisted his lips to the side, sighed, and placed him gently in my hands. He bent to tie his sneaker.

"Aren't you a little big for the playground?" Silver truck guy cocked an eyebrow at me.

"I'm a sucker for a warm slide." I held my hand over my eyes to block the sun.

"You take the SATs this morning?" He nodded toward my backpack on the ground beside the slide.

"Yeah, which is why I needed the warm slide. I think the AC here may have overcompensated for its high school cousin's incompetence."

"I didn't notice."

"Oh, so you were in there, too?" *Either he was a very young dad or a much older brother.*

"'Fraid so. Where d'you go to school?" he asked.

"Homeschool." The turtle poked its nose out then quickly returned to safety.

"Oh, wow. I met another homeschool kid last winter. He and his parents were RVing across the country, hitting every state. He said they wanted to show him what he was learning firsthand."

"Yeah, I've met a few kids like that."

"I can take him back now." Sebby held out his hands and I gently returned Mr. Aspire.

"Do I have time to take him on the spinny thing?" Sebby asked.

"Yeah, but I gotta get back to work and help Mom so only a few minutes." We both watched as he carried the turtle over to the mini metal merry-go-round and placed him far from the edge.

"That can't be good for the turtle," I said.

"Most kids want a dog or a cat, but Sebby has always played with the desert turtles." He turned to look me in the face and I noticed his eyes were the color of beach sand.

"He's your . . ." I purposely let him fill in the blank.

"Brother. My parents had me really young. By the time they were ready to try again, it took a while.

"Are you a senior at the high school here?"

"Yes. What about you? RVing through or live nearby?"

"Just moved here about a week ago."

"Oh, well, welcome."

"So where do you work?"

"For my family. We sell, rent, and fix RVs, kayaks, and boats."

"What do you do there?" My stomach churned for Aspire as Sebby spun him round and round.

"Whatever needs to be done." He shrugged and raised his eyebrows.

"I'm Lizzy, by the way." I held out my hand.

"Mateo." I felt his callouses as my hand disappeared in the girth of his and we made direct eye contact. My stomach flip-flopped.

"Mateo," I repeated, looking at his face again. "Italian for Matt, right?"

"I guess. I'm named after my grandfather."

"And Sebby?"

"Sebastian, after my other grandfather. So if you moved here, why not go to the regular high school?"

"We move a lot. It's just easier this way." Sebby had moved the turtle to a swing.

"Oh. Military family? I'm JROTC."

"No, but that's cool. Is that how you stay in such good shape?" Internally I kicked myself for saying that out loud.

"Uh, yeah. I guess." Mateo looked down at himself as if he wasn't aware he looked like he moved RVs with his bare hands. He shifted back and forth on his feet and looked over at Sebby. I stifled the urge to touch his bicep and trace the vein just below the surface.

"Sebby, we should go!" he called.

"Sebby groaned audibly. "Can I bring Aspire home?"

"No."

"But Winnie is lonely," he whined.

"No turtles in the truck." Mateo crossed his arms.

"Can you drive Aspire to my house?" Sebby crossed his arms and squinted up at me.

"Me? I don't have a car here. My dad's picking me up."

"Well, how about him, then? Can he drive Aspire to my house?"

"Sebby. Enough. Let that poor thing go. It'll be lucky to survive the day after what you just put it through."

"He likes playing with me." Sebby stomped his foot in the dirt. "Just 'cause you never have a girlfriend doesn't mean Winnie doesn't want a boyfriend."

"Okay." Mateo's face burned. "Nice to meet you, Lizzy. Maybe I'll see ya around." Mateo turned to go. Sebby stomped over and held Aspire out to me.

"Here. In case you want to drop him off. We're out past the Moose Lodge, right next to the hardware store. Just look for all the RVs."

I took Aspire. "I'll try my best," I said.

"Bye, Aspire." He dropped a kiss on his shell. I watched as they raced to the truck. Mateo faked a fall at the last minute so Sebby could win.

The minute my dad pulled up, I knew I had to convince him to let me drop off the turtle. Although I told my father we had to do it for the sake of turtle love, deep down I knew I wasn't trying to rescue anyone from loneliness but me.

My dad pulled into the gaping, dusty lot below the large sign reading T OR C RV. At the base of the sign's pole sat a hand-painted, stenciled, wooden A-frame sign reading KAYAK & BOAT RENTALS AND REPAIRS. A long, wide, sun-washed yellow stucco building stretched out to the right, in front of a massive metal-sided garage. To the left were covered racks of kayaks and small inflatable rafts. A tall black metal fence protected the inventory, which ran about thirty RVs long and ten deep. They varied in size, shape, and mileage by the looks of some of the more experienced peeking out from behind the shinier, newer beasts in front. The rows of everything from kayaks to RVs were military straight.

"Do you want me to come with you?" My dad pushed his

sunglasses onto his forehead to look at his phone.

"No, I'm good. I'll be right back." I hopped out of our white Highlander, balancing Aspire in one hand where he remained buried deep in his shell. I entered through the door labeled OFFICE. A bell announced my entrance and a tall raven-and-gray-haired woman smiled up at me with white crooked teeth. A display cabinet filled with numerous candies, sundries, sunglasses, lip balms, T-shirts, and sunscreens ran the full length of the office. She pushed readers onto her head, revealing eyes the same beach-sand brown as Mateo's. Years of kindly greeting customers lined her eyes and lips.

"Can I help you?" She walked closer to my end of the counter.

"Yes. I'm Lizzy and Sebby asked me to drop off Aspire for him." I nodded toward the turtle in my hand.

"Oh, goodness. Now he's asking strangers to bring him turtles? I swear we need to add Turtle Zoo to the sign." She set down some car part she'd had in her hands, wiped them on a rag hanging off the belt of her jeans, and held out a hand to me. "I'm Melissa but everyone calls me Mel."

I took her hand in mine and she gave it a firm shake. "Nice to meet you, Mel."

"Follow me."

I followed her, each of us on our own side of the counter, through another door. The counter continued on the other side, only shorter. This one displayed helmets for sale and also had a tablet register with a printer resting to the side. Half the long room displayed new and used kayaks, canoes, rafts, and life vests for sale, while the other held more rental equipment such as oars, life vests, and helmets. I noticed they had a fair amount of other camping supplies available for purchase as well, though only a small inventory of those items. I glanced over the pop-up tents, backpacks, and water shoes.

"Sebby!" she yelled, but only Mateo stepped out of a doorway I hadn't noticed before. I felt an unexpected tickle in my stomach at the smile he flashed when he saw me. His smile pulled his nose to the right.

"He's outside with the hose." Mateo nodded behind him. The entrance bell announced another visitor. Mel asked Mateo to lead me back to Sebby while she tended to the front. I followed Mateo through the giant repair area. The walls of the shop were lined with tools and supplies, methodically aligned and neatly labeled with terms like RUBBER MALLET or VISE GRIPS. The floors shined, ceiling fans whirled above, and a half-full bin labeled USED RAGS was the only sign that dirty work took place on the premises. A large RV towered above us, filling most of the bay. Beside us, a hatch on the beast sat propped open to reveal the mechanics of something that Mateo had been fixing.

"I can't believe you really brought him the turtle." Mateo's crooked-nose smile made me smile.

I shrugged. "I didn't want to stand in the way of turtle love." I followed Mateo's broad shoulders through the door at the end of the garage. The bright midday sun temporarily blinded us both. When my eyes adjusted I saw Sebby standing beside a large, elaborate, homemade cage. Two-foot-high clear plastic panels had been joined together to form a rectangle about three by four feet, with air holes drilled in multiple places. Sand and large rocks formed the majority of the floor except where a plastic bedpan formed a perfect turtle pool. The half-plastic, half-screened top lay off to the side. Sebby looked up from where he stood; he'd been arranging the rocks around the pool.

"Aspire!" Sebby yelled and ran to take him from me. "Winnie, meet your new boyfriend!" He gently placed Aspire next to two box turtles, one big, one small, sunning themselves on a large rock off to the right of the water. "And Charleston, meet your new best bro!"

"Sebby, aren't you forgetting your manners?" Mateo nodded toward me, raised his eyebrows, and widened his eyes at his brother.

"Oh yeah. Sorry. Thanks, Lizzy." He shot me a quick glance then refocused on his shelled friends.

Mateo shook his head. "Sorry. As you can see he's better with turtles than humans. Here, let me show you where you can wash that turtle off your hands." We walked back through the small door beside the giant RV-sized garage door and he stopped in front of a deep white utility sink.

"Here." He squeezed soap into my hands and turned the faucet on for me.

"Boy, you're really concerned about turtle germs, huh?" I teased.

"I do not want salmonella, thank you very much." He turned the water off and handed me a clean, neatly folded towel to dry my hands. When I handed it back to him, our hands touched and I studied his face for the reaction I felt in my chest. His eyes were unreadable. I stood staring at him for a moment too long. But just as it became awkward, Mel returned.

"Just Walter dropping off the mail. There's a letter from your dad." Mel handed an overseas envelope to Mateo.

"Is he traveling?" I asked.

"Deployed," they answered in unison.

"Oh." I didn't have a good response for that.

"Well, I guess I better get going." I shoved my hands in my back pockets and watched as Mateo ran his fingers over the edge of the letter. "My dad's in the car still."

"Are you new here?" Mel asked, digging through a small drawer of screws.

"Yeah."

"Mateo, you should take her to youth group tonight. Introduce her around."

Mateo blushed and shifted from one foot to the other. "Ah, sure. If you want?"

"I don't want to be a burden."

"Oh, it's no problem. He'd love to take you. Wouldn't you, Mateo?"

"Of course." His smile didn't quite reach his eyes and I worried I might be messing up his plans. But I hadn't met anyone my age in Truth or Consequences yet so I selfishly agreed to go. I told him my address, we agreed on a six-thirty pickup, and Mel walked me to the front of the store.

My dad didn't seem to notice how long I'd taken, or mind that I had evening plans. I suspected that meant he had plans of his own, which often meant he'd already met the latest in his ever-growing paper-doll chain of short-term girlfriends.

LIZZY

TRUTH OR CONSEQUENCES, NM
EVENING OF OCTOBER 11, 2014

Youth group consisted of sixteen high schoolers who gathered at the local minister's house to eat a home-cooked meal, play trust-building team-based games, hear a little "make good choices" scripture, and then head to one of the locals-only free hot springs to tempt one another into defying that evening's lessons.

Mateo gave me and a tall string bean, cocoa-skinned, chatty guy named Raj a ride. On the way to the hot springs I learned Raj had five sisters that drove him crazy, they ran a local high-end spa, and he liked to dance to pop music but preferred country if given the choice.

Everyone piled out of their cars, and promptly, and very nonchalantly, stripped down to underwear and slipped into the springs. The cloud-free night paired with a waxing gibbous moon made the scene a stage. I'd been skinny-dipping with friends in the past, but only girls and after I'd known them a while. I wasn't sure I was up for this type of debut.

"You don't have to get in." I jumped at the husky voice behind me. I turned to see the shaggy, purple-haired, waify girl named Fawn perched behind me on a big boulder. She still wore the flowy beige sundress I'd noticed her in earlier. If ever a name fit the person, hers was it. I fingered the edge of my navy tank top, trying to decide if I wanted to take it off among virtual strangers.

"You wanna cigarette?" Fawn asked, clicking her tongue ring against her teeth.

"No, thanks." I smiled.

"Mind if I have one?" she asked.

"No, it's fine," I said. She nodded, took out her lighter, and held it to the tip until it took.

"Where you from?" she asked, thoughtfully blowing her smoke away from me.

"All over. My dad likes to move around." I leaned against another big boulder. Off to my right, I had a perfect view of Mateo's firm, defined chest in the moonlight. I wondered what it would feel like to run my hands across his skin.

"Military or RVer?"

"Neither. Nomadic. My dad writes software and coding manuals. He can do it from anywhere." I watched as the group in the spring with Mateo passed a bottle of something around the circle. Neither Mateo nor Raj drank any before passing it along.

"That must be nice. I'd love to travel around." Fawn took another long drag and let the smoke out slowly in ascendingly sized haloes. "What about your mom? She mind moving?"

"Nope. She likes it, too. Only she moves separate from us."

"Oh. Divorced?"

"Technically, no. But might as well be. They both date other people. She works for FEMA. If there's a disaster, she's there."

"Do y'all ever meet up with all the moving around?"

"Sometimes."

"Do you text and talk and stuff?"

"No. I tried when I first got a phone. But days would go by before she could respond. She's usually in situations where either cell towers are out or there are far more important things to do than text your daughter back."

We sat in silence for a bit. Her smoking, me straining to hear the group conversation. They were discussing the SATs and what they needed for their dream colleges.

"If it makes you feel any better my parents live in the same house and I still don't hear from or see much of them. They are always working except when they sleep."

"Doctors?" I asked.

"Hotel and restaurant owners. Plus we own one of the gas stations. They always say they work hard so I can have a better life. But sometimes I think maybe my idea and their idea of 'better' and 'life' are different."

"Hey, new girl, why don't you get in?" a guy with limp but longish dirty-blond hair and a goatee yelled from the spring.

"Her name's Lizzy, Isiah," Fawn yelled. "And unlike you, some people don't strip to their underwear around people they've known for four hours."

I chatted with Fawn until Mateo and Raj got out of the water, ready to leave. Both had church and work the next day. Raj dominated the conversation as we drove.

"Mateo, where are you going? You drove right past my street," Raj yelled.

"I was going to drop Lizzy first." Mateo tightened his hands on the steering wheel, looking straight ahead.

"That's crazy. Then you'll be backtracking. Turn around at the 7-Eleven." Raj rolled his eyes at me and I smiled in return. "For a smart guy sometimes you don't think too clearly."

We dropped Raj and his absence felt palpable. I slid into the space Raj had vacated to give myself distance from the distraction of his body heat mingled with my own. I wasn't normally at a loss for words but my attraction to Mateo made me nervous.

"Fawn seems nice," I said as we waited at a red light.

"Yeah, I feel bad for her. All she wants is her parents to notice her, but no matter what she does, they rarely do."

"How long will your dad be gone?" I immediately regretted it when he drew back his shoulders and tightened his jaw. "Sorry, it's none of . . ."

"No, it's fine. It's a two-year deployment. He's scheduled to be back next fall." The lights of a passing car illuminated his face, and I saw his eyebrows were knotted.

"Does he get to come home for any holidays?" I asked as he turned onto the long, dark road leading to my street.

"He said maybe Thanksgiving this year."

"That's only about six weeks away."

"Yep." I couldn't tell if he didn't want to talk about his dad, wasn't happy to have him come home, or if he simply didn't want to talk to me. I racked my brain for a better conversation topic when he yelled, "Oh shit!" and jerked the wheel hard to the right. I slammed into the door, and the truck tipped onto two wheels, hung suspended for a few moments as if deciding whether to roll or return to four wheels. The air filled with the scent of burning tire. To my left, Mateo held tight to the steering wheel. A flash of a beige leg and dark hoof smashed through his window and back out, sending glass flying across the truck cab. The truck slammed upright, sending me hard to the left, testing the strength and effectiveness of my seat belt as we slid sideways a few yards before coming to a complete stop, perpendicular to the road and a few feet from a jagged rock formation looming over us like an angry giant.

"Are you okay?" I asked Mateo, my voice shaking like the rest of my body. He blinked, opened then closed his mouth without making a sound, then looked down at the shattered glass covering him, his eyes wide with shock. A high-pitched scream sliced through the night and our eyes widened in terror. I'd never heard a sound more disturbing. The image of the hoof jutting in and out of the car flashed into my mind and I thought, *Did we hit someone on horseback?* The screaming wouldn't stop. We both unhooked our belts and jumped out of the car. I ran around to his side and we both cringed in horror at the image of the back-half of the deer trapped beneath the front tire of the car. Its eyes, wide with fright and pain, reminded me of a spooked horse. Its tongue, covered in blood, curled in its open mouth as it emitted this hair-raising scream from deep in its throat. Mateo quickly opened his door, reached in to pull the keys from the ignition, climbed into the back, and unlocked a metal box installed across the back sixth of the bed. I felt vomit threaten at the back of my throat as I stood there, unable to help relieve this animal's pain. I knew Mateo moved swiftly and efficiently but it felt like an eternity as I watched him load the gun, flick off the safety, and put the gun to his shoulder. He instructed me to step back and look away. I stepped back but couldn't turn away. He took a deep breath, closed his eyes, and squeezed the trigger. I jumped at the pop of the gun, relieved that the screaming stopped, but haunted by the way it lingered in the air, mixing in with the scent of gun smoke, blood, and fear. The poor creature's head fell limp against the pavement.

Mateo emptied the gun, replaced the unused ammo, and returned them to the metal container. He locked it shut and hopped back down into the dirt to where I stood, staring, gape-mouthed, shaking, and unable to peel my eyes away from the terror frozen in the deer's eyes.

"Are you okay?" Mateo's calm voice felt jarring to my tortured senses. I nodded, but couldn't turn my eyes to his. He stepped around the deer and stood between me and it. I looked up into his eyes and found my pain mirrored in his. He reached out, pulled me into his chest, and wrapped his arms around me in a hug. I felt the pinch of tiny shards of glass poking at my tender skin where they were trapped between us. But the discomfort felt embarrassingly minor compared to what we'd seen this poor deer endure. We clung to one another, our breaths jagged, hearts racing. I heard in my head and heart our exchange of shared horror at what we'd witnessed, the role we'd played in its death, and the guilty relief that we were basically unharmed.

We released one another and turned to look at the fallen deer, still trapped beneath the tire.

"Here." He pulled his phone from his back pocket, tapped a few things, and handed it to me. The screen showed it was dialing a Roger Rightman. "Tell him we just hit a deer a half mile from wolf-fang rock and need his help."

While I made the call, Mateo backed off the deer, and drove the truck to a safer spot parallel to the road. Roger was a local cop and friend of his father's. Mateo helped him load the broken creature into the back of the police truck. We each explained what had happened, signed a report, let him speak to my dad on my cell, and Mateo's mom on his, and then were told we had to drive directly to the hospital to get cleaned up and officially checked over or he would send an ambulance to take us. My dad and Mateo's mom met us at the hospital. We were bruised and had a few minor lacerations but were released in under an hour.

Seven

LIZZY

TRUTH OR CONSEQUENCES, NM
HALLOWEEN 2014

Fawn invited me to a Halloween party that members of the senior class had thrown together at an abandoned warehouse outside the town limits. Apparently it had been a popular hangout spot for years. The relic straddles two redrawn town lines, making its jurisdiction fuzzy enough to allow both towns' cops to turn a blind eye. My dad dropped me off at Fawn's family's restaurant with a spit-shake promise I would call him for a ride if I couldn't find a sober, safe way home. The deer incident a few weeks earlier had shaken him a little.

Fawn made a striking Maleficent and I sighed with relief. Attending a Halloween party in a new town with new friends is a risky venture. Fawn and Raj both promised that everyone dressed up, but I'd still held my breath until Fawn stood before me, draped in a silky, high-collared black-and-purple dress with her hair masterfully formed into two horns on her head. Her lips and eyelids were lined in purple and black, a stark contrast to her pale skin.

"You look amazing!" I couldn't keep the awe out of my voice. "Did you do your own makeup?"

She waved off the compliment with a roll of her eyes, but my words prompted a rare smile and a rush of pink to her cheeks. "YouTube tutorial. The low light makes it look better than it really is." Fawn looked me up and down, taking in my oversized green sweater, leggings, and hat. "Are you a giant pea or something?"

"No. Look closely at my scarf." I held the ends out for closer inspection.

"A big black *N* and a big black *V*? I think maybe I missed a movie or something? Or are you a book character? I'm not a big reader."

"No." Through the restaurant window I watched a family dressed as the Flintstones pile into their car. I momentarily imagined them powering it with their feet.

"Nevada? You're Green Nevada?" Deep in thought, nose wrinkled, brows knitted, the black and purple turned her scrutiny sinister. A toddler, burning off energy as his parents ate, burst into tears near our feet.

"Quick, smile! You're scaring the children." I nodded toward the kid just as he'd been swept up into the safety of his father's arms.

"Oh, I get it!" The father smiled at us. "I'm *jealous* of a good punny costume."

Fawn lifted her eyebrow and cocked her head at me as the toddler wriggled away from his dad, raced back to his table, and into the comfort of his mother's arms.

"Say the two letters together fast," I coached her.

"NV," Fawn said. "NV, NV?"

"Green and NV?" She shook her head.

"Jealous?" the father offered.

"Dan!" His wife motioned him back to the table.

"Oh, duh!" Fawn pinched her lips together. "Green with envy. Got it."

"It's my safety costume. If nobody else actually dressed up, I could lose the hat and scarf and look basically normal." I shrugged.

"Oh just wait. Everybody really gets into it. Trust me."

Fawn drove like a maniac and I white knuckled the seat edge, my eyes glued to the road, on full deer alert. When we approached the warehouse, my heart sunk. There wasn't another car in sight, no light or sound emanating from the tired building.

"Are we too early?" I asked.

"Not at all." Fawn continued past the building for another

quarter mile before turning down a path-like pock-marked road. We wound around through the trees, the old Volvo bouncing and scraping the tips of branches with a disturbing squeal until suddenly we were in a big clearing lined with more than a dozen cars. Off to the left sat the backside of the warehouse. I still couldn't hear anything but the windows flashed with strobe lights.

The door opened to the loud bass line of a familiar song, loud enough to reverberate in my chest. We closed the door and walked through a curtain of fake bones to a room pulsing with masked, stuffed, coiffed, and painted people. A Mad Hatter danced with Winnie-the-Pooh, a pizza delivery girl made out with a male Madonna. I scanned the room for Mateo, but I didn't recognize anyone. The costumes made it nearly impossible.

"Come on!" Fawn yelled over the music. "Let's grab a drink." I followed her past a group of girls dressed as spices and a pregnant Statue of Liberty to a table with Solo cups, punch, chips, and a keg resting in a big tub of ice.

I took a cup of punch from Fawn and tried to sniff it without being obvious. It smelled like Hawaiian Punch. I took a tentative sip. It tasted like it looked.

"Do you care if we go over to the smoking section?"

I shrugged. "Sure."

I turned to follow her again when Shaggy and Scooby cut me off from Fawn.

"Heey. You're the new girl. Jenny or something?" Shaggy squinted at me or maybe his eyes were only that big. I couldn't tell.

"Lizzy."

"What are you? The Green Lantern or some shit?"

I looked after Fawn to see if she'd noticed the interception, but she'd already disappeared around a corner. I didn't feel like explaining it to Shaggy and could have kissed Raj when he swept in from the left, dressed as van Gogh, complete with red beard, pipe, and bloodied, bandaged ear.

"Hey, Isiah, you should go check out the haunted storeroom. I hear they stocked it with your kind of shrooms."

"Dude, no way! Come on, Scooby, let's get us some snacks."

"Thanks, Raj!" I sighed.

"Did you come alone?" Raj glanced around me.

"No, Fawn went to smoke. I got hijacked."

"Ah, well, you can hang with me. You like to dance?" He slipped his arm in mine, I set down my full cup of punch, and we joined a few other people I recognized from the youth group. I hadn't danced in public much but I'd spent my childhood dancing with my dad around the house. Our daddy-daughter dance parties faded out for a bit in middle school but came back with a vengeance once we had no TV again.

"You've got some moves there, Lizzy." Raj looked genuinely impressed. I couldn't help but smile as he grabbed me and swung me out and back into him.

"Look at you." I laughed as he whizzed me around, still holding his pipe in two of his fingers.

"Yeah, well, I took dance lessons for six years before we moved here from San Francisco." I felt him watching my face for a reaction.

"That's cool. Can't you do that here?" I leaned close to his ear so he could hear me over the music.

"I tried, but to be honest, the girls here basically made it clear a guy was not welcome in their classes." His hips, knees, and arms were flying, synced to the beat and incredibly smooth.

"What? You're kidding, right?"

"Nope, I am ashamed to admit I let a bunch of ballerinas bully me right out of the classes." He made mock boxing moves without missing a beat.

"That's awful. Maybe you should find some other guys to join. You know? Safety in numbers." He switched up his moves and I tried to mirror his footwork as best I could.

"Ha! Have you met the guys around here? You either play football or football."

Various people stepped in to dance with us for a bit, then wandered off. Fawn checked in with me to see if I needed an escape excuse, but I couldn't remember the last time I'd had this much fun. The freedom of flying around that cement floor, strobe lights flashing through the low lighting, the bass of the music pounding in my chest, I felt like a normal high school kid. Until I'd spun directly into the stone wall of someone's chest. I leaned back from the maroon-and-black paisley vest to take in the black suit and cape. A white mask covered most of one half of his face. My heart jumped into my throat when I recognized Mateo's strong cheekbones and jaw filling out the other side of his face. His normal sand-colored eyes were a dark brown glare, burning into my face. I felt a little chill ripple down my spine. His six-foot-three, bulky frame directing angry eyes from behind that mask were more than intimidating. I felt like that deer must have felt. Frozen, mouth open but all sound replaced by a racing heartbeat.

"Hey, Phantom, you lost? 'Cause, uh, you have willingly wandered onto the dance floor," Raj yelled, dancing up beside us. Mateo shifted his glare to Raj and in a blink the angry dark mud returned to the kind beach sand as he smiled at his friend.

"The whole place is a cement-floored warehouse. There is no designated dance floor."

Raj rolled his eyes at Mateo and turned to me. "A real hunk of humor, this one." He gestured with his thumb.

"Van Gogh, you're about to lose your ear again." I reached up to adjust his fake bandage. The bloody part had slid from over his ear to his forehead. His hair was damp with sweat. My back and neck were clammy as well. I'd removed my sweater earlier and tied it around my waist.

Mateo grabbed my hand from Raj's hair and briskly pulled me. "Let's get you guys a drink," he said and dragged me through the crowd to the table with drinks. *Why was he acting so weird?* An optimistic, possibly crushing-on-Mateo little voice in my head suggested he might be jealous of Raj. But I pushed that thought away; I probably had jealousy on my mind because of my costume. Having his big, rough hand wrapped tightly around mine had set my entire arm on fire. That same little voice squealed in protest when Mateo dropped my hand at the edge of the drink table. I scooped Hawaiian Punch into a cup and held it out for Raj.

"Oh, no thanks." He held his hand up. "I don't drink."

"It's Hawaiian Punch," I said.

"And grain alcohol." Mateo took it from me and set it on the table.

"Oh." I burned red. "I tasted it earlier and it tasted normal."

"Here." Mateo held out a water bottle for each of us.

"Yeah, grain alcohol has no flavor," Raj explained. "It's so dumb to serve. People end up drinking way too much. Seems like every spring somebody gets their stomach pumped. Not sure when they'll finally get smarter." We stood watching people trying to bob for apples. By the lack of success and the bouts of hysterics, we concluded that they must have had a few too many punches already.

I felt my phone buzz in my pocket and pulled it out to see I'd missed a few texts from Fawn and one from my dad asking if I needed a ride. I looked at the time and couldn't believe Raj and I had been dancing for almost two hours. This text was Fawn asking if I'd be okay if she took off.

"Everything okay?" Raj asked.

"Uh, yeah. Fawn wants to take off." I looked around the room to see if I could spot her horns in the crowd.

"Do you need a ride home?" Raj asked. A girl dressed as Goldilocks pulled her face out of the water, fake blond curls dripping, a big red apple clasped tight in her teeth. Onlookers cheered. "I'm sure Mateo can drop you, too."

Goldilocks ran over to her three bear friends, and leaned up for the biggest bear to take the apple from her with his own teeth—like Eve offering herself and the apple all at once.

"Mateo?" Raj nudged him with his elbow. Mateo jumped as if Raj had just brought him back from a distant place in his head.

"What'd ya say?" Mateo looked down at Raj.

"Lizzy. Can you give her a ride home later?" He spoke around the prop pipe he'd slipped back in his mouth. Mateo tipped his head at Raj and nodded. "Yeah, no problem."

A ripple of excitement zipped through my stomach at the thought of being alone in a car with Mateo again. I texted both Fawn and my dad to let them know I had a safe ride home. When I looked up I noticed Mateo looking back and forth between me and Raj, his brows pulled tightly together. I couldn't get a read on what he could be thinking.

Three girls dressed as paprika, ginger, and cinnamon swooped in, blocking my view of Mateo as they hair-flicked and giggled at him. I heard one say, "Love me, that's all I ask of you." And then they broke into song . . .

"In sleep he sang to me, in dreams he came,

that voice which calls to me,

and speaks my name.

And do I dream again? For now I find

the phantom of the opera is there

inside my mind."

Mateo smirked, but his eyes darted around the room. I found his discomfort humorous and didn't move to help. Besides, the "spice girls" harmonized together well. Raj appeared at my side, grinning from ear to ear. He raised his eyebrows at me, holding his pipe "Watson" style. "Think we should rescue him or hit the dance floor?"

Without waiting for an answer, Raj grabbed my hand and pulled me back toward the dancing area, leaving Mateo at the mercy of the trio of spice. We'd barely gotten through two songs when Mateo approached us. Once again, a stoic boulder disrupting the ebb and flow of the dancing crowd. How could he feel the music in his chest and not even tap his foot?

"Are you guys ready to go?" Mateo asked as if we weren't happily dancing.

"How about you dance one song with us and then we'll go," Raj yelled over my shoulder to be heard above the music. He swung me out toward Mateo so I landed right in front of him. Our eyes met for a moment, making my heart flip-flop before Raj jerked me back into his arms.

"I'll meet you at the truck," Mateo grumbled and with a flash of black cape escaped the grinding bodies surrounding him.

As we drove to Raj's house, he kept the conversation going, doing his own costume assessment: scariest going to Fawn; most true to self going to Isaiah and Lenny as Shaggy and Scooby; funniest to some junior dressed as a giant tissue box—a white pillowcase made his head look like a tissue coming out of the top, the logo artfully drawn on the front with the brand name BLOW ME.

"Most beautiful female had to be Mary Bloomburg." Raj pulled the bloodied ear wrapping off his head.

"Was she the blond girl in red?" I asked.

"Yeah, she's in our class. I'm pretty sure she was dressed as Jayne Mansfield."

"Who's Jayne Mansfield?" Mateo asked.

"Classic beauty who was the first Hollywood actress to have a nude scene in a film," Raj explained as Mateo took a corner too sharp, squeezing Raj tight against my right and Mateo on my left. I felt Mateo's leg tighten in reaction. I felt my own leg, arm, and shoulder, catch fire from the sudden close contact.

"I think she was a Playboy bunny, too, because she had bunny ears and a tail." I'd seen her. The girl stood out at the party. Her cleavage-promoting bright red dress accentuated her every curve. Plus, her baby-smooth skin, full lips, and vibrant blue eyes were memorable. I'd thought she was Marilyn Monroe. "I bet she's popular," I said.

Mateo shrugged. Raj said, "She's been with the same guy since middle school. Jeff is a couple years older and off at college someplace."

"I liked the guy dressed as an old fat lady with the puppy trapped in the butt cheeks of his skirt handing out the missing puppy flyers."

Raj shoved my shoulder with his hand. "Oh my God, that's hysterical. I saw the flyers but I never saw the puppy butt. Who was it?" Raj leaned forward to make eye contact with Mateo.

"Mateo glanced at Raj then quickly back to the road. "You got me." He shrugged. "I never even saw the flyers."

"Missing puppy. That's classic." Raj shook his head, his white teeth bright in the darkness.

"But I have to hand it to both of you," Raj moved on. "Lizzy, green with envy is quite clever. Gotta love a good pun. And Mateo, you are smoking hot in that mysterious *Phantom* mask and cape."

"Thanks." I squeezed Raj's leg and felt Mateo tense next to me again. Wow, maybe he did have a thing for me.

Mateo cleared his throat, shifted his shoulders, squeezed the steering wheel, and cleared his throat again. "Yeah, and thanks to both of you for your help with the Spice Girl situation. I really appreciate you having my back."

Raj laughed, threw his arm around me, and pulled me to him. "Hey, the dance floor was calling our name." I snuck a glance at Mateo and saw him flexing his jaw in the light from the dash. "Did you see Lizzy's moves? You gotta come with me to homecoming . . ."

Mateo slammed on the brakes and we all flew forward against our seat belts. My heart jumped into my throat and I scanned the road in front of us for a deer.

"What was it?" Raj asked. "Deer?"

Mateo shook his head, "Sorry. Not sure. Maybe a fox. You guys okay?" He didn't look at us as he returned to a normal speed. We both said we were fine, but my heart raced and the hair at the nape of my neck felt prickly at the memory of the screaming deer. We rode in silence until Mateo pulled into Raj's driveway. Raj opened the door and hopped down.

"Thanks for the ride, Mateo," Raj said then looked at me. "Think about homecoming. It would be way more fun to have you there to dance with." Raj winked and closed the door.

Mateo didn't move. At first I thought he might be mad but then I realized he was waiting to make sure Raj got inside okay. I unhooked the middle seat belt to move to sit in the seat Raj had vacated. It would have been odd for me to stay in the girlfriend seat.

"Wait." Mateo put his hand on my leg. I looked up at him. He'd removed the mask from earlier, revealing his entire square chin and high cheekbones, his smooth olive skin looked soft. Excited tingles spread through my stomach. Yet I felt like I might be missing something because his eyes grew dark with anger and he squeezed my leg hard.

"Wha—" I started to ask what the problem was, but he took my head in his hands and pulled my face to his. He crushed his lips into mine, kind of hard. The bottom dropped out of my stomach, like a runaway elevator. He pulled back a second, released my lips but his eyes remained closed. He returned his lips to mine again, this time more gently. I felt his tongue tentatively invite itself in. I escorted his with mine; my heart raced. He tasted like vanilla, and the gentle pressure of his full soft lips locked in mine sent my thoughts spinning. They felt even better than they'd looked. I slid my hands up to the back of his head, ran my hands through the prickly buzz cut, enjoying the feeling.

Mateo abruptly pulled away, released my head, and looked out the windshield then back at me. His eyes searched my face.

"I . . . was . . . um . . . was that okay?" he asked. "I mean, did it feel real to you?"

Very, I thought, but said, "Yeah. I . . . it was nice." I felt my face burn but knew he wouldn't see it in the darkness. He cleared his throat, then looked up at Raj's house like he'd just realized we were still in his driveway.

"We should go. Buckle back in," he said as if he hadn't just blown my mind with his kiss, then backed us down the driveway and took off down the road. We drove in silence for a bit, except for the sound of my heart racing in my chest. That sound echoed in my ears and my lips burned from his. I touched my fingers to my lips, then dropped my hands into my lap. I'm rarely at a loss for words but I couldn't think of anything to say. *Come on, Lizzy, ask him about something.*

"How is Sebastian's turtle zoo?" I asked.

Mateo turned toward me with a confused look. I got this odd feeling he was surprised to find me sitting there. Then he smiled and my doubts disappeared. "Good. He is working on building them a racing track. He said they told them they'd feel better if they had competitions." He shook his head. His smile filled his eyes this time, pulling his nose off-center. "He's an odd kid, but I love him for it."

"Did he go trick-or-treating tonight?" I'm glad I'd ended up staying in the middle seat because I felt the heat of Mateo next to me. I fought an urge to reach out and feel the tightness of his thigh against his black pants.

"Yeah. My mom took him to a friend's neighborhood since we don't really have any walkable neighbors." He turned onto the road to my house.

"What did he dress up as?"

"Guess." He lifted his eyebrows, tilted his head, and then returned his eyes to the road.

"Of course, a turtle." I laughed. As we approached my house, I noticed it was still dark and my dad's car wasn't in the driveway. I was relieved. I'd had a feeling my dad would sense something had happened and I wanted time to relive it myself before sharing it with anyone else.

"So," Mateo said as we pulled into the driveway.

"So," I said, rubbing my hands on my green pants, afraid to look at him, and hoping he would kiss me again.

"I've never had a girlfriend before." Mateo caught me off guard with that comment.

"Really? Why not?" I asked, then clamped my hand over my mouth. "Sorry. Was that rude?" I studied his face.

Mateo laughed. "It's fine. I know it's not typical. I just . . ." He looked straight out the window.

"It's okay. You don't have to explain yourself." I wanted the awkward feeling to go away. Did he mean he wanted me to be his girlfriend?

He looked back at me, cocked his head like a dog deciphering a new sound, and then opened his door.

"I'll walk you to your door." He hopped out and I unbuckled, but before I could do it, he opened the door for me. I took his hand as I jumped out and appreciated his big firm grip. How could every part of him send my body into overdrive? I couldn't remember ever being affected by a guy like this before.

"Thanks," I said and continued to hold his hand as we walked to my porch.

"I've never really had a boyfriend either. I mean in like fourth grade or something. But not like, ya know . . ." I took a deep breath. We reached my porch, climbed the steps, and then he turned to go, his cape swirled around him. I froze when he stopped, looked down where his hand still held mine, and turned back toward me. He looked down at his boots, squeezed my hand, released it, turned to go again, and I felt my heart sink.

Then he turned back, grabbed my hand to turn me to face him. With him a couple steps down, we were eye to eye, lip to lip. He leaned in and kissed me gently. I slipped my hands up into his hairline again, pulled him toward me. This time I deepened the kiss, wanting to keep his lips on mine as long as possible. I wondered if his heart pounded as hard as mine? He pulled back, opened his eyes, smiled straight at me, and my heart, breath, entire world froze for a splendid moment.

"Do you want to be each other's first?" he asked. I felt my eyes grow big and he quickly said, "First girlfriend, boyfriend, not . . ." He wrinkled his nose and closed his eyes for a beat. "Sorry, I wasn't suggesting . . ."

"It's okay." I saved us both from saying it out loud. "I know what you meant. And I should warn you my dad decides to move with great frequency and often with little notice. I have purposely not had boyfriends for this exact reason."

"That's perfect," he said, then, "I mean, that we both can figure this out together. Right? Less pressure or something." He shifted his shoulders again, looked at his black boots, then back up at me. "You can see I need a little help gettin' it right."

I laughed, put my hands on either side of his face, and said, "Yes, I'll be your first girlfriend." And feeling bold, I leaned in and kissed him again. I couldn't believe this was happening.

As he got into his truck he yelled back at me, "Do you want to tell Raj that I stole his homecoming date or should I?"

"I think that falls under the boyfriend's column," I yelled back and then floated into my house. I had a boyfriend. And could he kiss! I closed my eyes and put my fingers to my lips. I'd laughed at friends who claimed they'd never wash their face or hand again after their crush had kissed it. Now I understood. I didn't want anything to wash away the tingle Mateo had left on my lips. Best Halloween ever.

Eight

LIZZY

TRUTH OR CONSEQUENCES, NM
NOVEMBER 14, 2014

Mateo and I may have gone to homecoming together but I spent a large part of the night ripping up the dance floor with Raj. I felt bad but Mateo refused to dance. Both Raj and I felt guilty when he gave us the silent treatment on the drive home. He gave me a terse kiss at the door. I convinced him to let me make it up to him by making him dinner the following weekend.

My dad had plans so I hadn't even mentioned the date to him. In fact, at that point, I hadn't actually mentioned that Mateo and I were a couple.

Mateo knocked at the door, just as I pulled warm rolls from the oven.

"Come on in!" I yelled. The fresh, spicy-clean scent of his shampoo and soap announced his arrival before I turned to take him in. I almost dropped the cookie sheet when I turned to see him filling the door frame. A crisp tan T-shirt set off his eyes, tucked into his tight-fitting jeans, and slightly worn cowboy boots finished his look.

"Hey," was all I managed, because his presence had my stomach dancing. He filled the entire kitchen, shrinking everything in it to dollhouse size.

"Should I take these off?" he asked, nodding down at his boots.

"No." I may have overstated my protest. I set the rolls down. "You want a Coke?"

"Sure." He smiled and I turned toward the fridge, closed my eyes, and took a breath. My hands shook. He looked too good standing there all showered and smelling good. I grabbed the Coke and handed it to him.

"Thanks," he said. Our eyes met and a shiver rippled down my spine. "Is that barbeque I smell?"

"Yep." I turned to grab myself a Coke.

"My favorite." I could hear the smile in his voice.

"I know." I made myself busy putting the rolls in a basket, avoided looking at him too much. "Also pasta salad."

"You need any help?" he asked.

"Uh, sure. Can you grab the pasta salad out of the fridge and take it out to the table? Through there. I thought we'd eat outside since it's so nice." I pointed toward the sliding glass doors on the far end of the living room. I'd already covered the well-worn outside table with a plastic tablecloth from the dollar store. Dad and I had strung white lights all around the small covered deck soon after we moved into the place. It was one of our things we did to make any rental, no matter how shabby, feel homey at night. I already had them lit, though it wasn't dark yet. The table was set for two with the mismatched utensils and plates that came with the rental.

I followed behind him with the rolls, the pork, and my unopened Coke in my armpit. After a few moments of awkwardness, we fell into our usual easy banter.

"Oh, Sebastian wanted me to ask you if you would come watch his first turtle race tomorrow. He has the track all set up and six contenders," Mateo said, throwing his napkin onto his empty plate and pushing back from the table a little. I was pleased he had eaten a lot, which I hoped meant he had liked it. He'd said it was good.

"Of course. Although I will have to put my money on Aspire. I'm a little partial to that one."

"With good reason." He winked and I swear his long lashes tickled my insides.

"Hey, do you guys have horseshoes to go with the pit over there?"

Mateo nodded his chin toward the weather-worn wooden pit with the requisite poles on either side.

I shrugged. "Not sure. You wanna look around in the garage over there behind Dusty?"

"Dusty?" He tipped his head and raised an eyebrow.

"Oh, sorry—yeah. That's what I named the abandoned old Ford." I gathered the dishes to take into the house.

"I'm going to let that go for now." He shook his head. "Are you sure you don't want me to help you clean up?"

"I got it. Go see if you can find them before we lose all our light. I don't even know if the lights in there work."

He went in search of horseshoes and I quickly cleaned up and put away the little bit of leftovers. I finished before he came back so I proactively grabbed a flashlight and went in search of him in the garage. I opened the door with a noisy squeak to find him coiling an extension cord into a neat circle. I took in the jumbled mess of tools, abandoned furniture, old toys, an old lawn mower, some rusty bikes, and a few cracked plastic bins.

"Did you find them?" I asked.

"I found five of them." He gestured to the end of the counter where he'd put them in two piles.

"How many do we need?" I looked at the nicked and notched metal U's.

"Four."

"What are you doing with the cord?"

"Well, at first I was looking for one to use with a light out there, because I found a big job-site light and a box of new bulbs." I looked to where he'd placed the light at the end of the counter near the door. "But then I couldn't help but fix all these messed-up cables and cords." He leaned down to place the one he'd just coiled someplace out of my sightline. I stepped closer and saw he'd placed it into a bin where I assumed all the others were.

"Anyone ever tell you that you're a little OCD?" I asked, smiling at him.

He smiled and winked. "Four hands are faster than two."

I rolled my eyes, shook my head, smiled, and joined him.

"Is it your mom or your dad that gave you the neat freak gene?" I asked, mimicking his moves with the orange cord in my hand. His jaw tightened like it always did when I mentioned his father.

"That would be my dad. He's military in his approach to most things." He didn't elaborate any further than that so I let it drop.

"What about you? Your house is clean and organized. Is that you or your dad?" He plugged the end of the extension cord into itself, zip-tied it, and placed it in the bin.

"We make a good team. I mean, he taught me how to do everything, but we do it together. I don't remember if my mom cleaned or did laundry and stuff. She wasn't usually around long enough." I plugged my cord into itself like he did, but I couldn't get the zip tie to work right. It didn't catch.

"Try it the other way," he said. I did and it caught this time. "Why'd your parents split?"

"Lack of time together, I guess. My mom was never with us. And when she was, she really wasn't. It used to bother me a lot when I was little. I couldn't understand why she'd rather spend time helping complete strangers instead of us."

"I know. There's a part of you that is proud of them for helping people and having an honorable job. But then there is a part of you that wonders why they couldn't find a way to help people while also being at home," Mateo said.

"Has your dad been deployed a lot?" I purposely didn't look up from the work, hoping he'd be more comfortable talking in the darkened garage without me looking at him.

"Quite a bit. After nine-eleven he volunteered to go fight. I was four. I was so proud he stood up and fought for us; kept America safe at home. But when he kept re-upping, it got harder and harder to watch my mom struggle at home while he went off to fight."

"Did he come home often?"

"A few weeks here and there, between deployments. At first when he'd come home it felt like a holiday. He brought gifts, we'd get ice cream in the evenings, he'd teach me how to fix things. Mom would make all his favorite foods. They'd have trouble keeping their hands off each other. It sounds weird maybe to like seeing your parents like that. But I did. They looked so happy." He dropped his last cable in the bin and wiped his hands on his jeans.

"It's not like that when he comes home now?" I dropped my last cord in the bin and wiped my hands on my jeans. Mateo grabbed the bin and set it up on a shelf, out of the way.

"Not anymore." He wiped his face with his shirtsleeve, making his bicep bulge and my heart somersault. "Want to set this up and play?"

By the time we had everything ready, stars speckled the clear desert sky and the temperature had dropped. We grabbed sweatshirts and another Coke from the house before he explained the basic rules. The scoring sounded a little confusing to me but I figured I'd catch on once we played.

Mateo let me go first. My first shoe landed relatively close to the post, but my second flew far right, sending up a puff of dust.

"Oops." I bit my lower lip and looked back at Mateo.

"Not a terrible start." He flashed me an encouraging smile.

"Okay, hot shot. Show me how it's done." I moved back so he could step up to the foul line. He pulled his arm back, and gracefully tossed his first shoe. It hit the pole with a clank and twirled to a stop, perfectly placed. He didn't celebrate or boast. He simply grabbed the second shoe and did it again: a double ringer.

"Nice!" I said, and noticed he couldn't help but grin.

"Thanks."

"Oh, come on. No fist pump to the air or a woohoo? I'd be doing a victory dance if I schooled you like that." I pushed on his arm.

"Not going to jinx it. I get the feeling you may be a quick learner." He winked and I felt a warmness sweep through my chest. Why hadn't this guy ever had a girlfriend?

"I'm inspired by your blind—and I'd like to stress, *blind*—faith in me."

The next few rounds were a little better. I actually got a few points, but he would get at least one ringer every round. He was a few points from winning when I finally hit my first ringer.

"Yes!" I yelled and danced around. "I like the sound of that!"

"I knew it. Late comeback." He shook his head at me with that crooked-nosed smile. Then he proceeded to drop a ringer on top of mine, which apparently canceled out my ringer and cost me the game.

"What? No way." I stood, hands on hips, lips pursed. "Okay. Okay. Since you win you get to pick: round two or brownie break?" I held out his horseshoes to him.

"Depends. Did you make the brownies or buy them?"

"Whaaat? Made them, of course." I shook my head, incredulous. "Way better that way."

"Agreed. Looks like it's brownie time." He started toward the garage.

"Where are you going?" I asked.

"Putting this stuff away in case we're done for the night."

"Oh, okay. Thanks. You want me to help or should I get the dessert ready?"

"I got this." He unplugged the big lights and the night went pitch black for a moment.

We ate brownies and drank milk at the table under the white Christmas lights. Mateo sat at the end of the table and I took the chair to his right.

"Where is your favorite place you've lived so far?" Mateo asked.

"People always ask me that. I wish I had a better answer. There have been pros and cons to every place we've been. I like trying different foods in different places and meeting new people, but it can be hard to say good-bye."

"You must have friends everywhere. How do you keep up with all your Insta and Snapchat followers?"

"Well, I don't really. I have rules. Once I leave a place, I delete all my contacts for the people I leave behind."

"Seriously?"

"Seriously."

"That's harsh."

"It's better for everyone. I tried it the other way and I end up getting forgotten pretty quickly. I get sad. They feel guilty. Why bother?"

"Maybe when you were younger, sure. But now?"

"What about you? How come you've never had a girlfriend?" I raised my eyebrows. I couldn't be sure in the low light but I'd swear he blushed. He shifted in his seat and took a bite of a brownie.

"I mean you're not exactly unattractive." I looked at him beneath my lashes, unsure how he'd react.

"Right back at ya." He smiled, clearly being cheeky and locked his eyes to mine.

"I move too much." I stared right back.

"I work too much." Humor danced in his sandy eyes.

"Bullshit." I leaned in closer to his face, keeping eye contact.

"Same." He smiled that crooked smile and my eyes drifted to his lips. "I win," I watched them say before kissing his sweet chocolatey breath. I slipped my hands up to the back of his neck and he pulled me from the chair onto his lap where his gentle lips and tongue inspired back-to-back waves of stomach flutters.

Nine

LIZZY

Truth or Consequences, NM
November 20, 2014

My dad dropped me outside the T or C RV (T or C being short for Truth or Consequences), but instead of going in the front door, I walked around to the back, looking for Sebby. I'd made my dad stop to rescue a box turtle near the road on the way over. I knew Sebby would give him a good home. He'd been slowly adding on to his turtle zoo. He'd made them different rooms, and held regular races. He said they needed at least a week to recover and prepare.

I found Sebby refilling one of their four turtle pools. "Look who I just rescued from the side of the road, Seb!" I held out the medium-size turtle, who had his frightened head buried deep in his shell. "I thought we could call him Jayco. After the rig Mateo just fixed up and helped your mom sell." I squinted at him in the bright afternoon sun.

"Okay," Sebby said, gently taking the shell into his own hands. "Come see your new bed, Jayco." Sebby peered into his shell. I'd learned not to take it personally that Sebby rarely followed typical conversation guidelines. Mel, his mom, had explained that he had mild autism. He lived inside his own head more than we did.

"Why the hell was he even here?" I jumped at Mateo's angry outburst from inside the repair area. I glanced at Sebby but if he'd heard the yelling, he didn't acknowledge it.

"He had something to tell me." Mel didn't yell but her tone

implied controlled anger. I wasn't sure what to do. I didn't want to interrupt but I felt strange eavesdropping.

"I bet he did." Mateo slammed something loudly, maybe an RV door or hood.

"I don't have to explain myself to you, Mateo." I'd never heard Mel angry before.

"Are you still sleeping with him?" Mateo demanded and I quickly glanced at Sebby. He acted like he'd heard nothing.

"That is none of your business, Mateo."

"So you are." *Bam!* He slammed something else.

"Mateo. Stop."

"You promised Dad you ended it."

"How do you know what I said to your father? Were you listening to our private conversations?" Mel's voice cracked with emotion.

"He's never going to stay home now," Mateo yelled.

"Is that all you're worried about? Your father coming home? Because we both know that's probably never going to happen."

"He promised."

"Yeah, well, he promised me a lot of things and yet here we are. He promised when I was pregnant. He promised when Sebby was born. He promised when Sebby turned five. Forgive me if I don't believe his promises," Mel yelled and then I heard a door slam.

"Dammit!" Mateo yelled, followed by loud clanking sounds.

I wasn't sure what to do. I was stranded with no car. I glanced over to the turtle cages. Sebby slowly lifted one of their pools up and out of the cage without spilling a drop.

"Sebby, you need any help?" I walked closer to him.

"Mateo doesn't like Rooster." He began walking away from me, carefully carrying the turtle pool with both hands.

"Who is Rooster?" I asked, watching him as he carefully dumped the water off to the side, where it wouldn't roll back into his cage area.

"When did you get here?" I jumped at Mateo's voice behind me. I turned to look at him. His entire body looked rigid, ready to burst with the slightest touch, like an overinflated balloon.

"I . . . do you . . ." I looked off to the right at the rows of RVs, hulking metal soldiers watching us. "Follow me," I said and headed toward the intimidating inventory.

"Where?" Mateo asked, but fell into step beside me. I never answered and he simply followed me as I made my way past the long rows of new RVs toward the far back corner of the lot where a large old Coachman RV called to me. I turned to Mateo, shielding the sun with my hand as I looked up at his dark, stormy eyes and rigid jaw.

"Can this hold us if we climb on top with this ladder?"

He looked up at the top of the RV and shrugged. "As long as we avoid walking too close to the AC unit or the sunroof. Otherwise we could compromise the seals."

"So yes?" I asked.

"I guess. But why would we go up there?"

"Just humor me. Come on." I climbed up the little ladder and he followed. I walked as far away from the AC and sunroof as safely possible and sat down in the roof rack area, with my feet dangling over the rail. Mateo sat next to me but not within touching distance. We stared silently out over the many shades of brown and red that make up the desert floor.

"Did you hear all that?" he asked, still facing straight ahead.

"I take it your mom had an affair with some truck driver named Rooster?" I didn't look at him either. I felt his need for a little distance.

"Only Sebby calls him Rooster. He is fascinated by the colorful rooster tattoo that covers most of his back."

"Oh." I tried imagining how long it would take to get a tattoo that large and colorful.

"Does your dad know about him?"

"Yes. I think it's why he re-upped the last time. He was supposed to be done and come home for my high school years." He tilted his head, and raised his eyebrows.

"Maybe he'll make it back for your senior year?" I offered.

Mateo pulled a Swiss Army knife out of his pocket and used the

Phillips head to tighten a screw on the roof rack. "I shouldn't take it out on my mom. He's left her alone for most of the last thirteen years."

"Do you think they're even in love anymore?" I asked.

"Remember I told you how they used to be all touchy when he came home? It's not like that now. Even daily conversation was tense unless Sebby or I did the talking."

"Maybe he can't get over her having the affair?"

"No, it was like that before Seamus started coming around."

"Seamus? That's Rooster's real name?"

"Yep. Couldn't be more Irish. Probably pissed my dad off as much as anything." Mateo continued to make his way around to all the screws on the rack, tightening each one as he went.

"What do you want to happen?" I asked.

"I want my dad to come home so I don't have to stay in this town forever helping my mom."

"Couldn't she hire someone to do what you do?"

Mateo let out a puff of air. "Not for as little as I cost."

"But she still could do it, right?"

"Maybe. But that one person would have to learn a lot of different stuff. And then they wouldn't be able to help with Sebby and like, family stuff."

I carefully turned around so I could see him now that he'd moved completely behind me.

"This is my dad's responsibility and I'm tired of doing it for him," he said.

"Have you told your dad that?"

Mateo froze and knotted his eyebrows at me. "Would you tell your dad what to do?"

"No, but I do tell him how I feel." I had to squint up at him into the sun.

"Yeah, well, my dad doesn't talk about feelings." He went back to his work.

"Maybe your mom could get Rooster to help."

"Seamus? That would really piss Dad off."

"Well, maybe that would motivate him to come home? Sometimes we don't realize how much we want something until we're forced to let it go."

"And if he decides he can let it go?" Mateo's eyes locked with mine. His head temporarily blocked the sun, creating a halo effect.

"Then maybe your mom could move on," I said.

"And what about us? Do Sebby and I just move on?"

I felt the pain in his voice in my own chest. I knew exactly how it felt to have a parent choose other people and places over me.

"Mateo. Trust me when I say I understand your anger and how much it hurts to feel rejected. When I used to see some mother and daughter laughing together at the movies or in a store, or even fighting, I'd get completely enraged with envy. I'd ignore my father, refuse to eat his meals, hide in my room, complain about our life." I shook my head, still guilt-ridden at how awful I'd been at times. "I even pretended I didn't know him in a mall and demanded they call my mother to come get me."

"Ouch!"

"Yeah. I know."

"But you aren't angry with her anymore?" he asked.

"Oh, I'm still angry with her, but my dad helped me gain perspective." That day, after we'd gotten everything sorted at the mall with the police, my dad drove me to this big hill overlooking the town cemetery. From where we stood on the hill we could see from one end to the other.

He told me to look carefully at all of the different headstones and tell him which person I felt had been loved the most. The sheer number was overwhelming, and they varied greatly from stones the size of boulders with elaborate statues on top to the simple small N-shaped stones more common long ago. I finally settled on a giant white marble stone with a large winged angel reaching up toward the sky.

"That one?" I'd said.

"Are you asking or that is your final choice?" my dad asked.

I shrugged. "I don't know. It's impossible to know."

"Why do you think it's impossible to know?" he asked.

I shrugged, but he pushed me to explain.

"Well, I think that angel stone probably cost the most money so maybe that could mean they were really loved."

"But?" he prompted me.

"But if someone poor dies then they can't afford a big statue thing. So even if they have people that love them even more than the rich people, the small grave wouldn't show that."

"I agree. So look again and tell me what you think," he said.

I looked again and, thinking I'd figured him out, I pointed to a small headstone, off to the right. "That one."

"Because . . ." he prompted.

"Because even though it is in the section where the older graves are, it has a whole bunch of fresh flowers surrounding it. That means people miss that person enough to come visit and bring flowers," I explained, confident in this choice.

"Ah, that's good thinking," he said. "However, flowers arranged professionally like the ones placed on that stone are expensive. Maybe the person over there"—he'd pointed to a headstone a few rows away from my choice—"is actually more loved because their mourner had to pick those wild flowers lying next to the stone. Picking is more work than buying."

"True. Or maybe it's that really old one over there that looks like it may have been one of the first people buried here. They were truly the most loved but all of the people that loved them are also dead now, too."

"Ah, now you are catching on." He'd smiled and tweaked my nose.

"So there is no right answer, right? It's impossible to know who was loved the most?" I'd asked him.

"Correct. And just as it's impossible to know in death, it's impossible to know in life. And for many of the same reasons. Looking at a snapshot of a person's life cannot convey how sad or happy or loved they are. When you see other girls giggling with their mothers, I know you wish you had a mom like them. You feel like they are happier and more loved than you, because in that moment they look like they are. When I see you hurting like that, it hurts me. I want to take your pain away." He pulled me to him as tears threatened. My chest ached.

"Everybody has good and bad in their life. Orphans have no biological parents. Some children have mean parents or absentee parents. Yet, all of those children could be more loved or happier than some of those girls you saw laughing with their moms today. Your mom is not the mom you wish she would be. But it doesn't change the fact that she loves you. She does. Her way of loving is different than the moms you compare her to. She helps and has helped thousands of people during the worst moments of their lives. She believes those people need her more than we do. She believes she is being a good mother to people who need a special kind of mothering." He gently wiped away the wetness on my face.

"But we need her, too."

"And she gives us time with her sometimes, right?"

"Not like other moms do."

"No, not like some of the girls you saw today, but also not like the girl who lost her mom in an earthquake or the girl who was left on the steps of a church by a mother too poor to feed her."

"So you think I'm being selfish by wanting more?" I asked.

My dad dropped to his knees in front of me and took my hands into his. "No, sweetie, I think how you feel is completely normal. We all have moments where we feel like our struggles are harder than others. But my job is to remind you to be grateful for what you do have and help you find happiness in other ways. But ultimately we are in charge of our own happiness. If you are not happy, determine what could make you happy and work toward achieving it."

"You make it sound easy. If I think having Mom around all the time would make me happy and it won't ever happen, then what?"

"Hmm." My dad looked down at the ground for a moment then

back into my eyes. "Look at it like this. Do you think your mom would be happy if she gave up her work and stayed with us all the time?"

"Maybe," I said.

"What if I told you she did try that for two and a half years?"

"Did she?"

"Yep."

"And she didn't like being with us?"

"She did, sometimes. But she constantly worried that people were dying or suffering because she wasn't going to be there when they needed it. I know it's hard to understand. But I think your mom feels that it is a calling for her. She struggled with the guilt. She cried constantly. We agreed that wasn't healthy for her or you. Do you understand?" He rubbed my shoulder with his hand.

"You were afraid her sad would make us sad?" I looked up at his big brown eyes.

"Exactly." He nodded.

"I'm sorry I pretended you weren't my dad," I said.

Mateo quietly listened to me remembering this moment with my dad. "And that was it? After that you stopped missing your mom and being mean to your dad?"

"Well, not exactly. I didn't stop missing my mom, but I did stop torturing my dad. I realized I had been punishing the wrong parent. Just because my mom wasn't there to suffer the wrath of my anger didn't make it okay to transfer it to the parent giving me unconditional love."

Mateo sat down next to me again. "So you think I'm being too hard on my mom?"

I shrugged. "I think instead of demanding she stop seeing Rooster—"

"Seamus," he corrected.

"I like Rooster better. I think instead of taking out your anger and frustration with your father on your mother, you should work together to figure out how to run this place without your dad or you.

You have over a year to train someone to take your place when you go to college."

"And push my own father out of the business he started?" Mateo's eyes bulged.

"Mateo, your dad may have started this business but you and your mom run it. Does it require his salary to keep it going?" I asked.

"Some of it, of course."

"Well, I'm sure you could work out something."

"You make it sound so easy." Mateo didn't sound convinced.

"I'm sure it won't be easy at all. But at least talk to your mom about it instead of fighting with her. Save your anger for the right recipient."

Mateo put his arm around me, squeezed me to him, and kissed the top of my head. "You're kind of smart for a homeschooler." He laughed into my hair.

I elbowed him in the ribs. "Hey, that's not cool."

"You know I'm kidding." He tipped my chin up to his face and kissed me with a gentle, whisper-soft touch that left my lips and chest aching for more. When he pulled back, I slid my hands up his neck and around his head to bring his lips back to mine. I'd never experienced the need to kiss someone. At the same moment, as I'd felt the sun slip behind the horizon, pulling the last of the day with it, I realized I'd let him pull me past all my protective rules. I hoped my dad fell in love with Truth or Consequences or I'd have a real reason to be angry with him.

Ten

LIZZY

TRUTH OR CONSEQUENCES, NM
NOVEMBER 26, 2014

The afternoon before Thanksgiving, Mel, Mateo, Rooster—who had been coming around with greater frequency, and I were playing rummy at the small table inside one of the RVs. Mateo and Rooster had spent the day fixing its AC. Rooster jokingly suggested we made sure it was working properly by hanging out inside. Mel brought the cards, chips, salsa, and some drinks. Mateo and I took turns consistently beating them. We could keep an eye on Sebby through the windshield as he prepared a new racecourse for the next day's Turtle Turkey Trot or 3T as I've come to call it.

"Sebby!" A man's voice boomed from the side of the shop where Sebby worked in the distance. We all turned to see a man wearing camouflage cargo shorts and an army-green T-shirt stretched taut over his pecs and biceps. He dropped to his knee and held out his arms to Sebby.

"Oh God!" Mel said at the same time Mateo said, "Shit!"

Rooster stood as quickly as he could in the tight quarters. "I better duck out."

The rest of us stood. Mel nodded and followed him out of the RV, across the shop, and toward the front door.

"I better stall him," Mateo said flatly. The lack of excitement for their dad's return struck me as sad. Especially when I turned to see Sebby remained focused on constructing a wooden ramp, his dad's hug left unfulfilled. I couldn't decide whether to stay in the RV, follow Mateo, or follow after Mel and Rooster. If I hurried I could catch a ride with Rooster. But my curiosity overpowered my sensibility and I stayed where I was, watching through the windshield. As Mateo approached his father I noticed he didn't offer the same huggy welcome he'd tried on Sebby. Instead his father stood and offered his hand. Mateo paused, looked over at Sebby, then took it in his own. Mateo's dad was a few inches taller than Mateo, with the arms and chest of a weightlifter, shaved black hair and Mateo's chiseled face. I could see Mateo would only get better looking with age.

I couldn't hear what they said to one another but Sebby came over, holding a turtle out as his personal handshake. His father ignored the turtle but seemed to be looking over Sebby's elaborate turtle zoo. When his father didn't acknowledge his turtle, Sebby put him back in the cage and returned to his project. Brow furrowed, Mateo stood at a distance, his arms crossed as he and his father spoke. Mateo gestured toward the RV and his father squinted in my direction before heading toward the RV. I opened the door and met them at the entrance.

"Lizzy, this is my dad, Lieutenant Colonel Mascia. Dad, this is my girlfriend, Lizzy." Mateo announced the last part with such pride I felt a strange pressure to stand taller and meet approval. The colonel stuck out his hand and I shook it, a little more firmly than normal.

"Nice to meet you," I said, and smiled up at him. "Welcome home."

"Why thanks, Lizzy. It's nice to meet you. Really nice. I was beginning to wonder about this boy. You're the first girl he's brought home. Well, other than his friend Raj who is sort of like a girl." He winked at me. My jaw dropped and I looked to Mateo for guidance. Mateo's eyes narrowed at his father. Heat crawled up his neck and into his face, but he held his tongue tight in his clenched jaw.

"Did Mateo tell you, he got Woody working again?" I asked.

"Who?" The colonel furrowed his brows in my direction. He felt seven feet tall when he looked down at you.

"Woody. The old car you could never get to work," I explained.

"Lizzy likes to name cars sometimes. She means the old Model T convert." Mateo leapt at the change of subject but his body remained rigid with tension.

"And you got her going again?" For Mateo's sake I wanted to hear pride in his response but instead I heard doubt.

"Let's show him, Mateo," I suggested, desperate for this man to acknowledge his son's awesomeness. The old Model T was from the 1930s. His dad had bought it at an auction before Mateo was born, but hadn't ever gotten it started again. Mateo had rebuilt the engine, replaced parts, and cleaned and painted it until it looked like new. He'd planned to surprise his dad with it a few years ago, but his surprise had been overshadowed by the Rooster surprise. I couldn't believe he still hadn't shown him.

"He's probably too tired." Mateo shrugged.

"I want to see it. But first, where is your mom? Is she not here?"

"I'm here." Mel appeared through the door to the retail section of the shop. I noticed she had thrown her hair up and put on a little makeup. It struck me as odd that she made more of an effort for her husband than her boyfriend, or whatever Rooster was. Mel bit at her upper lip and took a tentative step forward as the colonel took a big step forward and pulled her into his arms. He gave her a crushing hug, then physically set her back a step from him, his hands on her arms.

"Let me look at ya. Damn, it's been a long time again, hasn't it?" he asked, studying Mel. Mel blushed and looked down at her feet. Mateo shifted uncomfortably back and forth on his feet beside me. "I see Sebby is still a little different, huh? I thought maybe he'd finally grow out of this?" And the colonel sealed his fate on my dislike list.

"Sebby is amazing." I couldn't help myself. "Why would you want him to grow out of himself?" I asked. And I took great pleasure in watching the heat rise in the colonel's face before he cleared his throat and pushed past Mel through the door.

"Looks like you haven't changed much around here." The colonel reached out and straightened a stack of river-rafting pamphlets on the counter. Mel shot me a quick smile and squeezed my arm before following after her husband.

"Why don't we grab Sebby and go for a ride before I drop you home." Mateo turned to get Sebby.

"Sure." Now I could understand why Mateo struggled over his feelings toward his father. From what I'd seen so far, he didn't seem very fatherly.

Eleven

LIZZY

TRUTH OR CONSEQUENCES, NM
JANUARY 9, 2015

The holidays flew by in a blur of small gatherings, handmade gifts, time with my dad, a postcard from my mom, and the painful, heartbreaking experience of being a spectator to the derailing of Mateo's family unit. I actually felt sorry for the colonel by the time he left.

Here is my take on the colonel. He wants to be a part of his family while he's in town, but his lack of participation in their daily routines and intimacies has made him a stranger. I witnessed him trying, but he had a knack for saying and doing exactly the wrong thing. I don't think he is a bad man. Nobody can expect to be absent for the nuances of life. He couldn't have known that Sebby refused to eat anything that had a brain, or that Mateo could tackle a three-hundred-pound linebacker without hesitation but couldn't get within a foot of a spider. He couldn't be expected to remember his wife stopped drinking caffeine six years ago when she realized it gave her migraines. And he certainly couldn't have known that surprising his sons with a father-and-son deer hunting trip would be the absolute last thing they'd ever want to do. I'm sure I wasn't the only one to notice the relief wash over the colonel's face and shoulders as he loaded himself into a friend's truck to head to the airport.

Rooster stayed away the six weeks the colonel visited, but pulled into the driveway less than thirty minutes after he left. I studied Mateo's face for his reaction to this apparent deception. As usual, his stoic expression gave nothing away. Mel, on the other hand, ran to Rooster, and all but jumped into his burly, tattooed arms. When Mateo and I noticed her stream of tears, we took Sebby and headed out back to give them space.

"Do you think your parents still have sex?" I asked Mateo. We were seated side by side on the top of one of the older-model RVs. We could see Sebby refilling the pools in the turtle cages in the distance. When Mateo didn't respond I turned to see his face, worried I'd pissed him off with my question. His eyes stared unfocused at nothing in the distance, like his mind was a million miles away from me.

"Do you think she told your dad about Rooster?" I looked at him again, but he remained unmoving.

"Okay. I guess we're not talking about it." I sat silently next to him as the sun crept higher in the sky. Minutes passed, maybe as many as thirty before he spoke.

"I asked her last night why she didn't just divorce him." He glanced at me, locking his sad sandy eyes with mine. "She said she couldn't."

"She still loves your dad?" I asked.

"Maybe. I don't know. She said she couldn't because she is too scared what could happen to him over there if he didn't have us to come home to." He looked back over the horizon.

"So, now what? She's with Rooster while he's gone and with him while he's here? What about next year when he comes home for good?" I asked.

"How the hell am I supposed to know, Lizzy? God! I don't have all the answers!" Mateo yelled. He quickly rose, climbed down the ladder, and stomped off in the opposite direction of the shop, Sebby, and me. I immediately felt like an ass for picking at his already exposed heart. Why couldn't I simply sit quietly with him once in a while?

Twelve

LIZZY

TRUTH OR CONSEQUENCES, NM
SEPTEMBER 28, 2015

Nine months later, Mateo, Raj, Fawn, and I sat outside playing Trivial Pursuit beneath the white Christmas lights, on my patio. A month into our senior year, we'd had a number of discussions about why I should attend the high school there for this last year instead of homeschooling. In the past I'd never had a big desire to attend the local school, but the idea of walking through the halls with Mateo, and eating lunch with this group every day had appeal. I usually had my homeschool work done for the day by lunchtime. The extra three to five hours waiting for them to get out of school or practice were less than exciting. Raj had started a dance troupe for his senior project and he really wanted me to join.

"Oh I forgot to tell you. Principal Rayner actually pulled me into his office Friday morning to discuss how I should really talk you into attending a real school!"

"He did not." I rolled my eyes at Mateo and rolled the dice.

"Swear to God." Mateo held up both his hands. "He felt the group setting would enrich your academic experience and offer you better opportunities to round out your college applications." Mateo said all this in a pinched-nose imitation of Principal Rayner's voice.

"I'm pretty sure his daughter would prefer you didn't ever step foot in her daddy's precious hallways given her preoccupation with making Mateo one of *her* enriching high school experiences." Fawn wiggled her eyebrows up and down and Raj laughed.

"Whatever." Mateo threw a pie piece in her direction and rolled his eyes.

"The principal's daughter has a crush on you." I smiled at Mateo. "Now that could make enrolling worth it," I agreed.

"Think how much fun it would be to—" We all looked up as my dad's car came flying up the driveway at a crazy speed. He slammed on the brakes, turned the engine off, jumped out, and slammed the car door. My dad rarely gets mad. He's about as mellow as dads come so we all sat in shocked silence. He slammed the front door, then stomped through the kitchen and living room and opened the sliding door to where we sat.

"Lizzy. We're done here. I'm getting the map and the darts. Kiss your friends goodbye. We head out in the morning." And he disappeared into the dark house.

The blood drained from my face, my vision went fuzzy like someone had depressurized my life cabin without proper oxygen flow, and my heart sank into my stomach like an antacid in water, causing a peptic-style cauldron of sadness. None of us moved or spoke for a good thirty seconds.

"Is he serious?" Fawn finally asked. We'd never stayed this long anywhere and now we had to pack up and go. I had Mateo and . . . I couldn't even wrap my head around it. Of course we were leaving. I always knew we would. What had I been thinking? I looked up from where I'd been wringing my hands in my lap to find all of them waiting for me to react.

I felt tears threaten as my throat and chest burned with restraint. I could only nod. I looked up at Mateo. As usual his face gave nothing away.

"Should we go?" Raj asked.

"Probably." My voice came out hoarse and felt too thick for my throat. Raj stood and the other two followed suit. I dragged myself up, dreading everything to come in the next twenty-four hours. I knew the exit drill all too well.

"Will we get a chance to say goodbye?" Raj asked.

I took a deep breath. "I'll talk to him," I managed.

Raj grabbed me in a tight hug, dropped a kiss on my head, and jogged through the yard toward Mateo's truck. Fawn squeezed my arm and followed. I turned to look up at Mateo. He took my hands in his and looked me in the eyes.

"Do you want me to drop them and come back?" he asked.

I nodded and he pulled me into his chest. This had been my happy place for months. How could I be expected to walk away?

A loud thump came from inside followed by a "Goddammit!"

"I better go," Mateo said and lightly brushed my lips with his before jogging to his truck.

I stood watching until long after his taillights had disappeared.

"Lizzy!" my dad yelled from inside. I took a deep breath, looked longingly at the horseshoe pit, Dusty, and our abandoned game before stepping inside to face "The Moving Map." The day my mom and dad decided it was better for all of us that she leave, my dad had gone out for a drive while she packed and spent one last afternoon with me. (An afternoon I only wish I could remember as I was two at the time.) My dad, depressed, wandered into an antique and trinket store. He came across a basket of various state maps and aimlessly thumbed through them until he came across a big map of the United States. He claimed he broke out in goose bumps when the idea of "The Moving Map" was born. He found an old dart set and came home much happier to announce that the two of us would be moving as well. From that point on, whenever something happened that my dad felt was a sign we should move, he'd pull out the map and the green dart (because green symbolized new and go and all things fresh) and wherever it landed (providing it wasn't in Alaska or Hawaii), we went.

Inside he'd taken down the odd print of a pig leading a pig marching band that had been hanging above the living room couch when we moved in. In its place hung The Moving Map. I looked at the map and dropped onto the couch with my arms crossed.

"Lizzy. What are you doing? I'm getting ready to throw." My dad's eyes were red, his hair more disheveled than normal, and I realized for the first time his left eye was swollen.

"Did someone punch you?" I asked him.

He took a big breath and let it out loudly. "Lizzy, come on. Move. I want to get this done, pack up, and go."

"I'm not budging until you tell me why we're moving. You once told me making big decisions when emotional is never a good idea."

"I'm not emotional."

"You also told me never to lie to you and you'd never lie to me."

"I'm not e-m-o-tional." He stretched out the word as if he were speaking in another language I may not understand.

"Sure. I'm still not moving until you explain the sudden urge to depart."

He glared at me. I glared right back.

"Fine. I decided to drop by Jane's tonight after I finished helping Harold put his new grill together." He stopped talking as if he'd explained everything.

"And?"

"And she wasn't there, but Greg was." He turned away and began to pace.

"She's seeing someone else, too?" I sat on the edge of the couch.

"Nope. She's married to him. Has been for nine years." He massaged his jaw with his hand.

"Wait, Jane is married?"

He looked back at me and nodded. "To Greg. Nine years. Two kids. Yep." He sighed and sat beside me.

"Wow," I said. "I didn't see that coming. Sorry." I studied his face as he studied his hands.

"Yep. Me, too, to both."

"But you've been seeing her for a long time. Where was her husband all this time?"

"Oh, just home. Apparently, *her apartment*"—he made air quotes with his fingers—"is actually her sister's place that she's been watching for her while she is on sabbatical in Peru."

"Ouch!" I wrinkled my nose.

"Yep." He raised his eyebrows and sunk into the back of the couch.

"But technically you are still married to Mom," I pointed out.

"Only because we have never bothered to go through the paperwork to correct it. Plus, I told Jane all about our situation before we got together. She didn't just omit her marriage and two kids, she let me believe she lived the single life." He stood up again.

"And you know how I feel about lies." He resumed his pacing.

"Deal breaker. Zero tolerance." I quoted his long-standing mantra. My dad could get over almost any mistake I made except lying. And the older I got, the more I understood why. "I'm sorry. I feel like I didn't really get to know her. You never really brought her here."

"Maybe, in the back of my head, I knew something didn't feel right." I followed him with my eyes, kitchen table to sliding glass doors and back again.

"Do you love her?" I asked, a little surprised. My dad held people at a distance even better than I did. He looked at me, his lips twisted to the side.

"I didn't let it get to that, but . . ."

"You let your guard down this time?"

"A little."

"Do you think if you stayed you would have fallen in love with her? Like finally-divorce-mom-and-stay-someplace kind of love her?" A surprising excitement shot though my chest at the possibility of a more permanent existence.

But my hopes had been dashed with the wide-eyed, *are you insane* frown that immediately filled my dad's face.

"You know me better than that," he said.

"Then why are you so upset?" I asked.

He came and sat next to me on the couch and his eyes grew serious. "Because of you. I haven't seen you this happy in a long time. You really like it here, don't you?" His brown eyes filled with sad concern. A look I had only seen him cast upon me. A look I hadn't seen in a long time. It used to make an appearance whenever I wished for a normal mom.

"I do," I admitted.

"And you have your first boyfriend. How can I make you leave?" He put a hand on my shoulder.

"Then let's stay." I shrugged.

"We can't." He squeezed my shoulder.

"Why not?"

He took his hand back and leaned into the back of the couch. "Greg will leave Jane and the kids if I stay."

"What? That's bullshit!"

"Lizzy."

"Sorry, but that's like blackmail or something. It sounds like it's their issue to figure out. It has nothing to do with whether we are here or not." I stood, crossed my arms, and looked down at him.

"That's not all." He looked up at me. I felt like we'd switched roles. Me the parent, him the kid.

"What more could there be?"

"She's the minister at the Unitarian church." His sad, apologetic eyes locked with mine. But it didn't help. I threw my hands in the air and fell back onto the couch beside him.

"Let me guess. Greg threatened her with exposure."

"She loves her work. She's very good at it." My dad shrugged.

"You've been to her church?"

"That's where we met." He cast me a sheepish grin.

"You don't go to church."

"A couple days after we got here, I heard the singing from the coffee shop where I sit and code. I wandered in and once Jane started talking I couldn't leave. She pulled me in with her open-mindedness and realistic views of faith in modern society. She's really mesmerizing on that pulpit."

"Wow. We really haven't been talking like we usually do." I shook my head.

"Sorry." He put a hand on my knee and squeezed. "Why do I suddenly feel like a Disney dad?"

"It's not *that* bad, but we clearly have some catching up to do." I lifted an eyebrow at him and he wrinkled his nose back at me. "Wait. If you met in church, how could you not know about her husband and kids?"

"Her church is here but her home is forty minutes away. Her husband doesn't do church. Their kids are young so he stays home with them. I would guess most of the congregation doesn't even know she is married with kids."

"What? This whole thing makes no sense. Why would her husband not attend her church when she is the minister?"

My dad threw his arms up in the air. "You can see why I feel like such an idiot."

"A lying, cheating minister? Boy, Dad, you know how to pick 'em." I dropped my head onto his shoulder.

"Any chance he's bluffing?" I asked.

"He seemed pretty adamant when he punctuated his words with a fist to my face." My dad released a heavy sigh.

"So that's it. Your mind is made up. We're leaving." I felt tears threaten again.

He put his arm around my shoulders and pulled me tight to his side. "Do you have a better idea?"

"Yeah. Stay here and let Jane reap what she sowed." I heard the venom in my own voice.

"She's a good person, Lizzy."

"Clearly."

"Have a little more faith in me, Lizzy. Would I have spent this much time with someone if she wasn't worth it?" He tilted away so he could look me in the eyes.

"Then let's stay and you fight for her." I held his eyes.

"And her two children? And then what about her congregation?"

"Isn't forgiveness what religion is all about?"

The doorbell sounded and we looked at the door, then back at one another. I glanced at the clock above the mantel. It was after ten.

"Oh, it's probably Mateo. I told him he could come back." I walked to the door and opened it to find a cop standing there. A chill ran down my spine and I held my breath. How many times had I feared this moment? My mom had been crushed or buried or drowned helping someone else escape.

"Is this the Lane residence?"

"Yes?" I basically whispered. My dad stepped up beside me.

"How can we help you?" he asked.

"Andrew Lane?" the officer asked, sizing my dad up and down.

"Yes. Is everything okay?" I heard the fear in his voice, too. I knew we were both thinking the same thing.

"This is for you." He handed my dad an envelope. Then he tipped his hat at us and said, "Greg told me to tell you to drive safe." He gave us a creepy grin that made his eyes look like glowing slits in his face. Another shiver ran down my back, but I let out the breath I'd been holding. It wasn't Mom. We stood there with the door ajar as the officer returned to his patrol car and drove off.

"What the hell was that all about?" I looked at my dad. "Who the hell is this guy you pissed off?"

"Greg's also a cop." He tore open the envelope and shook out the papers inside. I watched his face as he read them. Heat crept up his neck and his fingers turned white where he held the papers tight.

"What does it say?" I asked, my heart beginning to pound in my chest.

"We're being evicted, effective as of five o'clock tomorrow." He clenched and unclenched his jaw. I'd never seen my dad do that before.

"How can he do that?" I asked, then, "He can't do that." I sat down on the couch and crossed my arms on my chest.

"I don't know, Lizzy. As we just saw, the long arm of the law has a limitless reach when these guys band together."

"No wonder Jane works far away and pretends he doesn't exist. He must be an asshole. Do you think he beats her?"

"Lizzy." He glared at me.

"What?"

"Nothing," he said. He walked across the living room, slid open the sliding door, and stepped outside. I knew better than to follow. Oh how I wished it had been Mateo at the door.

Thirteen

LIZZY

TRUTH OR CONSEQUENCES, NM
SEPTEMBER 29, 2015

The night we left (my dad prefers driving through the night when we make a move. A practice that made me wonder, I eventually confessed, if we were fleeing from the law because he secretly robbed banks for a living. He found this hysterical and occasionally joked about hiding the loot or grabbing the guns as we packed for our next destination. Given the current departure circumstances we both refrained from any references to the law), Mateo sat, perched beside me on the back of Dusty. Mateo held my right hand in his left, slowly tracing the outside edge of my fingers with his finger. His hands dwarfed mine, the tip of my nails aligned with his middle knuckles.

"I know you don't feel lucky right now, but I'm envious of your freedom to leave," Mateo said.

"I can ask my dad if you can come?" I looked into his comforting beach-sand eyes, lifting my eyebrows in question.

"I think my mom and Sebby would have a small problem with that." He dropped a kiss on the top of my head.

"I'm going to miss them, too. Sebby probably won't even notice I'm not there anymore."

"Nah, he loves you. Besides, who is going to help him catch desert turtles now? 'Cause you know I'm not picking up those disease-carrying mini-motorhomes."

I laughed and leaned my shoulder against his. "You're not going to forget I exist as soon as you see our taillights, are you?"

"Well, Monica Rayner has been lingering by my locker lately," he teased, knowing I couldn't stand the passive-aggressive principal's daughter who'd taken our choice to homeschool as a personal assault on her daddy's good name.

"I'm serious." I turned to look him in the eyes. "I broke too many of my own rules with you and if you break my heart, it could ruin me forever. You promise you'll keep in touch?"

I sat straight up in bed, my heart racing. If I'd just paid closer attention instead of seeing and hearing what I'd wanted to, I'd have realized he never really did promise. And when I'd asked for his promise his eyes had widened, he'd swallowed hard, and my dad had called out for me to get in the car.

I'd just remembered the look of panic that had flashed across his face. He smiled down at me, pulling his nose off center. An ER doc had botched the stitching job after Mateo had fallen off his bike as a boy. The wave-shaped scar couldn't be seen from a distance and the crooked-nose smile that hadn't quite reached his eyes was the only true tell that something hadn't been quite right.

Fourteen

LODAN
LAKETOWN, NY
OCTOBER 17, 2015

Dr. Payne suggested we leave Kono with him one more night. Lizzy thought it had less to do with the welfare of the rabbit and more to do with an excuse to see my mom again. On the drive back home Lizzy reached from the backseat through the space between my seat and the door to squeeze my arm. When I looked back at her she grinned and slid her eyes toward my mom. My mother hummed along to the radio as she drove. Something I hadn't ever heard her do. I guess it was Lizzy's way of saying maybe my mom wouldn't mind seeing Dr. Payne again either.

Lizzy thanked us for the afternoon, but excused herself to do laundry and ran back to her house. I decided to take advantage of my mom's good mood.

"Hey, Mom, you know what we should do right now?" I asked.

"Get our laundry done as well?" She smiled and headed toward her room.

"No." I followed her into her bathroom where she was gathering her clothes from the hamper. "Let's look in the attic for my birth certificate."

My mom rolled her eyes, but smiled. "You are relentless." She headed toward the laundry room with her clothes. I followed. "But, fine. If you go get all your dirty clothes for me, we can look in the attic after I get the laundry started."

The access to the pull-down attic ladder was in the hallway outside my bedroom. I reached up, pulled the ladder down, flipped the light switch on the wall, and climbed up into the warm air. It smelled like old cardboard and vanilla. My mom must have put one of her air fresheners up there, too. Our house often smelled like the vanilla scent she favored. There were only a few bare bulbs for light. I let my eyes adjust as my mom climbed up behind me. I knew the layout well. My mom had a system. The entire left side had holiday bins and boxes lining a set of plastic shelving in a U-shape. They were only stacked about two to three feet high since the floors weren't built to handle too much undistributed weight. Each holiday had its own section, starting with Christmas on the left and ending with Thanksgiving on the right. When I was younger we would spend hours decorating for the holidays. I felt like she'd overcompensated for our lack of family with holiday decor.

The middle section in front of me held pieces of our life we'd outgrown or simply tired of but hadn't let go. The parts to my race car–shaped toddler bed, my mom's old nightstand, a child-size rocking chair, an old Wiggles beanbag, and an assortment of fans, lamps, and step stools I'd needed as a child. My mom headed to the right side where she kept "milestones and momentos," as she called them. There were multiple bins of my report cards, artwork, science and book-report projects, school pictures, favorite picture books, old yearbooks. She'd even saved my cast from when I broke my left arm in first grade. My homemade boxcar had been no match for the giant maple tree at the base of the hill near the school. If she could have fit it up the stairs, she'd probably have saved the boxcar, too.

She walked to the far right corner and began shifting bins around. I picked up a miniature dumbwaiter I'd constructed for a book project in fifth grade.

"If we still have it, it should be in that." She pointed to a dark corner. I stepped closer, stooping to avoid the sloped roof. A tarnished, ancient-looking safe rested on the center of three pieces of stacked plywood, probably helping to distribute the weight.

"It looks ancient. Did it belong to your parents?"

My mom shrugged. "It came with the house."

"So let's open it." I shrugged. *What was she waiting for?*

"I can't."

"Why not?"

"I can't remember the combination." She clenched her teeth, wrinkled her nose, but didn't meet my eyes. I cocked my head and studied her posture. She fixed her stare on the safe, but held herself tight, arms wrapping her chest. The only time she acted this way was when I asked her questions about my father. She never gave me any concrete information. She used the same phrases every time.

"Your father was an intelligent man. A teacher. We both made a bad decision that yielded the best possible result. You. If anyone had found out, he'd have lost his job. Your grandmother had died, your grandfather was remarried. I figured it was best if I moved someplace new and raised you. Eventually I landed here and the rest is our happy history." Whenever I asked for more details, she'd only give me the same story again. She said she didn't know my dad well enough to share his favorite color or food or car. I'd asked about everything and she'd given me a single paragraph. On my tenth birthday I'd gotten so upset at her lack of information that I'd stolen her car and driven all the way to town before she and her friend tracked me down. I'd left a note saying I'd gone to find my father, which was ridiculous because I didn't even know where to start looking. When I begged her to at least tell me what state he lived in, she'd say, "He only lives in our past, honey. Think of him like oxygen—you need it to live, but you can't see it." My head began to buzz with the familiar frustration and I clenched my fists and jaw to hold in my anger.

"Do you really not remember or you don't want me to see my birth certificate because of my dad?"

"His name is not on it."

"So why don't you want me to see it?" I yelled, causing her to snap her head in my direction. I rarely raised my voice.

"Honey, I didn't forget on purpose. Don't get upset." She sighed and moved beside me. "We can try all the obvious things," she said, resting her hand lightly on my arm. A peace offering.

"Let me try." I pulled my arm away, stepped past her, and knelt to take a closer look. The lock was old-school, not like the digital safe my mom had in her room where she kept spare cash for emergencies and her mom's wedding jewelry. It looked like a larger version of the combination lock on my locker at school.

"Does it work the same as a regular lock? Three turns right to clear, stop on the first number, left past the zero, then stop on the second, then right again to the third?" I asked, already turning to clear it and begin.

"I think so." She stood back a little so I had better light.

I tried my birthday, her birthday, her mom's birthday, her dad's birthday, her parents' anniversary. Nothing worked. Her phone rang from downstairs and she went to get it. I spent the next forty-five minutes trying to crack the code. When my frustration threatened to explode, I left the attic to Google other ways to open the safe.

A little while later mom knocked lightly at my door.

"Come in." I didn't bother looking up from my screen as she came in.

"Hey," she said tentatively. Clearly my heavy-handed keyboarding had made my frustration clear.

"Can I talk to you about something for a minute?" she asked, walking into the room and sitting on the edge of my bed.

"I'm listening." My eyes remained fixed on the screen.

"Can you take a break from that for a minute?"

I sighed loudly and turned in my chair to face her.

"So that was Jason on the phone..."

"Jason?" I asked.

She cleared her throat and crossed her legs at her feet. "Dr. Payne."

I crossed my arms and waited for her to continue.

"Anyway, Dr. Payne has this conference in Syracuse this weekend and he wondered if I'd like to go along since I know the area and..."

"I don't want to go away this weekend, Mom. I need to get that safe open."

She leaned back a little and I realized I'd raised my voice to respond. I'm not usually a yeller. "Sorry, but you know how important this is to me."

"I do. That's why I was going to suggest you stay here." I felt her watching me, gauging my reaction to this option.

"You're going to let me stay here alone for the weekend?" I asked.

"With some stipulations and Violet would come by to check on you periodically. Do you think you'd be okay with that? Because I don't have to go."

I looked at my mom and realized she was nervous. "Mom, are you worried about leaving me here?"

"Well, a little, sure."

"I'll be fine." I shrugged at her and then it hit me. My mom wasn't nervous about me. She was going away with a man for the weekend. She'd never even dated with the exception of that kayak date.

"Wait. You're okay with going away with Dr. Payne for a weekend?"

Her shoulders sagged a little and she looked up at me, her eyes full of confusion. For a moment I felt like she was the teenager and I was the adult.

"I don't know. He's a nice guy and he's funny and I . . . ugh." She fell back onto my bed. "It's been forever since I've been in a relationship. I don't know if I even know how to do this."

"Do you like him?" I asked, glad I couldn't see her face, because it felt a little awkward to discuss this with my mom.

"I think so." Her voice was barely above a whisper.

"Then you should go, Mom. What have you got to lose?"

"My dignity. And what if I get there and discover he is really annoying or chews with his mouth open or refuses to wear deodorant because of animal testing?"

"What? You're weird, Mom. It's only a couple of days. You're a nurse. I'm sure even if he has the table manners of a sow or struggles with personal hygiene, it can't be as bad as the bodily functions you face head-on, every day. Besides, you ate lunch with him and he's a doctor. If he wasn't gross then, I don't know why he suddenly would be now."

"I guess. I've only spent one afternoon with him and now I'm going away for the weekend? This is crazy." She jumped up from my bed and headed to the door. "I'm going to tell him no."

"No." I stood up to follow her. "Mom, you should go." I leaned against my door frame and she stopped at the top of the stairs.

"You think?" I noticed she was bouncing in place a little on her toes. This was excited Mom. I hadn't seen excited Mom in a while. As frustrated as I was with her about my birth certificate and the safe, I felt my chest tighten and I smiled at her.

"You want to go, Mom. I can tell. Just do it. I'll be fine."

She put her hands to her face and brought them to her mouth. "I'm going to. I'm going to go away for the weekend with a man." She raced down the stairs like she feared one of us would change her mind if she didn't immediately call to accept the invite. And I felt genuinely happy for my mom. Besides, she wouldn't be pestering me to do other things like laundry and I'd be able to concentrate on cracking the safe.

Fifteen

LIZZY

LAKETOWN, NY
OCTOBER 23, 2015

I don't know what time it was when I ran over to Lodan's house, but I knew it was late. Thankfully his mother wasn't home so I could run directly inside to show him the letter that I couldn't bring myself to read.

I sat on the floor of Lodan's room, leaning against his bed and I felt a small relief when he sat beside me and took the letter from my hand. The weight of what it could say was more than I could hold at that moment. Lodan turned it over in his hand and looked at the cover of the envelope. It had obviously been lost in the maze of our former addresses. We weren't always efficient about updating our snail-mail information. This could help explain the radio silence I'd gotten from Mateo. According to the date on the letter, he'd mailed it a few days after I'd left.

"I believe we may have uncovered the silent treatment mystery." Lodan vocalized what I'd been thinking. He did that sometimes; spoke my thoughts.

"What if it's a goodbye?" I asked.

"What if he's pregnant?" Lodan nudged me with his elbow.

"Not funny!" I snapped and yanked the envelope back from him. "If you're going to make a joke of this, then never mind." I began to stand, but he reached out and put a hand on my arm.

""Hey, Lizzy. Calm down. I'm sorry. I was trying to lighten the mood a little. You look like you're going to explode into a million tiny pieces with the slightest touch or misplaced modifier."

I looked down at the sincerity in his green eyes, handed him back the letter, and sat down beside him again. He threw his arm around my shoulder and gave me a side-squeeze.

"Now before we do this, can I suggest we use one of my mom's calming tricks?"

I shrugged. "I guess." Doubt and fear knotted tighter and tighter in my stomach.

"Okay. Let's go over the worst-case scenarios. If we prepare your psyche for all the worst outcomes you can think of, you are less likely to be blindsided."

"Seriously? I've been going through these scenarios since the first day I was ghosted."

"Great. Let's hear them."

"Well, the absolute worst can be ruled out given we have a letter to prove otherwise," I explained.

"Death?"

"Exactly. So that leaves serious injuries that could prevent him from digital correspondence."

"Paralysis, coma, that sort of thing?" Lodan asked.

"Yes. And we can probably rule those out, too, as this is his handwriting on the outside of the envelope." I ran my finger over his perfect penmanship.

"Okay. What's next?" Lodan rubbed his hand along my upper arm.

"He moved out of the country."

"Still possible. He could have left after he sent the letter."

"Yes. Then there is the new girlfriend possibility." I sighed shakily.

"And if that is what this says, how are you going to react?"

I closed my eyes and tried to picture Mateo with another girl. Fawn? I almost laughed out loud. That would never happen. I thought about Monica Rayner, the principal's daughter who had been crushing on him before I left. I imagined her looking up into

Mateo's sandy eyes and him gazing down into her freckled face. Bile gathered in the back of my throat. I shook my head.

"It wouldn't be good," I said.

"Okay. If that's what we read, what are we going to do?"

I shrugged again. "What can I do?"

"I mean, obviously that will hurt. So let's think of what we can do to help dull that pain."

"Like premedicating or something?" I asked, imagining the ibuprofen I'd take before getting my braces tightened.

"I like that. Premedicating. Yes."

"Okay. Well this would be a lot easier if I had experience in this area. But I've never had a boyfriend before Mateo so I don't know how to fix break-up pain."

"Yeah. I'm not any help there either." I saw the heat creep into Lodan's face and I gave his leg a squeeze.

"It's okay. We can figure it out together." He nodded and we fell silent.

"Google it?" we said at the same time, then laughed.

We pulled up a browser on his computer. He typed in "break-up survival methods" and the screen jumped from a website about safe cracking to a number of links to survival tips. He clicked on a top ten list from HuffPost. Basically it recommended three general categories of survival: physical, mental, and spiritual. Specifically I should meditate, eat right, exercise, avoid obsessing, and do nice things for others.

"I don't know," I said. "That all sounds like how to survive the long haul. What am I supposed to do in the first few minutes and hours of Lizzy without Mateo? I need instant pain relief."

"Okay." Lodan searched for instant solutions, but everything we read eluded to time healing my wounds.

"Ugh. This isn't helping." I threw myself facedown onto Lodan's bed.

"Okay, then let's do what they do in those relationship movies my mom likes."

"And that would be?" I asked, my voice muffled in his comforter.

"Ice cream." And before I could stop him, he'd run downstairs. He returned moments later with a pint of cookie-dough ice cream and two spoons.

"We need to step this up or our pain relief is going to melt," he announced, sitting back down.

"Okay. If it's not another girl, I guess it could be . . ."

"Another guy?" Lodan shrugged his shoulders.

"Oh," I said. "Um, I never thought about it. His best friend is gay, but . . ."

"How would you feel about that?" he asked.

I thought for a minute. I tried to picture Mateo kissing Raj, but I couldn't. I tried to picture him kissing Neil Patrick Harris. I still couldn't see it. "I don't think it's an issue." I shrugged.

"Okay. How about he can't do a long-distance relationship?" Lodan had made a good suggestion.

"That's the same as break-up, I think. I mean, I guess I could try to convince him otherwise. I don't know. What if he just doesn't love me anymore?" I'd spoken out loud my biggest fear. "Maybe he never did and when I was gone, he realized he didn't even miss me?" I looked at Lodan.

He gave me a half smile. "Then he's an idiot and you're better off without him anyway."

I threw his pillow at him. He blocked the shot and gave me a serious look.

"What?" I asked.

"It's time," he said. "The ice cream is melting. I'm ripping off the Band-Aid."

I nodded and he opened the envelope.

"Do you want me to read it aloud?" he asked, unfolding the letter.

I took a deep breath. "Yes." I climbed to the top of his bed, wrapped my arms around his pillow, and leaned against the wall as he paced the floor and read.

Hey Lizzy,

You know how you said Sebby wouldn't even know you were gone? Well, you couldn't have been more wrong. The morning after you left he asked me to take him to the playground at the school so he could let Aspire go back to where he came from. Then that afternoon he invited us to the first Annual Aspire Memorial Race. Before the race began, instead of playing the national anthem at the start, he played "Hurt" by Johnny Cash. And he continues to play it over and over again. If we all didn't find it so damn cute, I think we'd hide that old CD player he totes around.

Sebby isn't the only one who misses you. We all do. But I have done a lot of thinking since you left. The rooftops of the best-thinking RVs are all in tip-top shape. The thing is, from the moment you appeared in T or C my life has taken a giant right turn from where it had been bumping along. This new unfamiliar road has been amazing in many ways and scary in others. You have this way of making the people around you feel like anything is possible. For the first time in my life I found myself able to come up with more reasons why I should do something rather than why I shouldn't. Before I met you I made most of my life choices to please my parents or my friends or this whole town in a way. I've tried to do the right thing and be the person I knew everyone wanted me to be. I don't think that's a bad thing most of the time. At least not until I watched you guys drive away. I felt sad because I knew I'd miss you. Normal. I felt envious because I wished I was driving away from this town and toward a new adventure of my own. Normal. But the most overwhelming and confusing feeling I felt was relief—like someone had just hauled a giant 5-wheeler off the center of my chest. This is obviously NOT a normal reaction when saying goodbye to your girlfriend.

At this point Lodan looked up from his perch against his bed to where I sat squeezing the life out of his pillow. "You want me to keep going? Or do you want to read this in private?" I heard the pity in his voice and it made me angry and grateful all in the same breath.

"Just finish it," I said.

Lodan sighed. "Scooch over then," he said before moving beside me on the bed, his back also snug against the wall.

I hated myself for feeling this. I tried to ignore it, but I couldn't. Every time someone mentioned you it hovered there again, taunting me with the insanity of it all. Relief. I felt more lost than I'd been before I met you. And the thing is, when you were around I felt like I had found a sense of freedom. I'd found a way to let go. You helped me to see that I could go to college and pursue my own dreams rather than stay tethered to the business and my family obligations. Those are not my obligations to meet. Those are my dad's. And thank you, Lizzy, for helping me to see that and for encouraging me to be brave enough to take those steps. I am eternally grateful to you for that.

But still the relief. It confused me. I tried to decipher it from every possible angle. And here is the thing. Part of following the path others wanted (especially my parents and peers on this one) included having a girlfriend. That's what you're supposed to do in high school (at least around here). And Lizzy, you are easy to love. I hope that sounds like a compliment because it is. And I do love you. But I don't think I love you like a boyfriend is supposed to love a girlfriend. I wanted to love you like that. I had myself and everyone convinced that I could love you like that. And God, I hate saying all of this, because I know how much this will hurt you. But it is because I love you that I know I have to be honest with you about this. I know that's what you deserve and what you would want me to do.

You are smart and funny and kind and inspiring. I know you are going to do amazing things with your life. And I hope when the pain of this subsides we can find a way to remain friends and stay in contact because I know how having a person like you in my life will continue to help me be a better me.

I am working through some messy and complicated feelings right now. I guess I'm having a pre-adult crisis of sorts. Please for-

give me, Lizzy, for hurting you, for being dishonest with you about how I truly felt, and for dropping all of this on you when you have just moved to a new town where you don't have a good friend like you need and deserve to help you get through this. I am sorry.

I am not going to contact you again for a while. I think you need time and space to process this. And, like I said above, I am sorting through some complicated feelings of my own right now. I've even signed off all social media. I'm trying to get my head clear of all of the other voices and find my own voice. Please take care, Lizzy. I wish you nothing but good things. You deserve the world.

Your friend,
Mateo

We sat in silence. Lodan must have sensed my need to digest what he'd read. I felt oddly calm. I didn't feel tears coming like I'd expected. Instead I felt numb. I think that's the best description. Eventually Lodan reached for the ice cream, removed the top, scooped a spoonful, and held it out for me. I took the spoon and concentrated on the cold sweetness on my tongue.

We both took turns spooning the ice cream into our mouths, silently swallowing a whole pint of sweetness to help soothe the giant dose of shittiness I'd just had to swallow. Without saying a word, Lodan took my spoon, tossed the container, sat at his computer, and pulled up another safe-cracking site. After a bit I pulled a chair beside him.

"If we can't understand the mysteries of Mateo, maybe we can at least crack open a safe tonight," I said. I knew I wasn't letting myself absorb or feel Mateo's words. I couldn't yet. I needed to feel needed and Lodan needed my help.

Sixteen

LODAN

LAKETOWN, NY
OCTOBER 23, 2015

A couple hours later, Lizzy finally cracked the code on the antique safe and I hugged her so tightly she screeched, "Can't breathe!"

The code made no sense to me (4-22-20-2). Lots of twos for sure. Maybe my mom had set it wrong to start. Or maybe not. There was a stack of file folders inside the safe, a box of colorful, tangled jewelry I set aside, and a box of pictures that I didn't bother to look through. I had one mission and I was not going to get distracted. Lizzy hung back a little and let me look.

"Do you care if I leave you to look through this stuff?" she asked, standing, slightly stooped beneath the peaked attic roof. I heard the sadness in her voice and felt torn between comforting my friend and finally searching the safe.

"Do you want me to come hang with you?" I asked her.

"What? We may have just uncovered the Holy Grail! Dig through that thing. Besides, I think I need to process Mateo's letter alone." She started down the ladder.

"Thank you for cracking the safe, MacGyver."

"Who's MacGyver?" Lizzy asked as she headed down the attic ladder.

"I don't know. It's something my mom says whenever I figure out how to fix a problem."

"Oh, well, you're welcome. See you tomorrow."

"Night," I said as I leafed through the files looking for one that might contain my birth certificate. With each fruitless file I scanned, my excitement faded and my frustration grew. I began to suspect this safe contained nothing of ours. Everything here belonged to a family named Silverman. Near the last third of the stack I came across a picture stuck between two folders with tape remnants from a time it had been purposely secured elsewhere. My mom, about my age, looked admiringly at another girl, close to her age but taller. The other girl glared at the camera with her arms crossed on her chest, an incredulous subject. I turned it over and read *Heather & Sage*. This was a good sign. I dropped it into a file and continued looking. But after a few more minutes I had nothing. Angry, I began shoving everything back into the safe, mumbling under my breath, when another picture caught my eye. This picture showed my mom, younger than the other photo, with the same unhappy girl and my grandparents. I'd only seen them in the old photo my mom had on the mantel in the living room. They looked a little older in this picture, my grandmother closer to my mom's age now. It was stuck to an envelope. I peeled it off and turned it over. It had *1997* written in blue ink.

This had to be our stuff. I pulled out the small box of pictures and found more of my mom, my grandparents, and the unhappy girl. She never smiled in any of the pictures. Did my mom have a sister? Why hadn't she talked about her? Had she died? I flipped through a few more photos of people I didn't recognize, then a few of the unhappy girl with my mom and some guy. He must have been Unhappy's boyfriend. He often had a hand on her shoulder or his arm around her. My mom stood off to the side. I found a picture of Unhappy in a hospital bed holding a bundled baby. She looked like the most miserable mother I'd ever seen. I flipped through a few more and found a picture of a toddler playing with a big Tonka truck. I couldn't tell if it was a boy or a girl. I turned over the picture. It read *Michael, June 2000*. Michael. Did I have a cousin? I flipped through the rest of the pictures but there weren't any more of the boy named Michael. I set aside a few of the pictures to take downstairs and picked up the envelope. I pulled out the folded notebook paper and opened it.

Heather,
I came across this picture in my last move and thought you may want it. Remember how much he loved driving cars on our arms and legs like we were living highways? Hope you are still doing well. Maybe you could visit sometime.
Sage

Whatever picture she'd sent wasn't in the envelope anymore. I looked at the return address on the envelope. The only name written was Sage and she lived in California. Why hadn't my mom told me I had an aunt and cousin living in California? Did this have something to do with my father and why she wouldn't show me my birth certificate?

I didn't have time to finish processing what I'd found because I heard our front door slam open and footsteps pounding up the stairs. I'd glanced at my watch to see it was after midnight.

"Hello!" I called down the opening of the attic just as Lizzy stepped into my view. She had a big goofy grin on her face.

"Are you okay?" I asked her.

"Yes. And no." She tipped her head back and forth a little. "But I think I know what might help."

"Okay," I said, still looking down the open attic door at her.

"First tell me what you found." Lizzy climbed the ladder.

"Not my birth certificate," I admitted.

"You're kidding. After all of that, it wasn't even in there?"

"Nope. But I did find some family pictures and a weird note from my mom's sister, I think."

"I didn't think your mom had siblings." She sat down on one of my old stools.

"Neither did I," I said. I handed Lizzy the picture of my mom and her sister. "I think her name is Sage and I might have a cousin, too. Look at this one." I handed her the picture of the little boy playing with the Tonka truck and then Sage holding him as a baby.

"She's bubbling over with joy." Lizzy rolled her eyes and handed the pictures back.

"And then there's this letter to my mom from her sister. It's from a couple years ago." I passed it to her to read.

"So what do you think this all means?" Lizzy asked. "Why would your mom not tell you about them?"

"I have no idea. Maybe they had a falling out or something?"

"Did you ever meet your grandparents?" she asked.

"Nope. My mom's mom died before I was born. She didn't get along with her dad. He died a couple years ago. She went to his funeral in California, but didn't want me to miss school. Plus two plane tickets would have been too expensive. At least that's what she claimed."

"What about your dad and his parents?" She studied the photos closer.

"She refuses to talk about him." I couldn't keep the frustration out of my voice.

"I wonder if her sister knows who he is. I bet she does!" Lizzy's eyes lit up. She bounced her eyebrows up and down with a smile that made my stomach clench. I'd seen this expression before. She was about to tempt me to step outside my comfort zone.

"Whatever you are thinking: no!" I shoved the pictures into my back pocket and headed for the ladder.

"You haven't even heard what I'm thinking." We climbed down, folded the ladder back into the attic, turned off the light, and closed the door.

"I'm afraid to even hear it." I walked into my bedroom and we both flopped onto my bed, stomach first, side by side.

"Okay. If you don't want to hear my plan, then I dare you to text your mom and ask her if she has a sister."

"It's after midnight."

"So?"

"So, I'll text her in the morning."

"You just found out you have an aunt and probably a cousin. I'd text my dad immediately."

"She has to have a good reason for not telling me."

"Text her."

"No."

And before I realized what she was doing, Lizzy jumped off my bed, grabbed my phone off my desk, and ran down the hall into the bathroom.

"Lizzy, don't," I yelled and tried the door, but she'd locked it behind her.

"Too late!" she yelled back.

"Lizzy, this isn't funny!" I yelled and slid down the door to the floor. My stomach ached with a fear I'd never experienced. My mom and I had always been a team. But learning she'd neglected to tell me she has a sister had planted a seed of doubt about our relationship. She wouldn't tolerate dishonesty, yet wasn't the omission the same as lying? I ran my hands across my brush cut.

"Did she respond?" I asked.

"She's working on it. The three dots have been floating for a bit, like she is writing a long response."

I leaned my head back against the door. I heard the toilet flush followed by sink faucet as Lizzy presumably washed her hands.

"Still nothing?"

"Hold on. Um. 'Why?' She's asking why," Lizzy said.

"After all that she just said why?"

"Yes."

"Tell her I opened the safe and saw the pictures."

"I did."

"And?"

"Nothing yet."

"Bouncing dots?"

"Nope."

I stood to pace. Lizzy opened the door, stepped out, and held the phone up for me to read my mom's response.

> I'll explain when I get home Sunday.

I thought for a moment, then typed.

> Does your sister know my dad?

Nothing. I paced more. Then bouncing dots. Then they disappeared.

"Come on!" I yelled at the phone. Again the dots followed by:

> I'll explain Sunday.

"Great!" I yelled. I stomped back into my room and threw my phone onto the bed.

Lizzy picked the phone up to read her response. "I think that's a yes."

"If she's been lying to me all of these years, how do I know she'll tell the truth now? She has from now until Sunday to come up with whatever she wants me to believe."

"I think you're being a little harsh with her. Maybe it was your dad that caused the fight between them. What if he got your mom and her sister pregnant around the same time? Maybe your mom had an affair with your aunt's husband?"

"Seriously, Lizzy? That all sounds a little too reality television."

"What has she told you about your father? He was a teacher, right?"

"Yes, and he would have lost his job if people knew about me."

"How old was your mom when she had you?"

"Sixteen."

"Wow. Did she finish school?"

I shrugged. I'd never thought about what her life was like when I was born. I'd always focused on my father. "She must have. She's an RN now."

"Hmm. We gotta talk to your aunt. Where is that letter?" Lizzy had that crazy look on her face again and my stomach muscles tensed with her inevitably outlandish plan. I slipped the letter out of my jeans and handed it to her.

"Oh this is perfect." Lizzy squeezed my arms in her hands.

"You are scaring me a little bit right now." I wrapped my hands around her arms and shook them up and down a few times.

"We are going on a truth-seeking trip," Lizzy announced as she sat in my desk chair and woke up my computer.

"A what?" I asked, though I had a good idea.

"When does your mom get home?"

"Sunday afternoon."

"How old is her CRV?"

"Two years, but it doesn't matter because we are not going on a trip." I crossed my arms.

"Lodan. You want to know the truth about your dad and why your mom didn't tell you about her sister and is cagey about your birth certificate, right?"

"Of course, but—"

"And do you think I deserve to be dumped through the mail?"

"No, but—"

"We are going. We will stop to confront Mateo, and then go meet your family. Google Maps says it's only about forty hours. My dad and I have a twelve-hour hard limit without stopping for sleep. Can you miss school this coming week?" Lizzy ignored my protests.

"We cannot take my mom's car on a cross-country trip without her permission. How will she get to work?"

"I'm sure Dr. Payne will help her out or one of her friends will. Besides, my dad's car is overdue for some maintenance."

"I don't even have a license yet, remember? That's why we cracked that safe to begin with."

"Well, it's a good thing I have mine, then."

"Lizzy, we'd be gone for a week. I can't miss a week of school." I fell back onto my bed.

"To find your father. Of course you can." She lay down beside me.

"I can't." I covered my face with my hands.

"Tell me you don't have like a perfect GPA?" She pulled my hands away, hovering above me with those hypnotic big blue eyes.

"Exactly why I shouldn't risk messing it up." I closed my eyes.

"You have the flu. Plenty of people miss a week of school for the flu."

I didn't respond. I never missed school. I ran through what the next week entailed. I had a paper due in AP English but I could email that. I'd miss a couple quizzes and an AP physics test.

"I'll help you catch up. I promise." She said it as if she could hear my thought processes.

"Lizzy, we can't just show up at—"

"We can."

"We don't even know if she still lives at—"

"If she doesn't we will track her down from the new owners. Lodan, please, stop overthinking this. I would think a transportation enthusiast like you would be thrilled to go on a cross-country adventure."

"And what are we going to tell my mom and your dad?"

"The truth. I mean, what else? This is a truth-seeking trip. We can't start out with a lie."

"My mom will be crazed with worry." I felt a twinge in my chest. I hated to upset her. But then again, she'd brought this on herself in a way.

"Okay. I need to pack and we should sleep some. What time is it now?" Lizzy asked. We both read the time on my computer: just after one in the morning.

"Great. Let's roll out of here at six. My dad sleeps most soundly from about four to eight. He'll never hear us go." Lizzy jumped up and headed out the door to my room before I could even process this insane itinerary.

"Lizzy."

"Oh, and grab as much food as you can that doesn't require refrigeration, and money. Crap. Do you have money you can put toward gas and possibly a cheap hotel or two?"

"I have money saved for a car," I admitted.

Lizzy stopped at this and looked hard at me. "Look. I know that's a big deal for you. I have a decent savings account for college. Let's plan to use some of that first and we'll only tap into the car fund if we have to. Deal?"

"That's not fair to you. We can probably sleep in the car once we get to warmer climates. The seats fold down in the back and we could probably fit okay. You especially."

"I also have the emergency credit card if we get into a pinch."

"Lizzy, you do realize this is crazy." I ran my hand across my head.

She flashed a wicked grin, said, "It will be vintage," and waved before bolting down the stairs to get ready.

I rolled my eyes and grabbed a duffle bag out of my closet. Mateo was right, Lizzy had a way of making anything seem possible.

Seventeen

LODAN

LAKETOWN, NY TO ST. LOUIS, MO
SATURDAY, OCTOBER 24, 2015

"Are all of the songs on this playlist about dads?" she asked, keeping her eyes on the road while she took a long swallow of coffee from her thermal travel cup. She'd brought a full one for each of us, but I hadn't touched mine even after more than three hours on the road. When she asked, I'd admitted we were a tea household. She'd never met anyone who hadn't at least tried coffee. Well, at least nobody her age.

"Yeah, sorry, want me to change it?" I asked as a country singer sang about "keeping it between the lines."

"No, I'm fine with it. This song kind of fits the moment."

I didn't respond. I quietly watched the trees flashing by as we cruised down 90 West.

"I can't help but notice the songs all glorify fatherhood."

"I guess."

"I love that. You've never met him, yet you choose songs about great dads. I think most kids might be angry with their fathers and therefore gravitate toward dad bashing. Lodan Dawson, I do believe you are an optimist."

"What if I told you my next playlist is a dad-bashing compilation?"

"It is?" Lizzy turned from the road for a moment to check my face.

I gave her my best deadpan face until a small laugh escaped. "No, but I've never thought of myself as an optimist per se."

"Well, I think you are. And that's good because I prefer to spend time with positivity rather than negativity. I think both can be contagious."

I thought about this for a minute. Did I surround myself with positive people? I didn't *surround* myself, period. Before Lizzy, the only people I hung out with outside of school were my mom, her friends, and cyber friends. When I wasn't building or fixing something, I watched YouTube videos of other people fixing things or chatted with people online about the same things.

"I never really thought about it," I said. "I guess I used to hang out with kids when my mom had her day care. And this kid, Kenny, a son of my mom's friend, would come over with her. He stopped when we were around eleven or twelve. He always wanted to play baseball, and I always wanted to work on fixing a lawnmower or building a new section of my miniature town."

"Wait, you built a miniature town?"

"Yeah."

"Is it still around?"

"Yeah. I still add to it sometimes."

"Why haven't I been given a tour?"

I shrugged. "I don't know. I haven't worked on it in a while. It's in our extra bedroom."

"What's it called?"

"What do you mean?"

"The town. What's the name of your town?"

"Oh. Yeah, my mom used to ask me that. I never got around to naming it."

"Are you kidding me? That is kinda bizarre, you know."

"It never felt finished and I guess I figured I'd name it when it was done."

"That would have been the first thing I'd have done."

"Of course you would have."

"When we get back, can I help you name it?"

"Sure." I shook my head and looked at the Town & Country minivan we were passing. The body had a few rust patches. A toddler slept in a car seat. A woman, her mother probably, drove. I briefly wondered if that family included a father or if they were on their own, too. Then I glanced at my watch and felt a twinge of guilt tighten my stomach. My mom still wouldn't even know we'd left for another thirty or more hours. I wondered what state we'd be in when she read the note I'd left her on the kitchen table.

"Did you name all the stores and banks and schools and stuff in your town?" Lizzy asked.

"Um. Not really. I think it says 'bank' on the bank and 'school' on the school. You know, general labels."

"Well, if you are cool with it, I'm going to name them all."

"Sure. We can design signs for each building," I suggested.

"Cool." Lizzy's eyes lit up like I'd agreed to something exciting. Then again, Lizzy brought a level of excitement to everything she did. We drove in silence for a while, listening to the last few songs on my dad playlist.

"Hey, are you about ready for a bathroom break? It's three miles to the next rest stop. And maybe you could get one of the bottles of water out of the back."

"Sure."

"Do you mind if I drink your coffee since you clearly aren't drinking it?"

"Sorry." I felt bad she'd made the effort for nothing.

"No, actually it's good. More for me."

I beat her back to the car after the restroom and opened the back for the water. I moved one of the bags to access the cooler and discovered we had a third passenger. There in the plastic bin, snug in a nest of socks and fluffy white stuffing lay Kono. I shook my head, grabbed the water, and dug through the cardboard box of food items to make us peanut butter bagels for breakfast. Peanut butter and bread were two items I knew we'd be eating plenty of. Both of us had brought a family-size jar and plenty of bread products. As she pulled back onto the highway I selected an old Taylor Swift playlist my mom liked, hoping Lizzy might like it, too.

"You brought Kono?" I asked.

"Of course. As responsible parents we can't leave our infant home alone," she said, shrugging it off as normal to take a rabbit along on a cross-country trip.

"Of course not," I said and rolled my eyes. If she saw me or heard my sarcasm, she didn't react.

"We'll probably need gas and a bio break again in three hours. You good with that?"

"Sure. I'll make us lunch from our cardboard pantry."

"Sounds mouthwatering. I think we should call it the Cardboard Cupboard."

"Sure."

"That would be a kind of cool pop-up restaurant concept. Creative sandwiches made from everyday pantry items."

"Flavor may be an issue."

"Nah. We're two creative people. Surely we could come up with some amazing uncommon combinations."

I pulled a few items out of our Cardboard Cupboard and held them up to her. "Okay, how can we use fruit roll-ups and salted peanuts?"

"That's easy. Unroll the roll-up, sprinkle the peanuts inside, re-roll. Boom. You have a sweet and salty snack. We could call it . . . nut . . ."

"Nutsack?"

"Lodan!" Lizzy yelled, taking her bulging eyes off the road to look at me.

I felt my face get warm but couldn't help laughing with her. "Sorry, it just popped into my head."

"Okay, how about peanut butter chocolate chip bars and . . ." I dug through our random collection of snacks trying to find a nasty combination. "Aaaand . . . squeezy cheese." I held up the blue-and-red can of orange goo.

"Yuck. Who eats that stuff?" Lizzy squished her nose and twisted her lips in disgust.

"My mom loves it. When I was little she'd make little faces on crackers or the letters of the alphabet. She used it to help me and a whole bunch of the kids in her day care learn to read."

"Aw, that's cute. So you literally devoured complete sentences?"

"More like complete words. One letter per saltine. A sentence would be too much to eat." I tossed the squeezy cheese back in the box. "Okay, instead of squeezy cheese how about snack-size Nutella?"

"Much better! Open two of the snack bars, smear the Nutella on top of one, and make a sandwich with the other. Then slice them into bite-size finger snacks."

"Sounds kind of good. Should I make you a bite-size Barella?" I held up the Nutella.

"Nice! Barella. You aren't half bad at this. Maybe you should name your own town and its occupants."

"I don't know about that." I shifted in my seat.

"Well, either way, I think I will have a couple bite-sized Barellas if you split them with me."

"Coming right up."

I thought driving twelve hours would be a painful process, but with Lizzy and her random games or conversation, I couldn't believe we'd gotten over halfway when we pulled into another rest stop near Springfield, Ohio. It felt good to get out and walk around a bit.

When we got back into the car, I changed the playlist to an Eagles compilation. We rode in silence for a while, lost in our own thoughts until Lizzy spoke up.

"Do you think Mateo could change his mind when he sees me in person?" When I heard the doubt in Lizzy's normally confident voice I wanted to throttle this guy I'd never met.

"I know the thing to say here is of course he will, because it will make you feel better and fuel your hope, but . . . . . ." I hesitated.

"But?."

"In his letter he alludes to unnamed but difficult circumstances. I don't remember exactly what he said, but it sounded like he is struggling with his feelings about more than just your relationship." I tried to stay neutral.

"So you don't think this is a good idea? Me going to see him when he is obviously confused about a bunch of stuff?"

"No. I understand why you want him to explain face-to-face. I guess I think you should be sure what you hope to get out of this surprise confrontation. It sounds like you are hoping to pick up where you left off in the relationship." A large semi swerved slightly into our lane but Lizzy saw it and swerved out of his way as she laid on the horn.

"Wake up, buddy!" she yelled before speeding past him and out of his path of destruction. I watched out of the corner of my eye and waited as Lizzy chewed on the side of her lip and didn't respond for a few miles. "You're right. I'm expecting too much, I think, and probably setting myself up for more heartache."

"But you are going to tell him how you feel, right?" I turned to look at her profile.

"He knows how I feel." She shrugged.

"Maybe. It can't hurt to tell someone you love them, right? I mean maybe it can? I'm not the best person to ask about this stuff." I leaned back into my seat.

"Have you ever been in love?" Lizzy turned to look at me.

"Sure. The McLaren F1, the Ferrari F40, and I'd put a ring on a BMW 507 Roadster."

Lizzy cut her eyes at me and I felt heat creep into my face. I looked out the window as we slipped past another eighteen-wheeler.

"You give decent advice for someone who hasn't been in a relationship."

"Maybe that's why it's easy for me to express my opinion. I can do it without any of the painful parts attached to it. Or probably because I have no idea what I'm even talking about." I laughed.

"Has your mom had boyfriends before Dr. Payne?"

"Never. Well, I mean never that I can remember." I tried to recall anyone coming around other than her work friends. They were all female.

"She must have been lonely," Lizzy said more to herself than to me.

And out of nowhere I felt tears threaten. Why didn't I just wait for my mom to get home and ask her the truth? Didn't I owe her at least that? This was my mom we were talking about. She'd done everything for me. I swallowed hard, staying glued to the passing gray landscape out my window, afraid if I looked at Lizzy, I'd let the tears fall.

"When I was around seven, my dad dated this woman, Clarabelle, for a while."

"Clarabelle?" I asked, picturing a dancing cartoon cow.

"Yeah. I know, right?" Lizzy said as if she could read my thoughts.

"Dad got annoyed with me because I would ignore her when she came over. I mean, I was such a brat. She would speak to me and I would pretend like I couldn't hear or even see her, you know? Like she was a ghost or something. She'd be sitting on the couch or in a chair and I'd purposely, like, throw my coat over her head when I came inside. As if I could only see the piece of furniture. I got pretty good at it. Once we all went to the movies and I had to watch the seats while she ran to the restroom and my dad got popcorn. When they came back, I'd given her seat away. My dad was so angry that instead of changing seats, we left the movie. He knew that would upset me more because it was *Harry Potter and the Goblet of Fire* and I had been dying to see it. That was the height of my Potter obsession. I read and reread that series like a lifeline to a reality I preferred over my own."

"Yeah, I never got into the whole Harry Potter thing."

"What?"

"I know. It's strange. I guess I spent more time making stuff than reading at that stage in my life and then it was too late. I think we saw a few of the movies."

BEEEP, beep, beep. Lizzy laid on the horn then hit it two more times. I jumped in my seat.

"What?" I quickly spanned every window for a beep-worthy hazard and she hit the horn again.

"Jesus. What are you beeping at?" I yelled.

"You! I can't believe you didn't love Harry and Ron and Hermione and Dobby! Who doesn't love Dobby?" She hit the horn again and a gray-haired, wrinkled, purple-and-red-dressed cupcake of a woman, driving an old maroon seventies Bronco flipped us off as we flew past her. I grabbed the dash and braced myself.

"Okay. Sorry for my lack of literature love but please slow down so we live for another chapter or two in our own story!" I yelled.

Lizzy looked down at the speedometer, which I could clearly see from my side of the car had made its way past ninety and kept climbing. "Whoa! Whoops. Sorry." She backed off and eased her way over to the slow lane and to a safer seventy-five.

"Who knew this little CRV had it in her?" She looked at me, her nose wrinkled and a sheepish grin on her face.

"I think we should—" My thought was interrupted by the ringing of Lizzy's phone sitting in the console between our seats. I glanced at the screen.

"It's your dad." I felt my heart begin to race. "Should we answer?"

Lizzy scrunched up her nose and twisted her lips to the side.

"Yes or no?" I asked when she didn't quickly answer.

"No. Just text him that we are completely fine, following the normal road rules, and that I will text him when we stop for the night." She used her signal and pulled out to pass a red convertible Mini Cooper with two middle-aged bottle blondes singing and doing synchronized hand gestures to whatever music they played.

"Can't he just find you through your phone?"

"No. I turned it off. Didn't you?"

"No. But I can."

"You should."

"But what if something bad happens to us and they need to find our bodies?"

"Holy random dark thoughts out of nowhere!" Lizzy lifted one eyebrow higher than the other then turned back to the road.

"You never know." I shrugged.

"Just turn it off. If we die then we're dead and they will eventually put it all together."

"Fine," I said, grabbing my phone and severing my link to my mom.

"No word from your mom?" Lizzy read my thoughts again.

"Maybe she's actually having fun with Dr. Payne."

We rode in silence listening to The Eagles, guilt tearing at my insides like I imagined an ulcer must feel while Lizzy hummed along under her breath.

We were about an hour outside of St. Louis when my phone beeped with a text from my mom.

> Where are you? Violet said the door is locked, you didn't answer, and no lights are on.

"Oh crap. I forgot about Violet."

"Who?" Lizzy asked.

"My mom's friend who is supposed to check in on me. She's at the house and I'm not."

"Tell her you're with me."

> Me: I'm with Lizzy.
>
> Mom: Next door?
>
> Me: No.

"Where should I say we are?"

"Tell her we are going to dinner together." Lizzy shrugged.

> Me: We are headed to dinner.
>
> Mom: I'm missing your first date?!
>
> Me: NOT A DATE
>
> Mom: Are you sure?
>
> Me: Mom, I gotta go.
>
> Mom: Offer to pay. Love you.

```
Me: Love you.
```
"Dodged that bullet," I said.

"She's good?"

"She thought we were on a date and told me I needed to pay." I rolled my eyes.

"Aw, that's sweet. You can still buy me dinner if you want." Lizzy winked at me.

I rolled my eyes. "I thought we were using our daily food budget toward a hotel tonight."

"True. Let's compromise with takeout from the Cardboard Cupboard." She nodded toward our makeshift pantry.

"Sure thing. I'll cook."

It was dark by the time we drove onto the Eads Bridge to get a better view of the Gateway Arch in St. Louis. We hadn't heard anything more from either parent. About halfway across the bridge Lizzy pulled over and put on the flashers.

"We must document this moment," she announced and hopped out. I quickly unfolded myself from the car.

"We can't stop in the middle of the bridge!" I yelled but she walked to the side, ignoring me. I looked around for any cops.

"It smells like football and soccer and forgotten leaves." Lizzy smiled up at the arch looming above our heads in the near distance, her hair blowing out behind her in the wind. She'd put on my well-worn gray high school sweatshirt at our last gas break because we couldn't readily find hers and she'd had to pee badly. It came down to her knees. I couldn't help but think about how childlike she seemed standing there, her face to the sky, haloed by the streetlights above, drowning in my clothes. Yet, I felt like the smaller person in this adventure. Lizzy exuded a sense of control, like hidden within her small frame there existed a carefully coiled knowledge of how to navigate every challenge life hurled into her path. She turned her smile toward me.

"Isn't this cool? Our first major stop is the Gateway Arch. Beyond this point, somewhere out there, is our truth. For many people before us, this marked the end of one life and the beginning of a new one." She opened her arms into the wind.

"I like my life." I shoved my hands into my pockets.

"We can turn around. You can wait for your mom to explain and I can give up on Mateo."

A few cars sped by us, but nobody even beeped at us for disrupting the traffic flow. Maybe people did this all the time?

"Do you know that when they finished building this bridge back in the mid 1870s, to test its strength they borrowed an elephant from a local circus to walk across it?"

"Seriously?"

"Yep. The theory was that an elephant instinctively knew what could or couldn't safely hold its weight."

"The elephant test."

"Let me get a picture of you with the Arch in the background."

"I didn't realize the Arch lit up."

"I don't think it's always lit. Must be a reason. Last time we drove through at night, it wasn't lit up like this."

"Really?"

"Yep. What's it going to be, Lodan? Back to Laketown or through the Arch to whatever truth we discover?" She didn't look at me when she asked this question. She stared down at the water below.

I knew life in Laketown couldn't go back to how it was. I needed to know the truth. I wanted to find my dad, and I knew Lizzy needed to confront Mateo face-to-face. "No going back, now," I said. Lizzy turned from the water to face me again. I thought she would hoot and holler, but instead her small smile held a hint of sadness. The moment hung heavy upon us, like the gray fog of a permanent farewell.

And then with the honk of a distant car horn, Lizzy's smile spread across her face and she yelled, "Look at me and say 'truth-trip!'" She held up her phone to snap the shot.

"Okay, now a selfie with me." Lizzy flipped around so the arch was behind both of us. "You're going to have to bend down to my level, Lodan." I got on my knees, we wrapped our arms around one another, and leaned our cheeks close together to get both of our faces and the arch in the picture. Lizzy smelled like clean laundry, coffee, and mints.

I stood and we both turned to look out over the Mississippi flowing below us. There were a few tugboats and a riverboat docked in the distance.

"No matter what happens with Mateo, I think I'll be okay," Lizzy said without looking away from the water.

"Of course you will, Lizzy. You strike me as someone who will always land on her feet."

"Like a cat?"

"No, Lois, like Superman's girlfriend. Or maybe you're more of a Wonder Woman." I smiled at her and we both laughed.

"Thanks!" she said, "but never call me Lois." She grabbed my hand in hers. We both turned as a car blared its horn and someone yelled "JUMP!" out the window.

"Nice. Real hero there." Lizzy rolled her eyes.

"Have you ever dipped this hand in the Mississippi?" I asked, holding her hand up between us.

"Not in either of these states." She gestured to her right and left.

"Louisiana?"

"Yep. For one." She wrapped her arms around herself. The temperature had dropped.

"Well, tonight we are dipping our hands in the Mississippi of Missouri. Let's go before a cop puts an end to this trip when its barely gotten started."

We both climbed back in the CRV and crossed the bridge.

Eighteen

LIZZY

NEAR ST. LOUIS, MO
SATURDAY, OCTOBER 24, 2015

Late October in Missouri ruled out sleeping in the car so we drove a little farther to find a motel that fit our nonexistent budget. When it comes to motels, I think it's safe to say you get what you pay for. When we opened the door we were met with a blast of stale, smoky, musty air. It seriously smelled like we were camping out in the cavernous armpit of a chain-smoking, forgotten dragon.

"This is a strictly mouth-breathing-only kind of establishment." I wrinkled my nose and hesitantly set my stuff on the table. The floor was out of the question.

"Poor Kono, I hope her immature little lungs can handle it." I set her cage next to the ancient-looking television. The ancient beast had a massive two-foot humpback and wore a skin of dust. "I hope this isn't a canary in the coal mine situation." I nodded toward Kono in her cage.

"We'd be more likely to go than her. It's always the rodents that survive in all the apocalyptic movies and books."

"Are rabbits rodents?" I asked.

"Actually, you're right, they aren't. It may be the end for all of us here." Lodan looked around the dank room. "This is so vintage in all the wrong ways." He started to put his stuff on the floor then stopped and placed it beside mine on the wobbly coffee-stained plastic table.

"Do you think that bed comes with bugs?" I asked, grimacing at the thought of the little creatures making a carnival out of us while we slept.

Lodan volunteered to inspect. He approached the faded seashell comforter. There were a number of loose threads where the stitched pattern had come unraveled with time. "Any advice on where they hide?"

"Actually, I think you're supposed to pull back all of the sheets and check the mattress, both on top and underneath." I stepped a little closer.

"Cross your fingers. I'm going in." Lodan plunged his hand between the mattress and the box spring, grabbed the fitted sheet at the bottom, and yanked it up and back to expose the bare mattress. He jumped back as if he'd been shocked. "Oh God!"

"What?" I yelled, jumping backward.

"Nothing yet." He said it calmly, giving me a half-smile. I socked him on the shoulder.

"Jerk!"

He laughed and slowly approached the suspect mattress. He carefully peeled back all of the sheets until he'd uncovered the entire bottom half. "So far so good." He replaced the bottom sheet haphazardly and then peeled back the top.

"Anything?" I asked and stepped closer again.

"Weeell. Good news. I don't see any signs of bug activity." He stood back up, letting the bedcovers drop.

"But?" I wasn't going to fall for whatever his scare was this time.

"Either someone had a serious nosebleed or we are about to sleep on former evidence from a stabbing."

"What do you mean?"

"Check out that massive stain." Lodan held back the sheets and stood to the side so I could lean in and see. He wasn't kidding. A solid brown stain covered almost the entire top half of the mattress.

"Nasty!" I agreed. "Why wouldn't they flip the mattress or at least put that at the bottom?" I asked.

"Maybe this is the good side?" Lodan shrugged and raised one eyebrow at me, amusement flickering across his eyes.

I wasn't about to be the unadventurous princess. "Let's flip it then."

"Okay," he agreed.

"But let's roll up the sheets and blankets and set them on the TV stand dresser thing. I don't think we want them touching this floor." I pointed down to the threadbare collage of connecting stains, an early eighties rug that's closest connection to cleaning probably involved forensic chemicals, sirens, and badges.

We rolled up the bedding, set it to the side, and with a three count, held our breaths, closed our eyes, and turned our heads to the side (to avoid all of the dust—mostly dead skin) that we'd inevitably release into the air with the flipping motion. Once we felt the "dust" had settled, I said, "Okay, look now!" and we opened our eyes.

"Oh my God!" I covered my mouth and then quickly looked up at Lodan. His face and neck were beet-red. He looked up at me, started to speak, then shook his head, ran his fingers under his glasses at the bridge of his nose, and cleared his throat.

"Well . . . I guess . . . this . . ." He seemed unsure of how I was going to react and I immediately felt a need to put him at ease.

"Hysterical," I finished. I looked back down at the mattress. Someone had drawn a very life-like naked woman lying on her back. Her legs were spread wide in a frog-like pose, her arms bent up along the side of her head, and long locks of hair framed her face. This would be shocking enough if her face didn't so expertly depict a woman experiencing erotic pleasure and then the kicker: a hole had been made in the mattress right where you'd imagine it would be.

"You have to admit the artwork is impressive," I said and looked up at Lodan. Still flushed, he slowly met my eyes, then quickly looked back at the mattress, then back to my eyes again.

"I . . . let's . . . so many terrible jokes running through my head right now. We have to flip this thing back." Lodan reached to do it immediately.

"Wait. Let's flip it so that the stain is at the bottom, too," I suggested.

After wrestling with the monstrosity for a bit we finally got the mattress back in place, art facedown, stain at the feet, and bedding back in place.

"One more thing!" Lodan dashed back outside and came back carrying a red-and-black plaid blanket and holding up a canister of air-freshener as if it were the lit Olympic torch. "I just remembered my mom's handy-dandy car kit!"

"I love your mom." I hugged Lodan.

Lodan put the blanket over the questionable bedspread, then lay each of our sleeping bags on top of that while I bombed the room with air-freshener. It didn't completely kill the stench but it masked it to a more tolerable level.

We took turns in the bathroom, which was surprisingly clean given the rest of the room. In there the nostril-burning bleach level was somewhat comforting. The shower pressure may have been weak but it got hot. By the time we'd both settled side by side on our sleeping bags, phones charging beside us, I could barely keep my eyes open.

"You must be exhausted. Thanks for driving," Lodan said into the dark.

"Sure. You know, if you want to drive some, I'm fine with it. But I get it, if you're worried about messing up getting your license."

"I'll think about it. It's not like I don't know how. I've aced the online driving tests almost every time, I've built a plethora of miniature vehicles, and I've driven plenty of other vehicles around," Lodan said.

"Really? Like what?" I asked.

"Big Wheels, bikes, once a dirt bike, and most recently a kayak."

I laughed quietly. "You sound ready to me. Lodan, you're a lot of fun to hang out with. I don't get why you don't have a bunch of friends."

I swear I could hear him blush in the dark. "Lodan? Did you fall asleep?"

"No. I was just thinking of an answer. I guess it's my own fault. It's not like I don't interact with people at school. They used to ask me to hang out, but I was always working on a project and preferred that to hanging out with other people, I guess."

"Didn't your mom set up play dates and stuff?" I turned in my sleeping bag so I could see the outline of his face.

"We had a house full of kids all week when she had the day care. She probably wanted a kid break on the weekends. And then by the time she finished nursing school and did that full time, we'd already become set in our routines."

"I know you've never had a girlfriend, but have you had crushes on girls?" I asked.

Lodan made a humming sound as if his brain thought audibly. "Not that I recall."

"Do you like girls or are you attracted to guys?" I asked, then realized how personal that could be. "Sorry, you don't have to answer."

"No, it's okay. It's just I don't really know. Does that sound stupid?"

"No."

"Like on TV and in the movies, the characters are physically attracted to one another. One look, one touch, and they both seem to share a little secret about the other person. I've never looked at another person or touched another person and had a connection like that." I heard him swallow hard. "Do you think I'm asexual or incapable of attraction?"

"No. I think you just haven't met the right person."

"I don't know. As an almost sixteen-year-old male, I'm pretty sure sex is supposed to be all I think about."

"Maybe you're a late bloomer."

"Maybe."

I listened to the *thump thump* of the ancient heating system and thought through what he'd said.

"I think we should add it to our truth-seeking mission," I declared, turning to try and see his face.

He turned in his sleeping bag to look at me. "What do you mean?"

I ran my hand across the pokiness of his brush cut. "I mean let's make a point to find someone you're attracted to."

Lodan rolled away from me and onto his back. "I think we have enough to do already."

"Yeah, well, will you at least agree to be open-minded about it?"

"Do I have a choice?"

"Not really!"

"I didn't think so." He sighed and rolled over so that his back faced me.

I'd just drifted off to sleep when Lodan whispered, "What if the truth is awful?"

"About your family or who you find attractive?" I tried to make light of his question but it fell flat. I reached for his hand and held it in my own.

"Sorry." I squeezed his hand and he squeezed mine back. "If the truth is awful, then I promise to help you figure out how to make it okay again. But don't you think it's better to know the truth than to live a lie?"

"I don't know. I didn't think I've had much experience with lying. But maybe my whole childhood is one big lie. What if my dad doesn't even know I exist and if he had known we could have known each other all this time?"

"From what I know of your mom, she must have had very good reasons to lie to you. She obviously tries to do what she feels is best for you."

"I lay here feeling guilty, thinking I should call her and then I get angry and talk myself out of it. I don't know if I could forgive her if I learn I could have known my dad all this time."

"Try to get some sleep. Morning light always helps me have a more positive perspective on things. For some reason the negative voices in our heads are louder in the cover of darkness."

"I can't tune out the voices enough to sleep." I heard sad frustration in Lodan's voice.

"Here, give me your arm," I said and pulled his long pale arm across my stomach. I lightly placed my fingertips on his arm and slowly made small circles as I worked my way from his wrist to his bicep. "My dad used to do this to me when I couldn't sleep."

Our breathing slowed and at some point we both drifted off.

Nineteen

LODAN

ST. LOUIS TO JOPLIN, MO
SUNDAY, OCTOBER 25, 2015

"Yes! Yes! Yes!" My eyes flew open at the unfamiliar voice yelling in my ear. Or at least it sounded like it was in my ear, but when I turned to look, Lizzy had just bolted upright, too.

"Lodan?" She saw me and relaxed back into the bed.

The room remained dark. I looked at my phone, not quite five in the morning. I rubbed a hand over my eyes and the headboard next door began rhythmically slamming against our wall.

"This is nice." I could hear her sarcastic smile in the dark.

Then the "yeses" started up again with a few "Oh Gods" thrown in.

"Early start?" she suggested.

"Yeeesss!" I yelled, imitating our neighbor.

Lizzy hit me with her pillow and then leaped into action. We quickly took turns in the bathroom, packed up, and made hot coffee for her and tea for me before our neighbors probably even finished.

As I pumped the gas, Lizzy pointed to her phone. "You are so going to like where we end up today." She smiled at me.

"Will it have better art and an even more awkward soundtrack?" I asked, replacing the nozzle back onto the pump.

"Better art for sure and we can absolutely control the soundtrack."

"I'm in," I said sliding into my side of the car.

The miles of interesting Missouri landmarks along Route 66

passed quickly, including the town of Saint Clair's comical hot and cold water towers, and wacky signage on various hotel and eating establishments. I must have drifted off because next thing I knew Lizzy was shaking me awake.

"Lodan, look up." Lizzy's voice brought me around and I opened my eyes to a full view of very cool-looking waterfalls.

"Wow, where are we?" I asked, trying to stretch my legs as much as possible in the Honda's front seat.

"Welcome to Grand Falls!" Lizzy announced.

"Missouri?" I asked wiping the sleep from my face.

"Yep, near Joplin. Come on!" She hopped out of the car. I got out on my side and had to stretch on the gravel parking lot for a minute before jogging after her. This late in the fall the leaves made a crunchy orange, red, and brown carpet beneath our feet but the view a few weeks ago must have been spectacular.

"This is the largest continuously running waterfall in Missouri. Let's get close enough to feel the mist on our skin." Lizzy jogged until the landscape forced her to slow down. We carefully made our way through the slippery section and stopped to let the mist tickle our arms and faces.

"Take off your glasses and close your eyes," Lizzy commanded and I did.

"Do you like how this feels?" she asked.

"Yeah, it's nice. Feels like I'm communicating with nature or something," I admitted. I snuck a peek at Lizzy with one eye, but she had her eyes squeezed shut and her face turned up toward the mist.

"Keep your eyes closed, hold my hand, and just breathe with me, okay?"

I did as she asked. After a pause Lizzy said, "That little tickle of nature on your skin is but a fraction of what it feels like when someone you're attracted to touches your skin."

I smiled and looked at Lizzy. She peeked out of one eye at me. "What do you think?"

"It sounds nice." I smiled, slipped on my glasses, and then pulled her hand to swing her closer. She slipped a little on the wet rocks and let out a little surprised yelp, but we clung and balanced each other solid.

"Whoops, almost took us both down." We stood with our arms around one another, her damp eyelashes looking up at me and I thought, *I should want to kiss her or something at a moment like this.* But I didn't feel that at all. I felt happy to be with her, but nothing more.

"Why are you looking at me all serious?" Lizzy asked, her blue eyes studying my green.

"Nothing. It's embarrassing," I said and turned to go. She followed behind me until we were on the grass again.

"Tell me."

"It's just that . . . a moment like that. Shouldn't I have wanted to kiss you?"

"Just then? Sure. If you were *into* me. But obviously you aren't." Lizzy shrugged like it was no big deal.

"But you're absolutely adorable and I have such a great time with you and I can be completely myself with you. Isn't that what it's supposed to be like?"

"First of all, thanks for the high praise. Second, I don't think we can control these things. We love who we love. We want who we want. We lust after who we lust after." She reached out and pinched my ass for emphasis. I rolled my eyes and shook my head at her.

"Hath no fear my young Jedi, we will awaken the force in you yet!" Lizzy tilted her head and raised her eyebrows at me. "First one to the car drives!" And she bolted. I took off after her but stopped when I heard someone scream. I turned to see a woman near the deeper water to the side of the falls.

"¡*Ayuda!* Help! *Mi hijo se cayó al agua y no puede nadar!* My son. No swim."

I ran toward her looking at the surface of the water for the boy, but I didn't see him.

"Where?" I asked, ripping my glasses off, and ran into the freezing water. It dropped off quickly and I could understand why I couldn't see him right away. I swam out, reaching out in all directions, hoping to connect with the boy. After what seemed like an eternity, I felt him. I found his waist, wrapped my arm around him, and got his head to the surface. I made it to shore quickly and gently laid him on the ground. Lizzy dropped down beside him.

"I know CPR. I know CPR," she screamed. She tilted his head back, got them both in position, and covered his mouth. She carefully and efficiently shared her air with him, counted out the chest compressions, and after a few moments he coughed up a bunch of water and rolled to his side. He threw up some more water and burst into tears. His mother pulled the toddler to her chest crying, *"Oh gracias a Dios, gracias a Dios, Illijah."* She held him away from her to look in his eyes.

"Estás bien, chamaco? Estás bien?" Illijah nodded and clung to his mother, his body still shaking with tears and cold.

"Here, you better get him warmed up. *Muy frío*," Lizzy said and wrapped our plaid car blanket around the boy.

"Should we take him to the hospital and make sure he's okay?" I asked.

The mother squeezed him tightly to her oversized colorful knit sweater and shook her head. *"No gracias. No gracias.* We okay."

I looked at Lizzy. She looked at me and shrugged. We were both thinking the same thing. This poor mom was probably afraid to risk it because they were not legally in the U.S.

"Can we give you a ride home?" I asked, my teeth chattering. Lizzy handed me my glasses that had somehow survived my haphazard toss unscathed. They immediately fogged over when I put them on my face. Now that the adrenaline had subsided, the cold water, drenched clothing, and chilly October air had me literally shaking in my soggy sneakers.

"Drive tu casa?" Lizzy made a steering motion with her hands and pointed to our car.

"Sí, Sí, please." The woman nodded and stood up with her wrapped child. He had calmed in her arms. Lizzy got them settled into the car while I ducked off behind a few bushes to exchange my wet clothes for dry. I left my soaked sneakers off but planned to put socks on once I got in the car. I struggled to dress quickly as my entire body shook with cold.

"*Mi mombre es Lizzy,*" Lizzy said after we got headed down the road.

I pointed to my chest. "Lo . . . dan," My shaking voice split the name in two.

"Maria and Illijah," she said and her eyes filled. "*Gracias,* Mr. Lodan. *Gracias.*"

We turned down a long gravel road and then again onto a dirt road. The Honda bumped and heaved along without a problem. We turned around a bend and came across a small enclave of tents and shelters cobbled together with scrap materials. Clothes hung on lines between trees and a group of kids ranging in age from toddler to teen played soccer in a small clearing behind the houses.

Everyone froze in place when we rolled to a stop. Maria quickly opened the door and waved that it was okay and the kids returned to their game, but many of the adults remained still and watched us.

"*Gracias,* Lizzy. Mr. Landon. *Gracias.*" Maria nodded at us as she got out of the car.

"You're welcome," we both said. I hopped out of the back and again the place seemed to freeze, as if they held a collective breath. Then I climbed back into the front seat and they relaxed a bit again. Lizzy and I shared a sad look as she backed up to leave. We were about to pull away when an older child ran up to the car, carrying our blanket.

I rolled down the window and waved and shook my head. "You keep it." I said, but he kept trying to hand it to me. "No." I shook my head. "You keep it." I pointed from me to him and he got it.

"*Gracias,*" he said and waved. We waved to him and Lizzy headed back the way we'd come. We rode in silence for quite a while, only the blasting heater as our soundtrack. I finally got warm and Lizzy, who must have been sweating, turned it back to normal. We didn't really speak until we stopped for much-needed coffee and tea outside Tulsa, Oklahoma.

I stayed in the car due to a lack of proper foot attire. Lizzy leaned through the window to hand me the two cardboard cups of my hot tea and her coffee. Then she reached behind her to pull from her waistband a bright pink pair of pom-pommed house slippers.

"I splurged for your feet in case you wanted to use the bathroom. Hard to believe it but they were marked down to ninety-nine cents."

I smiled and promptly slid them on my feet. They were a bit small so a good chunk of the material meant to cover the tops of my feet was actually under my toes, but they were better than soggy sneakers.

"Thanks, Lizzy. Very thoughtful of you."

"You're welcome." She climbed back in the driver's seat and wrapped her hands around her coffee. "Mmm . . . French vanilla . . . yum . . . you are exactly what I needed." Lizzy held the paper cup to her lips like it contained precious nectar. My hot tea cup felt pretty good in my hands, too. We sat and sipped the hot joy into our bodies.

"Did that all just really happen?" Lizzy shook her head back and forth.

"I know. Kind of surreal, wasn't it? I still feel shaky but I think it's just shock wearing off or something. My insides are all jittery."

"Mine, too. You were amazing! Dude, you just saved a boy's life! I mean if we weren't there, that boy probably wouldn't be alive!"

"I don't even want to think about that. And you, you were all over the CPR thing. They didn't get it right with Lois Lane because you're clearly not the superhero-girlfriend type. You're more like Wonder Woman. Just saying." I flashed her a smart-ass grin.

Lizzy rolled her eyes. "Yeah, well, don't forget who my mom is. She does this stuff multiple times a day, all year long."

"Well, you definitely got that stay-calm-and-make-it-happen rescue gene for sure." I pulled the plastic lid off of my tea and blew on the surface.

"We make a pretty good team, Mr. Lodan." Lizzy smiled, turned the music back on, and we pulled back on to Route 66 feeling pretty proud of ourselves for before noon on a Sunday.

Twenty

LIZZY

MISSOURI TO TEXAS
SUNDAY, OCTOBER 25, 2015

I'd been purposely trying *not* to think about Mateo and what I would say when I saw him, but after I'd gotten over the shock of our impromptu rescue experience, my mind drifted back over my conversation with Lodan just before Maria yelled for help.

Mateo had been the first person who made my skin come alive with his touch. And I hadn't really thought about it in a while because once we'd been dating, I still felt a flutter in my stomach when we kissed or if I saw him unexpectedly, but it wasn't that same intense tingle with every touch that I'd felt in the beginning. But that wasn't what had my thoughts preoccupied. What had my thoughts preoccupied was what Lodan had said when we almost slipped together by the falls. He couldn't have been more right about the moment. Although he made it clear that he didn't have any desire to kiss me in that perfect movie-scene moment, I had felt that sparky excitement when he caught me in his arms. He had made my arms catch fire with his touch. Our lips had been inches apart and *oh shit* I had wanted him to kiss me.

"Lizzy!" Lodan yelled.

"What?!" I looked at him, heart racing, horror coursing across my brain. Did I say that out loud?

"Slow down!" Lodan yelled.

I looked down at the speedometer and again it was creeping toward triple digits. I immediately released the pressure on the gas and as the car slowed, so did my pulse.

"Sorry."

"No biggie. What were you thinking about? You should have seen the look on your face."

I felt my face heat up. "Nothing. That boy, I guess. How scary this day could have ended for his family."

"Yeah. It was good timing, I guess," Lodan said. "Want a snack?"

But before I could answer both our phones lit up. Lodan picked up both.

"It's our parents. Must be my mom got home."

"Let them both go to voice mail and start a group text with the four of us." I instructed. They can't easily stop us now, but they will want to know we are safe."

I saw Lodan hesitating. He looked longingly at his phone.

"Or you can talk to her if you think it will make you feel better," I said.

He heaved a big sigh. "No, I don't want to talk to her." He began creating the group text.

"What should I say?"

"Sorry we took the car without permission. Being safe. Back next Sunday. Will check in each AM and PM. Love you both," I recited.

Lodan typed and then reread it aloud. "Should we say anything about why or where we are going?"

"Your mom probably can guess the California part. My dad—"

Lodan cut me off. "Can probably guess the Mateo part.

"So hit send," I said and zoomed past a silver Subaru who kept changing speed.

Lodan's mom tried calling again and my dad didn't immediately respond. We ignored her call and then I got a text.

> DAD: `Lodan's mom is upset. Wants to call police. He isn't even 16.`

"Police? She's just trying to scare us. I know she wouldn't call." Lodan rolled his eyes.

"Are you sure? Because they could track us down pretty easily and then this whole trip is a bust." I felt a sense of dreaded reality wash over me.

"I'm sure. She's always had this strange aversion to cops. We got in a fender bender a couple of years ago and she begged the other lady not to call the cops. She offered her cash on the spot for barely a scratch," Lodan explained.

"And that didn't seem strange to you?" I asked.

Lodan shrugged. "Not at the time, no. I figured she didn't want our insurance to go up."

"Oh my God, Lodan. What if you are one of those taken kids? You know? Like your mom lost a baby or couldn't get pregnant or something so she took someone else's baby?" As soon as I'd said it I wished I hadn't. *God why didn't I think before I spoke sometimes?* I threw a hand over my mouth as if that could stop me from saying something worse. I saw him physically wilt into the seat beside me like someone had deflated his inner balloon.

"Lodan, I'm sorry. I'm an idiot. Don't listen to me. I'm sure that's not it at all."

He shook his head and pinched the bridge of his nose between his thumb and forefinger, his glasses resting on his forehead. "You know what, it's no big deal. It's fine. Really." He gave me a half smile, but it didn't even half fool me.

I took my scarf from around my neck and dropped it over our phones. "You know what? Let's just forget about family and boyfriends and just be us for the rest of today. Okay? Lizzy and Lodan and the open road."

When he didn't respond I switched over to the radio and searched until I found a country station playing Darius Rucker's "Wagon Wheel." I cranked it up and hoped we could both forget our mouths—what mine had said and what I'd wanted his to do to mine next to the waterfall.

Twenty-one

LODAN
TEXAS
SUNDAY, OCTOBER 25, 2015

I won't lie, what Lizzy said about my mom turned my stomach into a sewer. I'd probably be lying to myself if I didn't admit that her very words had been thoughts I'd refused to think more than once since we embarked on this venture. I guess hearing them spoken by someone else made it sound less crazy and therefore much worse.

I tried to recall all the things my mom had told me over the years regarding my family. Her parents: both passed. Her sister: never mentioned. My cousin: never mentioned. My father: a married teacher who supposedly wasn't worth knowing. Cops were to be avoided. A fire conveniently destroyed most family memorabilia. Did she avoid police and her family because she had taken me from someone? I decided the next time I had WiFi access I would do a little research.

I knew Lizzy felt bad for what she'd said and I was being a dick for not letting it go. I wasn't really mad at her. I knew my anger was misplaced, but by the time I'd mellowed enough to realize this, Lizzy seemed happily lost in her blasting country lyrics. I hadn't listened to much country but found I liked that some of the songs were mini short stories. The sound and message felt fitting as we got closer to whatever it was we'd learn by the end of this trip.

Lizzy turned down the music. "We're here!" she announced and eased the Honda off the road and onto the dusty shoulder.

"Where?" I asked, but then I saw the answer. There stood a line of half-buried colorfully painted Cadillacs.

"Cadillac Ranch," we said at the same time.

"Surprise!" Lizzy caught my eyes with hers and I could tell she wanted to know if I was still mad.

I beamed at her and grabbed her tightly to my chest. "Now this, my capeless heroine, is definitely vintage."

"So we're good?" She leaned back and looked up at me.

"We were never not good, Lizzy." I reached for her hand. "Come on; let's check these out."

"Wait. I have to grab something first." She opened the back and dug around a bit before pulling out a grocery bag.

"Okay, now we're ready." We walked along the iconic art, pointing out particularly well-done artwork or clever quotes like, "Always remember you are unique just like everyone else." The light was fading and it made for cool pictures.

"Hey, we need to hurry before it gets too dark," Lizzy said.

"Spray paint?" I guessed.

"Sorry. Couldn't find any in our garage but I did find some cool duct tape." We found a spot on the second-to-last car in the line that didn't have anything we felt would be overly missed. Then we used black duct tape to make a big fresh background.

"Yellow or green?" she asked, holding up one tape roll in each hand.

"Yellow seems somehow more fitting. Street signy, cautionary? Don't you think?" I asked.

"Works for me. Okay. Let's do this." We set to work creating our mark on the Ranch. When we finished we took a selfie in the fading desert light. Then we got back in our car to find a place to treat ourselves to a real meal, leaving our mark for the next visitors: SEEK TRUTH LX^2.

Twenty-two

LIZZY

TEXAS TO NEW MEXICO
SUNDAY, OCTOBER 25, 2015

We hadn't planned to drive all the way to Santa Rosa, New Mexico for dinner, but when we discovered an ad for a place called Tequila's Truth, how could we not make it our dinner destination?

Apparently either this place had the best Sunday night specials or we'd picked a local favorite, because we had to circle the parking lot twice to find a spot. We left the windows cracked for Kono, thinking a bunny in a bar was only acceptable when it was the Playboy type. By the time we got inside I was beyond hangry and I think Lodan was as eager to feed me as I was to eat.

When the hostess said it would be a thirty-minute wait or a seat at the bar, we did not hesitate to belly up. We asked the bartender what we could get into our mouths as fast as possible and she brought us chips, salsa, and the best guacamole to ever touch my tongue. Of course the flavor may have been slightly influenced by my ravenous state.

"Have you ever tasted tequila?" Lodan asked, looking over the extensive collection displayed along the shelves of the bar.

"Nope." I popped another chip into my mouth and talked around it. "But I have smelled it and I'm pretty sure the fact that it made my arm hair stand up means I wouldn't like it much. "You?"

"Haven't even smelled it. My mom never really drinks. In fact, I think besides the beer she had at Minnie's when we went kayaking, the only other time I've seen her drink was at a party her friends threw when she officially accepted a job as a nurse. And that was maybe a glass of champagne."

"Yeah, my dad doesn't drink a lot either. He sometimes has a beer or two at night or wine with dinner if he has a date."

Lodan dunked a chip in salsa and ate it.

"In T or C a lot of the kids drank but Mateo and Raj never did. Raj said he tried it once and first it made his face burn, then he spent the night over a toilet. Mateo refused to give up control to a substance."

The bartender placed a water in front of each of us.

"Ready to order?" he asked, looking a little annoyed. He probably knew we wouldn't be big spenders and we had good bar real estate.

"We'll take the taco six pack, please. Three bean, three beef," Lodan said, handing him back the menus.

"Have you ever been drunk?" I asked Lodan.

"No. I haven't ever had any alcohol." He motioned to the last chip.

"Thanks." I scooped up the last of the guac and ate it.

"What about you?" he asked.

"Once. When I lived in New Orleans. My dad and a date had opened a bottle of wine and only drank a glass before going out to dinner. My friend convinced me we should drink it. It tasted awful so we added sugar to it. It was still gross but we still drank enough to feel buzzy and laugh at stupid stuff. Then she got all sad about having a crush on her older sister's boyfriend. I got so annoyed by her that I pretended to fall asleep."

"How old were you?"

"Fourteen."

"Didn't your dad wonder where the wine went?"

"Yeah, he asked about it a couple of nights later when he went to get a glass for the same date."

"What did you tell him?"

"The truth." I shrugged. "I have always told him the truth."

"Didn't he get mad?"

"Not really. He actually thought it was hysterical that we added sugar."

"That was it?"

"I guess. Oh and he made me promise if I wanted to try alcohol again to ask him first and if he thought I might like it, he'd let me have a little."

"Wow. He seems pretty chill."

"I guess. Yeah. He's pretty reasonable. But then again I don't usually give him any cause for concern."

"Until now."

"Yeah. You must be a bad influence on me." I winked at him.

"Right." He shook his head and the bartender placed our tacos in front of us.

We inhaled our food and then decided to see if we could find an open pool table. We stood and watched a couple of guys annihilate their wives in back-to-back games. When I challenged them, the wives were all too happy to give up their spots to us.

"Thank you for saving us." A brunette with faded mom jeans and a short mom haircut to match, squeezed Lodan's shoulder. "What are you and your girl drinkin'? We'll buy you a round."

"Oh, we're fine. Thanks."

"Oh, come on. Let us buy you a beer at least? A shot? You look like a tequila kind of guy."

"Jill, let's do a shot with these cute young things. My mom is keeping the kids all day tomorrow."

One of the husbands, Joe, broke to start the game and sunk two stripes.

"Guess we're solids," I said. "I think she likes you, cowboy," I whispered in Lodan's ear and winked as I walked past him to take my turn.

We were down to one ball each and the eight ball by the time the moms returned. They were carrying a whole tray of drinks.

"I tell you. I don't miss doing this every night. I can barely carry these all the way over my head anymore," Jill said, twisting her plum-colored lips to the side.

"Yeah, and I don't miss getting grab-assed across the bar either," the other mom said.

"Oh, that I do kind of miss." Jill laughed, setting the tray on their table. "Joe here wouldn't grab my ass if I placed it between his fingers. They laughed, clicked glasses, and then handed each of their husbands a beer.

Lodan sank our last solid and the husbands didn't look too happy about it. We high-fived and the wives cheered us on.

"Hey, come do this tequila shot with us," the moms called out to us.

"No, thanks," Lodan said as he readied himself to sink the eight ball.

"How 'bout if you win on this shot, you drink this shot," Jill suggested.

Lodan ignored her and slammed the eight ball straight into the far corner pocket.

"Nice!" I yelled and high-fived him again. The bar had gotten progressively louder, darker, and even more crowded.

"Here." The moms shoved shots of tequila into our faces, then each grabbed their own. "Here's to you for puttin' them in their place." They both slammed the shots down their throats.

I pretended to take it, but actually dumped it on the floor when I brought it back down from my mouth. I tried to catch Lodan's eye to let him know to do the same, but when I glanced over at his face I knew he'd swallowed the tequila. His brows were knotted, his lips were pursed, and he looked like he needed a chaser fast.

"Here." Jill handed him a beer and he guzzled half of it down without even looking at it.

"Why would you willingly ingest that poison?" He shook his head, took another drink of the beer, and looked at me.

"How come it didn't bother you at all?" he asked.

I rolled my eyes and shrugged, trying not to draw attention to myself.

"Hey, this is pretty good. What kind is it?" Lodan asked, taking another big swig of the beer.

"Bud Light," Joe said and they all laughed.

"Vintage," Lodan said and they all laughed again.

"I hate to break up the party, but we need to get going. We have another long day of driving tomorrow."

"Aww, come on. Let's play one more game." Lodan finished off his beer and set it down a little hard on their table.

"Yeah, let your man have a little fun. It's the best way to keep them in line." Jill laughed and handed him the beer I didn't take.

I looked hard at Lodan and tried to give him a *come on* look with my eyes, but he was too busy listening to Joe explain how drinking actually helps his pool game.

I slapped Lodan on the back, a little hard, and said, "Thanks so much for the drinks. Have a good night!" He quickly drank most of the beer in his hand before setting it on another table as I all but pushed him toward the door.

We stepped out into the fresh air and it felt like heaven. "Why didn't you want to stay a little longer?" Lodan asked, his words coming out a little slower than normal.

"It's nearly ten and we still don't know where we're sleeping tonight." I headed toward the far end of the parking lot where we'd parked.

"I thought we'd agreed to try parking at that RV place we passed on the way here."

"Well, that's my plan, but I don't know if we'll be able to be very stealth if we let it get too much later."

"You're right." He plopped his hand on my shoulder. "You're always right, Lizzy."

"Well, I guess you can cross two things off your I 'never' list now: tequila and getting drunk."

I unlocked the car and we both climbed in.

"I'm not drunk and I'm never drinking tequila again. That stuff is nasty!"

"I told ya." I started the car, turned off the radio, and carefully pulled out of the lot.

"You drank it without even needing a chaser!"

"I pitched it on the floor. I tried to get your attention to have you do the same."

"Ohhh, that makes more sense."

"Okay, cowboy, help me keep an eye out for that turn. I can't remember if the sign was lit."

"Me neither, but I think maybe I am."

"Okay, and now it's hitting you."

"There," he yelled and sure enough, the sign was illuminated. I turned onto the road. The sign said it was a mile and a half farther. I did a drive-by to get the lay of the land.

"It looks like the RVs are toward the back and the trailers are all up front. We need to make it look like we belong to either an RV or a trailer."

"Well, there are more lights on in the trailers than in the RV section."

"I think I'll pull into the trailer part but try and park near the RVs. Help me watch for people."

"Okay."

"I drove slowly past a few trailers. One had a couple sitting on their porch drinking, but they didn't pay us any attention. I rolled past a few more and then turned onto a road that looked like it should take us to the RV area.

"Shit, security dude," Lodan said, and shrunk down in his seat like it would make any difference at all.

"Where?"

"Over there, he just turned down that little side road over there. He's in a little golf cart."

"How do you know he's security?"

"Because I saw his uniform when he drove under the streetlight over there."

"Crap. Maybe we should go someplace else."

"No. Let's just try and find a spot close to two different RVs. Then hopefully they will each think we are with the other people. Plus, I have to go the bathroom sooner rather than later."

I sighed. After driving all day the last two days, I just wanted to get out of the car. I drove as far back as I dared and found two RVs with a few trees between. Both were completely dark. One had two cars beside it but the other, the one closest to the woods, didn't have any.

"I think this could work. What do you think?"

"Looks good to me," Lodan agreed.

"Is that your brain talking or your bladder?" I asked.

"Both!"

"Okay, here goes nothing." I reversed into the wooded area so that the back of the car, where we planned to sleep, would be better hidden. I turned off the motor and lights just before the security guy turned in our direction.

"Get down," I whispered, and we both scrunched down as far as we could. This was much more difficult for Lodan's six-foot frame, but apparently it worked. We heard the guy continue past us and turn down the next pathway.

"My bladder is going to burst," Lodan whispered.

"Okay, climb out and crawl around to the shadows and go. I'll try and get the back set up. I'm going to put as much of the stuff in the front as I can, but we can't make it too obvious if he shines his light across it again."

Lodan did a decent job of staying quiet as he went to relieve himself and I managed to get most everything into the front. I had to put the Cardboard Cupboard in the passenger seat, and Kono's cage in the driver's seat but hopefully it sat low enough to appear empty so we wouldn't look too obvious.

I rolled down the side windows a little so we didn't steam up the car too much. That would be another dead giveaway.

By the time Lodan climbed back into the car, I had all the seats down and he helped me lay out the sleeping bags. He'd have to sleep with his legs curled up, but it wasn't too bad.

"That one RV has a mailbox next to it and you are not going to believe the name on the box."

"What?"

"Silverman. My aunt's last name! What are the chances?" He shook his head.

"We should take that as a sign we'll be fine parking here," I whispered. "I'm going to sneak out for a minute, try and brush my teeth with my mouthwash and also go to the bathroom. Okay?" I whispered.

"Do you want me to come with you?" he whispered back.

"While I pee?"

"It's not like I want to watch or anything. It's just dark and you're female and alone in a sketchy place."

I smiled at his chivalry. "Thanks, Lodan. That's very sweet of you, but I'm not going to go very far. Okay?"

"Okay, well, I'm timing you on my phone and if you aren't back in two minutes, I'm coming after you."

"That's barely enough time to brush my teeth. Make it four. Okay?"

"Okay, and do we have any of those pretzels left?" he said in his normal voice.

"Shh. In the pantry. But be careful. I have it all set up in the front."

When I climbed back in, Lodan was lying on his back, eating pretzels and looking up at the stars through the sunroof.

"Good idea," I whispered. I hadn't thought to push back the sunroof cover so we could see the stars. I put my stuff away and settled next to him in my bag.

"Pretzel?" He mouthed the word and held out the bag.

"No, thanks," I whispered. "I just brushed, remember?"

"Oh, yeah."

"Are you nervous about tomorrow?" he asked quietly.

"Yes," I admitted.

"What are you going to say?"

"I guess I want him to explain what he meant in the letter. Was he my boyfriend only because he thought having a girlfriend would make his dad happy? Or his mom?"

Lodan rolled up the bag of pretzels, apologized for the noise, then set them back in the Cardboard Cupboard and resettled next to me, his legs curled up to fit. He lay on his side facing my profile while I stared at the stars.

"I want to know if he ever thought of me or felt about me like I do or did or . . ." I sighed. "It hurts to really think about what he said. I mean *relief*? That's kind of harsh. While I had an atomic bomb exploding in my chest cavity as I drove away from him, he felt relief."

Lodan reached over and slipped his fingers through mine. "I don't know anything about this stuff, but maybe he wrote that letter to get you to move on."

"Obviously." I felt a flash of ache through my chest.

"No, I'm not explaining myself well. Slushy brain. What I mean is maybe this was an offensive letter: him pushing you away before you could push him away. You know what I mean?"

"I do. But I don't think it was that."

Lodan rolled onto his back and looked up at the stars with me. And all of a sudden I felt really stupid. I sat up quickly.

"What's wrong?" Lodan sat up, too and hit his head. "Ow! You okay?"

I laughed. "Ow, am *I* okay?" I put my hand to his head. "Are *you* okay?"

"I'm fine." I felt his head through his spiky hair for a minute but I didn't feel a lump. I locked eyes with him and felt that familiar tickle low in my stomach. I pulled my hand back and lay down.

"I just realized how stupid this is. What am I doing? Mateo couldn't have been more clear in his letter. He doesn't want me anymore."

"It's not stupid to want to hear how he really feels face-to-face."

"It is. It's like I want to torture us both."

"No. You're just getting panicky because it's so close to happening now."

"You think?"

"I know." Lodan lay down next to me again.

Neither of us spoke for a while and I figured he'd fallen asleep after all the alcohol. I closed my eyes and started to drift off when he whispered again.

"You asleep?"

"No," I whispered.

"Can I ask you a strange favor?" Then more to himself, "I can't believe I'm going to ask you, but . . ." He groaned a little then whispered, "Actually never mind. It's awkward."

"Seriously. Now you have to ask." I turned to look at him in the dark. He searched my face for a few seconds then turned back to the stars.

He took a deep breath, squeezed his eyes shut, and then whispered, "Would it be weird if I asked to kiss you so I can see if I feel anything?"

His question sent a little wave through my chest to my stomach where it currently continued to flutter. When I didn't immediately respond, he opened one eye and looked at me. I looked up at the stars.

"Sorry. Ignore me. It's probably the tequila."

I bit my lip. "It's fine. I'm just trying to understand. You want to kiss me as like, an experiment?" My heart began to pound a little faster in my chest.

"Sort of? But then when I say it out loud it sounds kind of awkward and mean since you have all these feeling going on inside right now. It's probably not a good time for you to help me with my issue. I guess I was just thinking maybe a kiss from a girl could somehow jump-start my attraction battery."

"So I'm the jumper cable in this scenario?"

"Um, no, I think you're the other car and your lips are the jumper cables."

And some evil little hormonal voice in my head whispered *or your tongue* and I said, "No," louder than I meant to.

"Sorry, sorry, yeah, it was a dumb idea. I think I must be drunk. We should sleep," Lodan said as he rolled over to face away from me.

I felt like a jerk. I'd embarrassed him. I put my hand on his shoulder and squeezed. "Hey, it's not a dumb idea," I whispered to his back. "I'm sorry. You just caught me off guard and my head is all over the place right now."

"It's fine. We should get some rest," Lodan said and I felt a new wave in my stomach, only this one was all guilt.

"Good night, cowboy," I whispered and he must have felt a little better because a minute later he whispered, "Good night, Wonder Woman."

Twenty-three

LODAN

NEAR SANTA FE, NEW MEXICO
MONDAY, OCTOBER 26, 2015

I woke up to Lizzy's phone alarm when it was still dark outside. My head hurt and someone had taken a shop vac to my mouth because I had no saliva to wet my swollen slab of a tongue. I found her phone before she could and silenced the alarm.

"Water?" I whispered and Lizzy handed me her travel water bottle. I could have kissed her. *Oh, God.* And with that thought, all of my other thoughts from the night before came back. What had I been thinking? *Asking Lizzy to kiss me?* Never. Drinking. Again. The big question is: do I apologize or pretend it never happened?

"We should get out of here while it's still dark," Lizzy whispered. "Do you need to do bathroom stuff first or should I go?"

"You go," I whispered and decided to pretend nothing had happened. I rolled up our bags and started to get the car back to our driving mode. I took my turn in the woods and then we held our breaths and started the car. Lizzy slowly pulled out of our spot and we crept our way back to the center of the RV park. We turned onto the road that would carry us out of the park and both let out a yelp when our headlights fell squarely on the security guy sitting on the back of his golf cart.

"Just don't make eye contact," Lizzy said. "And we will cruise on by." But the security guy stepped in our way and held up his hand for us to stop.

"Crap," Lizzy said. She came to a stop and rolled down her window at the insistence of the guard.

"Morning." The guard hitched his belt back into place over his gut.

"Morning." Lizzy smiled.

"You know, I don't recall anyone registering a red 2012 Honda CRV," he said as he gave Lizzy the stink eye. "You two lovebirds weren't using my good park to engage in deviant sexual copulative-type activities, were you?"

I had to bite back a laugh. Lizzy cut her eyes at me and covered a smile with her hand.

"Of course not, sir. This is my brother, Bill, and we just stopped by kinda late last night to say hi to our aunt, sleep in a bed, and get something to eat. You know."

"What are two young kids like yourselves doing so far from home?" he asked, pointing to our plates with his big flashlight.

"We're heading cross country, checking out colleges for Bill here. He's got a hell of a brain on him and my mom said it shouldn't go to waste."

"Don't your school help you do that kind a thing?" He wrinkled his forehead.

"We're homeschooled so we have to do it all ourselves." Lizzy smiled at the officer and gave him the full blue-eyed puppy look she used to convince me to do things.

"Lotta people doing that homeschool stuff coming through here." He shook his head like he didn't approve. "Well okay, I best let you get to it." He patted the side of our car and started to turn away from the window, but then he turned back.

"Say, who was it you said your aunt was?" He raised an eyebrow at Lizzy and gave her a stare down.

"Silverman," I said. "Mrs. Silverman."

He continued to stare at Lizzy for a minute like he was angry and then suddenly smiled at her. "I hope she gave you some of her muffins for the road! I've gained ten pounds since Sheil—er, Mrs. Silverman—moved in."

He smiled to himself for a minute, not moving.

"Well, we really need to get on the road, sir," Lizzy said.

"Oh yeah, you be careful," he said and waved us off as he climbed back into his golf cart.

Lizzy rolled up the window and we scooted out of the RV park like bandits in the night, holding our breaths until we got back to the main road.

"Woohoo! That was vintage, Wonder Woman. Let's find you some coffee!"

Twenty-four

LIZZY

TRUTH OR CONSEQUENCES, NM
MONDAY, OCTOBER 26, 2015

As soon as we passed the sign welcoming us to Truth or Consequences I simultaneously began to sweat and break out in goose bumps. Lodan must have sensed something because he reached out and put a calming hand on my shoulder.

"Remember, Lizzy, Mateo is a good guy. He won't be cruel. It's going to be okay."

"How do you know he's a good guy?" I snapped.

But Lodan just smiled at me and squeezed my shoulder. "Because you told me he was a good guy."

"Everyone will still be in school for hours. Why didn't we plan this better?" I asked.

"Show me where you lived," Lodan said. "I want to meet Dusty the worn-out old Ford."

I looked over at Lodan and he smiled, and again he squeezed my shoulder. "Do you remember everything I tell you?"

He shrugged. "I'm a good listener. Probably required as a child of a single mom. She vents. I listen. She feels better. I feel needed."

I drove Lodan around a little, pointing out different places I'd told him about. I purposefully avoided driving by Mateo's. That would be later. I drove past our old rented house. No cars in the driveway and everything looked exactly as we had left it. It hadn't been long, so chances were it was still vacant. I pulled into the driveway.

"Are we getting out?" Lodan asked but I already had my door open. I walked up to the windows and looked inside. The fridge was still propped open. Nobody lived there.

"Come on!" I gestured for Lodan to follow me. We walked over to the garage. When I got to the door, I turned back around. "Dusty, meet Lodan. Lodan, that's Dusty. Have a seat on his hood while I grab something."

When I came out, carrying the horseshoes, Lodan had half his body leaned into Dusty's window on the driver's side. "A 1977 Ford standard cab, long bed, automatic. Shame he's been neglected because the inside is in amazing shape besides the stockpile of empty Skoal containers. Probably rattlers living under the hood at this point."

"I knew you two would hit it off." I smiled, then held up the horseshoes. "Wanna play?"

"Sure." He fell into step beside me and we walked to the poles.

"You know how?" I couldn't hide the surprise in my voice. Lodan wasn't much of a physical sports guy.

"Nope." He laughed. "But you're a good teacher."

Turned out Lodan may be a physical sport guy in hiding. He had a rough start but then he consistently kicked my butt at horseshoes. My stomach hurt from laughing by the time we decided to call it quits and go get a cheap lunch in town.

Thankfully we didn't run into anyone I knew during lunch. We still had almost two hours to kill but I had a brilliant idea.

"Where are we headed now?" Lodan asked. "Did you get cold feet? Because I feel like we are heading away from town."

"We are, a little, but I think you'll like this." I smiled at him. We had the windows rolled down and it felt good to feel the wind on my face and in my hair. The smells in this town were happy smells for me. I got a little kick out of it when Lodan reached down and cranked a Keith Urban song on the radio. I think I may have turned the guy country.

When I pulled to a stop in what looked like the middle of nowhere, Lodan turned to me and raised an eyebrow. "You bring me out here to hog-tie and shoot me?"

"No . . ." I said. "Did you bring swim trunks?"

"We're going swimming?" He hopped out of the car.

"Yep." I smiled at him and lifted my eyebrows. "There are natural hot springs, just beyond that tree right there."

"Vintage." He quickly stripped down to his boxers and headed toward the water. "Come on!" he yelled over his shoulder.

"I gotta find my suit!" I yelled as I dug through my bag, trying to remember if I'd thrown one in or not.

"Who needs a suit? It's just us. Go in your underwear."

I rolled my eyes, tossed my bag back in, and followed him to the water. He slipped right in. "Woohoo!" he yelled, a big grin on his face. I smiled, quickly pulled off my shorts and shirt, and slipped into the water. Luckily I'd put on a black sports bra and underwear this morning so my underwear wasn't much different than a black bikini. I slipped in across from him, closed my eyes, leaned back, and tried to enjoy the therapeutic feel of the natural heat on my body. My lower back and legs were a little stiff from all the driving.

I opened one eye to peek at Lodan. He had his arms spread wide along the edge of the rocks, his head rested against a large boulder, his eyes were closed, and a big grin covered his face. I let my gaze drift down over his smooth pale chest. He had a sexy, lean look. Very different from Mateo, but it suited him. He must have felt me studying him because he opened one eye. I closed mine again and pretended to relax until I actually did.

"Hey, Wonder Woman?" Lodan's voice sounded sleepy.

"Yeah?"

"Did we ever text our parents this morning?"

And *bam,* just like that relaxation left the spring. I sat straight up. "Crap, they are probably worried sick." I started to stand but Lodan stopped me with his hand.

"Relax, I got it. You hang. I'll go do it now and come back, K?"

"There is no service here. Trust me, I know."

"So I'll drive down the road until I find some. Send it and come back."

"You want me to lie here and relax while you illegally drive around by yourself?" I looked up at him, shading the sun with my hand.

"I got it. Please? Let me do this, okay?"

"Actually, it would be good for me to have something to do. It helps keep me from obsessing over Mateo." I stood up and wrapped my arms around myself, fully aware that I was wearing only underwear.

"I'll come with you then," Lodan offered, also getting to his feet.

I looked up at him. "That's silly. I'll be right back. No sense in getting both car seats soaked."

"You sure?" he asked.

"I'll be back in like fifteen minutes, tops." I headed for the car. I turned the Honda around in the field and flew down the dirt road. It took me a few minutes to realize my speed was fueled by anger. Only it wasn't because of Mateo. It was because of Lodan. He didn't even react to me in my underwear and I sat there ogling him like some pathetic voyeur. What was my problem? Did it even matter anymore if Mateo wanted to be with me or not? Could I jump from one guy to another that easily? I must be some kind of harlot.

Twenty-five

LODAN

TRUTH OR CONSEQUENCES, NM
MONDAY, OCTOBER 26, 2015

I felt guilty that I hadn't fought harder to go with Lizzy, but those hot springs felt amazing after sleeping in a ball all night in the back of the Honda. Plus Lizzy hadn't seemed herself once we'd gotten to the hot springs. I was pretty sure the Mateo thing had her stressed. I just hoped she could drive away from there happier about the situation. It would have been horrible to drive that far and find no closure.

I closed my eyes, leaned back against the rocks, and breathed in the fresh air. I was drifting in and out of sleep when I thought I heard a car door. I stayed where I was, listening for Lizzy to approach.

I heard her getting close so I yelled, "I'd promise to pay for a hotel tonight if you bring me a water."

"I don't think this place has drink service," a deep voice said. I bolted up and opened my eyes. Hulking at the edge of the spring, all shirtless brown muscles, eyes, and eyelashes stood a complete stranger. My heart raced in my chest and I suddenly felt skinny, pale, and naked compared to this statuesque man.

"Sorry, didn't mean to scare you." He smiled down at me.

"It's fine," I said. "I think I was kind of asleep."

"Yeah, well, truth be told, you kind of spooked me, too. How'd you get here? I didn't see a car or a bike out there anywhere."

"Oh, my friend had to go send a text. She'll be right back."

"Ah. Yeah, there's no service here. Part of why I like it."

"Yeah?"

"Yeah. Good hiding spot."

I nodded, trying to imagine what this big guy could possibly have to hide from.

"But hey, I should go. I don't want to bust in on your time with your girl." He turned to go.

"Wait. Stay!" I yelled. Then embarrassed, I added, "I mean if you want. She's not my girlfriend. Just a friend. So not, you know . . . it's fine."

"You sure?" He cocked his head at me and locked onto my eyes. I got a little chill, which was odd in a hot springs and I had the feeling he was trying to ask me something with his eyes.

I didn't actually answer, with my voice. As for my eyes, I can't speak for them. He hung the T-shirt in his hand on a branch and climbed in across from me.

"So you must live here then?" I asked.

"Yep. Born and raised."

"Must be nice having a natural hot tub at your disposal."

"It is kinda nice, especially in the fall with football and you know."

"Yeah, well, I mean, not really. I've never played." I gestured to my sliver of a frame. "Obviously."

"Not into sports?"

"Not really." I cupped the water in my hands, making it shoot to the side.

"Computers?"

"Some, but more engineering I guess?"

"Wow, you in college?"

"No." I felt myself blush. Why was I blushing?

"Are you?" Because he looked like he could be for sure.

"No. Senior."

"What do you do besides football?"

"Fix stuff mostly. But it's funny you like engineering because I was just talking to our guidance counselor about this. I think it may be what I want to study in college. I already know how to take things apart and put them back together, but I'd like to learn how to build things. You know?" He leaned forward in the water toward me. I liked how his eyes got all bright and shiny when he talked about what he liked.

I found myself leaning in toward him more as I talked. "Yeah. I've been into building things since I was a kid."

"Really, like what?"

"You promise not to laugh?" I lifted both eyebrows at him.

"I'm not gonna laugh." He'd put his hand to his chest as if subconsciously crossing his heart.

"Most people our age do." I took a deep, shaky breath. "Well, it's just my mom and me so I used our extra bedroom to build a whole town." I held my breath, waiting for the laughter. Usually it didn't bother me much if someone laughed but for some reason I couldn't bear the thought of this guy laughing at what I love to do.

"Like a whole miniature town? Streets, buildings? Everything?"

"Yeah, electricity, running water, subway, that kind of stuff." I still couldn't gauge his response.

"Even a subway? Wow, that's impressive. I'd love to see that!" he said and I felt myself relax.

"I wish I could show you but it's a bit of a hike." I shrugged. We both jumped at the sound of a car door and quickly distanced ourselves a little by leaning back against the rock walls behind us.

There was an awkward silence so I said, "You know, I could probably film what I've built and post it if you wanted." I'd gone back to squirting the water by cupping my hands together.

"Yeah. That would be cool." He nodded. "What is the town called?" But before I could answer I looked up and saw Lizzy standing behind him with a horrified expression on her face.

"Lizzy." I smiled, excited to introduce her to my new friend.

"What?" the guy asked, thinking I'd answered his question.

"Mateo?" Lizzy asked and he turned to look. We all froze. I'm sure my face looked as horrified as theirs. I jumped out of the hot springs.

I felt like I had been consorting with the enemy or something. But then I wasn't sure what to do. So I stood there silently dripping.

"What are you doing here, Lizzy?" Mateo asked, standing. My heart went out to her as she stood there in her underwear, caught off guard. This was not at all how she would have imagined this playing out in her head.

"I just . . . we . . . so you met Lodan," she finally said, taking the focus off herself.

Mateo looked up at me. "Not officially, no. We hadn't gotten that far yet." He took a step closer and extended a hand. With me on the side and him in the spring, I towered over him. I watched the water trickle down his taut pectorals and when he firmly took my hand in his I felt a little chill go through me. Maybe it was the change of temperature from the hot water to the air. But I also became very aware of how light the material of my boxers was. I could feel my body reacting to something and I needed to either get back in the water or run for the car. I chose the car.

"Nice to meet you, Mateo. I'm gonna give you two some space," I stammered and ran. "I'll be at the car, Lizzy," I yelled back over my shoulder.

When I got to the car, I half-fell, half-leaned against it. I had a raging hard-on. I dropped my head into my hands, not sure how or what I felt. I took a few deep breaths and willed my body to return to normal. But then a warm happiness spread over every inch of my body because I finally got it. I'd finally felt attraction and Lizzy was so right: it couldn't compare to waterfall mist on my skin or anything else I'd ever felt. I laughed out loud. I couldn't stop grinning. I ran my hand back and forth across my chest because it heightened the tingly sensation of joy bubbles I felt there.

But then I pictured Lizzy's complete look of horror and my happiness quickly faded. I let it sink in that my first and only attraction experience was with my good friend's—hell, my best friend's—boyfriend, or ex-boyfriend. This could not be good for anyone. I opened the back of the Honda, changed into dry shorts, and sat in the grass.

I was confused, guilt-ridden, and still slightly aroused as I waited to learn what happened with Lizzy and Mateo.

Twenty-six

LIZZY

TRUTH OR CONSEQUENCES, NM
MONDAY, OCTOBER 26, 2015

When I pulled back into the hot springs, I was so focused on having taken too long and getting back to Lodan that I didn't even register the truck parked nearby. But I really wished I had because when I ran smack into Lodan and Mateo in the hot springs my world sort of seesawed for a minute. And poor Lodan, I must have scared him with my shock because he took off like a scolded child.

"Lizzy," Mateo repeated. "What are you doing here?"

I was glad he was in the water and I was on the ground, because he didn't have the usual height advantage.

"I came to see you." My voice was failing me and it made me angry. I wanted to sound strong. But it was hard when I'd been caught off guard in my underwear.

"You drove here from New York?" I couldn't tell if he looked impressed or put off by this major gesture.

"Yes." I squeezed my nails into my hands. Don't cry. Don't cry.

He rolled his lips into his mouth and back out. I knew he didn't know what to say. He looked down at his hands and then back up at my face. "I'm sorry, Lizzy. I swear I didn't mean for things to go like this."

And then I couldn't hold it back anymore. I started to shake and the tears came down my cheeks. Mateo got out of the water and wrapped me into his warm, big, muscular chest and I let him hold me. It felt good to be back in his embrace and I wanted to hold onto the feeling as long as I could. I breathed deeply the scent of his skin. And he gently rocked me back and forth as I cried. He didn't push me away. In fact, he dropped his face into my hair and gently kissed the crown of my head.

After my tears subsided I took a deep breath and without letting go I asked him, "Did you ever love me like a girlfriend?" I had my ear pressed to his chest and I felt his heart pick up its pace.

"Lizzy, I wanted to. I really thought I could." His deep voice vibrated against my cheek and a fresh round of tears started. I wanted to hate him, but I knew it wasn't easy for him to tell me this. I knew he didn't want to hurt me. I could feel it as sure as I could feel his heart racing.

He gently took my face in his hands and leaned back so he could look me in the eyes with his own beautiful sad brown ones. He wiped at my tears with his thumbs and I wished it didn't make my stomach flip-flop, but it did.

"Do you love someone else?" I asked, not sure I could take the truth. He closed his eyes and I knew his answer would gut me.

"I thought I did," he whispered. I dropped my forehead to his chest and took a deep shaky breath.

"Is it someone I know?" I asked. Then I shook my head. "Maybe you shouldn't tell me."

"This is a strange way to be having this conversation." Mateo pulled back a little. We were standing in very little clothing, talking about very intimate feelings. It felt raw. Harsher than maybe it could have in a different setting.

"Trust me, in all the hours I've had to imagine this, I would not have voted for this scenario either. But here we are."

"You're right. Here we are." Mateo released me and took a step back. He grabbed a T-shirt from the tree and handed it to me.

"Maybe this will help," he said.

"Thanks." I pulled his shirt over my head. It came to my knees and he gave me a half-smile. "Cute."

I couldn't smile back, too big a lump in my throat and ache in my chest.

"Like I said in my letter, I've been working through a lot of stuff. And I'm not trying to make excuses because I know this has been hard for you, too. I'm just saying you gotta let me ease into this because I . . . actually, I don't . . . maybe . . ."

"Was it the distance thing? The way I don't usually stay in touch?" I asked my feet because his beautiful face made my heart hurt.

"No. It started way before you left. This is something I've been fighting since before I even met you. I've tried so hard to be the son my dad could feel proud of, the friend and teammate everybody respected, and a big brother Sebastian could look up to."

I looked up in shock to see his eyes full of tears. I took his hands in mine.

"Mateo, you are all of those things. I can't imagine any reason you wouldn't be the poster child for what anyone would want in any of those roles you already do so well."

He let go of my hands and turned away with a sad laugh. "Role is a good word. For years I think that's what I've been doing. I've been playing the role of Mateo as I believed my family and friends wanted me to play that part." He turned to look at me. "But you changed all of that. You helped me see that the only way to be happy is to be honest about how I really feel. I have to stop blaming everyone else for how sad and angry I feel inside. It's my job to make myself happy."

"Yes," I said. "Absolutely, but I thought we were happy together." I felt my heart plummet into my stomach. "Did I imagine what I felt between us? Am I really that blind that it was all one sided?" The tears slid down my cheeks.

He took a step toward me, grabbed my hands in his, and dropped to his knees so that he could look me in the face. "I do love you, Lizzy, and I am grateful for almost every part of our time together."

"Almost?" I shook my head. "What do you mean?" He looked at me and I felt a jolt of concern in my chest because mixed in with the sadness, I saw fear in his eyes.

"Mateo, please, are you okay? You're scaring me now. Did someone hurt you?" I squeezed his hands in mine.

Mateo pulled in a deep breath, closed his eyes, curled his lips in, and then opened his eyes. "Lizzy, I'm gay. I can't love you like a girlfriend because I really only want a boyfriend." He let out a big breath, squeezed my hands, and stood up.

I'm not sure how long it took me to fully process what he'd said, but I know I didn't speak for long enough to make Mateo assume what my reaction must be.

Mateo paced back and forth, running his hand back and forth over his flat top. "You hate me now, don't you?" he finally said.

"What? No! God, no. I don't hate you. I just . . . I'm trying to wrap my brain around it."

"Do you?" Mateo started and stopped and I realized I needed to say something.

I grabbed his hands in mine and made him stop pacing. He looked at his feet. "Mateo, look at me," I said. He brought his eyes to mine and I could see he was holding in his emotions. "I would never hate you because you're gay. How can I hate you for being true to yourself? Please don't take my silence to mean anything other than time to absorb. I'm coming at this from a purely selfish angle, wracking my brain to think of how I could have missed obvious signs, but . . ." I squeezed his hands tightly. "Don't feel bad for being gay. I'm so happy for you that you figured this out because it must have been torture to have to pretend for so long."

"If you mean being with you? That was never torture, Lizzy. I do love you and I loved being with you."

"But kissing me and . . ." I put my hand to my mouth and I watched him realize what I'd just realized. I'd pressured him a few times about sex and he'd been very uncomfortable about it. Now I understood.

"I'm sorry, Lizzy. But now you can kind of get maybe a lot of things that didn't make sense during our relationship."

"But why be with me at all? You asked me to be your girlfriend.

You kissed me that night outside Raj's house . . . you . . ." And then I *did* get it all. My jaw dropped and I saw the reflection of my bugged-out eyes in Mateo's. The angry looks at the Halloween party, in his truck, at homecoming. He hadn't been jealous of *Raj* with me. He'd been jealous of *me* with Raj. "Raj. You're in love with Raj?" I put my hand to my chest. "Of course." I ran my fingers through my hair, twisted it into a long tight roll, then released it again.

"So what happened? Did you tell Raj?" I asked.

He nodded sadly.

"And how did he react?"

"Angry at first. He didn't believe me. Thought I was making fun of him or some shit. But I grabbed him and kissed him and that kind of made it pretty clear how serious I was."

"And did it feel right? Did you finally feel like you understood what it should feel like?" I asked.

He took a deep breath. "Yes and no." He went back to pacing.

"What do you mean?"

"Well, I think I've known I was attracted to men for a long time and so I'd built it up in my head that Raj and I would be perfect for each other because we've been such great friends forever and all, but when I kissed him it felt like kissing my brother."

"Oh."

"Yeah."

"And Raj?"

"Yeah. That's complicated because Raj didn't exactly have the same reaction I did."

"Oh, no. So now Raj is into you but you aren't into Raj."

"Pretty much."

"And does Raj know this?"

"Oh yeah. After everything I'd just been through with you, I couldn't make that mistake again. I couldn't hurt Raj like I'd hurt you. But . . ."

"It was already too late. The kiss changed everything."

"Everything."

"I'm sorry. Suddenly our break-up seems really simple compared to all of this."

Mateo gave me his crooked smile and pulled me to him for a hug. "I'm sorry, Lizzy. I know this has sucked for you, too."

"I am so glad I came to see you!" I said, and I felt a fresh round of tears coming. I tried to swallow them.

"Me too, Lizzy. I've missed having you to talk to. I could have really used your advice these past few weeks." Mateo squeezed me tight and dropped a kiss on my head.

"Do you think we can stay friends? You know, keep in touch?" I asked him.

"Wait, what?" He jumped back and held my hands out to the side. "Little Miss Sever All Ties would break her rules and STAY in touch with me?"

I smiled, rolled my eyes, and wiped the tears from my cheeks. "Okay, I deserved that. But I am serious. I'd really like it if we could talk and stuff. I miss our RV rooftop heart-to-hearts."

"Me too."

I sighed deeply and Mateo pulled me in for one more hug. I thought about all of the times he'd held me like this and wondered if it had been painful to pretend. If the person you thought loved you didn't feel the same *kind* of love (the I-can't-think-about-anything-or-anyone-else-when-I'm-in-your-presence kind of love), then was it ever really a true first love relationship?

"We should probably go check on your friend. We've been down here quite a while."

His voice pulled me back to the present. "You're right. Poor Lodan." And we headed back to the car where we found Lodan sprawled out, sound asleep in the grass in the shade of the car.

Mateo squeezed my shoulder and I turned to look at him.

"Hey, Lizzy. I haven't . . . um . . . told my family and stuff about all of this," Mateo whispered, folding his hands behind his head as if he wasn't sure where to put them. I tried to ignore the little thrill seeing his chest still sent through mine.

"Wait, what? Why haven't you told your mom?" I asked.

"My dad," he said, a shadow falling across his face.

"Oh. The whole tell-one, you've-told-them-both kind of thing." I opened the back of the Honda.

"Yeah. And you've met my dad. If you look up *homophobic* his picture is front and center."

"But you can't live in hiding, either." I locked eyes with him.

He closed his and turned away. "I've done it this long. I'm not ready for that step yet. Okay?"

"Of course." I had seen how insensitive his dad was about many things. "I get it. I just hate it for you." I went to put my hand on his arm, but held back.

"I appreciate that, but . . ."

"It's good. I get it. Lips sealed."

"Thanks." Mateo smiled and I felt it in my chest again. This was going to take some time to get used to.

"Well, we should . . ." I nodded toward Lodan, still asleep in the grass.

I opened the passenger door and closed it again: not hard enough to scare him, just enough to wake him.

"Hey!" Lodan sat up. "You're both still alive and unscathed."

"Yeah, sorry we left you hanging so long," I said.

"Here." Mateo reached out a hand to Lodan and helped pull him into a standing position.

"Hey, I gotta you know, go," Lodan said. "Be right back." And he dashed off into the woods.

"Okay? That was abrupt," I said as I moved things around in the car in search of my shirt.

"So how long are you staying? And where?" Mateo asked.

"Haven't made a definite plan yet. We have to be in California by Thursday."

"There's another ex you have to go see?" Mateo asked, winking. When I didn't laugh he scrunched up his nose. "Too soon?"

"Little bit." I stepped into my shorts and switched out his shirt for mine. "California is for Lodan. He's got his own mission."

"Ex-boyfriend to see?"

"What? What do you mean?"

"I don't know. Nothing. Never mind." Mateo cleared his throat as Lodan walked back into the clearing.

"Hey, is there poison ivy in New Mexico? I'd hate to drive cross country with an itchy rash!"

"Itchy rash or itchy ass?" I joked.

"Both!" Lodan scratched his chest.

"Actually, there is." Mateo shaded his eyes to look at Lodan in the sun. "Do you think you saw some?"

"No, I just had that awful thought mid-stream and now I feel all itchy."

"It's probably just from sleeping on the grass," I pointed out.

Mateo slipped his shirt back over his head and headed toward his truck.

"So, do you think it would be too weird to stay with us? You know we have loads of RVs available."

I looked at Lodan. He looked right back at me with a burning question-filled gaze.

"Do you think it would upset Sebby too much if we did?" I looked back at Mateo.

"We did just finally get him to stop playing that 'Hurt' song over and over again like a week ago." Mateo twisted his lips to the side like he was thinking. "I'm just kidding. Of course not. He'd love to see you and so would my mom. Why don't you at least come for dinner? Say around six-thirty. Then if you want to stay over you can. If you don't, no problem."

"Sounds like a plan! Thanks, Mateo." We both watched as he climbed into his truck and drove off.

"So, what happened?"

And I played back most of our conversation for Lodan and surprised myself by not crying once. Maybe, this scenario, one I didn't imagine at all, actually hurts the least. Our relationship didn't end because I wasn't loveable. It ended because I wasn't male.

Twenty-seven

LIZZY
TRUTH OR CONSEQUENCES, NM
MONDAY, OCTOBER 26, 2015

That night the universe conspired against us or maybe we all blame the universe when we try to do the right thing and it turns out all wrong. Lodan and I arrived right on time for dinner and Sebby ran straight up to me with his newest addition, Fleetwood. I held Fleetwood and made a point to introduce myself to him. Then I introduced Lodan. Sebby glared at Lodan and ignored his request to hold Fleetwood, but at least he still took him on a tour of the turtle zoo. I couldn't believe how much he'd added in the short time I'd been away. He remained with his turtles while we went inside to say hi to Mel.

Mel seemed a little distant when she saw me so I settled for a quick side hug hello. I noticed she'd colored her hair to hide the gray and wondered if that had anything to do with impressing Rooster. She didn't seem her usual warm fuzzy self but got Lodan and me each a lemonade while Mateo finished up in the garage with a customer.

I could smell she'd made penne à la vodka and saw a colorful salad set on the table. My mouth watered at the thought of a home-cooked meal.

"Mrs. Mascia, thank you for making us dinner. We haven't eaten a decent meal in days and my mouth is salivating just smelling this kitchen," Lodan said.

"Oh, I always make enough to feed an army. It's really no big deal to add a few place settings. It was nice of you to accompany Lizzy on the long trip to see Mateo."

"Actually, we're on our way to California to see some of his family so it worked out well," I explained. "Can we help with anything? Maybe set the table?"

"That would be great, thanks," Mel said. "I actually need to just do like two things in the office and then hopefully we can all eat. Okay?"

"Sure."

When she left the room I whispered to Lodan, "She's acting strange."

He shrugged. "She seems nice enough to me."

I shook my head. "Maybe I'm just tired."

Lodan and I set the table, and by the time we'd finished Sebby was seated with his hands washed, Mateo was washing his, and Mel arrived with a huge serving dish of pasta. Dinner went surprisingly well. There were no awkward silences. In fact Rooster joined us about halfway through and the three guys were quickly absorbed in conversations about fixing and designing cars, lawn mowers, and all things mechanical. I'd never heard Mateo or Lodan talk so much all at once. Sebby finished in record time and asked to be excused before Rooster had even finished serving himself.

"So how is your new town, Lizzy?" Mel asked.

"It's actually very picturesque, thanks. There is a nice-size lake and with the leaves changing it was a gorgeous fall. Lodan and I have kayaked on it a couple of times now. You'd love it."

"It sounds nice," she said. "Anyone hungry for dessert?"

Everybody agreed we needed to digest a little first. Plus, Lodan, Mateo, and Rooster wanted to go test drive the old Model T and apparently get Lodan's opinion on something else they were working on in the garage.

Mel and I cleaned up from dinner since they clearly had more fun stuff to do. We finished clearing the table, put away leftovers, then set to work on the dishes.

Mel was unusually quiet so I tried to make conversation.

"I like your hair. You look younger," I said, then quickly realized that could be insulting. "Not that you looked old before."

Mel smiled. "It's okay. Thanks. Hiding the gray does take a few years off." She rinsed a knife and handed it to me to dry.

"So, feel free to tell me to mind my own business, but I have to admit I was a little surprised when Mateo said you'd be coming for dinner tonight," she said. I watched as she aggressively scrubbed a dish that looked clean, her yellow gloves sloshing the soapy water.

"It's fine. I know you guys talk about everything, anyway," I said. Mel handed me the dish to dry. "Plus, I felt better about him breaking up with me once I talked to him in person." I crossed the kitchen to put the dish in its cupboard.

"Wait, what do you mean? He said he broke up with you because you admitted you had acted on feelings for someone else." Mel knotted her eyebrows and wiped a chunk of hair out of her face.

I felt a wave of anger rush up my spine. "What? He told you I cheated on him?" I asked as I grabbed the dish towel back off the counter.

"Oh God," Mel said. "Why did I open my big mouth? It's really none of my business."

"But I didn't cheat on him. I wouldn't do that." My chest felt tight and I knew my face and neck were red hot. "Mel, you know me better than that."

"Well, I thought I did. And that's why I thought it was odd that you'd bring your new boyfriend here so soon after. Mateo has been an emotional mess."

"Mel, *he* broke up with *me*. He thought *he* loved someone else." I twisted the dish towel in my hands until it began to pinch my skin. "And Lodan isn't my boyfriend. I came here hoping Mateo would change his mind and stay with me."

"So you didn't cheat on him?" She looked up from washing a colander.

"No!" I felt my face flush. "I swear. I wouldn't do that. He thought he loved Raj," I said just as Lodan and Mateo walked back into the kitchen.

Mel's eyes grew twice their normal size and she clasped her yellow gloved hand to her mouth, wet suds dripping down the glove. I quickly realized what I'd just done and threw my hand over my own mouth, a whole new flame zipping up my neck and face.

"Lizzy!" Lodan said my name like a parent shocked by their child's behavior. I felt guilt and regret twist like a knife in my gut.

We all looked at Mateo who turned to glare at me, veins popping in his forehead and neck, his hands fisted at his side. If I didn't know him, I'd have been afraid he'd hit me. Instead he simply turned and slammed out the kitchen door.

We all stood in shocked silence for a beat. "I . . ." What could I say? That secret had not been mine to share. "Mel, I thought . . . I'm sorry."

She turned to me and her eyes softened. She put a hand on my shoulder. "No, Lizzy, this is my fault. I shouldn't have gotten into yours or Mateo's business. I'll go talk to him. Please don't leave. Just . . . just don't go yet, okay?"

She pulled off her gloves, set them on the counter, and followed after Mateo. Lodan didn't say a word. I could kiss him for that because one word and I would have lost it. He simply slipped on Mel's gloves and picked up where she'd left off with the dishes. We finished up in silence. Both of us knowing that what I'd done was awful and nothing either of us could do or say would put the words back in my mouth. I really did not like myself at that moment.

Twenty-eight

LODAN

TRUTH OR CONSEQUENCES, NM
MONDAY, OCTOBER 26, 2015

The timing of everything that night couldn't have been worse. When we first arrived for dinner and Lizzy introduced me to Sebby, I was worried it would be a long, uncomfortable night. But as soon as we all sat down to eat, things took a turn for the better. Mateo amazed me with his knowledge of mechanics. I felt like I'd finally met someone who spoke the same language. He knew exactly what I meant by twin engine trucks and a side versus a downdraft carburetor. I felt like I'd finally found my people. And Rooster had years of experience with large diesel engines. I could have talked to them for hours.

I helped Rooster and Mateo with a holding tank they'd just replaced in an RV. They had differing opinions as to what had caused the tank to fail in the first place and needed to fix the issue for the owner so that it didn't happen again. I actually disagreed with both of them and pointed out what I thought had caused the issue. You'd have thought I'd discovered the key to time travel. They made me feel like a mechanical genius. This all may sound trivial to the average person, but I'd never had anyone fully appreciate me doing what I loved.

Rooster had to fix something on one of Sebby's turtle cages so he told Mateo and me to take out the Model T without him.

I'd seen a Model T on the road before but I'd never been up close enough to study one or ride in it. For a moment I felt like I could have ended the trip after this ride and still felt happy. I ran my hand along the back of the leather seat, and admired the pristine royal-blue paint job.

"Wow, this is absolute vintage," I said.

"Thanks. My dad bought it a while ago and never got around to getting it running. I finally learned enough to take a crack at it. Rooster helped me with a few things recently and now she purrs right along."

He adjusted a mirror. "She has a Cleveland engine with comp two-sixty-eight cam, tunnel ram with two Holley four-fifty C.F.M. Carbs."

"C-6 automatic transmission?" I asked as I admired the inside.

"Yep." Mateo leaned against the driver's side. I could feel him watching me admiring the car and it gave me the same stomach thrill as the first few seconds after a roller coaster begins its plunge down a steep peak.

"Ready to go for a spin?" Mateo asked, getting in on his side.

"Absolutely." I climbed into the passenger side and wow, the seat was barely built for two. The left half of my body tingled with heat where Mateo's right shoulder, hip, and thigh pressed tight against mine.

I rested my fists on my knees, my palms sweaty and tense. I felt him smile over at me but I didn't dare look at him and kept my eyes focused straight ahead. He pulled out of the garage area where it lived, crossed the RV lot, and pulled onto the main road. He reached down and put on the radio, which was tuned to an oldies station. My heart raced and I couldn't control the perma-grin on my face as the wind tickled across my head. We drove in a small loop, making it maybe a twelve-minute round trip, but I don't think my heart stopped racing the entire ride.

He pulled the car back into its spot and asked me if I wanted to drive it.

"Man, I'd love to," I said. "But I'm not sixteen quite yet." I rubbed my palms on my jeans.

"Who will know?" When he flashed me that crooked smile and

caught my eyes with his I thought for sure he could see exactly how much I wanted to do anything as long as he did it with me. I bit my lip and ran a hand across my head. *Did his words have double meaning?*

"I really want to, but I probably shouldn't," I said.

"No problem. Another time," Mateo said and I thought (*hoped?*) I heard disappointment in his voice as he got out of the car. I got out on my side and helped him put the cover back in place before we headed back outside. The desert sky had grown dark and starry. I guess I was following him a little too closely because he turned around suddenly and we landed chest to chest, our faces inches apart. We must have been near the same height because our eyes were dead on track. I swallowed hard and heard him take a quick breath in and hold it. Probably a few seconds passed but it felt like an eternity we both froze. And then Mateo took my head in his hands and pulled my lips to his. I didn't dare breathe. My chest ached as I kissed him back. He smelled like cologne and he tasted like toothpaste. I felt his kiss from my lips to the soles of my feet in waves of hot prickly chills. My stomach felt sick and warm all at once. I put my hand up to his head to pull him closer and our kiss deepened. I heard a quiet low groan come from the back of his throat and I felt my entire body react. I couldn't believe I'd been missing out on this feeling forever. And I didn't want to let go. Mateo reached behind me, closed the garage door, and then crushed my body with his against the door. Our teeth clashed and Mateo laughed and pulled back to look at me. I looked him in the eyes and then I ruined it all with my conscience.

"God. I don't want to stop. Like ever." I laughed a little, looked at the ground, then back at his caramel-brown eyes. I rested my forehead against his. "But . . ."

"Lizzy."

"Yeah." I closed my eyes, willing myself to be a good friend. "She's still in love with you."

"I know." He pulled his head away and banged his knuckles against the door a few times, next to my head. "Why is life so complicated?

Why can't we just like who we like and kiss who we want to kiss?"

"I don't think it's usually this complicated. But I don't really have anything to base it on," I admitted.

"Oh God. You gotta stop that," Mateo said and stopped my hand with his where I'd been running it over his chest without even realizing it.

"Sorry." I pulled my hand away and slid it into my pocket.

"We should probably get back in there," Mateo said but neither of us moved. A warm breeze brought a sweet, dusty, desert smell.

"Have you seen Jayco?" We both jumped apart at the sound of Sebby's voice. My heart leapt into my throat at the thought of him possibly having seen us.

"Hey buddy," Mateo said, shooting me a look. "How long you been standing there?"

"I can't find Jayco. I set him down for a second while I put the lid back on the girls' cage and then I forgot and had to pee and then I remembered but he's gone."

"We'll help you find him, buddy," Mateo said. He looked at me again and I smiled then looked at the ground, afraid everything I felt would be obvious to Sebby, and there sat a turtle, right next to the garage door.

I bent down, picked it up, and said, "Sebby, is this Jayco?" as I held the turtle toward him.

Sebby's face lit up. He gave me an odd look, gently took Jayco into his own hands, peered down its shell, and said something I couldn't hear. I stood up and flashed Mateo a hope-he-didn't-see grimace. Sebby wandered back into the darkness.

"Well, you probably scored a few points right there," Mateo said. "But you might want to wash your hands. Those things carry diseases."

"Really?"

"Yes, I think Sebby is magically immune, but I wouldn't risk it if I were you." He briefly ran a finger down my arm, causing my breath to catch in my throat. Then he headed back toward the house, me on his heels. This time I left a little more space between us.

Just before he opened the kitchen door, he looked around, grabbed my face, dropped a quick kiss, then said, "Gonna hold you to that 'another time.'" But his smug smile disappeared as soon as we stepped inside to hear Lizzy accidently turn his life upside down.

Twenty-nine

LIZZY

TRUTH OR CONSEQUENCES, NM
MONDAY, OCTOBER 26, 2015

Lodan and I finished the dishes, cleaned the counters, scrubbed the stove, and they still hadn't returned. I made coffee in case we were still doing dessert. We sat at the table, both on our phones. I sent our parents an update that may or may not end up to be true. I wasn't sure we had a safe place to sleep and were done driving for the day, but I hoped we could still stay. I looked up at Lodan when my group text dinged into his phone.

He reached across the table, squeezed my hand, and gave me an encouraging half smile. It helped ease the clench in my gut a little. I read through the latest headlines without really comprehending anything.

We both jumped when Mel opened the door to the kitchen. She looked like she'd been crying.

"Hey," she said with a sigh. "Thanks for finishing the cleanup."

"Sure." Lodan answered for us both.

We waited for Mel to lead the conversation. She poured herself a coffee and leaned against the counter.

"Is he okay?" Lodan finally broke the silence.

"He will be." Mel tried to smile at us but it faltered halfway. "He's scared about his dad."

"Why do you have to tell him?" I asked.

"I don't have to tell him, at least not right away. But eventually we do. Mateo can't keep pretending to be someone he isn't."

"Are you mad that he's gay?" Lodan asked, surprising all of us.

"Of course not!" Mel set her full coffee on the counter. "Not mad at all. Concerned for him. Heartbroken that he's kept this inside so long. Hurt that he didn't come to me. Scared for him to face a path that will be more challenging. But we can't help who we love." She turned away from us for a minute, and I saw her back begin to tremble.

I stood up and gave her a hug. "I'm so sorry this is how you found out." She hugged me back. "I had no right."

"Lizzy, I know you didn't mean any harm." Mel pulled away but held my arms. "It's good this happened. I think Mateo is actually relieved that I finally know. He's just concerned about his father."

"Then don't tell him," Lodan said.

Mel wiped the tears from her cheeks and took a shaky breath. "I won't for now. But when he is ready Mateo needs to tell him. He can't live his life as a lie anymore. He will be miserable. He should be free to have relationships and feel love like the rest of us. This is a small town, if Mateo comes out, his dad will find out anyway. Mateo should be the one to tell him."

Lodan stood up. "Well, for the record, Mrs. Mascia, I think you're an awesome mom for being so cool about this." He put his hands in his back pockets and shuffled his feet around.

"Thanks, Lodan. I love Mateo no matter what. It doesn't matter to me who he loves as long as he's happy. And that person is good to him."

Lodan smiled and blushed a little. He seemed to be acting a little odd tonight but then again it was an odd night.

"Well, I don't know about you guys but I'm ready for an early night. Let me show you where you can sleep, and then I need to get Sebby in the shower before bed."

We followed Mel out to one of the RVs parked close to the building. It was one of their rentals that they kept hooked up to power and water so they could demonstrate for customers how everything worked.

"When I thought you were a couple I was hesitant to have you together in here but I don't think Mateo would be up for Lodan as a roomie tonight, so I hope you're okay in here together."

"Oh, we've been sleeping together the whole trip," Lodan said, then blushed. "I mean in a geographic sense not . . . you know."

Mel smiled at his obvious discomfort and patted him on the shoulder. "I got what you meant, Lodan."

"Thanks, Mel, for dinner and this and for being so nice about everything," I said.

She pulled me to her for a hug. "Of course, Lizzy. And I am so sorry about the whole cheating thing. I should have known better. We've really missed having you around here."

"Do you think Mateo will be willing to talk to me in the morning? I'd really hate to leave with things like this between us."

"He has school tomorrow so he'll be up by six. What time did you guys plan to leave?" Mel asked.

"Probably around then," I said, looking to Lodan for confirmation but he seemed a million miles away in his own head.

"I'll have coffee ready and you'll probably find him in the garage. He usually keeps his hands busy when he's upset."

She showed us how everything worked and we settled in for the night. It was nice to each have our own separate bed for a change. I closed my eyes and wondered if Mateo would be able to sleep tonight. Why did the truth have to hurt sometimes? I closed my eyes and willed Mateo to forgive me by morning.

Thirty

LODAN

TRUTH OR CONSEQUENCES, NM
MONDAY, OCTOBER 26, 2015

I couldn't believe Mateo and I had almost been bunkmates for the night. The thought both terrified and excited me. I wondered if his mom had told him of her plan and how he'd felt about it if she did. I smiled in the darkness, remembering our drive and the kiss that followed. Was it just Mateo or could other men make me feel like this? I felt like he'd awakened something inside me, making my whole being hum with happiness. But then I thought of the pain Mateo must have been feeling and it sent me down that same thought train. How would my mom react when I tell her I think I'm gay? And was my father gay? Was that what happened between them? What if that was why she wouldn't have anything to do with him? My mind buzzed with questions that I hoped could be answered, at least in part, in a matter of two days.

√hirty-one

LIZZY

TRUTH OR CONSEQUENCES, NM
TUESDAY, OCTOBER 27, 2015

Instantly wide awake, I struggled to find my phone in the dark. It was just past five thirty in the morning. I lay there a bit, then decided to take my blanket with me and watch the sunrise from one of my favorite spots. I made my way down the rows of RVs to the back right corner. And I was about to climb the ladder to my favorite RV when I saw two figures sitting on top of the RV two down from mine. I heard Mateo's laugh and studied the other figure as best I could in the dark. Lodan? I couldn't decide whether to let them know I was there or listen to what they were saying. Were they talking about me? Why were they up so early?

I crept closer to try and hear what they were saying. I stopped at the base of the ladder to the top of the RV where they sat. I couldn't see them anymore but I listened.

"My mom didn't really encourage me to do any of that stuff. Little League, football. I never asked and she didn't either," Lodan was saying.

"I'm surprised a coach didn't try to recruit you for basketball or something," Mateo said.

Lodan laughed, only it sounded funny, different from when he laughed with me. "Yeah, well, the coaches were also PE teachers so they knew how useless I was on a basketball court."

"Well, if they saw your moves under the hood . . ." Mateo said but never completed his sentence. They fell oddly silent and I waited for them to speak again. But the longer I waited the more uncomfortable I felt for eavesdropping. So I cleared my throat and yelled up to them.

"You guys are up early," I said before grabbing the ladder to haul myself up. I adjusted the blanket around my neck. I heard a couple of thumps.

"Lizzy?" Lodan's voice sounded scared.

"No, it's Rosemary's baby coming to seek revenge," I joked sarcastically.

"When did you wake up?" Lodan asked.

"Just a few minutes ago. I couldn't go back to sleep so I thought I'd watch the sunrise." I finished the climb and stepped onto the hood. Lodan stood off to the side and Mateo had his screwdriver out tightening something.

Lodan looked back and forth between the two of us. "Um . . . I'll go see if I can help with coffee."

"You don't have to leave," I said, feeling a little guilty. Mateo had sounded perfectly happy talking to Lodan.

"No, you two should talk." And he hurried down the ladder and disappeared into the darkness.

I sat down next to where Mateo was working.

"I thought you told me you already had these in tip-top shape," I said, referring to his comment in the letter.

"You know me. Check and double-check," he said.

"Mateo, I am really sorry. I swear I didn't purposely do that." I put my hand out and touched his arm. He looked up at me and my heart kicked up a notch when his eyes met mine. Would I ever feel normal around him?

He put down the screwdriver and took a seat next to me. "I know, Lizzy. I know you wouldn't purposely hurt anyone. I just wanted to do that on my terms, you know?"

"I know and I'm sorry I took that away from you."

"The timing is bad. My dad is coming for Thanksgiving. In fact he could be here as soon as tonight."

My heart sank. "Oh God, Mateo. I really messed things up, huh?"

"I think my mom would have no problem keeping it a secret from a distance, but with him right here . . . It's not right to make them have secrets for me."

"Is there anything I can do? I feel terrible." I wrapped my blanket tighter around myself and stared out at the first hint of light in the distance.

"I can't let you take all the blame, Lizzy. I did lie to my mom about us. And she was being protective of me when she thought you and Lodan were together."

"I guess we created a tangled mess."

"That we did."

"Are we going to be okay after this?" I asked, hoping we could stay friends.

Mateo put his arm around me and I snuggled into his chest. "Yeah, we're going to be okay, Lizzy. Who could stay mad at you?"

"You'd be surprised," I said and felt tears of relief fill my eyes. I tried to hide them but Mateo knew me too well.

"Oh, Lizzy, don't cry. I'll figure this out."

"I'm sorry. I'm just so relieved that I don't have to drive away feeling worse than I did driving in."

"My mom has been completely awesome about everything. And I am relieved to be able to be open and honest with her about how I feel. I hated keeping things from her."

"I'm sure she was most upset that you hadn't been honest with her."

"Yeah. Hurt really."

"How did you and Lodan both end up out here so early?" I asked.

"Guess we both couldn't sleep. He told me a little about his situation. I hope California is good to him. It sounds like things could go either way." The pink morning light continued to slip higher in the sky, bathing us in a soft light.

"Yeah. He's a really good guy. I hope he doesn't get his heart broken," I said.

We silently watched the sun come up, me still cocooned in Mateo's arms. I knew for him it didn't have the same meaning it did for me. But as the sun climbed higher in the sky, I forced my heart to try to remember it needed to let him go. "I have no regrets, Mateo, I'm glad you were my first boyfriend," I whispered. He didn't say anything but hugged me tighter.

"Lizzy, you changed my life," he finally said. "As scared as I am to face my father, I've never felt more at peace inside my own head."

The good-byes were rushed because a neighbor's dog had gotten loose and headed straight for Sebby's turtle zoo. It took three of us to catch the big retriever-shepherd mix. He didn't mean any harm but he evaded us like it was the best game. By the time we got the dog on a leash, Sebby calmed, and the turtle cages back in order, they were late for school and we were late to leave. Quick hugs, a few tears (me), an exchange of contact info (Lodan and Mateo), a few Sebby-insistent turtle kisses (me, Jayco, and Fleetwood), and we all headed to whatever the next few days had in store for us. And none of us could have predicted just how crazy things would get.

Thirty-two

LODAN

NEW MEXICO–ARIZONA
TUESDAY, OCTOBER 27, 2015

We put on a country station and rode in silence, both lost in our own thoughts. I'd thought I was dreaming when Mateo tapped on the RV window near where I slept early this morning. I'd looked out the curtain and there he stood, finger to his lips, his phone lighting his face in the darkness. I grabbed my phone, sweatshirt, and shoes, then quietly snuck out past a sleeping Lizzy.

"Morning?" I whispered to Mateo, a ball of excitement unraveling through my body when he flashed his smile at me.

"Sorry. It's early," he whispered and motioned for me to follow him away from the RV. We walked in silence to the far right of the RV park, lost in the shadows of the hulking beasts. Eventually he stopped and turned toward me. "Is Lizzy okay?" he asked.

"Yeah. Just angry with herself and worried about you," I said, looking down and kicking the dirt with my shoe.

"Hope this is okay. I couldn't sleep and I didn't know if we'd have a chance to talk in the morning."

"Yeah, sure." I looked up at him quickly then back down because my heart began racing again. "I'm glad you did." I looked up at him again and knew I'd said the right thing when he let out his breath and relaxed his shoulders again.

"Good. Are you okay with, you know?" Mateo asked.

"Yeah," I said. "I've never." I felt stupid. "I didn't, or well, I wasn't . . ."

"Sure if you were gay?" Mateo finished for me.

I creased my forehead and dared a check of his eyes to see how he felt about that.

But he didn't look amused or surprised. He just looked right back at me with kindness that made me swallow the fear that had gathered in my throat. His eyes had the flutter in my stomach churning again.

"I couldn't believe it when I saw you in the hot springs. This feeling came over me like you were waiting for me or something." Mateo shook his head, looked down, and kicked at the dirt. "Sorry that sounds really . . ."

"Gay?" I laughed and he did, too.

"I can't believe you're the Mateo I've heard about and hated for weeks."

"Wait, you *hated* me?" Mateo knotted his brow.

"Yes. Lizzy just got your letter a couple days ago so we thought you'd ghosted her," I explained, putting my hands in my pockets, rocking back and forth on my heels.

"But I sent it like a day or two after she left." Mateo ran a hand over his flat-top. "She must have been really pissed."

"And sad," I pointed out. "Hence the hate thing."

"I hope you don't still feel like that?" Mateo looked up at me. The juxtaposition of his strong, muscled body and his vulnerable eyes made me weak in my knees.

I didn't trust my voice to speak so I shook my head. Mateo took a step closer and I could feel his breath on my face. He'd brushed his teeth again and I hoped it was because he wanted to kiss me. But then I felt a jab of guilt when I thought of how this would hurt Lizzy. My thoughts must have showed on my face because Mateo took a step back again.

"Come on," he said. "Let's sit up here and watch the sun come up."

"Yeah? Can it hold both of us okay?" I asked.

"Oh yeah." He began to climb the ladder and I followed him. We stood awkwardly for a minute on the roof until he sat on the edge and motioned for me to sit beside him.

I wanted to sit close but I felt like that was giving him mixed messages. Honestly I didn't know what I wanted or maybe I did know but I felt too guilty to act on it.

But Mateo didn't wait for me. As soon as I started to sit, he reached for me and pulled me to him. I didn't even bother to try and resist. I'd never known a feeling like this in my chest and I didn't want to push it away. It felt too good.

We made out, barely allowing the other to breathe, chests crushed together, hearts pounding, his hands cradling my head as mine traced the muscles in his back through his T-shirt. We got so carried away we almost fell off the roof.

"Woah." Mateo grabbed at me as I started to slip. That fear adrenaline rush was nothing compared to the adrenaline rush of Mateo. We both laughed and lay back, side by side, our backs against the roof, legs over the edge, his fingers looped into mine. I couldn't remember a time I felt happier. My lips and face buzzed from his touch. A sweet flowery smell drifted through the early morning air.

"I wish I lived here," I said, looking at the fading stars.

"Me, too," he echoed and squeezed my hand.

"I've never met anyone that gets as excited about cars and building things as I do," I said.

"I know," he agreed. "Funny we were brought together by Lizzy."

I groaned a little. "Now I feel guilty again." I sat up.

"Sorry." He sat up as well.

And then we got to talking about cars and the town I'd designed and built and I told him I didn't know my dad or if my mom had been honest with me about anything. We had just drifted back to talking cars again when Lizzy shocked us both by appearing at the bottom of the ladder.

I looked over at her profile focused on the road. The fresh air coming through her car window blew her blond hair around her face. She looked like a car model with her bright blue eyes and girl-next-door wholesome face. I wondered what she'd think if she knew what we'd been doing not long before she came upon us. She felt me looking and gave me a sweet Lizzy smile before turning back to the road. I felt like a deceptive jerk, but I'd be lying if I said I regretted even one heart-racing moment with Mateo.

Thirty-three

LIZZY

NEW MEXICO–ARIZONA–NEVADA
TUESDAY, OCTOBER 27, 2015

I pushed through all the way to Flagstaff, Arizona without stopping. Then we grabbed gas and split a veggie burger and fries at a cheap dive near the gas station. We were both ruined now that we'd had good food again and the thought of peanut butter hadn't appealed to either of us. Mel had sent us off with some freshly baked muffins but we'd devoured them miles ago.

I hadn't told Lodan where our next surprise stop was this evening. I couldn't wait to see his face. This had been the quietest leg of our trip so far. With each mile I put between myself and Mateo, the better I felt about everything. I worried how his dad would react, but I kept realizing all the signs I'd missed. I even began to wonder if maybe I'd pushed our relationship to be more than it really was based on my notion of what it meant to be boyfriend and girlfriend. I hoped next time I had a chance to love a guy, I let the relationship follow its own course.

I looked over at Lodan beside me. He had his feet up on the dash and thumped his hand on his thigh to the beat of the Taylor Swift song playing on the radio. He had a small secretive smile on his face and I wondered what had him feeling happy. Would we become a couple? I looked back at the road and thought about how I'd wanted him to kiss me earlier in the trip.

A horn blare made us both jump. Someone had cut off the car in front of us and the driver had apparently wanted to express his or her distaste. Lodan sat up and put his feet back on the floor.

"Where are we staying tonight, Wonder Woman?" Lodan asked as he dug through the snacks.

"It's a surprise," I said and lifted my eyebrows.

He laughed. "You and your surprises." He pulled out a granola bar. "Want half?"

"Sure," I said and reached out to take it from him.

Three hours later, Lodan was sound asleep, his head resting on his sweatshirt against the window.

"Wake up, cowboy," I said as we pulled up in front of Buffalo Bill's Resort and Casino. He sat up and stretched but when his eyes landed on the giant Indian headdress with a buffalo head in the middle his eyes grew wide.

"No way! Are you kidding me right now?" His face transformed to kid-on-Christmas happy. He let out a whoop, grabbed my head, and planted a big smacky kiss on my forehead. "You ARE Wonder Woman!" He laughed.

We parked the car. Lodan opened his door and got out. "Are we staying here tonight? Can we afford it?"

I got out on my side, stood on the edge of the door so I could see him over the car door and hood. "So, I made us a reservation but we are supposed to be twenty-one because it's a casino and stuff."

"Okay, so how do we pull that off?"

"Well, I brought along some stuff for us to wear if you're game." I walked around to the back and found the other bag I'd packed.

"Ooh, Wonder Woman, did you bring your super suit?" He lifted his eyebrows up and down at me.

"You wish!" I pulled out the best part of his costume. "Nope, but I did bring this for you." I held up the cowboy hat my dad had purchased (and frequently) wore a few years ago when we lived in Texas for four months.

"Vintage!" Lodan grinned. "Is it ten gallons?"

"Not sure, cowboy, but here, try it on." I tossed it his way.

He caught it, bent his head down, put it on, then looked up at me with a wink. "Howdy, partner."

I rolled my eyes. "Okay, now throw this jacket over your T-shirt." I tossed him a leather jacket I'd borrowed from my dad's closet. It would be a little short on Lodan since he's a few inches taller than my dad, but I knew with Lodan's shoulders it would make him look more filled out. And hopefully older.

"It's boiling out here. But okay." He rubbed his face and adjusted the hat on his head.

"It will be air-conditioned inside."

"I don't have to wear a fake mustache, do I?" He slid the coat on and I had to admit, he did look bigger and a little intimidating until you saw his sneakers.

"Okay, lastly, put on these." I handed him some worn cowboy boots. My dad loved them so I hoped he hadn't been looking for them.

Once he had it all on, I felt like he could pass for older if he didn't talk too much. "Okay, you may want to take off that coat while you wait for me to get ready. I have to put on some makeup." I rolled my eyes because I'd never liked the feel of crap on my face.

"Okay." He took off his hat too and settled in the passenger seat, door ajar to wait.

I put on my only tight-fitting, low-cut dress that gave the illusion I actually had a little cleavage. The dress was black but my cowboy boots were red. I tied a cool choker with three turquoise stones set in, in the middle around my neck. It was a gift from my mom. I'd never worn it or even opened the makeup kit I was about to use.

"Do not laugh. But I have to pull up a video on YouTube to figure out how to put on my makeup," I warned Lodan.

"No laughing here. I use it all the time to learn how to do stuff."

I looked through the options and selected one. But it looked easier than it actually was.

"Damn it!" I groaned. "Can you toss me the wipes from the front? I already used up all the ones in this kit."

"Don't get mad, but do you want me to try?"

"Putting on my makeup?" I looked up at him as he walked around to where I was sitting in the back of the Honda, holding a mirror and resting my phone in my lap.

"Seriously, I have painted countless little cars and people and buildings. I have a steady hand."

"Okay. It can't be any worse than what I've been doing." Lodan took out the cooler to use as a seat for himself and I stayed seated on the edge on the tailgate. He watched the video all the way through and then went to work. Just like the woman in the video, he started with a foundation, then eyeshadow. He was so intent on what he was doing that it didn't even feel strange. He tipped my chin up with his hand and told me to close my eyes as he carefully painted a thin line of black eyeliner along my lid. Then he had me look up while he carefully applied eyeliner underneath. My eyes watered briefly but he dabbed the tears gently away with a tissue. We struggled a bit with the mascara because I kept blinking and then we couldn't stop laughing. It is very hard to put on mascara while laughing. He brushed on a little blush and stood back to look at his work. He shrugged.

"You definitely do not look like the good little girl next door anymore." He tilted his head. "You still need lipstick. Can you do that part on your own?"

"Yeah, sure. Where did you put the mirror?"

He handed me the mirror and I couldn't believe how well he'd done. "Wow, if engineering doesn't work out for you, you could do this for a living, Lodan."

"No thanks," he said. "Can you imagine all the bad breath you'd have to contend with?"

"Oh god, does my breath smell?" I asked, horrified.

"No." He laughed. "I swear it doesn't, but I imagine it happens a lot."

I piled my hair on top of my head, pinned it into a messy bun, clipped on some dangly earrings from an old Halloween costume, and stood for Lodan to inspect.

"What do you think? Twenty-one?"

"I think so," he said. "I'm probably not the best judge. Hey, won't they check our IDs?"

"Got it covered."

"What? How? he asked.

I shrugged. "Von."

"Who?" Lodan raised one eyebrow higher than the other.

"Von." She looked at me strangely then laughed at herself. "Sorry, you call him Ryan."

"Ryan Braun? From Laketown?"

"Yeah, we FaceTime and Snap and stuff off and on since you introduced me to him at Minnie's that day," I admitted.

"Oh. Why didn't you ever mention him before?"

"I got the feeling you weren't a big fan so I just didn't. Sorry."

"It's fine. I don't care who you're friends with, Lizzy. And I don't not like him. He's not a bad guy. Just different from me I guess," he said, putting the jacket back on.

"Sorry, I should have told you. Anyway, he got me IDs we can use." I grabbed my bag and fished the IDs out of my wallet.

"I'd just be careful because his girlfriend is not a nice person. I'm sure she would not like your talking to him."

"Yeah, I got that impression. Here." I handed him his ID. It was a decent match. The guy in the photo had a full head of hair, green eyes, and was six foot three. It was good Lodan's head was shaved.

Mine was more of a stretch because it said I was five foot eight. But based on the parking lot, this place looked like it could use the business so hopefully they wouldn't care that much.

We locked up the car, grabbed our stuff, and headed to check-in. Scary thing was this place didn't cost much more than our dirty mattress motel, so who knew what we'd find on the inside.

We got checked in no problem. The guy behind the counter barely looked at us as he swiped my credit card and took my ID. He didn't even ask for Lodan's. We went to our room to drop our stuff.

We were both happily surprised. It was a nice room with two beds and even a hot tub bathtub.

"Wow, how much did this cost, Wonder Woman? Isn't your dad going to be pissed to see this on the emergency card?" He opened the shade to look outside at all the lights.

"It wasn't that expensive. So shall we do what we came to do?" I asked.

"Yes! Desperado, here we come!" He took off his hat, bent at the waist a little, and gestured to the door, hat in hand. "After you, milady."

We made our way out to the roller coaster and he took in every detail, spouting facts left and right about its structure, history, everything. A woman behind us actually thanked him as we got on the ride because he'd kept her kids entertained with his knowledge as they waited in line.

Lodan whooped and hollered on every twist, turn, and drop. We rode three times in a row and then stopped to split a drink.

Out of nowhere Lodan grabbed me and hugged me tight to his chest. "Lizzy, you are amazing. I can't believe all the work you put into this for me. Thank you!" His flushed face was glowing in the lights and I hoped that whatever was waiting for him in California wouldn't take the happiness out of him. Because when Lodan smiled like this, it made me feel all bubbly and happy inside. He didn't deserve to be sad.

"You're welcome. Trust me, watching you on the ride made every moment worth it. Even letting you apply my makeup."

We wandered around the casino and played a few cheap slot machines. We didn't really win anything but we didn't really lose much either.

"Lizzy!" Lodan came almost running back from his bathroom break.

"What? Dude, chill! Adults don't run in casinos unless they stole something."

"Sorry, but I have someone you have to meet."

"Seriously? You made friends in the bathroom?" I cashed out my six dollars and change, hopped off my stool, and followed Lodan through the maze of lights and sounds. He stopped in front of a plump woman with dyed red hair, thick blue eyeshadow, and thickly painted lips that matched her hair. She had on a paisley housedress with glittery ruby-red slippers. She sat on a stool in front of one of the push-button slot machines, methodically pushing the button over and over as her money continued to creep up. Her total had just slipped past four hundred dollars. I was speechless.

"Lois, meet Lois!" Lodan beamed back and forth between the two of us.

"Hi, hon. I'd shake your hand but I am in the middle of a winning streak here and if I break my rhythm it could all go to hell."

"No problem," I said, smiling and cutting my eyes at Lodan. "I'm just honored to make your acquaintance. You're the one and only Lois I've ever met."

"Well, aren't you two the sweetest things. What are you doing in this place?"

"We're on a truth-seeking trip," I explained. "I needed to find out the truth behind why my ex broke up with me and Lodan is trying to find out if he has a secret aunt and cousin and possibly meet his father." It all sounded a little crazy when I spit it all out at once.

"Your last name isn't Kardashian, is it?" Lois asked and laughed at her own joke. "You got a camera following you around or are you posting to some blog or something?" Lois had just flipped over into the five hundred dollar range. But she didn't miss a beat with her button.

"No, this is just for us." We watched her work for a few minutes before Lodan spoke.

"Well, we should stop distracting you. Thanks for meeting my Lois, Lois. She's always wanted to meet one and you made her wish come true today."

"Well, good luck on your truth-seeking trip," Lois said. "Family is crazy. You never know what you may discover when you pull back the bedsheets of generations."

Lodan started to walk away and I yelled, "Wait! Lodan, can you take a picture of me next to the other Lois?"

"Good idea," he said. "Lois, do you mind?"

"Not as long as I don't have to stop what I'm doing."

I stood as close to her as I dared without distracting her. She smelled like roses. Lodan snapped a couple shots.

"Hey, why don't you take one of my lucky horseshoes with you? It sounds like you could use a little," Lois said. "They are right there on that little table to the left of me."

"No, we can't take your luck away," I said.

"Oh, you aren't takin' mine. I have a few extras. Please, it will bring me luck to share with you."

Lodan walked around her and picked up a miniature pewter horseshoe.

"Thank you, Lois," I said. I'm so happy to have met you."

"Good luck!" she said and we left her to her streak.

"Vintage!" Lodan said, holding up the little horseshoe.

"Thanks, Lodan."

"Hey, we are pretty good at making one another's wishes come true. Don't you think?" Lodan asked me.

"Yes, we are," I agreed. "And right now, I am wishing for my head on a pillow."

"Your wish is my command, Wonder Woman."

It took me so long to scrub my face clean from the makeup that Lodan was sound asleep by the time I came out of the bathroom. I looked at him, smiling in his sleep and hoped this was a happy family reunion in California and not a sad disappointment.

Thirty-four

LODAN

CALIFORNIA (FINALLY WE MADE IT!)
WEDNESDAY, OCTOBER 28, 2015

We sang along to "California," the theme song from the old series, *The O.C.* as loud as we could as we crossed the state line into California. Neither of us had seen the show but both of us knew the song.

As it faded out and moved on to the next song, Lizzy, the wind fanning her hair around her face like corn silk, smacked the wheel with her hand and yelled, "I can't believe we did it! We just drove across the entire country!"

"And you know what?" I yelled back.

"Yes, I do," she laugh-yelled. "It's VINTAGE!"

I nodded my head along to the beat. "You said it, Wonder Woman."

Our enthusiasm waned when we hit the two-ten freeway and traffic slowed to a crawl. There is nothing worse than having the very end of a long trip inch along due to traffic.

Lizzy turned down the radio. "What's our plan when we get to your potential aunt's?"

"Well, assuming it is still her address, she is indeed home, and actually my aunt, I have no idea," I said, only half joking.

Lizzy braided and unbraided her hair, steering with her knees since we were virtually at a standstill. We'd heard on the radio wildfires had caused some closings and evacuations that had caused a backup. We could see the black smoke in the distance.

"I guess I'll start by introducing myself as her potential nephew and ask if she has a sister named Heather Dawson."

"Let's play worst-case scenario." Lizzy fanned herself with a flattened cracker box. We could have put the windows up and the air on, but we were both sick of stale car air.

"Let's rule out the obvious. She doesn't live there anymore and the new owners have no idea how to contact her."

"She does live there but she isn't your aunt because your mom doesn't have a sister and we are sitting in this crazy traffic for no good reason." Lizzy beeped her horn three times quickly for emphasis, setting off a horn chorus for a few moments.

"Or my mom is not really my mom, but Sage is her sister and she knows about my mom abducting me. In an effort to keep her sister out of jail, she locks us in her basement until my mom gets there and they can decide what to do."

"Okay, we're going dark now, huh?" Lizzy drums her fingers on the steering wheel. "Or your mom is your mom, your sister is your aunt, but your cousin is actually your brother and your uncle because your father is also your grandfather!"

"And if that turns out to be the truth, I think I will seek out a hypnotist who can help me permanently erase all knowledge of it from my brain and replace it with a better, less *Game of Thrones* version." I shifted to stick my bare feet out the window.

"Careful, it would suck to lose a foot in traffic."

"They're inside the side mirror so as long as you don't sideswipe anyone in this Autobahn-paced race, I should be safe."

"It would really suck to go back to school next week having gained the truth only to have lost a foot."

"Shall we sing?" I couldn't stand the idle sitting because it was giving me too much time to think.

"I'm in. Any requests?" Lizzy asked.

"'Sweet Caroline.'"

"Perfect. Oh wait, look on my phone for the playlist called Check Mix. It should be on there. I can't believe I didn't think to play it sooner."

"Check Mix?" I asked.

"My dad made it for the last part of our drives when, just like right now, you feel like you can't take another mile. Check as in the game of chess and then mix is obvious."

"Cute. Okay . . . Here we go. Don't leave me hanging, I am expecting a duet, not a solo performance here."

And we spent the next fifty-five minutes and twelve miles to our destination probably annoying anyone else with windows down as we belted out all the best sing-along songs on my dad's well-timed playlist.

When we pulled up outside the yellow stucco, black-trimmed two-story house there was a newer model silver Volvo station wagon parked in the driveway.

"Should I come in with you? Go get a coffee? What do you prefer?" Lizzy asked.

"Come to the door with me. If she's a woman home alone, she's more apt to answer the door to me if I have a cute wholesome Girl Scout next to me."

Lizzy rolled her eyes and opened her door. "I'll take Wonder Woman over wholesome Girl Scout any day."

As we walked up the sidewalk Lizzy whispered, "My bladder really hopes your aunt lives here and doesn't think it's weird if I need to use her restroom in the first five minutes of our arrival."

"Why are we whispering? You think she can hear through walls?" I asked.

"Well, Wonder Woman can, can't she?" Lizzy whispered.

"Actually, I don't think so but you know what I just realized?" We stood at the bottom of the front steps, but I didn't move forward up them. "Wonder Woman has a lasso of truth. Isn't that kind of ironic?"

"Very, but you are stalling. Walk up the steps and ring the bell." Lizzy took the first step. I followed her and reached out to ring the bell.

We waited. A small dog barked a few times. Then we heard footsteps approaching the door. A guy with salt-and-pepper hair, wearing a yellow button-down shirt dotted with small hot dogs, a pair of golf shorts, and flip-flops, opened the door, holding a little Chihuahua who let out an additional couple of yelps then stopped.

I froze.

"Hi," Lizzy said. "Mr. Silverman?"

"No." He studied us both, looking us up and down.

"Oh, did you happen to know the former owner, Sage Silverman?" Lizzy proceeded.

"What is this about?" the man asked.

"Well, my suddenly mute friend, here"—Lizzy cut her eyes at me—"Lodan, thinks she may be his aunt and wanted to meet her and find out some more information about his family."

The man studied Lodan for a minute, his eyebrows knitted. Lodan shifted uncomfortably underneath his scrutiny. He opened the door farther.

"Why don't you come on in? Sage is at an appointment but she should be back in a few minutes if you don't mind waiting."

"Wait, so Sage Silverman does live here?" I finally spoke up as we followed him into the entryway.

"Yes." He turned, set the dog down, and held out his hand to me. "I'm Dale. We've lived together for years but never married." The dog walked around in little circles, barking. Dale shook Lizzy's hand.

"Lizzy," she said then Dale picked the dog up again to stop the barking. "Gem, it's okay. Calm down." He rubbed the dog behind the ears. "Let's sit and she'll calm down." He gestured for us to have a seat on the puffy gray leather sofa.

"Actually, would you mind if I used your restroom? We've been sitting in traffic for a while," Lizzy asked.

"Oh sure, down that hall, first door on the right, light's on the right, too."

Lizzy headed for the bathroom while Dale and I sat on the sofa.

"So, did you have a long drive?" Dale asked.

"Today wasn't too bad but we've been on the road since Saturday morning," I explained.

"Where are you from?" Dale asked.

"A small town in New York called Laketown." I tried to scan the room for pictures without being obvious but only abstract art hung on the walls.

"Wow, you guys had quite a trip. We used to live in Syracuse, New York."

"Is that where Sage grew up? Because that's where my mom grew up."

"As a matter of fact, she did. Is your mom's name Heather?" Dale asked.

"That's right, Heather Dawson," I said as Lizzy walked back in the room.

"Oh, I knew her when she was Heather Silverman. I guess we didn't know she'd married."

"She didn't. I thought Dawson was her maiden name."

Dale looked uncomfortable. "Maybe we should wait for Sage before we get into all of this."

"Sure. Sorry," I said but then I couldn't help myself. I've had so many questions burning in my head for years. "Do you know why my mom and Sage don't talk?"

Dale looked toward the front window as if he could will Sage to pull in. "I think you should wait and ask Sage that one. What did your mom tell you about it?" Dale tried another tactic.

"She didn't," Lizzy answered. "That's why we're here. We found all these old family pictures and stuff in this locked safe and Lodan's mom was out of town and refused to explain until she got home. Lodan was afraid that gave her too much time to come up with another story so we hopped in the car and drove to ask Sage ourselves."

"So do your parents know where you are right now?" Dale asked, looking even more uncomfortable.

"Exactly where, no. But we have been texting them morning and night to let them know we are safe."

"But they don't specifically know you are here?" Dale asked again, glancing at his watch, then to the driveway.

"My guess is Lodan's mom has figured it out and she hasn't sent the cops after us for taking her car without permission or anything so we took that as a sort of nonverbal permission granted," Lizzy explained.

"Can I get you kids something to eat or drink while we wait? I'm afraid we don't have much soda, but I do have tea or coffee if you'd like." He stood to walk into the kitchen. Gem got up from her bed by the couch and followed him.

"Coffee for me and tea for him if that's okay," Lizzy said. "Thanks."

"Do you think he's my dad?" I whispered to Lizzy.

She shook her head.

"Do you both like milk or sugar?" he called from the kitchen.

"No both black is fine," I called.

"No signs of a cousin. Did you see any pictures in the hallway?" I whispered.

Lizzy shook her head again then asked him herself. "So Dale, do you guys have any kids?" We heard a little bang as he dropped something.

"No, no kids for us," he yelled back. And then Gem started barking like crazy and ran into the living room.

We heard another car door but the front window shades were drawn. A few moments later a woman with a black-and-gray bun, a long multicolored skirt, and a flowy, white shirt and Birkenstocks came in through a side door.

"Dale," she called as the dog ran in circles barking. "Whose red Honda is that out front?" But before any of us answered, she'd noticed us seated on the couch. We both stood to greet her.

"Hi," she said and her voice sounded just like my mom's. She scooped up Gem to stop the barking and dropped her purse on the floor by the entryway. "Are you students of Dale's?"

"Uh, no." I adjusted my glasses on my nose. "I think I may be your nephew." I felt tall and awkward and unsure whether to shake her hand or hug or what.

"My nephew?" She looked up at me, one eyebrow raised and her head tilted just as I'd seen my mom do hundreds of times.

"Yes." I held out my hand. "I'm Lodan and this is my friend, Lizzy." I nodded my head in Lizzy's direction as Dale walked in with two steaming mugs. But Sage didn't shake my hand, instead she stepped strangely close to me and studied my face. "Dale, can you . . ." and without any further direction he took Gem from her hands. She reached up and placed a noticeably shaky hand on my face as her eyes welled up with tears. "Michael?" she whispered, her throat thick with emotion.

"Sage." Dale set down the dog and grabbed Sage's other hand. He gently removed her hand from my face and got her to take a step back. He remained next to her holding her hands. "Did you say your name is Lodan?" Dale asked.

"Yeah," I said. "Dawson. Lodan Dawson."

Sage let out a little yelp and clenched her fist to her stomach.

"How old are you?" she asked me.

"I'll be sixteen in December," I said.

Sage's eyes grew wide. She threw a hand to her throat and said, "Oh my God." She half fell but Dale caught her and eased her over to the chair across from the couch.

"I can't believe this. Dale. Michael." She held her hand over her mouth, tears streaming down her cheeks, as she stared at me. "I think I'm gonna be sick. I'm . . ." She ran down the hallway past where Lizzy had used the bathroom and through another door which she closed behind her.

"What's wrong?" I asked. "I'm sorry, I didn't mean to . . . I didn't think." I didn't know what to say and I didn't really understand what had just happened.

"Did you say you'll be sixteen in December?" Dale asked.

"Yeah. December seventh. Why?"

The color drained from Dale's face as he ran a hand through his hair. "Jesus," he said. "I'm sorry." He stood. "I'll be right back in a minute. Drink your . . . I need to check on Sage." And then he, too, disappeared into what I presumed was their bedroom. Gem ran after him and began barking outside the door until they opened it a crack to let her in and promptly closed it again.

"What in the hell just happened?" Lizzy whispered.

"I have no idea," I whispered back, "but she is definitely my mom's sister. They don't look a lot alike but they have all the same mannerisms. It's freaky and cool all at the same time."

And then everything got a little bit crazier because the doorbell rang. I looked at Lizzy. She looked at me and shrugged. Lizzy walked to the front window and peeked out the blinds.

"There's a Chevy Malibu with California plates parked behind us," Lizzy whispered. Nobody came out of the room to get the door and the bell rang again. The dog barked nonstop.

"Should I get it?" Lizzy asked.

"I don't know." I shrugged.

The bell sounded again but before anyone could answer it, the door opened and my mom stepped into the room, followed closely by Lizzy's dad.

"Mom?" I said, standing as Lizzy said, "Dad?"

My mom rushed to me and wrapped me in her arms. "Oh, thank God, you're okay." She stood back to look me over but remained holding my hands. "My God, you look different. Did you grow?"

Lizzy hugged her dad. I pulled my hands away and took a step back. Anger shot through me. "What are you doing here?" I asked.

"I wanted you to hear the truth from me," my mom said.

"And how do I know that what you tell me this time is the truth?" I asked her.

"I guess you don't. But I'm pretty sure Sage and Dale will be able to help make you believe it."

"Lizzy, maybe we should go get a coffee or something," her dad suggested.

"No way," Lizzy said and she walked over to grab my hand. "I'm not leaving him here alone like this." And I squeezed her hand in mine, more grateful than ever that she'd made this trip with me.

"Fine, then I guess I'll go get some coffee and you can text me when you think I should come back with the car," he said. "But don't you dare take off again. We will talk about this road trip thing later." He gave Lizzy a stern look and left.

"Where's my sister?" my mom asked. I pointed to the bedroom door. My mom took a deep breath. "Stay here," she said. She knocked lightly on the door then disappeared as well. Lizzy and I stood there dumbfounded.

"I'm beginning to wonder if Narnia's on the other side of that door," Lizzy said.

"I can't believe they flew out here to check up on us," I said.

"I can't believe you haven't busted into that room and demanded to know what in the hell is going on."

The door flew open and Sage, face swollen from sobbing, tears still streaking her face, came stomping out and into the living room, followed by my mom and Dale.

"Tell him what you did, Heather. I want to watch you tell him what you did," she yelled. We all looked to my mom and she closed her eyes for a beat. When she opened them she said, "I'll tell you all, everything. But you might want to sit down. It's a long story." My mom had never looked so tired.

"I am not sitting down until you tell him," Sage said, venom dripping from her tongue.

"Fine," my mom said, "but you all have to promise I can explain my side of the story."

"Oh, I'm dying to hear it," Sage said, her eyes shooting daggers at my mom, "but first you tell him!"

"For Christ's sake, tell me what?" I finally yelled.

"Sage is really your mom and I saved you from her when you were two and raised you as my own." Her voice broke at the end and she began to sob. I felt the blood drain from my face and I tightened my hands into fists, forgetting that Lizzy's hand was still in mine until I heard her wince from the pressure. I let her go and then I dropped onto the sofa.

"Saved? Did you just say 'saved'? Dale, did you hear her? You stole him!" Sage spat. "Stop crying. Tell him the worst part, Heather. Tell him how you did it."

"There's more?" Lizzy said and sat beside me. She ran a comforting hand back and forth across my back as I tried to comprehend why my mom would steal her own sister's child.

And then my mom explained her whole unbelievable story.

Thirty-five

HEATHER (MRS. DAWSON)

SYRACUSE, NY
FALL 2001

The stench of baby poop filled my nose as I unlocked the door and stepped into the living room. I couldn't see very well in the dark so I made my way to the light, slid down the dimmer, and turned it on. Nobody was there, but the smell drew me toward Lodan's Pack 'n Play. As I got closer I saw his dirty pull-up and what could only be described as a post-poop finger-painting party. It looked like Lodan had enjoyed himself. I couldn't believe Sage would leave this mess.

"Sage!" I called out, but not too loudly as I didn't want to wake Lodan. Then I noticed a smear of brown on the sofa cushion, and then another on the arm. My heart began to race as I followed the poop trail into the kitchen. A Lodan-sized brown footprint began at the threshold and made a few steps before stopping mid-kitchen, leaving a little less each step. I called out again, "Sage!"

No response. "Michael Lodan!" This time I yelled, but still nothing. I ran up the stairs to Lodan's room only to find an empty crib. I ran past my empty room, the empty spare room, and then back down the stairs to check Sage's. To get to her room, I cut through the kitchen; racing so quickly that I almost missed the tiny pink cherub foot peeking out of the pantry doorway. I hadn't noticed it ajar before. "Lodan!" I whispered. I didn't want to scare him.

Heart in my throat, "Please, please, please," I whispered as I gently pushed the door open.

There, curled on his side lay Lodan, wearing only the shirt I'd dressed him in after bath time. The material had bunched up to reveal his plump tummy. I placed my hand on his chest and sighed with relief at the steady thump of his heart. A box of Cheerios lay scattered on the floor around him. He'd dragged his bathroom stool into the pantry, probably to reach the cereal. Besides the Cheerio stuck to his cheek, a brown poop smear on his thigh, and his dirty hands, he looked unscathed. I filled a sippy cup with milk, then began to wash his hands and face. He woke with a cry and as soon as his face and hands were clean I gave him the sippy cup to calm him. After a quick bath, he thrust the cup at me and said "More." That was unusual at this hour.

"Did you eat dinner?" I asked him as I pulled up his pajama pants.

He shook his head and said, "Gwapes?"

I could not believe Sage had just left him in his Pack 'n Play. I settled him in his high chair with some safe-sized grape chunks and another sippy while I cleaned the rest of the mess. When I passed Sage's room on the way to the laundry, I could hear muffled music. I loaded the washer, peeked at Lodan, then slammed open Sage's door. She lay on the bed, headphones on, the volume set high enough to hear Kurt Cobain's voice. I marched over to her and pulled the earphones away from her ears.

"Sage!" I yelled, but she didn't wake up. I shook her. "Sage!" Nothing.

Goose bumps prickled my arms and neck. I lay my head on her chest and thanked God when I felt the slow rhythmic beat. I grabbed the cordless, dialed 911, and bolted for my purse as I spoke with the operator. I raced back to her, trying everything they asked. After I had her turned on her side and confirmed her mouth and throat were clear, I texted Dale. Luckily he lived a few houses down and sprinted into the front yard just as they were loading Sage into the ambulance.

"Sorry, I just saw your message. What happened?" Dale asked.

"I'm not sure but we think she may have taken too many sleeping pills."

"Twuk." Lodan pointed to the ambulance.

"What can I do?" Dale asked.

"Are you sober right now?"

He held up his hands. "Yes, completely. I've been working on a paper."

"Can you watch Lo . . . Michael for me while I follow her to the hospital?"

"Sure. Of course." I handed him Lodan. "He really just needs to go to bed. Can you handle it?"

"No problem. You go," he said as the ambulance pulled out into the street.

"Thanks." I kissed Lodan on the head and ran inside to grab my purse. "Read him something from the bookshelf in his room. He probably won't make it through one." I jumped in my mom's Honda Civic. She'd had it less than a year before she died and it still only had about ten thousand miles on it. We both had a license, but neither of us liked driving it much. I was relieved that the battery wasn't dead.

At the hospital, they were able to induce vomiting, which probably saved Sage's life. I later learned that she had taken way too many sleeping pills. She'd also chased them down with beer and vodka, which complicated matters. Luckily, she was going to be fine. The worst part was I didn't dare leave Lodan alone with her anymore. We were incredibly lucky he hadn't gotten into anything worse than his own feces and Cheerios. But I also couldn't stay with him constantly either.

That night I began brainstorming an escape plan. Lodan couldn't grow up with a mom like Sage. He deserved better. Although I had saved quite a bit of money, I needed a lot more to move and get settled in a new place. I called my dad and told him I needed money for college. He deposited money into both of our accounts monthly and paid Sage's tuition as well. I convinced him to put my tuition money into my bank account along with the money he already gave me each month and I would handle the bills. I'd given him no reason to distrust me so he agreed pretty easily. Sage remained angry with my father for getting remarried and moving away (not that she spent any time with him before that), and I knew that meant they never spoke. This worked to my advantage. I asked Sage if she cared if I sold mom's car for tuition money. She didn't even bat an eyelash.

I never sold it. I parked it in the driveway of one of my co-workers at the diner with a FOR SALE sign on it and my cell number. She lived on a busy road and I'd told her I thought I'd have a better shot selling it there. Whenever they called I purposely asked for too much money. It worked like a charm.

Then I had to figure out how to get Sage to let Lodan go. Obviously I haven't painted a pretty picture of her here, but when Sage acted like her old self, her pre-mom-dying self, she was really good with Lodan. She taught him new words, read to him, told him about all of the different flowers in the lawn. She pulled our old train set out of the attic for him one day and made a little course around the kitchen floor. Lodan loved it. He laughed and clapped and repeated "more" and "again" over and over; never tiring of tracking the train's path as it looped and curved around the kitchen floor.

But when she was bad, she was really bad. She'd close him out of her room. He learned to drag his stool from the bathroom to her door to reach the handle and open it. It was adorable. But instead of seeing the magic in his brilliance and recognizing his need for her, she picked him up, handed him to me, and closed herself back in her room. Maybe what I decided to do was too drastic and wrong, but I was eighteen and desperate to save Lodan from Sage. And looking back, I can admit maybe I felt entitled to Lodan. I did all the real work to take care of him. I was more of a mother to him than she was. He even called us both Mom. I never bothered to correct him and neither did she. The hardest part of my plan was how to hide Lodan for a big chunk of time. And the lengths that I went to were a little crazy.

One of the houses I passed on my way to the diner advertised a day care program. I sometimes stopped to watch the children play and thought it would be nice for Lodan to have the opportunity. This was exactly what I needed. He could be in good hands for hours. A couple of weeks before our big escape, I knocked on the door. The woman who answered the door was very nice. She and her mother had been running the small day care out of their home for six years. I asked if I could sign him up for only a month, explaining that we'd be moving away after that. I told them I had left a bad home situation (not a complete lie given that my dad did basically abandon me). They were very kind and helpful. I told them I preferred not to give our real names for safety reasons. It wasn't a problem at all. I told them his name was Lodan Smith and introduced myself as Heather Smith. I began taking Lodan with me during my lunch shifts. I'd drop him at the day care while I worked and pick him up after. I was worried he would cry when I left him, but he never did. They had a little play area with a Matchbox car city. They said he played there for hours, sometimes with other kids and sometimes alone. This piece to the plan worked better than I'd hoped. Sage thought I took Lodan to a play group for parents and children during this time. She had no idea I was working and he was in day care.

Dale played the pawn in my plan. Growing up, my mom used to take us to Green Lakes State Park on warm summer days to swim and build sand creations. I mentioned this to Dale one afternoon as we played with Lodan in our backyard. (Without the loving care of our parents, the beds had grown unruly. I mowed the lawn on a regular basis, but I couldn't bring myself to tend to the beds, too.) I hinted to Dale it might be good for Sage to visit the park. She'd gone inside to nap. She'd been almost giddy with a renewed vigor for life after she came home from the hospital. Eventually she sprung a leak and day by day she deflated into herself like a neglected kiddie pool. Dale took the bait and a week or so later announced he planned to treat all of us to a beach picnic the following Monday. He knew it was my only day off and forecasters had predicted an unusually warm day for April in Syracuse. He told us to be ready by eleven.

Monday morning I told Sage I had to run a few errands and asked her if she was okay to watch Michael.

In an unusually happy mood, she scooped him up, swung him around, and said, "Of course. We will prepare for our adventure. Right, little prince?"

And as I stood in the doorway watching her with him, I almost lost my nerve. But then I pictured Lodan on the pantry floor and reminded myself these moments were too rare for Lodan to be safe.

I took a bus to my friend's house to retrieve the car. I parked it in one of the side lots near the playground and beach area at Green Lakes State Park. I placed it far off to one side, hoping Dale wouldn't drive or park near it. Then I took the bus back to the campus area and walked home. It was almost eleven by the time I got there.

Dale had bought a CD of silly kid songs like "Wheels on the Bus" and "Old McDonald" and even Sage sang along. We sat in the warm spring sun, ate fried chicken and pasta salad, and skipped stones into the glimmering water. Dale and Sage snuggled on the picnic blanket as Lodan played with Matchbox cars in the sand. There were a few other couples and families with young children enjoying the day, too. But, being a Monday, it was relatively quiet.

"You guys have Michael if I go for a run?" I asked. Since age thirteen, I ran a few times a week to help with my asthma. Then daily to cope after my mom died. Most recently, it was back to about three days a week. Dale ran with me on occasion. Sage never exercised. She ate and slept so little, I doubted her body could have handled much more than her trips to campus and back.

"You want to come, Dale?" I asked, certain he wouldn't leave Sage.

"No, thanks." Dale didn't even look up from driving Lodan's police cruiser along the curve of Sage's thigh toward the sensitive intersection ahead. Sage was halfheartedly protesting, but I could tell she enjoyed the sensation as well as his attention. She'd accused him on multiple occasions, lately, of focusing more of his attention on Michael than her. At that moment, I needed him to focus on Sage.

I took off on the trail until I fled their line of sight, then I cut into the woods and doubled back around toward the beach area. I watched as they made out on the blanket and patiently waited until Lodan looked my way. I held up his big plastic Tonka truck and waved it until I got his attention. Just as I'd hoped, he stood up and started toward me. The whole plan could have fallen apart right then. If Lodan had said anything to them or yelled to me, I'd be toast. Plus, I had to get Lodan to come all the way to me and away from their view quickly and unnoticed by anyone. I told myself this was Lodan's chance to pick his own fate. If they stopped him or saw us, Lodan was meant to be with Sage. But if they didn't, Lodan was meant to be mine.

As soon as Lodan reached out for the truck I grabbed him and swung him and the toy into my arms. I ran as fast as I could for my car, buckled him into the car seat, and bolted. I sang silly songs to keep him happy and me from losing my shit. My heart raced and my head buzzed like I'd OD'd on Starbucks. I prayed I could make it through the next couple days without messing this up. My cell phone rang about ten minutes into the drive and I saw it was Sage. I felt incredibly guilty and awful for doing this to her, but I knew I had to do it for Lodan. I ignored the calls and dropped him at his day care, having previously alerted them I'd be later than normal as I was packing for our move. He ran off to his Matchbox tracks and I raced back to the car. I had four missed calls from Sage and two from Dale. I knew they had to be frantic by now.

I drove to the pre-booked hotel, parked the car in their garage, and grabbed a cab back to Green Lakes. By the time I got dropped off, I had been gone for just over an hour. The park rangers and a local cop were already on the scene. I made a quick stop by Dale's car to slip my phone through a window he'd left cracked open to keep it cool. Then I summoned all my resolve and repeated in my head: *do this for Lodan, do this for Lodan* as I raced over to where everyone was gathered around Sage.

"Sage, what's going on?" I asked.

"Do you have Michael?" she asked, her eyes pleading.

"You had him. I went running," I said.

"Oh God." She fell against me. "He's gone, Heather."

"What do you mean, *gone*? Where's Dale?" I gently set her down on the sand.

"Looking for Michael."

"How long has he been gone?" I tried to sound scared.

"Where have you been? We called you a million times."

"I got a little lost because I forgot my phone."

"He was playing right here." Sage stared at the spot as if she could will him to reappear.

"He's probably in the woods or playing with his cars someplace," I said.

"We've been looking for an hour." Sage glared up at me.

"Sorry. I didn't . . . I'll go help." I couldn't watch her suffer and keep it together.

Sage nodded, her eyes fixed on Lodan's abandoned car lot. She'd drawn her knees to her chest, and rocked slowly back and forth.

I took off for the woods near the beach. I couldn't look at her, knowing what I was doing at that moment. *Do this for Lodan. Do this for Lodan.* What I was about to do makes me sound like a monster, but I had to leave little room for doubt. I made my way to the edge of the lake, away from any of the other search parties, and reached into my shorts to pull out one of Lodan's tiny sandals. One of the pair he'd been wearing that morning. I'd switched them, along with his clothes, before dropping him at day care. The sweatshirt tied around my waist hid the bump in my spandex. I made sure nobody was close enough to see, and held it under the water. I rubbed the sandal around on the bottom a little to make it look slightly tattered, then tangled it in the tall grass to keep from drifting. Hopefully someone would discover it before it washed away.

I made my way along the water farther. All around me complete strangers were yelling for Michael. The happy couples from earlier walked through the woods calling out to a boy I knew was safe and sound. The parents with young children held tight to their own as if whatever had taken Lodan lurked nearby, waiting to snatch another. I felt evil, but I kept repeating in my head: *this is for Lodan*. Besides, there was no going back now. I could not explain this away to anyone. I knew I had to play my role as panicked sister. I imagined Lodan really was missing; I thought about the last day with my mom. I channeled the guilt I still felt for debating her into agreeing that morning to allow me to go to a friend's after school, not knowing I'd never speak to her again. I worked myself into a sobbing, panicky mess just in time to come across Dale.

"Heather! Did you have him?" Dale looked at me, desperation and perspiration dripping down his face.

"I went running." I lied to his face. "I left him with you."

"I really thought he had to be with you." He grabbed my arms hard in his hands and shook me a little. "He was right there. Right next to us, playing with his cars." He dropped my arms and turned to look out at the empty lake.

"Oh my God!" an older woman yelled. We all turned to look at where she stood, pointing in the water. Dale ran to her side. I followed. The cop asked everyone to step back as he approached the shore.

"What is it?" I yelled. "What did you find?"

The cop used a long stick to pull the dripping sandal out of the water. He slipped it into a plastic bag he'd produced like magic.

Sage came out of nowhere and snatched the bag from the cop. She took one look, grasped it tight against her chest, and crumpled to the ground howling, "Noooo! Please God, no."

Dale went to her and wrapped her in his arms. I didn't know how to act. I knew if this were really happening I'd be screaming at them, blaming them, hitting them. But I couldn't make their pain any worse than I already had. I dropped to the sand myself. As I watched my sister I felt her pain in my chest. I ached for her. Silent tears rolled down my cheeks as I heard arrangements being made around me for a dive team to search the lake. I briefly wondered how long we'd have to wait before they simply declared him gone. I couldn't watch my sister suffer through this. I'd break. I'd give in.

"Excuse me, Miss . . . Miss?" It took me a few minutes to realize a cop was addressing me.

"Are you the aunt?"

"What?"

"Of the missing boy. Are you Michael's aunt?" *No, I'm his mom.*

"Uh, yes." I wiped my eyes. "Yes. Why?"

"Well, we need you to confirm that the lost article of clothing is in fact Michael's."

"What?"

"You see sometimes, in these situations, the moms don't think clearly. Jump to conclusions. See things not there, you know? Can you take a look and confirm?"

"Uh, sure." I followed him to Sage where he asked her to show me the shoe. She looked at me with eyes of shame. "I'm sorry, Heather. It's my fault. You told me this would happen. You told me to watch him better."

I couldn't speak. Thankfully Dale wrapped his arm around her shoulder. "It's not your fault, Sage. Kids run off."

"Miss?" The cop was still waiting for my confirmation. I hadn't even realized I'd taken the bag with the shoe into my own hands. I looked down at the lonely sandal. I couldn't imagine if this were ever really all I had left of him. My tears dripped onto the bag. I nodded and shoved it at the cop. I couldn't stare my own trickery in the face a second longer.

"We should keep looking," I announced and headed off down the beach. I left Dale to console my sister and the cops to handle the rest.

By four that afternoon, most of the original families and couples had left the area. Clouds had moved in to transform the sky to a dark, threatening tone of gray that better suited the current mood on the beach. A collection of local volunteers, cops, rangers, divers, and dogs were searching the lake, the shoreline, and the woods surrounding the area. I'd made a point to let Dale and Sage know I'd forgotten my cell in his car, in case they later wondered why I never responded to their attempts to contact me. Neither responded to anything or anyone. Dale would walk the shoreline, the woods, stop by to comfort Sage, then return to the search. Sage sat motionless on the blanket we'd spread for our picnic earlier. She clutched the bagged sandal to her chest, rocked, and stared ahead at the rescue boats and divers in the lake. I remained silent as well, afraid anything I said would give me away. It was easier to follow along behind strangers in a search party than to sit with the pain I'd cast upon my own flesh and blood.

I panicked when I saw two local news crews appear in the parking lot. Luckily the cops kept them from getting too close. I began to fear the day care would see the news and recognize Lodan. I never considered this making the news. But of course a toddler disappearing at the beach was a hot headline. I prayed something more pressing would bury the story enough to keep the day care crew from seeing it. At least he'd be known as Michael Silverman to the media and Lodan Smith to the day care. It wasn't ideal, but it was too late now.

As four sped toward five I began to get nervous about getting back to pick up Lodan. How could I leave the scene without it looking odd? And then I had a brilliant idea. I'd had severe asthma as a child. My mom made multiple trips to the hospital with me until we eventually discovered it was allergy induced. After six years of allergy shots, using an inhaler, and running to build my lungs, I rarely had an attack unless I experienced emotional distress. I hadn't had one since my mother's funeral five years prior. But this was exactly the type of event that triggered it. It was risky to fake because I could actually prompt a real attack, making it very difficult to get to Lodan by six. I looked at my watch: ten minutes to five. It was now or never. I had followed this search group a decent distance from the beach and decided a run back would help with my cover. If I ran without a puff from my inhaler, my breathing wasn't great anyway.

"I'm going to check on my sister," I announced to the group, so my sudden bolt didn't seem completely odd. I took off at as fast a pace as I could manage without falling on the underbrush or a tree root. I purposely took in too much air too fast as I ran. By the time I'd reached the area where the woods ended and the sand began, I felt myself getting dizzy. *Don't overdo it, Heather.* I paused and bent over to stop the world from spinning, then headed for Sage and Dale. They were talking to a cop. As I approached the blanket I began breathing in short shallow breaths. I made a bit of a show of bending to try and catch my breath.

"Miss, are you okay? Did you find something?" the cop asked.

I shook my head, grabbed at my chest, and wheezed out, "Can't . . . breathe."

Sage perked up. "Her inhaler. She needs her inhaler!"

"Where is it?" Dale asked me.

I shook my head, continuing to take the short shallow breaths. I felt myself swoon and the cop grabbed me. "Forgot . . . home," I managed.

Sage yelled out, "Does anyone have an inhaler my sister can use? She's having an asthma attack!"

"I didn't know she had asthma. She runs all the time." Dale looked pale and distraught. His happy picnic had become a nightmare.

"She used to have it worse as a kid, but now it only happens when she's really stressed. Last bad one was at Mom's funeral."

I heard the cops and park rangers asking around for an inhaler. They all had medical kits but none had an inhaler.

"What do we need to do?" the cop asked.

Sage said, "Usually we take her to the ER, but . . ." I knew Sage was torn. How could she leave without her son?

"I'll take her," I heard Dale say.

I shook my head, "Stay . . . Sage . . . help," I said and again felt a wave of dizziness. I had to stop this soon or I really would be in trouble.

"I can take her." A younger cop stepped up to me. "Can you walk?"

I nodded. "But what about . . ." I didn't want to say Lodan. I needed everyone to think of and refer to him as Michael.

"We have everyone doing everything they can for your nephew. You'll be more help to him if you're well," the cop said.

The cop ran to get his patrol car as close as he could and helped me into the back. He threw on the lights and we made it to the hospital in eighteen minutes. I know because I watched the clock like a hawk. My breathing had returned to normal by the time we arrived, but luckily, the cop was distracted by a call he'd taken. He left me with the check-in clerk and a "You good?" before heading out the door. I began answering the woman's questions with bogus information until I saw him pull away from the curb.

"You know, I'm actually feeling a lot better. Can I just sit for a minute and then decide if I need a doctor? I have no insurance and can't really afford another bill."

"Don't matter to me none, as long as you don't go dyin' in my waiting room." The woman shook her head at me and waved me off. I walked out of her line of sight and cursed the fact that my phone was still in Dale's car. I spotted a young couple waiting. He had his hand wrapped in a bloodstained cloth. She ran her nails back and forth along his back as she flipped through a magazine with her other hand. "Excuse me, I left in a panic without my phone. Could I use yours to call a cab?"

The woman looked at the guy for a second, then shrugged, dug in her purse for her phone, typed in her password, clicked to bring up the number pad, and handed it to me.

"Uh, you don't happen to know a number for a cab, do you?" I asked. The woman rolled her eyes but took her phone back for a minute, then handed it back to me.

"It's ringing. But if you want cab fare, too, you're out of luck." She looked back down at the magazine in her lap.

The cab pulled up to the day care at a couple minutes past six, but I had worried for nothing. There were two other vehicles parked in front to get their kids, too. Apparently, running late was common. I held my breath through the entire pickup process, praying the news of a missing toddler did not come up, or, worse yet, that no pictures of Lodan had surfaced yet. I quickly piled us into the cab.

"Tacci." Lodan clapped his hands. How he knew what a taxi was, I'm not sure. But he clearly liked it. He repeated the word a number of times on the drive to the hotel.

We took the elevator to our temporary hideout. I couldn't pack much of Lodan's stuff because Sage may have noticed. I'd bought a handful of things at a garage sale a week ago: the car seat, clothes, and an impressive bag of used Matchbox cars. Lodan played cars as I flipped through local news stations with the sound set low. My two main concerns were someone from the day care recognizing Lodan as Michael and having Dale and Sage believe the note I'd left on the fridge this morning when I ran inside for the purposely forgotten bag of beach toys.

Sage,

I just can't stay in this house without him. He's everywhere I look. I'm staying with a co-worker. I'm sorry.

H

I hadn't thought out the part where I left the beach before them. I worried it would be odd for me not to mention that I was feeling better after the asthma attack. But there was nothing I could do about it now. I had to hope they assumed my note meant I was fine and they left it at that. If they tried calling, my phone would only ring in Dale's car. I couldn't even imagine how they would be able to leave the beach with Lodan's empty car seat.

I made dinner in the little kitchenette, fed, bathed, and read Lodan to sleep next to me in the bed. My nerves were shot by the time the local news came on again. I imagined every sound in the hallway was the police coming to find us. I'd started to drift off to sleep when my sister's pale, shocked face filled the screen. The camera zoomed in on her and Dale standing beside our picnic blanket. They looked numb as a cop explained something to them. I turned up the volume a little more and listened.

"... earlier, on the scene. René, can you tell us what has happened there?"

"Yes, Sandra, it's a grim scene here where a beautiful beach day has turned to a gray tragedy for this mother and her boyfriend. Her two-year-old son, Michael Silverman, wandered off during a picnic. The local police, park authorities, and beachgoers combed the area in search of the toddler. Things took a sad turn when a woman discovered one of the missing boy's shoes floating in the lake. They called in divers, but hadn't found any more signs of Michael before thunderstorms forced them to halt the search until morning."

"Do police suspect any foul play here, René?" the plastic-faced anchor asked.

"They haven't ruled it out but the canine unit couldn't pick up his scent past the edge of the beach. Sadly, they believe it's likely Michael wandered off and fell into the lake."

"Well, our thoughts and prayers are with Michael's family tonight. Such a scary situation for them, René."

"Yes, police are asking anyone who may have any information or may have seen Michael on the beach this morning to please call the Fayetteville Police Department at . . ." I felt the blood drain from my face as a picture of Lodan appeared on the screen. But I looked quickly back and forth between Lodan snuggled beside me and the boy on the screen. Luckily Sage rarely took pictures of him. She must have given them one off her phone, but it was at least six months old. I remembered the day well. He'd learned how to climb all the way up the steps to the second floor. The picture captured him mid-crawl, about halfway up, looking over his shoulder toward the camera with a triumphant and devilish smile on his face. He'd already outgrown the red pants and truck shirt, and his hair had darkened and grown significantly since then. I let out a sigh of relief. Thank goodness with all my planning I'd been too busy to keep his hair trimmed like I usually did. You'd have to know Lodan pretty well to connect the two boys. I went to sleep relatively confident the day care wouldn't suspect the truth.

The next day I dropped Lodan without a hitch, parked a few blocks away, and made my way home for what I hoped would be the last time. Guilt weighed on me and each stair on the porch felt like climbing in quicksand. I had to play this right.

I opened the door and yelled for Sage.

No response.

I headed toward her room, part of me dying to turn around, race back to my car, and never look back. But this was Sage, who'd let me slip into her bed during bad thunderstorms, helped sneak me into PG-13 movies with her friends, the only other person in the world who had been abandoned by both of our parents. And now I was about to abandon her again. The least I could do was tell her goodbye.

I knocked on her door, but I couldn't hear anything. I opened the door a crack. She lay on her side, headphones on, staring at Lodan's well-loved Thomas the train stuffed toy. It was his favorite and he'd asked for it repeatedly last night. I couldn't take it, it would have been strange to have it missing.

I sat down on the end of her bed. Sage pulled her legs farther up into her chest, wrapping the toy in her arms. We sat like that until I couldn't take the waiting any longer. I reached down and pulled her headphones off her ears. She let them slide clear.

"Hey," I said.

She didn't respond. I could hear Depeche Mode leaking out of the earpieces.

"Where's Dale?" I asked.

"Class; big test." Her voice held no emotion.

"Have the police gotten any new information?" I asked.

"No. Doesn't matter. He's gone."

I didn't know how to respond. I knew if this had all really happened the way it did, I would be slicing her to bits with a tongue lashing. But I couldn't do that knowing I'd already caused her enough pain.

"Why aren't you yelling at me? Telling me you told me so." Her dark eyes flashed anger.

"I can't."

She sat up in her bed. "Why not? Just say what you want to say. Tell me again how I'm an unfit mother. How I neglected him. How I let my own son die." She had her face close enough I could feel her stale sleep breath. Tears rolled down her face. She grabbed my upper arms and began to shake me. "Tell me how I ruin everything and everyone in my life."

I didn't know what to do. I wanted to run, but could I leave her like this? What if she took too many pills again? What if she didn't do it by accident this time? "Is Dale coming back?"

"Not if he's smart." She gave me one final shove and fell back on her bed.

"I don't know what to do." I spoke the absolute truth.

"Go. As far away from me as you can and never look back."

"Sage."

"Don't even look at me. I know all I will see is blame and hate. And that's what I deserve." She bolted off the bed and ran to her closet, Mom's old closet. "Take whatever you want to sell and go." She began pulling all of the jewelry out of Mom's jewelry box. "I don't need any of it except the house so I can lay here and rot in hell for what I've done."

"You're not even making sense." I watched as she grabbed an old cloth overnight bag and began shoving the contents of Mom's jewelry box into it. She grabbed my phone from her nightstand and tossed it in, too.

"Nothing makes sense in this world, Heather. Haven't you learned that yet? I can't have people in my life. I need to be alone."

"Sage . . ." Now that she was telling me to go, I felt like maybe this was all wrong. It may be better for Lodan, but who would take care of Sage?

"Heather, I am begging you. Please, if you won't do it for me, do it for Michael. I can't look at you without . . . I just can't have you near me right now." She shoved her headphones over her ears, closed her eyes, and rolled into a ball, facing away from me.

I sat with her for a few minutes, taking in her thin, frail frame on the bed; the dark, disorderly room; the picture of Sage and Lodan from last Christmas. I stood and gave her one final look. "Good-bye Sage." I squeezed her arm. But she didn't respond. I took the bag of jewelry and my phone and left.

I quit my waitressing and babysitting jobs over the phone. Nobody made a fuss given the circumstances. Then I picked up Lodan, paid my bill, and said good-bye to the day care. By the time Lodan woke up hungry for lunch we were twenty minutes from our new home. I chose Laketown solely based on a conversation I'd overheard at the diner months before. The family was moving from Syracuse to the small town because the dad had been hired as their school superintendent. Their teenage daughter complained about changing schools the last year of middle school. Her twin brothers seemed oblivious to anything but sword fighting with their cutlery as the girl's parents described the quaint, tranquil town of Lakewood.

"The school is small enough you could try any sport you wanted, Tia, and probably make the team. In the summer you can go tubing and waterskiing at the lake. There is this cute main street area with little shops and our house is going to be twice the size. You even have your own bathroom connected to your bedroom."

"But isn't it going to be all farms and tractors and cows and stuff?" In spite of her obvious disdain for this turn of events, their daughter, Tia, had a sparkle in her eyes as she ran her hands through her cute pixie-cut.

"There is some of that, too," the mother admitted. "But wait 'till you taste the cheese they sell. Their cheddar has won tons of awards."

"The cheese? A little nugget of advice, Mom, thirteen-year-olds don't take comfort in a new home based on the accolades of the dairy products," Tia said.

The dad sighed and got up to take the boys to use the restroom. I refilled the mom's coffee, as she leaned close to her daughter and said, "Right, well, how about this? It's been my experience that when a cute girl moves into a small town, the guys, bored with the girls they've known forever, line up to meet the new girl."

Tia's face lit up at this declaration. "That's way better than top-rate cheddar," she said. Her mom relaxed her shoulders, and smiled back.

I don't know why but I began fantasizing about raising Lodan in this quaint small town where he could play any sport he wanted and we could spend summer days at the lake. So when I decided to execute my escape plan, there was only one destination I considered as our new home. The rest, you basically already know.

Thirty-six

LODAN

CALIFORNIA
WEDNESDAY, OCTOBER 28, 2015

We all sat, speechless, with the exception of a shaky sob or an incredulous or shocked expletive from Dale or Sage. Lizzy held my hand through the entire emotionally charged confession, squeezing at points, rubbing my fingers at others. By the time my mom finished speaking I felt like I imagined a marathoner felt after the high had worn off: physically and mentally exhausted. I had so many questions but I couldn't wrap my mouth around any words. Kono's cage rested beside Lizzy and she had been uncharacteristically restless. As my mom rationalized her crazy decisions, I felt like Kono understood my desire to escape and run away from this unbelievable reality. Even the dog, accidently closed in the bedroom, barked and scratched like she was desperate to escape.

"Isn't anybody going to say anything?" my mom finally asked, looking specifically at me. "Lodan, you understand all I wanted to do was protect you and make sure you had a happy childhood." She moved from the sofa and knelt down before me, trying to get me to look her in the face.

I refused to look at her and sank back into the couch to put as much space between us as I could. Sage had curled into a ball in the chair across from the couch where she rocked quietly back and forth. Sage. My mom. That was my mom. I couldn't quite comprehend it. I didn't look a thing like her with my fair hair, skin, eyes. Nothing.

Every time Dale tried to comfort her, she shrugged off his touch.

"You've had a good life, haven't you, Lodan?" my mom asked, now on her knees at my feet. The dog scratched at the door and her barks had taken on a whiny, howling pitch at the sound of sirens blaring nearby.

"I'm sorry," Lizzy said, "I didn't want to interrupt but have you all heard a phone or an alarm sounding off and on? I think it may be why the dog is freaking." Dale jumped up from where he'd been sitting on the floor beside Sage. Lizzy stood to look out the window while Dale looked around for the beeping phone. "I think Lodan and I left our phones in the car but"—Lizzy peeked out the blinds—"I think we need to get out of here."

Lizzy sounded scared and I turned to where she had the blind pulled away from the window. Through a smoky haze, loaded cars sped past the house. "People look like they are leaving."

"The fire!" Dale yelled from the kitchen. "The wind shifted. We need to get out of here, now."

"I'll get Gem!" Lizzy yelled, already halfway down the hall to the dog. I grabbed Kono's cage.

"Do we take anything else?" I asked.

My mother and I looked to Dale. Sage hadn't moved from her balled-up position in the chair.

"Your emergency kit. Medication. Important papers. Passports. Cash. All electronics." Lizzy spouted off a list; Gem had finally, thankfully, gone quiet in her arms. The phone sounded again. Dale ran toward the bedroom.

"Don't we need to go?" my mom said. "How far away is the fire?"

"My dad!" Lizzy yelled. "I left my phone in the car. Lodan, come on. We gotta go. I gotta call him."

"Sage!" my mom yelled. "Come on, we need to go!" Sage didn't respond. She looked asleep with her eyes open.

Dale came running back into the room carrying a duffle bag over his shoulder. "Why haven't you guys left? Go! Authorities will tell you where to go. We'll find each other later."

"What about Sage?" Lizzy asked.

"Will she fit with you?" Dale asked.

"Yes!" Lizzy said. "Come on, Sage!"

When she didn't move I handed my mom Kono and lifted Sage off the chair." I shifted her until I had her cradled like a child. She was surprisingly light. She wrapped her arms around my neck but didn't speak. I headed to the Honda.

"Do you need help hooking up the hose? Moving propane from the grill?" I heard Lizzy yell.

"I got it! Go!" Dale yelled. "Please!" Lizzy looked back at the house, probably torn about leaving without Dale. It looked like *War of the Worlds* around us. Black smoke filled the air. People had abandoned stuff on their lawns, like it hadn't all fit in their car. The houses around us had no cars in the driveway, when I caught a glimpse of the fire in the distance, I felt the hair on my arms spike and my heart kicked into overdrive. This was surreal. A single car sped by, the backseat full of stuff and a couple in the front.

I dropped Sage into the open side of the backseat. Lizzy shoved the Cardboard Cupboard into the back then took a seat beside Sage, Gem on her lap. My mom took the wheel, I took the passenger seat with Kono on mine. Mom started the car and we headed out of the neighborhood.

"Can you hand me my phone, Lodan? Lizzy asked.

I unhooked it from the charger and saw that she had a number of missed calls and texts. We drove in silence, breathing heavily.

"Shit, the call won't go through. The system must be too taxed," Lizzy said.

"Send him a text just in case," my mom suggested. "Maybe it will eventually get through."

"I did," she said.

The smoke got thicker and it felt like the road was taking us closer to the fire.

"Oh my God!" Lizzy voiced what we all felt as we turned a corner out of the direct smoke but so that we could now see the cause behind it. One street away houses were engulfed in flames shooting high in the air, cars burned. Everything in its path.

I felt my mom accelerate, then back off again. We couldn't go much faster because the smoke and flying embers made it difficult to see. A few minutes later (or maybe it was a few seconds later I can't be sure because time became non-finite) we turned a corner and the flames were reaching out into the roadway from the vegetation on the side.

"We're going to die!" Sage yelled, prompting a fresh round of barking from Gem.

"We're going to be fine," Lizzy said. I looked back to see her face and she'd pulled the dog into her lap where she whispered to him. I turned back around just in time.

"Mom!" I yelled just as she swung the car hard to the right. A burning branch bounced off my side of the roof.

"What are you doing? Why are we driving right into the fire? Where's the fire department? Someone needs to help us!" Sage continued to yell.

"You okay, Mom?" I asked, ignoring Sage. I could barely see ten feet in front of us. Flames licked at either side of the road where the trees burned and embers dotted the smoky space around us.

"I've got it." She remained focused on the road, her hands white with their grip on the wheel.

Sage mercifully stopped yelling but then began to hum to herself. I could feel the outside heat warming the car.

"Do you see something ahead?" my mom asked, slowing even more. I stared into the smoke-filled windshield. Embers dotted my view like stars in a night sky. I saw a shadow of something.

"Stop!" I screamed and my mom slammed on the brakes so hard the rear of the car skidded back and forth quickly. Sage shrieked; Gem let out a yelp.

"Everyone okay?" my mom asked, giving us all a quick glance.

"Why are we stopping?" Sage yelled.

"There's something in the road," my mom started to explain.

"Shit, reverse!" I yelled as flames shot up into the sky mere feet from the hood of our car. A fallen tree, engulfed in flames blocked the road.

"We're going to die," Sage repeated as Lizzy leaned up between the seats and my mom put the car in reverse.

"Is that a tree blocking us?" Lizzy asked.

"Oh my God. I can't do this." Sage began to cry. "We need Dale."

"Can you drive a bit in reverse? I saw a turnoff to the left a little way back," Lizzy said.

"How far? I don't know if I can see much without headlights." But she'd already begun backing down the way we'd come. Orange flames threatened at the road's edges, stopping only from lack of vegetation to feed on.

I watched out the front while Lizzy directed her from the back and Sage hummed and cried.

"More to my side," Lizzy guided. "Okay, good. Straighten it out. Keep going."

"Is that it over there?" my mom asked.

"No. Just a non-burning patch. I know I saw it. This is good. You got this." Lizzy's calm reassurance counterbalanced Sage's panic.

"A little right, good. Keep going," Lizzy continued. I held my breath. *What if we couldn't find a way out? Would we burn inside the car? Would it explode?* I forced myself to focus on escape.

"Straighten out the wheel again," Lizzy said. "Good. Good. Okay. Keep going," Lizzy coaxed. Gem continued to bark. Sage continued to hum. Both sides of the road were a black and orange blur. I felt like we were trapped inside a burning tunnel.

"There it is," Lizzy yelled. "Back up a little farther then you can turn into it." My mom floored it backward and quickly whipped us onto the other road. We drove as fast as she dared down the gravel road, flames reaching toward us from both sides.

"I just want to get out of heeeeeerrrreeee." Sage cried out. Gem barked and Lizzy whispered gently to the dog, trying to keep her as calm as possible.

"You're okay, Gem. We're okay," she said.

I watched out the front, trying to make out the road ahead in case my mom missed something. I prayed for no more fallen trees. My heart raced and I gripped the dash, my face as close to the windshield as possible for better viewing.

"You're doing great, Mom," I said.

"We need a way out. Look for a way out of the flames."

"I am," I said.

"What are we going to do? I don't want to burn to death!" Sage whined. I quickly looked behind and caught sight of the fear in Lizzy's face. The hair on my neck and arms stood out as fear and panic threatened to take control.

"What is that?" Lizzy yelled and I turned around as we passed what looked like it could have been a large sign. Flames had reduced it to a charred, disfigured version of itself. A moment later my mom yelled.

"Is that water?" She slowed to a crawl.

"I think it is!" Lizzy yelled. We continued down the road and it opened into a parking area. In the distance was a body of water. As we pulled closer we could see a couple small wooden buildings off to the right, and a metal rack for kayaks and canoes.

"Oh my God," my mom said.

"We have to find a boat or something," Lizzy said. My mom pulled to a stop near the edge of the parking area. The flames hadn't reached the buildings yet but the grassy field between the woods and the buildings had just begun to burn.

As soon as we came to a stop, Sage opened her door and ran for the lake.

"Where are you going?" Lizzy yelled. "Wait. We have to get a boat or something!" Sage kept running until she was in the water.

I jumped out and raced around to the front of the building, looking for a boat or anything we could use.

"Anything?" my mom yelled from the other side of the building.

"No!" I yelled as the flames ate their way through the vegetation, closing in on us. I blinked into the smoke and tried to cover my mouth.

"Try all the doors!" Lizzy yelled. I could hear my mom coughing somewhere in the smoke.

"Hey, are you okay?" A voice I didn't recognize yelled as I vainly pulled on another locked door.

I looked in the direction of the voice. It sounded like it came from the water.

"Over here. What are you doing here?" I jogged toward the water. Was I hearing things?

"Hello?" I yelled.

"Hey, over here. In the water. Do you need help?"

And out of the smoke came a small wooden rowboat with two kids. They both wore high rubber boots, shorts, T-shirts, and bandanas that revealed only their eyes. One had short curly red hair under a baseball cap and the other had a single black braid down her back. Both had blue eyes. They looked like modern teen pirates.

"Are you real?" I asked.

"You better hurry and get in. We gotta get out of here." The redhead's voice was muffled under the material.

"Mom, Lizzy, come toward the water. I found a boat!"

"Wait, how many of you are there?" the redheaded girl asked, rowing in closer to the shore.

Lizzy appeared out of the smoke, carrying Kono's cage, now covered with a sweatshirt. My mom followed close behind, her shirt pulled up over her mouth and nose.

"You okay, Mom?" I yelled. She nodded but I could tell she was struggling with her breathing. "You guys get in the boat, first," I said. "Sage!"

"Another one? I don't know if *Lil Dipper* can hold all of us," the redhead said.

"Sage, where are you? We have a boat!" I yelled and we all jumped as a large tree fell in the distance, taken down by the flames devouring its trunk. I walked along the shore until I spotted her a few feet out, just standing in the water. When she wouldn't respond to her name, I scooped her up and carried her back to the boat. By the time I'd climbed in, the top of the boat rested only inches from the water's surface.

"Once we get farther out, some of y'all may have to get out and swim a bit," the redhead warned. As we slowly made u way across the water, we watched in horror as a burning branch landed on the roof of one of the wooden buildings. My mother coughed and wheezed in the thick smoke, but she didn't complain. We kept our shirts up over our mouths and noses. The girls paddled slow and steady. Looking back I should have offered to paddle, but I think I was in shock.

"Is this a lake or a pond or what?" Lizzy asked.

"A reservoir." The dark braid spoke for the first time.

"Will we be able to get someplace safe on the other side?" my mom asked.

"There's a bunch of houses and roads and stuff not that far from where we keep our boat."

"We can't thank you enough!" my mom said.

"Well, we aren't there yet," the redhead said. And we all jumped as something exploded behind us. We didn't know if it came from one of the buildings or our car, but even the dog stayed quiet for the rest of the trip across the water. I looked from Lizzy, gently stroking the dog, to my mom, her gaze fixed on the water in front of us, her breathing wheezy but better, and finally at Sage, who remained wrapped into herself, knees under her chin, eyes squeezed shut and I couldn't help but wonder how different my life would have been if Sage had been in charge of keeping me safe.

Thirty-seven

LIZZY

LOST IN CALIFORNIA
WEDNESDAY, OCTOBER 28, 2015

We'd left everything not living in the car, but I was okay with that because I knew we were incredibly lucky to have survived. Teri and Karen, the girls that came to our rescue, remained oddly calm and nonchalant about having saved our lives. I wasn't sure if it hadn't registered with them yet or if they simply approached life in a black-and-white life-on-the-farm-mind set of sometimes living creatures survive, sometimes they don't; no sense wondering why. I found it humorous that *Karen*, the redhead, seemed to *care* the least.

Lodan had to hop out of the boat a little way from shore. He swam until he could stand and made his way in to help get Sage and his mom out of the boat. Heather's breathing had gotten much better once we got away from the thicker smoke. I handed Gem and Kono to Lodan before leaping to the shore.

"Well, we better get home for dinner," Karen stated as if we'd simply gone for a joyride in the boat.

"Wait," I said. "How do we get to like a shelter or whatever?"

Karen kept walking as if I hadn't spoken but Teri shrugged and said, "I guess you could call someone from one of the houses here. We're on our bikes."

I wasn't sure if that meant to follow them on their bikes or what. "Can you give us directions?" I asked.

"Oh, yeah. See that break in the bushes over there? That's the start of a path. Follow it until you hit the avocado trees on your right, turn left, pass the goats, then you will come out behind a barn. That's the Cortez farm. They'll have a phone." She turned away to help Karen lift the boat onto the wooden boat rack. They didn't say anything else.

We followed them on foot as they rode their bikes until the gap grew too big. They never looked back. The entire encounter felt otherworldly. The walk probably took us about thirty minutes. The farther away we got, the lighter the smoke in the air. I don't remember anyone talking as we walked. Poor Lodan had to be chafing in his wet jeans. Sage's shirt and skirt were still soaked. Her white shirt had become translucent, revealing a beige bra beneath. Sage carried a subdued Gem, and Lodan carried Kono. I worried about the amount of smoke inhalation the young bunny had endured. When I'd peeked under the sweatshirt earlier, I'd seen his soft furry chest steadily rise and fall. When we came upon the farmhouse, Heather and I climbed the recently replaced wooden steps onto the porch while Lodan and Sage waited beneath a tree in the front yard. Sage sat down on an overturned milk crate and held Gem tight in her lap.

I reached up to knock on the door. We waited, listening for footsteps or any sign of life on the other side. After three attempts and a semi-obnoxious knocking session, the door finally opened to reveal a shriveled, stooped, older woman wearing a housedress and bright orange Nike sneakers. She greeted us with a gap-toothed friendly smile.

"Hi," Heather and I said in sync and we all three laughed.

"We had to boat across the reservoir to escape the fire. Do you have a phone we could use?" Heather asked. The older woman nodded, gestured for us to follow, and turned to walk back into the house. I glanced back at Lodan and Sage, before following her into a small, tidy living room to a phone connected to the wall. She handed Heather the portable receiver and nodded.

"Thank you," Heather said as she took the phone.

"Who are you going to call?" I asked.

"Actually," she said, handing me the phone, "can you call your dad? I don't know a number for anyone local and I'm sure this isn't a 911 situation."

"I'll try." I dialed my dad's number and held my breath as I waited to hear his voice. But all I got was the digitized voice mail version of my dad.

"Hey, Dad, I wanted to let you know we are all safe, but we are stranded at a farm. I hope you are okay. I don't have my cell so I will try you again when we get someplace else. Love you." And I disconnected.

"Know any other numbers?" I handed the receiver back to Heather. She replaced it in its base on the wall.

"Ma'am, do you know how we can get back to town?" Heather asked.

But before she could answer, the door swung open and a black-haired, brown-eyed woman and two Labs came bounding into the room. The brown Lab beelined it for me and the black one headed straight for the lady of the house. I briefly feared he'd barrel through her, but she made a sound with her mouth and the dog immediately halted and sat before her. I reached out to pet the brown Lab's eager face, and caught her rewarding the black one from a stash in the pocket of her housedress. I bent down to scratch my handsome suitor's neck and was quickly rewarded with a wet kiss to the face.

"Mud!" chastised the coal-haired woman. "I'm so sorry." She had her arms full of groceries.

I waved her off as I scratched him beneath his ears. "I don't mind."

"Let me help you with those." Heather reached to take a bag of groceries. Lodan came through the door, carrying a case of beer and another bag of groceries.

"What's the black one called?" I asked as they all headed into the kitchen with the bags.

"Chomper. But don't let the name fool ya. He's big but well-behaved. Unlike Mud. We're still working out his kinks."

"Are there any more out in the car?" I asked as she came back into the living room.

"Nope, your friend Lodan got the last of it. Thanks."

"I'm Lizzy and this is Heather." I extended my hand.

"Pauline." The woman shared a firm handshake with each of us before making the dogs sit for the treats in her other hand.

"Sorry to bother you. Your mom?" I gestured toward the woman who had quietly slipped away.

"Aunt," Pauline corrected.

"Ah, yes, she let us use the phone, but we are sort of stranded. We got trapped trying to outdrive the fire. Two girls helped us boat across the reservoir but it meant abandoning everything including our car and phones."

"Yeah, Lodan filled me in. I can give you a lift into town if a few of you don't mind riding in the back of my truck."

"We would be grateful," Heather said.

"Do you know if they have a school or someplace set up as a shelter?"

"I don't. But I can find out," Pauline said. "Just let me get these two fed, watered, and settled and I'll make a call and get you there."

By the time Pauline dropped us off at the church-turned-shelter, night had fallen. We thanked her and got in line with the other temporary homeless escapees. Sage and Gem had ridden in the front with Pauline and Heather while Lodan and I rode in the back. I was worried about my dad and held Lodan's hand for comfort and support. I knew he had to be reeling inside with all we'd just learned. I could tell he didn't want to talk about it. Not yet, anyway.

At the shelter, we found a spot on the floor of one of the Sunday school rooms. We scored Sage and Gem a beanbag while the rest of us sat on the carpet. Sage remained silent. Pauline had made sure Gem got food and water but I made the humane decision to leave Kono with Pauline. I doubted the shelter would allow bunnies in cages. It hadn't been fair for me to drag him through all that we had. She promised she'd take good care of him and I believed her.

Lodan and I had Heather maintain our spots while we went in

search of human food and to see if my dad had ended up here too. I knew he had to be beyond worried that he couldn't reach me.

"You okay?" Lodan asked me as we waited in line for provisions.

"I wish I had a way to reach my dad. I don't know why but I feel certain he is fine. I want him to know I am, too."

"Hopefully he got your voice mail by now and knows you were headed to one of these places." Lodan pulled me to him for a side hug and left his arm around me. I leaned my head on his upper arm.

"The good news is, I think my pants are almost dry," he said.

"This is good news," I agreed.

He squeezed my arm. We both quietly watched the people around us all experiencing various emotional states. A few kids tossed a football; an older couple leaned against a wall, silently holding hands, their pale faces nervously watching the crowds around them; a mother sat on a folding chair, a blanket covering her chest and one shoulder. Small shoes poked out the end of the blanket. As she breastfed her baby, her toddler sat playing with a set of keys. Her husband paced and talked on his phone. An older woman cried quietly a few people behind us in line. She'd been unable to get home to her cat before the area was evacuated.

"Do you think we almost died today?" I asked.

"I think we were lucky today." He squeezed me again.

"I hope Dale was lucky, too." I felt guilty we hadn't all left together. "Do you think Sage is silent because of you or Dale or both?"

"I don't know what to think. I tried talking to her when you went inside to use the phone, but she wouldn't even look at me."

"I can't imagine how she feels. She thought you were dead and clearly blamed herself."

"I have so many questions to ask her but she won't even look at me."

"Ask your mom," I suggested.

"Because she's proven to be an honest, reliable source." He pulled his arm away and ran his hand across his hair. I noticed it looked longer than he normally wore it.

We'd made our way to the front of the line and gratefully accepted the granola bars, snack cracker packs, and waters. We took the long way back to Heather and Sage in hopes of spotting my dad or Dale amongst the crowd, but if they were in a shelter, it wasn't this one.

One of the volunteers stood on a chair and announced donated blankets and pillows had arrived if anyone would like to help hand them out. Lodan and I quickly offered to assist. I couldn't stand the sitting and worrying. It felt better to be able to do something.

I went in one direction and Lodan loaded up his arms and headed in another. The mound of donated bedding was impressive. It renewed my faith in humanity. People were grateful for the supplies and I noticed many of the younger children, exhausted from the trauma of the day, had already fallen asleep without any creature comforts.

I'd just gone back for my third round, when I heard someone calling my name. "Lizzy Lane! Is there a Lizzy Lane here?"

I turned, my heart pounding, to find the loud, gravelly voice came from a small middle-aged woman with short, choppy brown hair wearing a fleece, jeans, and barn boots.

"Right here." I waved to get her attention as I made my way closer to her.

"Oh hey. You Lizzy Lane? Wendy's kid?"

"Yeah. That's me. How do you know my mom?"

"We've worked together here and there over the years."

"Why is she looking for me?" I asked, now standing right next to her. She was one of the few adults as short as me.

"Your dad called her. She called around and got me. Here, use this to call them both and let them know you're okay." She handed me a phone. "You can bring it back to me over there in that office next to the chapel when you're done. I'm Pat."

"Okay. Thanks Pat," I said, already calling my dad. I listened, waiting for it to make a connection and felt my body relax at the sound of his voice.

"Hello?"

"Hey, it's me. I'm okay. I'm at a shelter. Where are you?" I shot my update at him in quick bursts.

"Lizzy. Thank God." I heard him sigh with relief. "I'm in a shelter, too. A school. By the time I realized the fire had changed directions and headed toward you guys, it was too late for me to get back to you. I tried calling but nothing was going through. Did you all get out okay?"

"Yeah. Well, I don't know about Dale, actually."

"Who's Dale?"

"He lives with Sage, Heather's sister."

"Oh. I've tried calling your phone. Did it die?"

"Yes, probably a hot painful death. It was abandon with Heather's car."

"You guys had to leave the car?"

"Yes. It's a long story, but we are all safe."

"Okay. Well, tell me the address of where you guys are and I'll find out if I can come to you."

"They already started turning people away so let me ask Pat. Hold on. I have to walk to her."

"Okay. And make sure to ask her if it's safe for me to drive from here to where you are right now or if we need to wait until morning."

"I will. So you called Mom to track me down?" I asked.

"Yes. Call her next and let her know you're okay."

"I will. Is she here helping with the wildfire shelters?"

"No. I didn't catch where she is."

"Oh."

I put my dad on with Pat and she explained how he could safely get to where we were, where he should park, and to give her name to get into the church. I asked Pat if I could call my mom next but she said she'd already let her know I was safe and my mom had told her to tell me she was glad and would talk to me another time soon. Apparently she was busy doing something more important than talking to her only child who had just narrowly escaped death by fire.

Lodan and I continued to help the other volunteers. I can't speak for Lodan, but I'm guessing that focusing his efforts on helping others helped keep him from facing the odd truth he'd learned about his background. As I helped sort food donations, I watched as Lodan comfortably chatted with a cute college-age girl. I'd heard her ask him to help take her frail walker-dependent grandfather to the men's room. I couldn't put my finger on the change I saw and felt in him, but something had shifted overnight. He possessed an outward confidence that had been absent before. I would have bet he physically stood taller. I couldn't understand how learning his past was a lie could have this impact. Or maybe. Was I attracted to him? Was that what had changed? *My* perspective? I *had* thought about kissing him a few times.

"Excuse me. Do you work here?" A small blond boy wearing a Scooby-Doo shirt, shorts, and Crocs pulled on my arm.

"Umm, sort of. What's wrong?" I bent down to his level.

"My mom went into the bathroom a while ago and hasn't come out. Can you go tell her I'm hungry?"

"Do you like peanut butter crackers?" I asked, handing him a package from the supplies.

"Yes, but my mom said never to eat food from strangers unless I ask her first."

"That's good advice. I'm Lizzy. What's your name?"

"Paul."

"Okay, Paul. Let's go find her and ask her if you can eat them." I took his hand and walked toward the restrooms. I tapped Lodan on the shoulder on my way. He'd moved on from the college girl and grandfather to a middle-aged woman and her dog.

"Hey, can you keep an eye on this guy while I find his mom in the bathroom?" I asked.

"Sure." Lodan smiled and bent down to the boy. "Do you like dogs?"

Paul nodded but stepped closer to me and squeezed my hand tighter. I bent down next to him, too.

"Hey, Paul. It's okay. This is my friend, Lodan."

Lodan stuck out his hand to shake the boy's but the boy turned his face into my hip.

"Hey, Paul," said the woman with the dog. "I'm Nancy and I have two sons of my own. Would you be okay hanging with me and Rex while she finds your mom?"

Paul turned to study Nancy, but stayed attached to my leg.

"Rex misses my boys' attention and would probably love to have you pet him." Nancy ran her hand over the golden retriever's head. Rex's tongue hung out the side of his mouth as he happily accepted being the center of affection.

Paul looked up at me, shrugged, and reached out to pet Rex along his neck.

"You okay here with Nancy, Paul?" I asked.

"I guess."

"Great. What's your mom's name?"

"Lynn."

"And what color is her hair?"

"Like yours."

"Okay. Good. I'll be right back with your mom."

I bypassed the small line at the bathroom door, letting them all know I was only looking for someone. When I got inside, I looked around for a blond motherly woman, but nobody fit the part.

"Lynn?" I called out to the closed doors of the stalls.

"Yeah?" A voice, thick with emotion, came from the handicapped stall.

"She's been in there a while, wailing away." A pretty brown-skinned woman with dyed red hair and mile-long eyelashes locked eyes with me in the mirror. She was applying makeup. "I've been standing here for at least fifteen minutes and she was at it when I got here." She outlined her lips with a vibrant pink.

"Thanks," I said as around us the women went in and out of the other three stalls, keeping their thoughts to themselves. I knocked gently on the door. "Lynn?"

I heard a sniff followed by a blow. "I'm sorry. I just. I just can't," she said, her throat hitching with a fresh round of sobs. I looked around at the other women but nobody made eye contact.

"I told you," the woman at the mirror said. She'd finished her work and was busy packing her brushes and makeup into a bright red makeup bag.

I spoke to the door in a low voice. "Lynn, your son Paul is worried and sent me in here to get you. Can you come out and show him you're okay?"

"Do I sound okay?" she wailed, followed by another large blow.

Another woman in line, wearing workout clothes that she clearly used for that exact purpose with a dark, tight ponytail and a tattoo on her neck that read UNBREAKABLE also spoke up.

"Listen, lady. I'm sure whatever or whoever is making you so sad you can't even face your own son is awful. But you could cry alone outside or in a closet or something and not be keeping a lot of other people from taking a much-needed piss. This line is backing up out here mainly because of you."

A few other women nodded in agreement. And a woman a few people back said, "Amen."

The door opened and Lynn, an attractive blond woman with mascara-streaked cheeks, hazel eyes, wearing a shockingly tight and glittery dress, bare feet, and a large purse stepped out of the stall. She towered over me but was tiny excluding her large chest, which the dress struggled to contain. She clutched a pair of neck-breakingly high silver stilettos and a roll of toilet paper close to her chest.

"I'm sorry. It wasn't busy when I came in." She threw her shoulders back and marched out the door with me right behind her. A few people clapped as the door closed behind us.

"Hey. I'm sorry, but Paul was worried." I gently touched her arm at the elbow.

"Is he okay?" She looked at me, concern softening her features.

"Yes. Hungry." I tried a smile, hoping she would too but instead she burst into tears again. The raw emotion attracted the attention of the people camped out near the end of the hallway.

I spotted a door farther down. "Hold on," I said and checked inside. It was a small janitorial closet. "Come in here for a minute," I suggested as I hit the light. She stepped in beside me and closed the door. The yellow industrial mop bucket made the space tight. Cleaning supplies, toilet paper, and paper towels lined the shelves.

I took the toilet paper from her and rolled out a chunk. "You might want to wipe away the mascara before you go get Paul," I said and reached up to wipe at her smeared makeup. She didn't protest and took deep shaky breaths as I put her face back in order. Her eyes were still red and puffy but she didn't look like a complete train wreck. She didn't look much older than me, which struck me as crazy given she was already a mother.

"Much better," I said, stepping back to look her over.

"Thanks."

"Sure. You okay to go out there now?"

She took a deep breath and the tears glistened in her eyes.

"Okay, okay. Don't start again. Deep breaths. Take deep breaths."

She looked up at the ceiling, keeping the tears from slipping down her face again. "It's just that I don't know what I'm going to do and when I look at him I get panicky," she explained.

"There are lots of people here who can help you, I'm sure."

"I don't think so. My house is ashes. Nothing left. I tried to get back to it and they wouldn't let me."

"You have insurance, right? You can rebuild."

"Yeah, well, the house isn't the issue."

I felt a little wave of nausea. Had someone died in the house? "Oh God. I'm so sorry. I shouldn't . . ."

She looked at me strangely and then said, "Oh. It's not what you're thinking. Nobody died."

"Oh."

"I was just really effing stupid."

"Okay." The small space and the exhausting and emotional day began to catch up with me, and I was losing patience with this woman who wouldn't go calm her young son.

"I kept my cash at my house, you know." Her throat grew thick with tears again and she looked up at the ceiling and waved her hand in front of her face to keep from letting them spill over. "Eight years. Gone. Shaking my ass for all those perverts. All of it. Ashes!" Lynn clutched at her stomach. "It makes me sick. What am I going to do?" She began to take slow, heavy breaths as she tried to contain her emotions. She looked at me as if I, a homeschooled teen, might have the answer to this impossible question.

Not sure of how to respond and unable to contain my curiosity I asked, "How much was it?"

"I always said I'd get out when I reached half a million. That was my goal, fifty a year. Ten years and out. Paul would still be too young to really know and we could start over with a good nest egg, you know? Maybe go back to my parents and where I grew up."

I did the math and felt sick for her. Eight years. Four hundred thousand dollars. Holy shit.

"Was it in a safe?"

She shook her head. "I had a roommate with a drug problem and a boyfriend with a blowtorch. I caught them trying to get into my safe. I kicked her out, but after that I put it where nobody would think to look."

"Freezer? That could survive," I guessed.

She shook her head again. "I had to have a bigger spot. A few months ago Paul spilled milk all over his oversized beanbag. It wasn't one of the kind you can wash. No matter what I tried, it smelled like sour milk. I bought Paul a new one and put the old one in the attic. But before I did, I emptied out most of the beans and thought I'd found a foolproof new hiding spot."

I didn't know what to say. I had no idea what it would feel like to lose something I'd spent eight years getting. Eight years ago I'd been nine. That seemed like a really long time.

Lynn ran her fingers under her eyes and took another deep breath. "Take me to Paul."

We walked out to where Paul sat between Nancy and her dog. He leaped up with a big smile at the sight of his mom. He ran into her arms and held tight. Lynn looked up at the sky again over his shoulder, fighting the tears.

"I offered Paul some crackers," I said, pulling them back out of my pocket, "but he wanted your permission first."

"Thanks," Lynn said, taking the crackers and handing them to Paul.

"Hey, have you seen my friend?" I asked Nancy.

"Lodan? Yeah. He said to tell you he went to check on his mom."

"Great, thanks."

I wished Lynn luck and headed back to where we'd left Lodan's moms. I felt sick for Lynn and all she had lost. I searched for my dad as I made my way through the groups of stranded people. I felt an odd combination of guilt and relief. The church represented wall-to-wall stories of loss and difficult days ahead. We could have died today. Some people probably did. How could I have thought being ghosted by my boyfriend was such a big deal? The harsh slap of perspective almost stung.

Thirty-eight

LODAN

CALIFORNIA
WEDNESDAY, OCTOBER 28, 2015

When I got back to my mom, Sage and Gem were sound asleep on the beanbag, and my mom was coloring in a bible-studies coloring book with a little girl.

"How are you doing?" My mom looked up at me. I set down a bag of water bottles and snacks.

I shrugged as the little girl looked up from a partially colored nativity scene and said, "I'm Clara and you must be Lodan. My grandma went to the bathroom so I'm coloring with your mom. What's in the bag?" Only she said it all in one long, fast sentence.

"Hi, Clara," I said and sat on the carpet beside them. "There are some snacks and water. Feel free to help yourself." Clara pawed through the bag.

"Where's Lizzy?" my mom asked, having resumed coloring.

"Helping someone," I said. "Is she okay?" I nodded toward Sage.

My mom looked up at me and I could see tears in her eyes. "Dale got word to her through a first responder and one of the people in charge here. He is fine and very lucky. He couldn't get out and literally had to hold off the fire with the garden hose. He said the houses on either side burned to the ground, but Sage's house and one of their cars miraculously survived."

I shook my head at their unbelievably random luck. "And what about the other stuff? Did you guys talk?"

"Not yet . . ." She took a shaky breath, sniffed a little, and then reclaimed her voice. "Maybe it will be better once we are out of here."

"Dale isn't my dad, right?" I pulled my knees up to my chest and could still feel damp patches on my jeans and smell the musky scent of wet sneakers. To my left, Clara read through the ingredients on each of the different cracker packages.

My mom furrowed her brow. "No. Don't you . . . I mean . . . is that really your first question?" Her eyes searched my face.

I felt anger bubble in my gut. "There are so many, I don't even know where to start." My jaw ached from the restraint of trying to maintain a civil tone. "But we obviously can't talk about it all here." I motioned to Sage and little Clara.

"Hey." Lizzy appeared out of nowhere and plopped down beside me. She must have sensed the tension because she immediately filled the silence. "Did Lodan tell you my dad is on his way here?"

"No, but that's great news, Lizzy. I knew he'd be okay." My mom's smile looked more like a pained grimace. "Did you hear that Dale and their house are safe as well?"

"No. That's a relief." She looked pointedly at me.

When my mom immediately made herself busy with coloring again, Lizzy mouthed to me, "Sorry, did I interrupt something?"

I shrugged and shook my head at the same time.

"Hi, Lizzy." Clara held her hand out. "I'm Clara and all of these crackers have BHT or some other preservative in them so we really shouldn't eat them." Lizzy shook her hand and shot me an amused look. Clara set the bag aside and resumed coloring.

"That's good that you read the ingredients. Listen, do you think it would be okay if I colored with you while Miss Heather and Lodan go check on something?" Lizzy picked up a blue crayon.

I flashed Lizzy a *what are you doing* look.

"They need someone to check that janitor's closet just past the bathrooms for any helpful supplies." Lizzy gave me a loaded look.

The thought of closing myself in a closet to confront my mom felt like a recipe for emotional combustion.

"Actually, I was thinking some fresh air might be a good idea." My mom must have read my mind.

"It won't be very fresh out there with all the smoke," Clara declared. "But I know you're just trying to talk about stuff away from me. It's fine. My adults do it all the time, too."

We all couldn't help but smile at Clara's forthright nature.

When we stepped out into the night air, it wasn't clear or smoke-free, but it was cooler than inside and the darkness felt better suited to the matter at hand. A few smokers were gathered off to the side of the door, but we wordlessly continued past them and toward the back of the church grounds. When it became clear that the playground was in use to entertain kids, we continued beyond it and along the paved path.

"So, who really is my dad?" I asked.

"Your dad. Again." She sighed. "He's a professor. Sage had a thing with for him for a few months in college. He was married so she never told him about the pregnancy."

I stopped walking. "What?" I couldn't believe this. "So my dad doesn't even know I exist?"

My mom halted. Shaking her head, she shrugged. "Not as far as I know."

I felt a heated pressure explode through my limbs. "That is complete bullshit." I kept my voice in check but I wanted to scream it in her face.

"No, I'm serious. He never knew." She looked at me with a matter-of-fact expression like we were discussing random acquaintances instead of my dad.

"I'm not doubting that. Jesus. The bullshit is he never got the chance to decide to meet me or not. You took me away from my real mother but only after she kept me away from my father. What the hell is wrong with you guys? What did your parents do to you that made you do this to me?" Tears wet my face and it made me even madder. I didn't want to cry. I wanted to punch something. I turned to run farther down the path and found myself surrounded by a small graveyard. I heard my mom calling after me, but I ignored her and kept running. I stopped when a misstep on a pinecone jarred my ankle. I picked it up and hurled it at the trunk of its mother tree, the irony not lost on me. I picked up a few more and hurled them at their mother. By letting them fall, this massive pine had lost the ability to help or harm her pinecone children. But they could still hurt her if I hurled them at her trunk with enough force. I whipped another as hard as I could. It barely nicked the edge of the trunk before sailing off into the dark night.

I thought about Mateo and his parents. How he lived in fear of being himself in front of them. I thought about Lizzy and how her mom didn't even get on the phone to speak to her after she could have died. Weren't parents supposed to protect us from pain, not cause it?

"Lodan." I turned to see my mom. It hadn't taken her long to catch me; she quickly caught her breath. "Please, can we talk about all of this?"

I whipped another pinecone at the trunk. *Thwack.* "I want to meet him."

"I understand." She stood, her arms at her side. I could see fear in her face and I felt an odd empowerment like our roles had flipped now that I knew what she'd done. I held a power over her. I wondered if this combination of confession-based empowerment and hurt had been the impetus for horrendous and selfish decisions made by political leaders and jilted lovers throughout history. After reading about it and questioning its feasibility I understood exactly how it felt to love and hate someone at the same time.

"I asked you a million times about my dad. You knew how important it was to me."

"Yes, but I couldn't tell you who he was or let you meet him without telling you the whole story. I didn't do it to hurt you. I did it to protect you."

"You did it to protect *you*," I corrected. "Because you are a criminal, a kidnapper, and a big fat liar. You didn't want to go to jail. It had nothing to do with me." I whipped another pinecone, completely missing the trunk altogether.

"I didn't. Do you think it was easy what I did? I started a whole new life from scratch. I did everything I could to give you a good life; to raise you in a safe and happy place. If I had left you with Sage, you wouldn't have ever been safe."

"Why did you have to take me away to keep me safe? Why couldn't you have helped her raise me? Or why not ask my dad to help?"

"Sage was dangerous to herself and to you. Your father was a married professor who'd gotten his student pregnant. I'm pretty sure he wouldn't have signed up to help raise you."

"You could have given him the option."

"I wasn't much older than you are now, Lodan. I did what I thought was the best thing for you."

"How dangerous could she have been?"

"She mixed drugs and alcohol all of the time. Sometimes she'd go days without leaving her room for more than a quick trip to the bathroom. I couldn't risk something happening when I was at work."

"Kidnapping and faking a death weren't risky? Did you ever stop to think about what would have happened to me if you'd been caught?"

She'd begun to cry and I liked it. It made me feel better to make her feel worse.

"I worried about it constantly when you were young. I changed our names, avoided my dad and anything to do with Sage. I made sure we weren't in newspapers or online or anywhere they could accidentally come across us."

"What if she goes to the cops now?" I asked. "Or what if Dale does?"

"I don't know." She wrapped her arms around herself. "At least you're grown and I kept you safe."

"What if I went to the cops?" I knew that was going too far. I saw in her eyes how my words cut through her like a knife to her back. How could this person she'd raised turn on her so easily? I'm ashamed to admit it felt good to keep making her hurt more. Once I got started I couldn't stop myself.

I took a step toward her and looked her right in her crushed, tear-streaked face and threatened her. "I'm going to find my dad and I'm going to tell him what the two of you have done to us." She flinched and turned away from me, her back shaking with harsh sobs.

"I thought I raised you to be more forgiving," she whispered.

"I thought you raised me to be truthful," I shot back. And then I didn't want to be there anymore. I couldn't stand myself like this. I turned and ran, away from her, away from the graveyard and the shelter, away from everything that reminded me of who I should be and how I should act. I didn't want to be this mean, angry version of myself. I felt bile threaten at the back of my throat; like the hurt and spite needed to be physically expelled from my body, but as much as I hated the feeling, I swallowed it back and kept running. I couldn't let it go that easily. I wouldn't let it go at all. Looking back, maybe I should have. Maybe if I had stopped and let it all out right there at the base of the tree, things would have turned out better for everyone.

Thirty-nine

LIZZY CALIFORNIA
ALMOST THURSDAY, OCTOBER 29, 2015

My dad arrived soon after Lodan and Heather left. I introduced him to Clara and she immediately became his best friend when he produced a huge fresh salad and a few other organic, preservative-free snacks he had purchased on his way there. I may have failed to mention that my dad had become a health food nut three homes ago when he dated a nutritionist. He had mellowed some since the initial habit overhaul, but he still stuck with organics and non-GMO when he could.

Heather came back before Lodan and from the look of her puffy red eyes, things had not gone well. Everyone else fell asleep around us, but Heather and I wordlessly waited for Lodan to return. I didn't ask her what happened and she didn't offer. We played round after round of rummy in the dimly lit room, only whispering about the game itself.

We both looked up when Lodan did return. His fists were clenched, his jaw set, and his eyes filled with anger. He didn't say anything to either of us except, "I'm going to sleep." He lay next to me on the rug, turned his back to us, and attempted to cover the middle portion of his long body with a small candy cane– patterned donation blanket. Heather looked at him, clearly heartbroken, and whispered she needed to do the same. I lay there between them in the dark, certain neither of them were asleep and felt guilty for my role in bringing us all to this point. I wondered for the first of many times to come if sometimes the truth shouldn't always be told.

Jordy

LODAN

CALIFORNIA
THURSDAY, OCTOBER 29, 2015

It took me a few seconds to wake up enough to recognize the face in mine. The room around us was still dark and quiet. Sage held a finger to her lips and motioned to follow her.

"You'll want your blanket," she whispered, and I saw she still had hers wrapped around her. I quietly followed behind her as we tiptoed past the groups of people sleeping haphazardly throughout the church. We slipped out a side door into the night.

"What time is it?" I asked her.

"Almost four. Early. Sorry. I don't sleep much usually," Sage said. Her voice shook like a middle schooler about to present to a class of peers. I realized I made her nervous.

"It's okay. Are you feeling better?" I asked.

Sage closed her eyes for a moment, opened them, and reached out to pull my face closer to hers. I had a moment of panic, thinking she wanted to kiss me but then she stopped when our faces were a couple inches apart. She studied my face and I felt my heart pound in my chest.

"I can't believe you're practically a man." She caressed my cheeks with her thumbs. "You look just like your father." She smiled but her eyes looked through me for a beat before she released me and turned her back, tightening her blanket around her shoulders.

"You're probably relieved Heather raised you after meeting me like this," she said.

"Did you ever tell him about me?" I asked.

"Franz?" Sage asked, looking back at me.

"Was that his name?"

"Your father? Yes. Franz Kemp."

"Franz," I said to myself. I hadn't ever tried that one on for size when I'd imagined his name. "Lodan Kemp." I shoved my hands in my pockets.

"Lodan." Sage shook her head. "Did you know your real name is Michael? Only Heather called you Lodan."

"Michael?" I looked at her to see if she was joking but she wasn't. "Michael Kemp."

"Michael Silverman. I never listed a father on your birth certificate. He never knew about you." I heard an air of defensive pride creep into her voice.

"Why didn't you tell him?"

Sage sighed and shrugged. "He was married. I didn't love him or want to be with him. You were . . ."

"A mistake?" I finished for her, surprised at the onslaught of unexpected sadness.

"Unexpected," she corrected me.

"Were you sad when you thought I died or were you relieved?"

Sage's jaw dropped and hung for a moment before she threw up her hands to cover her mouth. She slid her hands down, looked away from my eyes, and twisted her fingers back and forth in front of her.

She finally spoke. "I didn't handle your leaving well."

"Why?" I asked.

"What do you mean, why?" She drew her brows tightly together and I heard the defensive anger in her voice.

"Well, it sounded like you weren't into being a mom and didn't really want me around most of the time."

"Is that what Heather told you? That is not true." She raised her voice for the first time. She began to pace, her long skirt swishing along with her. "Your mom has no idea what I went through after I lost you because she abandoned me, too."

"You told me to go." We both jumped at the sound of my mother's voice in the darkness.

"I'd just lost my son. I said plenty of ridiculous things. You didn't even stick around for the funeral or anything."

"There was never a funeral, Sage, so don't try that line on me."

"Well, there would have been if you hadn't left me to deal with everything by myself."

"Sage, you told me to take Mom's jewelry and leave you alone. You told me to never come back."

"I did not. I would never say that."

"You did."

"When did I ever say that?"

"The next day after, you know." She nodded her head in my direction. "I came to see how you were doing and found you alone in your bed."

"I had probably taken a bunch of sleep meds. How could you take anything I said seriously?"

"Always with the drugs. Why do you think I got Lod—"

"Michael," Sage interjected.

"Lodan, out of there."

"I had postpartum, Heather. I would have gotten better. I did the best I could."

"It wasn't good enough. Not for him. He deserved more."

"Oh, like you? He deserved you because you were so much better for him? You stole him and ran off to raise him on a high school diploma and a pack of lies. You left me to believe I'd let my own baby die? Tell me how that is better?"

"You know that as sad as you were to lose him, you were relieved as well. You didn't—"

Sage flew at my mother and smacked her face with a loud snap of skin on skin. I froze. My mother put her hand to her face and stood shocked, her mouth hanging wide open. The two sisters glared at one another, both breathing hard.

"You ruined my life." Sage's voice broke with emotion and I heard the tears before I saw them. Sage crumpled onto a small bench along the walkway. "You ruined everything."

"That's not true. You've had a great career and won academic awards. You've written tons of articles and you have Dale. You've had a good life. I've followed it all." My mom sat beside Sage on the bench.

"How would you know? You're basing it all on what you can Google. You've never come to visit. You never called, wrote. I've only seen you once in fourteen years and that was at Dad's funeral for six hours. Everyone left me. First Mom, then Dad, then Michael, and finally you. Dale is the only one who has stayed. And God knows how he can stand to live with me." Her body shook with deep sobs. My mom slid closer and put an arm around her.

I looked around and shifted on my feet. This didn't feel like a conversation I should hear.

"You always acted like you didn't care. I tried calling you for months, then on holidays and your birthday for years, and you would never talk to me."

"Not true," Sage said.

"Yes, Sage. It is true. Dale even tried to get you to talk to me, but you refused. You told him I reminded you too much of Michael and you couldn't see or talk to me anymore. You pushed me away."

"Only after you took him away," Sage said. "I thought I'd let him drown."

"But you moved on and did fine."

"Do I look like I'm doing fine?" Sage looked up at my mom and my mom looked away.

"I'm sorry. I thought you were fine. I never knew. I just thought . . ."

"You just thought about yourself and what you wanted. You never thought about how this would kill me inside and mess up Michael's life."

"I tried to do what I thought would be best for both of you. It wasn't about me." My mom shook her head.

"Mom, I think you did do what you wanted. You couldn't have worried about what it would mean for Sage or for me. Because if you had, you wouldn't have done it."

"What are you saying? You have no idea what you are talking about. Do either of you know what it's like to take the greatest care possible to protect and care for a baby and then come home to find him unfed, and asleep in his own feces while his mother is passed out in the other room?"

My mom stood and began to pace in front of the bench. "I vowed I'd never leave you alone with her again. I could never risk your life. I wasn't there when Mom died and I wasn't going to make the same mistake twice."

"It was one bad night and it was an accident." Sage smacked her thighs with her hand. "And Mom had an aneurysm. That wasn't my fault."

"I didn't say it was. I just . . . I should have been there. If I'd have been there . . ."

"What?" Sage stood, and her blanket fell to the side. She faced my mom, halting her pacing. "If *you'd* been there instead of me you could have somehow saved Mom? You think I *let* mom die?"

"That's not what I'm saying." My mom turned away from Sage.

"Well, it sure sounds like it to me." Suddenly Sage turned to me. "What do you think, Michael? What does it sound like to you?"

I took a step back, held up my arms, and shook my head.

"Leave him out of this." My mom's voice held a threatening tone I'd never imagined coming from her.

"Ha!" Sage laughed. "Right. Leave him out of this. Sure. This"—Sage motioned to the three of us with her hands—"this is all about him. You took my child. Michael was mine, from my own womb. My only child I was able to have ever. And you took him from me."

"I saved him from you."

"Saved him? I was young and a new mom. Wasn't I allowed one mistake?"

"It wasn't one mistake!" my mom shouted and I looked around to see if anyone else had come outside. "Do you really want me to do this? You rarely fed him or bathed him and never changed his diapers. I did all of that. Do you want me to list all of the times I came home to a disaster? And how many times he pulled at your pant leg, snuck into your room, cried out for you in the night and you ignored him."

"I didn't."

"You did. Or you'd pick him up and hand him to me because you were too tired or too drunk, or too busy with school."

"I did not."

"You did."

"How do you think that would have affected him? Huh? If he grew up rejected by his own mother again and again?"

"Stop it."

"No. You can't blame all this on me. Do you think it was normal that he called us both Mom?"

"And you loved that, didn't you?"

"I did. I did love it, because I loved him like I was his mother. But you didn't, you—"

Sage jumped at my mom, but this time she stopped her hand before it connected with her face. They both froze.

Sage leaned in to my mother's face with contained anger in her voice and fire in her eyes and said, "Don't you dare say I didn't love my own son. I did love him. You don't understand anything."

"Then explain it to me." My mom dropped Sage's hand and stepped away from her to stand beside me. "Explain it to him."

"I . . . I can't." Sage dropped down onto the bench again.

"Because you know I'm right. You didn't want to be a mom." She stepped closer to Sage.

"I did. I always did. I still wish I could, but . . ." Sage shook her head, tears streaming down her face.

"There are no buts in motherhood. It's all or nothing. You can't be a sometimes mom."

"I didn't mean to be. I just wasn't ready. Mom was . . . Mom was like perfect, you know? She knew everything about books and music and science and cooking. She taught us how to do everything with such ease and patience. She loved being a mom. And I kept waiting for it to come out in me, to feel the happiness that she had for being a mom. But I just couldn't. I felt empty." She shook her head and looked up at me. "I'm sorry. I couldn't find that happiness. I hated myself for it. And sometimes being with you just reminded me of how awful I was for you. I'd marvel at your green eyes looking up at me all bright and full of questions and all I could think was how I had no idea how to give you the right answers. You were like this fresh, blank sheet of paper that everyone expected me to fill with just the right words, only I had no idea what those words were or where to find them."

Goose bumps crawled across my skin, yet I felt hot as my world teeter-tottered before me. All I kept thinking was this woman with the hippie clothes and freckles is my mother and yet she could be anyone. I felt sorry for Sage, sure. I could see how much she was hurting, but I'd expected to feel more of a bond toward her. I'd dreamt of meeting my real dad so many times and every time I imagined we'd see each other and experience a mutual immediate connection. Now, standing here with these two mom possibilities, I only felt connected to Heather. Now, more than ever, I wanted to meet my dad. I needed to know if we'd have a special connection. But I'd also never been more scared to meet him than I felt at this moment. What if I'd done all of this for nothing? What if after everyone knows the whole truth, nobody is happy?

"I think I need to walk," I announced and handed my blanket to my mom.

"I'm sorry. I didn't mean to upset you." Sage looked up at me.

I shook my head. "No, it's fine. You didn't. It's not about what you said. I just need to move."

"Do you want me to come with you?" my mom asked.

I shook my head. "No. I have to sort through some stuff."

I watched her struggle to bite back whatever she really wanted to say. "I'll be back," I said and turned to head down the dark path, toward the graveyard.

I hadn't gotten far when Lizzy jogged up beside me.

I rolled my eyes at her. "Did my mom send you after me?"

Lizzy shrugged. "She was worried you were upset."

I nodded and she fell into step beside me. I loved that she could sense I didn't want to talk. And it was nice to have her there beside me again. For a moment my thoughts turned to Mateo. I'd been so sure what I'd felt toward him must have been what love felt like. Now I felt foolish for thinking that way. I realized maybe the only true test of love is to have someone disappoint you in one of the worst ways imaginable. If you still love them in spite of the pain, that is true love. My mom had made a horrific decision that changed so many lives forever, but I'd had a great childhood. I was still angry for the lies and for keeping me from my dad, but I couldn't help but love her.

I reached over and dropped a kiss on Lizzy's head.

"What was that for?" She stopped, grabbed my hand to stop me, and looked up at me.

"Nothing. Just a thanks, I guess." I searched her face. She was looking at me strangely and before I could work out the expression, Lizzy reached up and pulled my lips to hers. I quickly stood tall to pull my lips away. "Lizzy."

She let go and took a step back, covering her face with her hands. "I'm sorry. I thought maybe you . . ." She shook her head and peeked over her through her fingers at me.

"It's okay," I said. "I just wasn't expecting it and I think . . ."

"I know. You don't think of me like that. I could tell as soon as I . . ." She closed her eyes and looked at the ground. "Embarrassing."

I kicked at the ground with my shoe. "Don't be. It's okay. I did think I wanted you to do that a few days ago, but . . ."

"But now you don't." She looked up at me, her eyes questioning mine.

"I think . . . no, I'm *sure* I prefer guys." I bit my lip, waiting for her response.

"Oh my God!" Lizzy swung away from me and looked up at the sky. "What is wrong with me? Why do I keep kissing gay guys?"

I took a step closer to her. "I'm sorry. If I could pour your personality into a six-foot muscled male version of you, I'd be a complete goner."

"Thanks? I think." She shot me a sidelong glance.

I nudged her shoulder with mine and she smiled.

We started walking again and I thought we were good until she asked, "Wait, when did you figure all this out? Last we spoke you weren't sure. How are you suddenly so confident about . . ."

And with the dread that comes with watching an inevitable disaster unfold, I cringed as each emotion played out on her face as she reviewed the possible opportunities for me to confirm my attraction to men: amusement turned to speculation turned to realization turned to hurt.

"Lizzy, I should have told you." I stopped walking and grabbed her arm

I could see her fighting back tears. "How could you?" I felt the hurt and disappointment in her eyes from the pit of my stomach to deep in my chest. She pulled away from me.

"I'm sorry." I reached out for her, but she backed away.

"Wow." She bent over and took a few deep breaths. "Talk about an emotional sucker punch."

I put my hand on her back, but she shrugged it off.

"The attraction was there before I knew who he was."

She held up her hand. "Don't. Please. I really can't. I just need . . ." She stood up and looked around us. It was still dark but dawn was approaching enough to make out shadows in the distance.

"I gotta . . ." And she darted off across the graveyard. I debated what to do and eventually followed her. By the time I caught up to her she was halfway up a big tree.

"What are you doing?" I yelled up to her but she didn't respond as she continued her climb. Eventually she stopped and dropped down to hang upside down from a large branch.

I flashed back to the day we met. She'd been hanging upside down in the big tree between our houses.

"Okay. You do whatever you've got to do. I'm just going to sit right here and make sure you don't fall out of that tree and break something."

She didn't respond. I didn't expect her to. So we stayed there as dawn fought to break, but the ash-filled sky wouldn't let even the sun warm our silence. I knew she'd come down when she was ready. What I hoped was that her new perspective would take her to the same realization I'd had about my mom: in order to feel true hatred toward someone, you have to love them first. The tougher question was how to move past the hate to forgiveness. For this I had no answer.

Forty-one

LIZZY

CALIFORNIA
THURSDAY, OCTOBER 29, 2015

I hated him. I mean I hated them both. I couldn't decide who I hated more as I hung from that tree, allowing all the blood to fill my brain, willing it to ooze into the very section that contained all of my feelings toward both Mateo and Lodan and wrap them in a protective coating that kept them from making my heart and stomach ache with their betrayal. Instead I felt the pressure causing a pounding headache. But that transfer of pain was mildly helpful.

I couldn't hate them. I thought back over the short time we'd spent in T or C on our way here. When I came upon Mateo and Lodan in the hot springs, I had been too caught up in my own feelings to recognize all the obvious signs of their attraction toward one another. And then later at Mateo's house I'd found them together on the RV. Had they spent the night together? My stomach churned with jealousy and rejection. I'd trusted both of them and they went behind my back. Hadn't they even been discussing me when I found them? I couldn't remember what I'd overhead. What an idiot. My face burned with humiliation at the thought of how I'd just thrown myself at Lodan.

I opened my eyes and found Lodan remained at the base of the tree. Would it be weird between us now? Then I caught myself. What was I thinking? Who cared if it was weird? He deserved it to be weird. He and Mateo had created this mess. But the two of them together? It sucked. It hurt in my chest. I'd found these two amazing people that made me laugh and who I genuinely liked spending time around. They were kind and smart and everything I could ever want in a friend. Why did I have to ruin it all by breaking my own rules? Just when I'd thought I could handle the Mateo breakup, they throw this curve ball at my heart.

Forty-two

LODAN

CALIFORNIA
THURSDAY, OCTOBER 29, 2015

"You might want to close your mouth."

I tried to swallow, but I had desert mouth. I looked up at Lizzy, my neck protesting from the odd angle I'd had it in my slumber.

She handed me a bottle of water.

"Vintage." I took a long drag, partially because I needed the water and partially to gauge Lizzy's mood. I massaged the knot in my neck with my other hand.

"You now have about two minutes before the poison kicks in, forcing the muscles in your body to attack themselves. You'll seize, slip into a coma, and die."

"Harsh," I said.

"Warranted." She crossed her arms and raised her brows.

"Debatable." I crushed the water bottle.

"Justified," Lizzy returned.

"Penitent."

"Better."

"Forgiven?" I locked my pleading greens onto her sad baby blues.

"Deliberating."

"I am sorry I hurt you, Lizzy. And I hope you can forgive me but I also hope you can understand a little, too."

She groaned and pushed against my chest with both her hands. I stumbled back a step. From the force. "I'm too angry to understand.

I know it's immature and selfish but I can't help it. I'm wallowing in my self-pity. I bring you together and you two ride off into the sunset without me."

I cocked my head at her. "Lizzy, we're not riding off anywhere together. We live thousands of miles apart."

She threw her arms up in the air. "Oh, even better. You betrayed me for a one-night stand!"

"Lizzy."

"Lodan."

"Wonder Woman."

"Don't call me that."

"Would it make you feel better if Mateo and I did start a long-distance relationship?"

"Did you?" She turned to look me in the eye.

"No." I threw up my arms in surrender.

"Good."

"What will make you feel better?"

"I don't know."

"That helps." I shoved my hands into my pockets.

"I'm not supposed to be helping you make me feel better."

"Ice cream?"

She let out a snide laugh. "Good luck with that."

"I will ply you with ice cream if it will help you feel less sad and more willing to forgive me."

She rolled her eyes and gave me a half smile.

"Ha! Was that a smile?" I pointed at her face.

"No!" She turned away but I could hear the smile in her voice.

"I think that was a forgiveness smile." I crossed my arms and rocked on my heels.

"Visions of dairy heaven induced that smile." She continued facing the opposite direction.

"Look, you can't stay mad at me because I need your help."

"Ha, you want me to help you now?"

"Yes. You're the best truth-tripping partner I've ever had and I still have truth to tell."

"I'm the only truth-tripping partner you've ever had."

"Exactly. I can't do this with anyone else."

"Not even Mateo?"

"Not even Don Henley."

"Wow. I feel so honored." Sarcasm dripped from her tongue.

"You should. You should feel special. *Wonder*ful even."

"Don't call me that." Lizzy shot me the stink eye.

"Please?" I gave her my best impression of the doe-eyed look she used to move me to action.

"Did the moms tell you who he is?" She stopped walking.

"Franz Kemp." I stopped beside her.

"Franz?"

"I know. Not sure what to make of that."

"Is he German?" Lizzy asked.

"I don't know anything other than his name and that he was a professor at Syracuse University around the time I was born."

"Wish we had our phones." She resumed walking. We'd reached the playground behind the church where a handful of kids of varied ages played tag on the equipment. The space beneath the slide served as a jail for those unlucky enough to have been caught.

"I'd love to use my dad's phone but I'm guessing he is going to be suspect of anything we do. He's still a little pissy about the whole unsanctioned trip across the country."

"Yeah, I guess it's a little harder for my mom to get too upset with me for sneaking off, huh?"

"I bet the church has a computer or two in one of the offices. I wonder if my mom's friend Pat would help us get online." Lizzy had the spark of adventure back in her eyes and I couldn't have felt more relieved to see it. I didn't dare ask for a verbal confirmation, but I had a gut feeling she'd decided to forgive me for Mateo. Or at least set it aside for further consideration after we'd finished what we'd started. We locked eyes for a moment and my chest warmed at the thought of how once again Lizzy rose above her own pain to help me. At that moment as I stood, a sliver from suffocated in the smoky gray aftermath of fires within and around me, I'd found comfort in the determined, benevolent face of my first best friend.

Forty-three

LIZZY

CALIFORNIA
THURSDAY, OCTOBER 29, 2015

Pat proved quite helpful. She got us online in exchange for our help driving around to pick up and drop off supplies in the area now that the fire had been 60 percent contained. The access to wheels became an even sweeter proposition when a quick search yielded only one Franz Kemp, formerly a professor at Syracuse University, currently VP of research and development at Neurospective Incorporated headquartered in Pasadena, California.

I clicked on a link and a middle-aged Lodan appeared on the screen. "Dang. Take a look at your future self, dude." I clicked to display his full bio.

"Apparently your dad collected degrees and awards before leaving the world of academia." I scanned through his many accolades in the fields of physics, engineering, and neuroscience. "But look, he's been in California for at least a decade. Kind of makes you wonder if Sage followed your dad to California. It seems improbable they would both live and work this close to one another by chance." I turned from the computer to look up at Lodan where he leaned over my shoulder.

He tipped his head, and pierced his lips as he read the screen. "Especially since they both work in the field of neuroscience." He continued reading. "No family mentioned."

I tried a few more searches but everything focused on his

career. There was no mention of a personal life anywhere. He had a LinkedIn account but no other social media that I could find. He'd authored a number of articles in various academic and scientific journals.

"I can't get his home address unless we want to pay for it, but we could easily swing by his office while we are running around for Pat. One of the pickup spots is near the center of Pasadena. According to Google Maps it's less than eight minutes from your dad's office." I looked back at Lodan again. He pushed his glasses up the bridge of his nose with his finger, stood up, and ran his hand over his overgrown brush cut, never taking his eyes off the screen.

"Let's do it," he said.

"Yeah?" I asked.

"Yes."

"Awesome!" I jumped up and threw my arms around him. "This is amazing." I couldn't imagine what it would feel like to know he'd be meeting his father for the first time ever in less than an hour.

Heather looked physically ill when we told her our plan, but she knew she couldn't do or say anything to stop Lodan. She agreed with us that we didn't need to share our plans with Sage. After our discussion earlier, she hadn't spoken much. She focused on Gem and remained rather still on her beanbag. Her blank stare and listless body became a ghostlike presence within our group though her thoughts and feelings were anything but translucent.

The biggest hurdle in our quest stood directly before me, his arms crossed and his eyes doubtful. My dad had insisted we needed to talk and we'd walked the path, passing the playground and cemetery to my thinking tree. At some point I'd come to think of him as Oscar. He had a big scar about five feet up his trunk where something had struck him hard enough to leave an offset oval divot in the outer bark layers.

"Dad, I know that you're mad that I didn't ask before making this trip. And I am sorry, but I told you I felt the reasons were solid. If I had told you, I know you would have felt obligated to tell Heather. I needed to confront Mateo. I needed closure. And Lodan. I know you don't know the whole story but trust me, Dad, when I tell you it was imperative that Lodan make this trip and learn the truth about his parents."

"What if something had happened and I didn't even know where you were?" My dad traced the tree's scar with his finger, but he looked directly at me.

"I don't have a good answer for that. I could say that every day something could happen to Mom and we rarely know where she is."

"That's diff—"

I held up my hand. "I know. She's an adult and I'm a kid. I get it."

"I know in a matter of months you'll be eighteen and legally can do what you want, but I still want to know before you embark on a trip across the country." I heard the anger under the surface of his words, but my dad rarely raised his voice toward me. It was a skill I envied and hoped to one day emulate. I took a deep breath.

"Do you remember when we left T or C and I asked you why you didn't at least consider fighting for a relationship with Jane?" I tilted my head up at him.

"Yes."

"You told me no matter how you felt or what she said, it couldn't work. You said if the primary layer to a relationship isn't truth, then all the feelings and beliefs built upon it are vulnerable."

"Exactly." He nodded.

"You can work hard and try and smooth out the lies with layers of apologies and good faith, but ultimately in the back of your head, you can feel the crack of the lies looming underneath: a constant threat to the smoother surface."

"Good to know you were listening so intently." He crossed his arms over his chest.

"Lodan found out his entire foundation was formed in quicksand. I couldn't stand by and let him sink. We both needed truth. I threw him a line and we have kept each other afloat."

My dad tilted his head at me and pulled his eyebrows together.

"Are you in love with him?"

The directness of his question caught me off guard. I felt my face and neck turn red and I self-consciously looked around, though I knew we were alone beneath the tree.

"He . . ." I wanted to tell him he preferred guys, but I couldn't make that mistake again. That wasn't my story to tell. I didn't think Lodan had told his own mother. I couldn't tell my dad. "It's complicated. But we do not have a physical relationship if that is what you are asking."

He relaxed his arms and I heard him release his breath.

"And where is it you want to go now?"

"To meet Lodan's father at his office in Pasadena. It's right near where we have to stop for Pat anyway."

"Does his father know you're coming?" My dad wrinkled his forehead.

I shook my head. "His father doesn't even know he exists."

"Ohh." My dad wrinkled his nose and half-whistled. "That's a hell of a surprise."

"We know."

"Have you done worst-case scenario?"

"Not specifically, no."

"What if there is security at the building? How will you get in?"

"I'm not sure if you've noticed but I can be pretty persuasive." I flashed him my wide-eyed, help-a-girl-out look to punctuate my point.

He rolled his eyes. "Lizzy, convincing your friends or your father is a little different than convincing security."

"True, but I'm also pretty sure if the security guard knows Mr. Kemp at all, he will take one look at Lodan and recognize him as his son."

"You know this is life-altering news you two plan to deliver. Has he considered how this could change his father's life if he has a wife and other kids?"

"Dad! Are you suggesting he shouldn't tell his dad he exists?" I couldn't believe he'd feel that way.

"Not at all. I'm simply concerned you could be taking this all too lightly."

"Too lightly? We borrowed a car without asking, lived on peanut butter and crackers, slept in odd places, and drove thousands of miles!" I yelled.

"Okay. Okay. Calm down. I'm playing devil's advocate. That's all." He patted at the air as if to say bring it down a notch.

"Look, Pat is waiting for us. Can we go or not?" I asked, completely out of patience and frustrated at my father's reaction.

He sighed, tilted his head, and put his hands on his hips. He locked eyes with me. I held his gaze, arms crossed, standing strong in my resolve.

"Dad. Imagine one of your exes kept a son from you for sixteen years. Wouldn't you want to meet him if he had been looking for you?"

He sighed, closed his eyes for a beat, and shook his head. "Of course."

I threw my hands in the air. "Then there's your answer. Please help me, help him to do this." And I used my ultimate weapon: I threw my arms around him and squeezed, my head resting on the middle of his chest. "Pleease!"

He groaned, put his arms around me, and bent to rest his chin on my head. "You have no phone. How will you contact me if you end up in jail?" he asked but I heard the defeat in his voice.

"They give you a landline call," I said, not letting go.

"Fine."

"Thank you!" I pulled away, then hopped up to give him a kiss on the cheek.

"Here." He held out forty bucks. "Please make good choices!"

"Thank you. I promise we'll be careful."

I turned to run to find Lodan, then turned back. "Hey, we didn't tell Sage about this yet so please don't mention it. Okay?"

"I won't lie if she asks directly," he said, his eyes and tone serious.

"I know." I turned to leave and threw back over my shoulder,

"Maybe you should try avoiding her until we get back."

He shook his head and gave me a wave, which I returned before turning the corner out of his line of sight.

Forty-four

LODAN

PASADENA, CALIFORNIA
THURSDAY, OCTOBER 29, 2015

We made two stops for supplies before entering the city of Pasadena. The closer we got the slower time moved and the faster my heart raced.

"Okay, you're getting that squinchy-faced panicky look you get," Lizzy said. "Let's play worst-case."

"I can't, I'm too nervous." I rubbed my sweaty palms on my jeans.

"Okay, I'll do it and you listen."

"I mean, look at me. I'm meeting him in clothes I've worn for two days straight, after escaping a fire and wading in a reservoir. I haven't showered or used deodorant. What was I thinking?"

"You do have a point." Lizzy gave me a once-over as she stopped for a red light.

"But I can't not do this. I'm this close." I looked out the window at a couple of young, uniformed Boy Scouts with latex gloves picking through trash cans.

"Okay, I've got an idea. Let's go to the next stop first and then we'll meet your dad."

"Okay." I knew better than to ask her questions. She wouldn't tell me until the plan was upon me.

I focused on finding a good song on the radio as she drove.

"Oh go back, I love that song." Lizzy yelled.

"'Jingle Bell Rock'?" I asked.

"Yes. Please."

"Sure." I went back a couple of stations, turned it up, and let it play. Lizzy sang along and it helped calm my nerves to listen to her singing as we rode. Traffic in California was a nightmare. I made a mental note to be thankful the next time we made it from home to the store in eight minutes.

We left the holiday station playing and "Frosty" had just begun when Lizzy pulled into a faded orange stucco strip mall with only a Subway and Goodwill left standing amongst the vacant storefronts.

"This is us," she announced and we both got out. Inside Goodwill, the volunteer told us to drive around to the back of the building where the supplies for the shelter were bagged and boxed for us to take.

"I'll move the van," Lizzy said, "you need to shop." And she bolted out the door before I could protest. The air smelled musty, like the basement of our town library.

What does one wear to meet his father for the first time? Especially when said person hasn't showered in a few days? I made my way to the men's section and began sorting through various shirts. Hawaiian? Too touristy. Sweater? Too hot. Full suit? No. Not me at all. I just wanted a fresh shirt and jeans. I spotted a circular rack with jeans divided by waist size. I fingered through the thirty-fours, but most of them were too short. I needed a thirty-six in length.

"Any luck?" Lizzy appeared from the back of the store.

"Not really," I admitted.

"How about this?" Lizzy held up a black leather jacket covered in lots of metal. "I think it's very 'Don't give me any shit!' Don't ya think?" She winked at me, then put it back.

"I'm going to try these on." I took two pairs of jeans in my size and headed for the changing room.

"Okay. I'll hand you in some shirts if I find any," Lizzy announced, already flipping through the rack of shirts I'd abandoned earlier.

By the time we pulled up in front of my dad's office, I had transformed into someone as presentable as possible given the circumstances. Thanks to Lizzy's dad's forty bucks we were able to purchase a black collared polo shirt, jeans, deodorant, two toothbrushes, and toothpaste. We both used a fast-food restaurant bathroom to clean our teeth, pits, and faces. It wasn't perfect but I felt a hell of a lot better when I took a final look in the mirror.

"Remember, this is just like the casino. The key is to act like you belong here. Okay?"

"Yep. And in a way I do. Right? I mean he is my dad."

"Worst-case scenario or are we going in cold?" Lizzy asked as she fed the meter with change we'd found in the ashtray of the van.

"I can't think too much. Let's go before I lose my nerve." I stood as tall as possible and we walked through the revolving doors to the security desk at the front.

A twentysomething dark-haired girl approached the desk ahead of us.

"Hi." Her voice had a husky, seductive tone and a touch of an accent. "I'm here for Dr. Kemp. He said I'd need a temporary pass for four weeks for the study."

"Name, please?" The female security guard didn't look up from the screen in front of her.

"Michelle Burrows." Her black hair was pulled into a tight high ponytail and she wore a black pantsuit and heeled boots.

"Yes, Ms. Burrows. One moment please." The guard got up and disappeared through the door behind the desk.

I looked at Liz and wordlessly we both walked past the desk and rounded the corner to head in the direction of the elevators. She pushed the up button and my heart raced as we both watched the light indicate its descent from the eleventh floor. By the time it reached the lobby and we'd stepped in, we could hear Michelle's heels clicking their approach on the marble floor.

I pushed the button for the eighth floor but it wouldn't stay lit.

"Can you hold it, please?" she called out and Lizzy put her hand out to stop the door. I kept hitting the button but it wouldn't take. I tried another, but it didn't work either.

"Did you forget your pass?" Michelle asked. She stood close to my height with her heels and for some reason her eyes reminded me of a giraffe's from the zoo when I was little. Her lashes were long and her eyes big and brown.

"Oh crap!" answered Lizzy since I'd frozen. "I left mine in the car. Do you think your dad will be mad?" Lizzy grabbed my arm and gave me a loaded look.

"Um, I . . . he . . ." I drew a blank as Michelle studied my face for a few beats past normal.

"It's cool. I got it. Going to eight, right?" Michelle slipped her pass through the reader, the button remained lit, and we began our ascent. All I could think was I was seconds from meeting my real father.

"Is Dr. K your dad?" Michelle asked but I couldn't find my voice. I wiped my palms on the backs of my jeans.

"You here for the study?" Lizzy asked, trying to take the focus off of me because I'd suddenly lost the ability to form complete sentences.

"Yes. I can't believe I get to finally meet him in person." Michelle's face flushed.

"I didn't realize he had a son." Michelle turned her focus back to me. "You favor him." She reached out and pulled my glasses up off my nose. Then just as quickly she released them and snapped her hand back. "Sorry. That was rude of me. It's just that—"

The elevator door opened and Lizzy held her arm out. "After you." She looked directly at Michelle.

"Thanks." Michelle squared her shoulders and stepped into the hallway. Lizzy shot me a look and mouthed "wack," as we trailed her past a few unmarked doors. At the end of the hall a glass door etched with NEUROSPECTIVE INCORPORATED and their logo (a hand and face curved around a brain), opened when Michelle's slid her pass through the reader.

Another young, black-haired, ponytailed girl with giraffe eyes stood to greet Michelle.

"Does he clone them?" Lizzy whispered to me.

We listened as she welcomed Michelle.

"I have to get Michelle set up in intake. Are you both here for the application consult or just you?" She looked at Lizzy.

"Just me. He's my ride." Lizzy rescued me again.

"Great. It shouldn't take more than thirty minutes once she gets in there." She focused her big eyes on me. She hesitated a beat past awkward before handing Lizzy a clipboard and disappearing down the hall with Michelle.

"What should we do?" I asked Lizzy, who was staring down at the clipboard, her eyes wide as she read through the document.

"Lizzy. Should we go look for his office or something?" I asked.

"Yes," she said abruptly, setting the clipboard back on the desk and grabbing my hand. I followed her down the hall and at some point she released my hand. The doors had no windows or any clear indication of what was behind them. Lizzy continued down the short hall and turned with the speed and stature of someone who knew where they were headed.

"Lizzy," I whispered. "Where are we going?"

"Just follow my lead."

She turned the corner and we both looked up as my father stepped out of a door at the end of the hall.

"Dr. K!" Lizzy used the nickname Michelle had used in the elevator. He turned to look our direction.

"Yes?" he said with a slightly deeper version of my voice. My heart raced as I took in the tall, older version of myself. His build hinted at hours in a gym or some other physical activity. I couldn't move, breathe, think. I stared. It's a powerful moment when you meet another person that shares your same features and literal DNA when you weren't born experiencing this luxury daily. I didn't resemble my mother or Sage in any outwardly noticeable form. But this. My dad. The physical tangibility of it blew me away for a moment. It took me a minute to realize both Lizzy and my dad were staring at me expectantly.

"Um, hi, I'm Lodan. Your . . ." I cleared my throat. "I'm your son,"

I said. He opened his mouth to speak but then stopped, leaving it slightly unhinged as if his thoughts overrode his words. I watched as he wordlessly processed this information. Whatever emotion my appearance evoked within him, his face gave nothing away. He briefly looked at Lizzy, then back at me. He tilted his head, let out a small chuckle, and motioned toward the door he'd been headed toward when we stopped him.

"Why don't you two step into my office." I could hear traces of an accent in his voice.

Lizzy and I exchanged a glance and then followed him inside. His office felt sparse and modern. The word neutral came to mind. The walls were a light gray. Four or five oversized black-and-white close-up photographs of everyday objects were the only artwork on the walls; a button, a house key, a dime, and a paperclip. He motioned toward the gray leather sofa along the left wall.

"Have a seat. Can I offer you a bottle of water or soda or something?" We both looked to the left of the door we'd come through where he pointed toward a mini-bar area similar to a hotel room. Across from the door sat his small, white, lacquer desk which held only a small laptop and a water bottle resting on a square black coaster.

We both declined his offer of a refreshment and took a seat on the sofa. He took a seat across from me in a black leather chair. Between us was a marble-and-silver coffee table with a stack of black pleather coasters in the center.

"Well, I must say this is a shocking development," Dr. K began and again the slight accent sounded odd to my ears. I'm not sure why. Maybe because in all my imagined meetings I'd never thought about how he'd sound.

Lizzy lifted her eyebrows at me expectantly and I knew she wanted me to talk but I still hadn't come back from the odd enchantment cast over me by seeing myself in another person.

"I'm a little embarrassed to have to ask this, but who is your mother, Lodan?" And my stomach did a little flip at hearing him say my name.

"Sage," Lizzy said. "Sage Silverman."

"Ah, yes. Syracuse. That would fit. Sage. That would make you around fifteen, sixteen?" he asked.

"Sixteen in December." I'd finally found my voice.

There was a knock at the door and then the woman from the front desk popped her head in the door. "They are ready for you in intake, Dr. K," she said. If she was surprised to find us in the room, her face didn't show it.

"Ah yes, I suppose they are. I think . . . I think we may need to reschedule Ms. Burrows."

"Okay. Should we begin tomorrow instead?"

"Yes. Please extend my apologies and beg my forgiveness. Thank you." And she stepped out and quietly closed the door behind her.

"Dr. Sage Silverman. Odd. I swear I have seen her fairly recently at a couple of engagements. Excuse my bewilderment but I didn't realize you existed nor did I realize she had any children. But clearly as you sit before me an adolescent version of myself, the actuality is undeniable."

His reaction had me speechless. I felt his eyes assessing me in an odd way; like he was mentally charting my eye and hair color, height, weight. It felt clinical. It was unnerving. This must have been what it felt like to be at the other end of a microscope.

"You must live nearby," he stated.

"No, actually we drove here from New York state. I grew up with my mom, well, her sister. My aunt, I guess."

"Ahh. Well, that certainly makes it much more understandable. Yes. Okay." He nodded and rested his hands on his lips.

An awkward silence fell over the room.

"Do you have any other children, Dr. K?" Lizzy asked and again I felt a rush of gratitude that she could carry on like a normal human.

"Uh, no. No. I didn't. Well, that is to say I had never planned to reproduce. I know too much about the brain. Occupational hazard you might say." He nodded again.

"Did you ever get married?" Lizzy pressed.

"No. I didn't plan for that either." He shifted in his seat and then smiled at me oddly.

"Well. Looks like your plan has got a little hitch in it," Lizzy said.

"Yes. It does." Dr. K turned his smile on Lizzy and he shook his head. I couldn't tell if he looked more awestruck or amused.

"Lodan likes to build things and he knows a ton about cars and engines and all things mechanical. He built an entire miniature town with running water and electricity. He's pretty amazing."

Lizzy had begun to ramble and I couldn't do anything but sit and blush and wonder at this man's reaction. I felt a weight building in my chest, and a coldness spread just beneath my skin, though his office was comfortably temperate. In a few imagined scenarios of this moment my dad had tried to deny me or forced me to leave. Then other times he was homeless, even dead. But this. This I hadn't been prepared to confront.

"Did your mom come with you?" Dr. K asked. I wasn't sure what Lizzy had been saying before that. I couldn't get out of my own head.

"Did you mean Sage?" Lizzy asked. "No, why?"

"It would be interesting to hear why she chose to never tell me about this . . ." For the first time since we entered his office he seemed at a loss for words. "Um, this byproduct situation."

Lizzy's mouth dropped open. She glared at Dr. K. "Did you just call your son a byproduct?" Lizzy demanded.

"I didn't mean . . ."

"Then why did you say it?"

"I simply . . ." Dr. K began, clearly taken aback by Lizzy's anger, but she cut him off again.

"Lodan is your son." Lizzy stood abruptly. "Maybe Sage didn't choose to share that information with you at any point during the past sixteen years, but he is a person that you helped create, sitting here in flesh and blood with feelings and hopes and dreams. One of which has always been to meet you. And you have the audacity to sit there and treat him like a *byproduct*. A byproduct. He is not a hypothesis you got wrong. He's your child. Don't you want to know who he is? What he's been doing for the past sixteen years? His favorite foods and color and where he wants to go to college?" Lizzy's face was flushed, her hands fisted, and a mere sliver of blue edged the dark anger in her eyes.

"It's okay, Lizzy," I said, standing. I put an arm on her heaving shoulder.

She turned to me. "It's not okay, Lodan. You deserve better." She turned back to my dad and seethed. "You should be ashamed."

Then she abruptly marched to the door of his office. "I'll wait for you in the lobby, Lodan. Take your time." She opened the door and left.

"I like your girlfriend. Tenacious." He smiled at me.

"She's not my girlfriend," I said and felt like my own anti-hero. Lizzy had stood here and defended my honor and I all I can do is define our relationship. "She's my best friend but we aren't a couple," I elaborated.

"Well, I think she may feel differently. She is quite taken with you. That's in the genes, son. Women love Kemp men. My father, your grandfather, was married seven times."

"Is he still alive?"

"Sadly, no. You'd have liked him. He was an engineer."

"How would you know who'd I'd like?" I asked. How dare he assume anything about me?

"Well, I just meant you'd probably have much in common since you are interested in engineering and building." Dr. K cleared his throat and looked at his watch.

"Am I keeping you from something?" I couldn't keep the anger out of my voice.

"Not yet. We have ten more minutes." He smiled and I wanted to punch him in his perfect white teeth.

I threw my hands in the air and dropped them again. "So that's it? I come and tell you I'm your son and you give me thirty minutes and what? You want me to leave and go back to life as it was?"

"Lodan, what did you expect to happen when you came here?" Dr. K asked.

"I don't know. I thought you'd be angry or excited or possibly deny it could be possible, but this . . ." I waved my hand at where he sat, fit, ironed to perfection, and smug. "It's like . . . like my existence is an amusement to you."

"Well, it is in a way. And again I ask, what would you prefer to have happen, now? Did you need money for college? A new car? Back child-support pay?"

"I don't want money. I guess I just thought, or hoped we'd get to know each other. Maybe hang out sometimes? You know, make up for lost time."

"I spend eighty percent of my time here. Working, peeling back the hidden layers of human addiction. When I'm not here, I sit on panels, attend conferences, lead discussions, and make appearances as a guest speaker. On the rare occasions when I have free time, I have a long list of friends I am overdue to meet for a meal or drink. You live across the country, attend school, and have hobbies and a girlfriend . . ."

"She's not my girlfriend."

"That's right. You said that. Sorry. I imagine you still spend significant time with her given her territorial reaction to me. I simply can't imagine how we would manage to *hang out*, as you so eloquently suggested. Can you?"

"So that's it? I tell you that you have a son and you don't want to do anything about it? You're going to move on to your next meeting, go on with your day and life like nothing has changed?"

"Lodan, nothing has changed. Really. Has it? You continue to exist as you have for the last sixteen years and I continue to do the same. You already said you don't want money. You look like you have had the support you needed to become a man. In two years you will legally be a man. I don't see the need for me to mess up what looks like a perfectly good childhood."

"But you're my father."

"More like a sperm donor, really. In many species you would have struck out on your own years ago. The parent's role is to provide nourishment, teach their offspring the skills needed to eventually live on their own, and protect them from harm until then."

The admin knocked at the door again and peeked her head in. "Dr. Polska is waiting for you in conference two," she said with a quick sympathetic glance in my direction.

My dad stood and I did the same. He held out his hand to shake and dumbfounded I simply shook it; numb by the entire experience.

"Best of luck, Lodan." And he turned and walked out the door.

"Would you care for anything to drink before you go?" the admin asked.

I shook my head, too despondent to speak. I followed her back to the lobby where Lizzy was waiting. She stood near the elevators and pushed the down button as soon as she saw me.

"Have a good day!" the admin said in an overly sweet and encouraging tone.

Lizzy shot her a dirty look as the elevator opened before us. She sat down, her head blocked by the protection of the computer monitor.

We stepped in. A tall, suited man feverishly texting on his phone stood off to the side. We silently rode to the bottom. Lizzy reached over and squeezed my hand with hers. This trip had not turned out how I'd imagined. My real mother was a basket case; my mom who raised me, a criminal; and now this. My father was . . . I couldn't even come up with a word to describe him.

The elevator came to a halt and we walked silently across the lobby and out the revolving door to the sidewalk. Lizzy and I climbed into the van and she turned to me and said, "Undemonstrative." Again as if she'd read my mind. "Sorry, I know he's your dad but I've never met someone so unaffected in my life."

"The first word you thought of"—I looked her in the eyes—"and it's a good one." She pulled into traffic. "Has demon right in the middle."

"I'm sorry, Lodan. I hope you were okay that I left you. I wanted to punch him in his smug smile and I didn't think that would be good for anyone." We were sitting at a light.

"I don't know what to think," I admitted. *Or feel,* I thought. "I can't go back to my mom and her questions right now."

"I understand, but we have to get this stuff to the shelter." She motioned with her head at the full load in the back.

"I know. And you should, but I think I need to just be alone for a while."

"Okaaayy," Lizzy said. I don't know what she was thinking because I stared out my side window at the blue of the sunny world around me. The light changed and we drove on in silence for a bit.

Lizzy came to a stop and said, "Okay, this is your stop. I'll be back to get you in two hours." I looked up and saw she had illegally pulled over by a row of parked cars in front of a small park. In spite of my mood, I gave Lizzy a grateful half-smile.

"Thanks, Lizzy. Can you handle my mom?"

She cocked her head and rolled her eyes. "Rhetorical." She gave me a half-wave, pulled into traffic, and disappeared down the road, leaving me to decipher my truth.

Forty-five

LIZZY PASADENA, CALIFORNIA
THURSDAY, OCTOBER 29, 2015

A whole lot of shit (sorry, had to be said) went down in the last twenty-four hours in California. Too many secrets held too long had spilled, or more like vomited all over Lodan's concept of self. Upon my return to the shelter, I told his mom he had needed some alone time to think. Heather couldn't sit still and asked me questions I couldn't answer about what he planned to do and how he felt. Thankfully my dad came to my rescue by enlisting her nursing skills to assist in a monkey bar misstep bleeding knee and elbow. Thankfully Pat let me take the van again if I promised to gas it up and drop a few items at another shelter. My father insisted he ride along this time and since I needed him to pay for the gas, I couldn't really argue.

When I pulled up to the park, Lodan sat alone on a bench under a tree. Other than a quick hello to both of us, he didn't speak as we drove. Once again my dad filled the empty air with practicality.

"I booked us all flights back tomorrow afternoon on the only non-stop flight that could accommodate us. Our car is at the airport so we can all ride back to Laketown together."

"I'll pay you back," Lodan said.

"Maybe it could be an early birthday gift?" I gave my dad a hopeful, give-the-kid-a-break look.

"Sure. When is your birthday?"

"December seventh," I answered for him.

"Seventeen?" my dad asked.

"Sixteen," I answered again and gave my dad a look that I hoped conveyed my thoughts: *stop, clearly he doesn't want to chat.*

He must have gotten the hint because he reached down and turned up the Cyndi Lauper song on the eighties station.

By the time we pulled into the church, the sun had set. Lodan silently helped us unload a few more bins of supplies we'd brought from the other shelter. It was impressive how quickly the communities had gathered items and food and coordinated getting what was needed to each location. Once we'd unloaded, we went back to our temporary home base. I could tell Lodan was reluctant to face his moms. I hated to see him so sad and had an idea that I knew would either be brilliant or a complete disaster. I went with my gut, coerced my dad's phone from him one more time, and stepped out to make a call.

Forty-six

LODAN

PASADENA, CALIFORNIA
THURSDAY, OCTOBER 29, 2015

A couple hours at a park were not enough time to sort through the deluge of mind-altering truths I'd learned in the past few days. Each discovery within itself could have had me spinning for a week. To get it all at once made it impossible to separate my feelings about each person.

"Where did you go?" My mom looked awful. Her hair, pulled up in a messy pile on her head looked greasy, and she still wore the same clothes she'd been in through the entire fire ordeal. I noticed wrinkles on her face I hadn't seen before.

"I needed to think," I said. A mom-looking woman sobbed loudly in the other corner of the room while a couple of people rubbed her back and tried to comfort her.

My mom followed my eyes and said, "They just found out about an hour ago that their whole street burned. They lost everything but what they brought here. They are both teachers with only a few years to retirement. She told me they had just paid off their house with money from his father's passing."

I nodded, feeling guilty for being upset when I had a home to return to, filled with things from my whole life. We both hung our heads. I knew she must have felt the same guilt.

My mom told me she had volunteered the two of us to go help break down boxes in the back and put them in the recycling bin. I knew it was her way of getting me alone to talk. We worked beneath the outside light near the Dumpsters. The rotten, slightly sweet smell of waste emanated from the two overflowing garbage cans to the right of the recycling. I made a point to breathe through my mouth. She gave me the box cutter while she used a pair of scissors to slice through the tape.

"Are we going to be okay?" my mom asked me. I knew she must have been dying to ask me about my meeting with my father.

"Have you talked to . . . Sage or Dale?" I asked.

My mom sighed, tossed a flattened box into the bin, and nodded. "I didn't know she was like this. That she wasn't doing okay. I've followed Sage's career online and she's done well as a professor, doing research and winning awards. She's published in tons of journals. I thought she had made a good life for herself."

When I didn't respond, she continued. "I thought she'd been *relieved*."

I winced. "That I died?" I briskly sliced my box cutter down the seam.

She stopped mid-cut on the box in her hands. "It sounds so horrible now. But I convinced myself that this was a better life for all of us. I truly didn't think she wanted to be a mom. I think I was too young to understand. Now I can see she probably had postpartum or maybe suffered from depression even before she had you. We didn't know as much about all of that back then."

"But to pretend I died. To plant my shoe. Mom. You have to admit. It's . . . it's bat-shit crazy stuff." I tossed my box into the bin.

"I know. I'm the one who did it and I can't even believe I dared do it." She held the box with one foot and folded it smaller.

"What if one of them tells someone?" I asked. "What are we going to do?"

"I will have to take whatever punishment I get." She tossed her box into the bin.

"They'd put you in jail, Mom." I slid the box cutter through tape.

"I know. Trust me, I have lived with that looming shadow for fourteen years."

"You seem so calm about it."

"I've had plenty of time to think about this. And honestly, at least now, if it came to me going to jail, I know that you'd be fine. More than fine. Look, you drove across country with barely any money. You are basically grown." Tears clouded her eyes and slid down her face. "My job is done. You are an amazing person. I'm so . . ." She sniffed and swallowed a sob, "proud of who you are." She wiped at her face and I fought the urge to hug her.

Instead I bent to pick up another box. I wasn't ready to completely forgive her. She returned her focus to the box at her feet.

We worked in silence for a few boxes. Our rhythmic cutting and folding a stark contrast to the random cadence of the happy screams and hollers of a few kids still playing on the church playground off to our far right.

"Well, I met my dad today." I didn't stop my work and she didn't either. After a minute with no response I realized she was withholding her comments until I told her more.

"I look like him." I paused for a moment then added, "Well, an underfed and less fit version of him with fewer wrinkles."

Still silent.

"He was kind of a dick."

Nothing.

"Actually, correction. He *is* a dick."

Slice. Fold. Silent.

"Aren't you going to say I told you so?"

She stopped folding and gently placed her hand on my arm. "Is that what you thought I would say? Do you think I wanted your dad to be a dick to you?"

"Well, that way you don't have to worry about him trying to take me away, right?"

She closed her eyes for a moment. Then smiled and shook her head back and forth.

"I'd be lying if I didn't confess that I've always worried that if your father knew about you, he would try to take you. However, for your sake I'd rather he not be a dick. I know how long you've wanted to meet him. I know how important it's been to you. And I can imagine you had this built-up version of him in your head. It's probably almost impossible to not be disappointed. So, truthfully? I'm relieved for my sake that he didn't decide to sweep in and be the hero dad. But for your sake I kinda wished everything I'd heard about him wasn't true."

"He looked at me with distant amusement, like I was a punch line to one of life's long-running jokes or something."

My mother moved to hug me and I let her. I hugged her back and it struck me as odd how small she felt in my arms now. Me, the child, bigger than her. When had I last let my mom hug me? Why did I stop? I felt tears threaten but swallowed them and gently let her go. She wiped tears from her face and bent to pick up another box.

"How did you get so smart, so young?" she asked.

"Do you think he just needs time or do you think he really doesn't care he has a son?"

"I don't know, honey. I can't imagine meeting you wouldn't have a big impact. Maybe he needs time to process it. It's funny how time can change your perspective on things. Especially things that are family related."

"You mean like you and Sage?"

"For one. Yes."

My mom and I each threw our last box into the bin.

"Maybe we should invite Sage and Dale to come visit us in Laketown?" I suggested as we headed back toward the door and inside.

"I think it would be great if she could handle it." She pulled open the door.

We entered to find the main room as we'd left it: filled with piles of belongings, cots, and people. But now instead of the normal busy movement of people with no place to go, they all appeared frozen like a twisted fairy tale. We quickly discovered what held their shocked focus. A tall, disheveled, pale woman, wearing a navy business suit, her hair cut painfully short, wearing ugly chunky heels, and yelling hysterical nonsense tore through her luggage, throwing stuff to either side.

"Where are they?" she yelled, turning on the group closest to her. "Who took 'em? She fixed her steely gaze on a couple of middle-aged women who took a step back and pulled their frightened children closer.

"What's going on?" I asked a kid near me who looked about twelve.

"I guess that lady thinks someone took her stuff?" He shrugged.

"Who took my pills?" she yelled, pointing a long red-tipped finger as she scanned the crowd like the Wicked Witch staring down Dorothy and friends in *The Wizard of Oz*. "I need my pills!"

Pat quickly approached her with another volunteer. As the volunteer gathered the woman's stuff back into her luggage, Pat forcefully escorted her into the back office. The woman continued to throw accusations and stabbing stares at the people she passed.

As soon as the door closed, everybody went back to their own business. After a quick stop to wash our hands, we made our way back to our little corner in the shelter. We found Clara, Dale, and Lizzy playing cards.

"Where's Sage?" my mom asked.

"Out for a walk," Dale answered, not looking up from his hand.

"Hey," Lizzy said. "Mrs. Dawson, can you take over my hand? I wanted to show Lodan something."

I shot her a look but my mom readily agreed. They switched spots and I followed Lizzy back outside. At the door, we passed the group of kids running in from the playground.

We walked over to the swings. I sat while Lizzy remained standing.

"What's up?" I asked, her eyes level with mine and sparkling with amusement. I recognized the look. She was pleased with herself about something. "What are you up to now?" I asked, my heart kicking up a notch with a mixture of fear and anticipation.

"Don't get mad. Here." She handed me a phone.

"What?"

"I gave Mateo an abbreviated version of the last few days and . . ." She spoke quickly.

"Wait, what?"

"He's expecting your call."

"No way," I said, shoving my hands into my pockets. "I'm not unloading all my crap on him."

"I already did that. He knows all the crap. You can just use him as a sounding board."

"But why him? He barely knows me."

"That's why it's perfect." She dropped the phone and I quickly jammed my knees together to catch it in my lap.

"Password is off and his number is in contacts!" she called over her shoulder as she made a dash back to the shelter.

"I'm not calling!" I yelled after her.

"You're welcome!" she yelled back before disappearing inside the door.

I stared down at the phone in my hands. Mateo. Just thinking his name sent heat through my body. I shifted on the swing and looked around quickly as if somebody may have witnessed my instant involuntary arousal. I wished he were here in person, then just as quickly was grateful he wasn't. What if once I'd left he'd felt differently about me? What if what we'd felt had been only because we had nothing to lose? I was just passing through.

I jumped when the screen lit up in my hands: Mateo's name with a heart emoji. Lizzy's love that we both betrayed. I wondered briefly if there was a broken heart emoji. I didn't text much, let alone use emojis.

I locked my jaw, closed my eyes and answered. "Hey."

"Lodan?" My heart slammed in my chest. His voice. My name.

"Yeah," I managed.

"Hey."

"Hey," I repeated.

"Is this okay? That I called? Lizzy thought . . . Well, you know." And I heard the shakiness in his voice. He was nervous too. I felt a wave of relief. Nerves meant he cared what I thought.

"It's fine. I mean good. It's good," I stammered.

"Good," he repeated.

"So your dad turned out to be an asshole." He dove right in.

I smiled. "Pretty much." I dug my toe into the dirt beneath the swing.

"Well, mine can be one, too."

"Yeah."

"But at least you finally got to meet him."

"Yeah." Dr. K's smug smile flashed through my mind.

"It has to be better to at least know who he is," he said.

"I guess." God, I sounded like an idiot.

"And your mom. Wow! I thought I had a well-hidden secret. Your mom is like *Dateline* deceptive."

"I know. My life is kind of messed up." I looked up at the starless night sky.

"Nah. Not messed up, just different than you thought. But you're still the same person and really so is your mom. And she made you who you are, which I happen to think is pretty awesome." A nervous laugh followed. Then he cleared his throat. "I mean . . ."

"Thanks. You're pretty awesome yourself." I blushed, the compliment sending a momentary shiver of pleasure through me.

"So, Lizzy gave me a quick version of everything, but no details. What is your real mom like?" he asked.

"Well, it's kind of hard to know. A lot has happened since we met so she's been pretty emotional the whole time." I watched a man and a woman step outside the distant side door of the church.

"Do you look like her?"

"Not at all," I said.

"Too bad for her."

Another blush. "I look like my dad though. Only he's built more like you than me. You know . . ." I cleared my throat. "Fit and muscular. Like he works out a lot." The man and woman by the back door shared a cigarette. Their body language led me to believe they were not a couple.

Mateo laughed.

"What?" I asked.

"Lizzy said she wished she'd punched him. I'm just visualizing little Lizzy slamming her fist into a tall, muscled you. She'd have to stand on a chair or sucker punch him in the gut."

"Knowing her, she'd probably go for his balls." As soon as the word left my mouth I felt my body react. Why did I have to say something so sexual?

Mateo was quiet for a beat and I wondered what he was thinking.

"I wish I was there," he said.

"That's what I was thinking right before you called," I admitted.

"Really?"

"Really." I wiped a sweaty hand across my thigh.

"I told my mom," he said.

"About what?"

"You."

My stomach flipped and I twisted on the swing, making the chains wind around one another.

"What did you tell her?" I asked.

"That I understood about her and my dad and Seamus." Mateo paused, then added, "You know, Rooster."

"What do you mean?" I felt that tickle in my stomach. The one that felt better than waterfall mist on my skin.

"Well, I told you how my parents couldn't keep their hands off one another when I was younger and then it stopped and then I saw how my mom was with Seamus. She acted like she had with my dad, only different. Or maybe because I'm older my perspective is different. Anyway. I understand why she can't stay away from Seamus but yet she is afraid to leave my dad."

"You think she loves them both?"

"Yes. But in different ways. I love Lizzy, but not in a couple-like way. I love her as a friend. She helped me feel better about myself and taught me how to adjust my perspective on life. But . . . you." He sighed and my heart jumped in my throat. I froze the rocking swing in place and swallowed hard.

Mateo groaned and I pictured him running his hand across the top of his brush cut. "You make me want to jump in my car and drive to California." He said this all really fast.

I didn't know how to respond.

"Oh God. I'm freaking you out, aren't I? You have all this heavy stuff going on and . . ."

"No." I took a deep breath. "You're not freaking me out. I swear."

"I know we just barely met."

"Yes. But I think I know what you mean. When you got in the hot springs with me I finally understood what writers write about in books and movies and stuff." I squeezed my eyes shut, cringing. "God, that sounds super cheesy."

"No, it's nice."

"I know you have known you were into guys for a long time. I wasn't sure until I met you." I couldn't believe I'd said that out loud. "Now I'm probably freaking you out."

"No. I'm flattered. That's, I mean. Wow. That's cool." Mateo sounded sincere.

"What did your mom say?" I asked.

"She cried and hugged me and said she was worried."

I felt my heart sink. "Worried?"

"Not because of you. She liked you."

"Oh." Relief washed over me.

"Sorry. No she is worried about the whole distance thing and my feelings distracting me from college and stuff. Typical mom worries. Not that I think of you as a distraction."

"Your attraction distraction," I said, then wanted to kick myself.

I'm such a nerd. Thankfully, he laughed.

"Yes. My AD."

"Well, maybe it's better that I'm a distant distraction then." Though I felt the opposite.

"Ouch. So you're my D-A-D?"

"Your dad?" I asked. Another woman had joined the smoking circle.

"No. God no. Distant attraction distraction. But you do bring us back to what we should be discussing. I'm not supposed to be talking about how I feel. I'm supposed to be helping you feel better."

"You are," I insisted.

"Really?" Mateo asked.

"Really. Lizzy made another good call."

"She does that," he agreed.

"Yeah. I hate that we hurt her. That she's probably sitting inside, feeling a little left out." I wound the chains of the swing even tighter, lifting the swing higher from the ground.

"It does suck. But she is so amazing. You know she'll meet some lucky guy," Mateo said and I heard a few voices in the background.

"Yeah." I wondered where he was calling from.

"And if he hurts her, he'll have to deal with us," he said.

"Pretty sure you may be the only one that poses a threat. But perhaps I could belittle him with words."

"Okay, stop changing the subject. Tell me what you want to do about your dad."

"What do you mean? What can I do?" I asked

"He's your dad. Dude, you're going to let him off that easy?" I heard Mateo walking and the other voices faded.

"He made it pretty clear he wants no part of my life." I recalled being deemed a byproduct.

"He has no other kids, right?" Mateo closed a door on the other end of the line.

"Yeah."

"He just doesn't get it yet."

"What do you mean?" I let the swing unwind, taking me in backward circles.

"Adults that don't have kids, don't get the kid thing."

"How do you know? Do you have a kid?" I asked, mostly joking.

"No. But I have a Sebby and a Rooster," he said.

"I'm not following."

"So Rooster never wanted kids. He had a ton of older siblings, grew up poor, was frequently bullied, and pushed aside. He decided he'd never have kids."

"Then he met your mom and Sebby." I filled in the blanks.

"And he said it is his biggest regret in his life."

"Luckily he has you guys."

"Exactly. He told me he had no idea what he was missing until he hung out with us." I heard a touch of pride in his voice.

"I can't picture him talking about all of this stuff." I pictured the tattooed, weathered guy I'd met.

"Yeah well, my mom went to bed early with a headache one night and he found my dad's scotch. He let me try it. I hated it. But he really likes it. Anyway, he was kind of drunk I think," Mateo explained.

"Oh. I think I get that a little. I got a little drunk one night on our way here." I switched the phone to my other ear.

"I bet you were funny." I could hear the smile in his voice.

"I have no idea." I shook my head.

"Anyway, Rooster literally said he can't imagine his life before us. Like what he did with his time and stuff."

"But Rooster is nice and funny and basically a normal human. My dad, though, he seems like he doesn't even believe in real emotions." I sighed.

"Show him what they are," Mateo suggested.

"How?"

"Make him hang out with you."

"I can't make him and I don't even know that I want to hang out with a guy like him." The side door closed and I saw the smokers had gone back inside.

"Well, you should think about it. Sometimes I hate my dad, but I can't imagine him not being in my life," Mateo admitted.

"Maybe. Isn't he supposed to be home soon?" I asked.

"Maybe." His voice tightened.

"Are you going to tell him?" I asked.

"My mom said I have to." He sounded grim.

"I wish I could be there when you do," I said.

"Me too. But then again, maybe not. Who knows what he'd do to you?"

"You think he'd hurt me?" I tried to picture a bigger soldier version of Mateo.

"I don't know. He has a bad temper, lots of guns, lots of training, and I don't think you'd be the first guy he's taken out."

A chill ran down my spine. "Okay. Feel free to leave my name out of it."

Mateo laughed. "Yeah, well, I hope I'm exaggerating."

"I haven't told my mom yet either," I admitted.

"How do you think she'll react?"

"I think she'll be cool about it." I went back to twisting the swing chains.

"Yeah, she's not really in a place to judge."

"True. She'll probably be bummed I'm not with Lizzy. She loves her."

"My mom, too," Mateo said.

"You know my mom could go to jail if Sage or Dale tell anyone what she did."

Mateo didn't say anything.

I pulled the phone from my ear and checked the screen before I asked, "You there?"

"Yeah. I'm just thinking about it. How I'd feel. What I might do," Mateo said.

"It's messed up." I looked back up at the sky again, searching for any sign of a star.

"It really is." His voice had genuine concern and I wished I could see his face.

"But she's my mom. Basically. And she's a good person."

"Who kidnapped her sister's son and let a whole bunch of people think he died," he pointed out.

"To protect me." Why was I defending her?

"Was your real mom that dangerous?" Mateo asked.

"I don't know. I guess she did drugs and drank and didn't want to take care of me most of the time."

"Is that what she's like now? Like an addict or something?"

"Not really. I mean, she's a professor and published and won awards and stuff. She can't be too crazy." I let the twisted chains go again, lifted my feet, and the swing circled free.

"Yeah, I Googled both of them after Lizzy called. Both your real parents seem pretty successful."

"Yeah, but she seems emotionally unstable and he seems emotionally . . . I don't know. Defunct."

"Makes you wonder what they talked about when they hung out." Mateo's tone was teasing now.

"Maybe they didn't talk much," I suggested.

"True."

Again the sexual charge hung in the air. I cleared my throat.

"Have you talked to Sage or Dale about what they plan to do?" Mateo asked.

"No." I began twisting the chains again.

"Maybe you should. I'm guessing you don't want your mom to go to jail. They might listen to you and do what you want."

I heard Mateo's mom call for him in the background.

"It's weird, you know? I don't feel any connection to Sage like I do to my mom. You'd think there would be some kind of primal connection to your biological mother over your aunt."

"Well, you'd think that men and women would only be attracted to each other since reproduction is necessary for the existence of the human race. Biology is obviously not as black-and-white as math."

"Clearly," I agreed.

"I think you need to talk to Sage," he said.

"What if she wants me to move to California and live with her?" I voiced one of my fears.

"You'd be closer to me." I heard his mom call him again. "Sorry. Selfish thought," he said.

"Not close enough to really make a difference. Besides, I don't want to live with strangers. I want to stay with my mom, finish school, get my license. God, do you realize all of this happened just because I wanted to get my license?" I shook my head and switched ears again.

"Listen, I don't want to go but I have to. I have two oil changes to get done and then a ten-page paper I haven't really started for AP English."

"That sounds so nice and normal." School felt a world away.

"Talk to Sage. And when you get a phone again, call me." I heard him pass through a door again.

"If I get a phone again. I'm not sure how we will afford to replace two phones and a car."

"Insurance?" Mateo suggested.

"Hopefully." I twisted the swing chains another turn, pulling myself higher off the ground.

"Mateo?"

"Yeah?"

"I'm glad Lizzy had you call. I was worried that . . ."

"We just imagined all those feelings because we didn't have to ever see each other again?"

"Exactly," I said, letting out a breath. He really got me.

"Yeah, Lizzy said she thought you'd think that. It's real, Lodan. And I plan to make sure we see each other again."

My heart raced at the thought. It kicked into high gear when I heard something and unwound the swing chains to check behind me.

"Lodan?"

"I'm here." I didn't see anyone but I had that feeling that someone was there. I squinted into the darkness between where the light pole halo ended and the tree border began.

"You do want to meet up, right?"

"Yes. Absolutely." My heart raced at the thought.

"Good. You scared me for a minute."

"Sorry. I thought I heard someone coming up behind me. But I guess I got my mom's crazy."

"Better hope it's not my dad," Mateo teased.

"Funny."

"Okay, well. When you get access to a communication device I better be your first connection."

"Good luck talking to your dad if that happens before we speak again," I said.

"Thanks."

"Okay." I let out a breath.

We both sat silent for a few moments. I could hear him breathing and found it comforting. Maybe he was as reluctant as I was to sever the line. Eventually he did. I sat there staring down at the screen even after it went black.

"Hey." I jumped at the unexpected voice behind me. As I untwisted back to the natural swing position Sage walked out of the shadows and sat on the swing next to me.

"Hi," I said and then felt heat creep into my face as I wondered how much of my conversation she'd heard. Had I said anything really bad about her?

She began to swing next to me. I watched her, my eyes tracking her as she slowly gained momentum and height.

"Your mom and I used to have a swing set in our backyard."

I didn't respond.

"I'd go as high as my legs could pump and then jump into the pile of leaves we'd raked for just that purpose. She would swing and jump, too. But she never dared jump at the peak of the swing like me. She always had to wait for it to slow down to a safer height before leaping. I wasn't nice about it either. I called her chicken. Dared her to do it for Popsicles or candy or whatever I thought might tempt her. She never gave in. She took the safe jump every time."

"Sounds like mom," I said.

"Studies often show that the firstborn is the more cautious child while the younger siblings are more likely to be risk takers. Not in our family. If it was risky, I tried it. Heather held on to the railing while I went straight off the rails.

"But I knew she envied me for taking risks. I read it in her diary once." She locked eyes with me briefly. "I know, what a jerk, right? Reading my sister's diary?"

"She always tried to get me to keep one," I said.

"Yeah? Me too. She said maybe I should write down some of the crazy things I wanted to do rather than actually doing them."

"Sounds safer." I shrugged.

"Sure. Safe, but boring." This was a new side to Sage. Even her voice sounded stronger.

"But then she surprised us all. Safe Heather. She took a risk so daring, so completely unbelievable, I almost fell for it myself." She swung in silence for a moment.

"You know how your grandmother died, right? Brain aneurysm. It's quick. Here one second looking completely healthy; gone the next. But I was there. My mom took a step, a freshly picked tomato in her hand, and then this look came over her face. Like someone flicked a switch that turned her off. She said one word and before I could even take one step, she dropped to the floor like one of those kid toys that stand rigid or fall by pushing the button on the bottom that tightens and releases the springs. Have you seen the ones I mean? We had a Pinocchio one."

I didn't answer but she didn't wait.

"Anyway. My mom did say one thing right before she hit the ground. You know what it was? Heather. I was standing right there in front of her and she said Heather. As if her dying thought wasn't of me or her husband but precious little fragile Miss Safety."

I remained still on my swing, not daring to move. Trying to imagine watching my mom die.

"I know you grew up without a dad. And that is sucky. Of course, he is kind of sucky." She clucked her tongue then continued. "When my mom died, it was like someone drained all the color out of life. She made everything fun. Brussels sprouts were baby lettuce, church a fashion show with singing, the frickin' dentist meant one-on-one time over hot fudge sundaes after." She looked off into the dark, sniffed, then turned her eyes back on me.

"And she was brilliant." She began to swing again. "Way smarter than my dad. Smarter than anyone I've ever met. Well, except maybe your father, but he barely qualifies as human. And then she just left. Poof. Like the color tube blew on our TV set. We went from a colorful, happy family home to a gray, three guest bed and breakfast. We did not function well as a tripod. My life went from perfect to shitty and hasn't really ever recovered."

She stopped again suddenly and looked at me hard.

"Your dad. He loved how broken I was. Loved studying my brain. He picked through our conversations like a malnourished boy picking turkey from the bone. He savored each morsel as if he alone could consume me and I would come out the other side of his magnificent brain whole again. All back in one happy normal piece. Once he'd gotten all he could from me and it became clear I was beyond repair, he moved on to another young, attractive, tattered cut of meat. But, surprise, instead of a cure he gave me you. Foolish me. I thought you were like some kind of sign from my mom. Like, this guy really had been important to returning my happiness. He provided the seed I needed for the person that would make me happy about living again. You were going to put the color back in my life. And God, when you were born: this tiny thing. Long but lean; like you are now, in a way. With those green eyes. My mom's eyes. Another sign. You didn't cry, which I didn't know at the time but can be a bad sign. It wasn't. You were perfect."

She smiled and even in the dim light I saw the shine of tears in her eyes.

"I looked down at you and braced myself for the color to return; to feel its warmth embrace us. Instead I felt . . ." Sage laughed. "Numb. For weeks, then months. Numb. I tried to be like my mom. I tried so hard. Harder than I've tried to do anything. They gave me drugs. They turned numb to tired and then when I woke up, numb. Every time I looked at you, I saw her looking back at me; asking me why I couldn't be like her."

She looked off into space another moment, then another angry laugh. Her head lolled on her neck like it was hard for her to hold it in place.

"But Heather? She knew exactly what to do. She became Mom. And it was so damn easy for her. She got the color. I remained stuck in gray and she got your color. I hated her. Despised her. But then she'd make you laugh. Make you so happy and I was so grateful she took care of you. I felt guilty. And poor Dale. God, how he tried. He loved you, too. Was so good with you. Some days he'd talk about the three of us being a family and if I'd had enough to drink and no pills, I'd see it. I'd believe it. The color danced right there within my reach. But I'd turn my back on it every time."

The way she talked made me nervous, like she was drunk or something.

"That day at the lake. It was like that, too. The day started all sunshine and color and hope and happiness. Then in came the gray clouds and you were gone. I remember the very last thing you said to me. You were driving these little Matchbox cars around on my arms and legs. And you drove up to my shoulder. You stopped the little ambulance right next to my cheek. You leaned down and fixed your green eyes on mine. You rested your tiny hand on my other cheek and you said, 'Don't be sad.' And you smiled." Sage wiped at her cheeks. "And then I guess you must have run to Heather who we now know tempted you into the woods with a Tonka truck and all her color."

She began to swing. She pumped hard and giggled. I began to feel nervous that she might jump like she used to or something. I wanted to run inside but I didn't dare leave her.

"But you know what, Lodan? I have secrets, too. Yep. Your mom, she thought she had all the secrets but I got more. You want to hear them?"

I wanted to run inside.

"You don't talk much, do you, Michael?"

I shrugged. "I guess."

"You guess or you guess not? Let's play truth or dare. Have you ever played?"

"Once or twice as a kid."

"Your choice: truth or dare. But remember I'm not Miss Safety like your mom. So choose carefully." She continued to pump and swing with a crazed abandon.

"Truth," I yelled.

She laughed for a second and I thought she might jump anyway. Then she dropped her feet down and dragged herself to a stop. I winced as I watched her legs, sure they would snap. But they didn't.

"Good choice." She turned in her swing to look at my face. "Remember how your mom said she came back to check on me and I sent her off with our mom's jewelry?"

"Yes."

"I knew. When I sent her away, I knew what she'd done. I knew the whole plan. Oh, she had me fooled at the lake and when I got home I thought you were dead. I really did. But then I started thinking and something felt off. If you were really gone, she would not have left that lake. She would have been the last person to give up on you. Yet, she took off to take care of herself. Asthma attack, my ass. The other thing about your mom. She is very organized. She has patterns that are easy to follow. I bet she still changes out her purse once a year and relives each little scrap as she does it, doesn't she?"

I nod, still caught on the "I knew."

"She did a decent job of pulling it all together. She really did. But she forgot to grab her diary. She must have gotten it when she came back 'cause I never saw it again. But she forgot to take it when she took you. And I found it that night and read every little detail of her fucked-up plan. I thought about calling the cops. I thought about showing up at her hotel door. She even had the addresses of three of the places written in the diary. It wouldn't have been hard to find you guys."

"Why didn't you?"

"Because, Michael, I am not my mother, and I am not my sister. I turn my back on the color every damn time and run straight for the darkness. I took a bunch of pills, drank too much. Passed out. And your mom woke me up. It was so funny to see her so guilt-ridden, so frightened. This was Heather taking a risk. The mother of all risks. One word and she would have caved. I saw it in her eyes. She still wasn't sure if she could go through with it."

She twisted in the swing, her head loose on her neck, her hair drifting into her face.

"Sage?" I felt a chill run up and down my back. "Are you okay?"

"I'm fine." She laughed but her words slurred.

"Do you want me to get Dale?"

"Dale?" She spat his name out like old chewing gum. Then she repeated, "Dale," and began to cry.

I stood to get help.

"Sit down," she yelled. I jumped but complied.

"I'm   not   done."

"Sorry, you just seem a little . . ."

"Fucked up? Yeah, well, that's nothing new. But I need to finish my T-R-U-T-H." She whispered the letters.

"Did Dale know?" I asked, suddenly realizing how shocked he'd been when we met.

"No. God, no. Do you think he would have let you go?" She laughed. "No, poor Dale was fooled by both Silverman girls. Oh wait. Heather is a Dawson, now." Sage fell into a fit of giggles. I began to slide off my swing and sneak away when she turned her eyes on me.

"Do you know where she got your last name? From her favorite TV show at the time, *Dawson's Creek*. Kinda cheesy, huh?" Her head lolled again. I held my breath and debated what to do.

"I better wrap it up before I fall outta this swing." She wrapped her arms around the chains and linked her hands together. "Where was I? Oh yeah. Your mom. She sat at the end of my bed, like my mom used to do each night before bed. She was talking but I wasn't really listening. I wasn't really seeing her. I felt my mom there. And I swear I had this moment. It sounds crazy, but I heard my mom's voice as clear as you talking to me right now. I mean in a way it was Heather sitting there. But then it wasn't and my mom, she said, 'Let him go, Sage. Let them both go. If you let them go, I'll stay with you.'" She looked at me, tears streaming down her face. "She told me to do it and I believed her. I thought she'd bring the color back if I let you go. So I did. I let you both go."

She looked down at her feet twisting in the dirt, her hands still tightly entwined to keep her arms wrapped around the chains. I saw her back shaking with sobs and I felt sorry for her. I felt an ache in my chest. I'd never witnessed a sadness this dark.

"But you know what?" Her voice was small now, whiny. "She lied. The color never came back. Mom did sometimes. When I really needed her. But she lied about the color, Michael. Heather got to keep you *and* all the color."

I couldn't take it anymore. I stood up. "Sage, let's go inside. Come on. Let's find Dale."

And like a magician, Dale walked out the door of the church.

"Hey, over here," I said.

He jogged over and as he stepped up to her swing Sage swung forward then back, letting go and falling back like an exhausted child dropping into bed. We each caught a shoulder and gently set her back onto the playground dirt. Dale blocked the swing with his body.

"Sage? Honey. Did you take something?" Dale asked.

"Not me. Heather. She took all the color."

Dale glanced up at me. "How long has she been like this?"

I shrugged. "I don't know. At first she seemed fine but then she started acting kinda drunkish. Maybe ten minutes ago?"

"Sage, what did you take? I didn't think you had your pills on you."

"I don't want to do this anymore, Dale. I'm tired and look, you have Michael back. You don't need me. Mom misses me. She says it all the time." Dale looked at me and I saw the fear in his eyes. "Go inside, have them call 911 and find out what kind of pills that lady is missing."

I sat there frozen in place, trying to catch up.

"Go! Call 911 and find out the pill type. Jesus, kid," Dale yelled.

I leaped up and ran for the building. "I'm sorry," I yelled. And as the door closed behind me I heard Sage yell, "I'm not sad anymore, Michael."

Forty-seven

LIZZY

LAKETOWN, NY
FRIDAY, JUNE 21, 2019

I picked up a small stone and threw it up to click against Lodan's window. Nothing. I found another and tried again. The shade flipped up, then the window and then a voice.

"Lizzy!" Mrs. Dawson leaned out the window, her hair pulled back in a braid. She wore a green fuzzy robe. She waved her hand toward the house. "Come in and meet me in my room."

I'd been hoping for Lodan but was eager to see Mrs. Dawson as well. I ran around to the front and let myself into the kitchen. Wow, I thought to myself. She had torn down the wall between the living room and opened up the kitchen. Updated white cupboards and high-end appliances brightened the inside. The brick fireplace had been painted white. An unexpected wave of nostalgia brought the prick of tears to my eyes when they fell on a black-and-white photo of Lodan and me standing in front of Massachusetts Institute of Technology (MIT) in Boston. I pulled it down to study it closer. He'd just started growing his hair long. It partially covered his eyes where they locked on the camera. Our arms were cast around one another. I wore a flowered sundress and high ponytail and he proudly wore an MIT T-shirt. The tourist we'd asked to snap the shot had caught me mid-laugh, looking up at Lodan and pointing to where he had dripped ice cream down his front. The drip had transformed the "I" into a mini cone on his shirt. We'd just had a debate as to how he could love coffee ice cream but still hate coffee as a beverage. It had been another one of our road trips the summer after my backyard high school graduation and right before his senior year. We went college shopping for him, and MIT—his first choice and current home—had been our last stop. I'd left the next day for Costa Rica.

"Lizzy?" Mrs. Dawson called from her room. "I'm in here."

I set the frame back on the mantel, wiped the unexpected tears away, and went to find her. I knocked on the door lightly before opening it to a completely updated version of her old bedroom. The walls had been stripped of their old flower wallpaper and painted a light gray. The worn multicolored Walmart rug and mismatched cover and pillows were gone. The current rug, chair, and duvet cover were complementary shades of gray. This room felt calm, comfortable, and peaceful. Her pillows and a painting I'd sent her for Christmas my first year in Costa Rica brought a nice touch of color to the room.

"Wow, the house looks amazing!" I said and she turned to wrap me in a big hug.

"It is so great to see you! How can a year pass this quickly?" She held me away from her. "I'd hoped to see you when I visited Lodan in Boston, but I suppose you needed to visit Alex in Costa Rica," she said.

"Yeah, sorry. It was the only chance I had to go see him last semester," I replied.

"And a good place to escape to during the end of the winter months," Mrs. Dawson said.

"This is true," I agreed.

"Lodan should be back in about an hour. He went to get Mateo at the airport."

"I thought Mateo got in last night?" I watched as she applied mascara in front of her mirror.

"His flight was canceled. Mechanical issue with the plane." She looked at me through the mirror.

"Surprised he didn't ask them to let him take a look at it." I laughed.

"When do you head back to Boston?" she asked.

"I'm here a week, but then I have to be back to work and move all my stuff."

"That's right. The three amigos back together again. Is Alex okay with you living with two guys?" She opened her closet and began to slide hangers along the rack, searching for something to wear.

I hesitated. Did I want to talk about Alex? No, not yet. "Yeah, he's met them both." Best to keep it simple for now. I slipped the hair tie off my wrist and pulled my hair up into a loose bun.

"Good for you. We were disappointed he couldn't come for the wedding," Mrs. Dawson said.

"Yeah. Sorry. This is a busy time of year for him. He runs five different kids camps in three-week intervals. I feel bad I can't help him this year, but there is a visiting professor at Boston College whose class I really wanted to take this summer. Besides, Alex found a replacement for me."

"I love that you follow your own path. You all have. I don't feel like any of you compromised your education for a relationship." She pulled out a blouse and stepped into her bathroom.

"I can't keep up with where you all are with your schooling. Will this be your sophomore or junior year this fall?" she yelled through the door.

"My work in Costa Rica counted toward sociology credits, so after my summer work I will be a second semester sophomore. If I take classes next summer, I can graduate the same year as Lodan and we can have one big party."

"That sounds fun. But I'm in no rush. I'll see you all even less after that." She stepped out wearing jeans and a shirt.

"You could come visit us," I suggested.

"We will." She squirted perfume on herself, then on me. I didn't remember her wearing perfume in the past.

"Do you need help with things today before the rehearsal dinner tonight?"

"Always." She smiled. In fact, do you want to ride with me to pick up some chairs and tables I'm borrowing from the church? I had planned on the boys' help but it looks like it's you and me. This is Jason's last day in the clinic before being gone for two weeks."

"I'd love to."

"Oh, and are you okay staying in the office again? Mateo and Lodan are in his room and Emerald City continues to expand in our guest room."

"Any exciting new additions to the booming metropolis?" I asked, peeking through the ajar door to his creation.

Mrs. Dawson headed down the stairs. "Who knows? He and Mateo have been converting it all into a self-sustaining green city."

"I heard. I guess the name is fitting." I followed on her heels. "They make quite the team."

"And relentless in their pursuit of green." She opened the door to the office where she'd made up the sleeper sofa for me and laid out fresh towels. "They have me down to one small bag of trash a week. Composting is a pain, but my garden loves it." She gestured toward the lush lawn and small garden.

"Thanks for letting me crash here again. I'm going to go grab my stuff and then I'm all yours," I said and dashed out to the car. I was a little disappointed the boys hadn't returned yet. I really needed their advice and the sooner the better.

Forty-eight

LODAN

LAKETOWN, NY
FRIDAY, JUNE 21, 2019

As I'd waited for Mateo's plane to come in, old fears had resurfaced. What if after months apart we'd both changed so much that our chemistry had changed? What if our spark had faded? He'd been in Germany doing his first of two co-op positions required for his degree in civil engineering. He'd moved to Boston to attend Wentworth Institute of Technology the year before my acceptance to MIT. Our families had initially been concerned that his choice had been driven by its proximity to my dream school. I'm sure it didn't hurt, but his initial interest stemmed from a lengthy conversation with the admissions woman he'd met at a college fair. Either way, he had thrived at the school and become deeply passionate about helping the world go green.

    I watched as a heterosexual couple said good-bye outside security. I envied the ease with which they could publicly display their emotions without fear of repercussions. The woman looked a little like a young Sage, with her free-flowing colorful skirt and long dark hair. A fresh wave of worry momentarily pushed Mateo out of my mind: seeing Sage again.

    Luckily, four years ago in California, they had gotten Sage to the hospital in time. However, as Heather and I had waited with Dale while doctors pumped her stomach and stabilized her, Dale painted a grim picture of the side of Professor Sage Silverman's life that hadn't come up on Google. Dale explained her long history with depression and delusional disorder, including six suicide attempts, even a two-year stay in a psychiatric facility. The latter was prompted by another overdose after attending my grandfather's funeral. Sage truly believed my dead grandmother had returned when my mom took me. She held conversations with her and insisted Grandma guided her as needed. Dale confirmed Sage had tried to tell him on a number of occasions that I was alive and living with her sister in a small town in western New York. He had assumed it was part of the delusion. My mom had taken it all very hard. Dale confessed that as hard as it had been to lose me and as angry as he'd originally been with my mom, he had to admit that Sage would not have been able to handle motherhood. They made their peace. Dale did not see how anyone would gain by the authorities learning the truth. My mom stayed in touch, sometimes through Dale if Sage was having a hard time. I hadn't seen her since California. It had been cowardly of me. But everyone would be at my mom and Dr. Payne's wedding.

The latest group of arriving passengers had begun to file out of the gate area toward the baggage claim. I scanned the crowd for Mateo, my heart pounding, my mouth dry. I needed a mint. I dug around in my pocket for my Tic Tacs, took them out, and shook one into my mouth. When I looked up again Mateo filled my view.

"Hey, handsome," he flashed that dimpled, crooked grin and I immediately realized how foolish I'd been to ever doubt how he'd make me feel. He pulled me to his broad, firm chest and we hugged tightly for a moment. I still had a few inches on him in height, but he had a few inches on me in the chest. I breathed in his scent of soap, deodorant, and a musk unique to him. This never got old. He pulled back and brushed his lips with mine. I longed for more, but we'd learned early on in our relationship that PDA invited unwanted attention. We'd been harassed once outside Fenway by a trio of big, drunk, angry Red Sox fans. We were walking back to Mateo's student housing after a few drinks with his classmates. I hadn't even realized we were holding hands until they began to taunt us. At first we ignored them. This wasn't the first time we'd been verbally chastised for our relationship. Usually people got bored when we didn't react and continued on their way. But these three began to follow us. When we picked up our pace, so did they.

"I think these homos need a lesson in sex education," one yelled.

"Yeah, the birds, the bees, and broken knees." They all laughed and Mateo squeezed my hand and cut his eyes at me. I knew he'd been in fights before. And he held his own, but he and I both knew I wouldn't fare well in a fight. We weren't far from his place, but the last thing they needed was his address. One of them chucked a partially full beer at us, and it soaked the back of my shirt before dropping to the ground. Another empty can followed, clipping the back of Mateo's head. He stopped and turned around. I stopped next to him, turned, and said, "Don't. They aren't worth it."

"Ooh, the big one's gonna get us, boys." The jerk's teeth were crooked and stained yellow.

"I don't know if we can play. My dad told me I couldn't hit girls." They all found this hilarious.

But then I saw the smaller bald guy pull something out of his boot and with a flick, the light from the street pole glinted off a blade. A hot chill ran through my body as fear commanded every hair on my head to attention.

Without moving my lips I whispered to Mateo, "Knife. Run." And I charged straight toward them for the first few paces before I quickly dodged to their right, into the street, and sprinted as fast as I could down an alley that I knew dropped us out near a couple of the more popular bars. We needed to get into a crowd fast. Mateo followed my lead and I'm sure could have outrun me. When we looked back, the men hadn't even bothered to chase us. But we blended into the crowd for a few blocks before walking the long way around. We'd turned a ten-minute walk into thirty. All because we'd casually held hands on the walk home.

I scanned the baggage claim area to see if anyone had been offended by our embrace, then pointed to his backpack. "Is that it or did you check one?" I asked.

"This is it." He hitched his backpack higher on his shoulder.

"Where are your glasses?" Mateo asked.

"Oh, I forgot. Surprise!" I raised my eyebrows up and down. "Contacts."

"I thought you hated them?"

"I do, well, I did. I pushed through it and they're fine now. No biggie."

"And you cut your hair," Mateo said.

"You don't like it?" I asked, running my hand through the side. I'd worn it long and usually pulled back in a ponytail for the last few years. But the other day I went in for a haircut and spontaneously told him to cut it short again. It remained longer on top.

"I do. It's kinda sexy, that floppy top bit." He raised his eyebrows at me and my entire body reacted. Heat flooded my face.

"Glad to see I can still make you blush." We pushed through the doors to the outside.

"I love these smaller airports," Mateo commented.

"It'd be better if they flew a few more places direct," I said, breathing in the contrast of warm fresh air and idling cars.

"So how's our best girl?" Mateo asked as we headed toward short-term parking.

"I haven't seen her yet. She was due in this morning. She stopped on her drive back to see her dad somewhere on Keuka Lake."

"Is that where he's living now?" Mateo asked.

"He's stayed six months now," Lodan said. "Apparently, the girlfriend from Atlanta moved with him."

"Wow! That's new." Mateo scanned the lot.

"I know," I said, stopping beside a green Jeep Wrangler. "But I think Lizzy feels better about him having somebody. She still feels guilty that he's alone."

"His choice. Where's your truck?" Mateo looked around.

"This is us." I unlocked the passenger door.

Mateo laughed and shook his head. "Let me guess, you got it for nothing."

"I did. And I made fifteen hundred off the truck, which is much greener now."

Mateo tossed his bag in the back and climbed in.

"You started the whole car greening thing." I climbed into the driver's seat.

"And created a monster." Mateo squeezed my leg.

"A Jeep will be fun for the summer. Maybe we can take it to the Cape." I started the car.

"Right. Like any of us will have time or money enough to go away."

"Rent will be split three ways now," I pointed out.

"Yes, but Lizzy will also have us signed up for a million evening and weekend commitments for whatever her most pressing causes are this summer."

"True." I noticed he'd left his hand on my knee. A comforting distraction. "I bet your mom and Sebby were glad to see you." Mateo had gone home from Germany to spend a week with them.

"Yeah. It was nice. She spoiled me with all my favorites. Sebby continues to amaze. He's such a cool kid. And thank you for the perfect Christmas gift. You were spot on about the aquaponics thing. He's really into it. You gotta see his system. It's amazing. My mom is not as thankful. She's not a fan of the odd collection of bathtubs he's now using for the fish."

"Bathtubs?" I laughed.

"Yeah, and the cherry on top? A toilet." He raised his eyebrows.

"Nice!" I said.

"Pink!" His smile widened to dimple length.

"Vintage!"

"That was all Rooster. I'm pretty sure my mom gave him a decent dose of the silent treatment for that one."

"So they're good?" I leaned out the window to pay for parking.

"Great. He only drives overnight hauls if they need a sub. He's on site full time, living and working side by side with my mom."

"That's great."

"Yeah, I haven't seen her this happy in a long time." Mateo sighed as we pulled onto the highway.

"It's too bad they couldn't have come to the wedding. I think our moms would have a great time together," I said.

"Nobody to man the shop. Plus, you know Sebby and routine." Mateo tried to adjust the AC.

"I know. It's all good. Hopefully my mom and Dr. Payne can visit them sometime," I said. "The AC isn't connected. Natural cooling only." I rolled my window down.

"Of course." Mateo shook his head and rolled his down, letting in a blast of fresh air.

"So, have you made any progress in the dad department?" Mateo asked me.

I sighed. This was not our best topic. "Not really. He keeps sending checks but he doesn't respond to my letters."

"Are you still not cashing his checks?"

I shot him a look.

He shrugged. "Just asking."

"And my mom and I finished paying off the car, too."

"I thought you said you had payments through August?" Mateo asked.

"I was going to but I made the money on the truck, remember?"

"Sweet. I still say he can't be completely defunct if he was kind enough to ship you out a new car."

"I won't disagree that it saved our asses, but we didn't ask him for anything."

"Yeah, well, I could kiss Dale for guilting him into it."

"You better not kiss Dale. Or any guy but me," I said and flipped on the radio.

He shot me a look, leaned in as if to kiss me, and teasingly turned back toward the radio to switch the station.

"So that's how it is," I said. "Maybe you'll have to sleep in the office and Lizzy can bunk with me."

"As if." He rolled his eyes at me and I liked that he and I both knew we wouldn't be able to keep our hands off each other as soon as we were alone in a room together. I just hoped that would be sooner than later.

Forty-nine

LIZZY

LAKETOWN, NY
FRIDAY, JUNE 21, 2019

The guys showed up at Dr. Payne's house five minutes after we'd finished setting up all the chairs in his lawn for the sunset ceremony the following evening. I loved that the lake where they'd shared their first date, kayaking with us, would serve as the backdrop to their vows. Lodan had built them a wedding arch that we'd secured on the dock. The attendees would be seated on the lawn but the bride and groom would stand at the front of the dock, under the arch. Mrs. Dawson and I were standing on the dock when the boys ran up behind us. Lodan scooped his mom into the air and Mateo snatched me from behind and headed to the edge as if to toss me in.

"Don't you dare, Mateo, or my foot may brain damage your future children," I warned. My foot was in perfect position to connect with his family jewels. He dropped me so quickly I almost fell. He reached out a steading arm. I smacked his shoulder, then gave him a proper hug. His touch didn't give me butterflies anymore, but I did feel a rush of love at the sight and smell of him. He'd told me a dozen times how grateful he is that we stayed close friends in spite of how he'd hurt me. I couldn't imagine life without either of them by my side. Though it's often been only in spirit the past few years, I looked forward to our year ahead together in Boston. Well, I had been looking forward to it until recently.

"Feeling neglected!" Lodan interjected and I realized that I hadn't released Mateo.

"Sorry." I turned and hugged Lodan. "Lost in my head for a minute."

"Bet that's an entertaining spot," Mateo said.

"Where?" Mrs. Dawson asked, slipping into the conversation.

"Lizzy's mind." Lodan gently tugged on my ponytail.

Mateo let out an approving whistle. "Wow. Lodan." He stood admiring the wedding arch. Lodan had rescued a chapel's large curved window frame. The glass panes were gone but the curved wooden insets gave it an elegance. On either side of the tall window stood rescued barn doors. He'd sawed an *H* out of one and an *E* out of the other. He'd whitewashed all the wood to make it more cohesive. He'd used pine boughs, white and silver ribbon, and solar-powered lights to form a romantic, decorative garland. The calm, glimmering lake could be seen through the window and letter cutouts. The solar lights would make it a nice backdrop even after the sunset. "It's perfect." The pride in his eyes and voice made me momentarily envious. Not that I wanted Mateo to look at me like that, but to have someone I loved look at me like that. They had no idea how lucky they were.

"Thanks. Dr. Payne helped me." Red crept into Lodan's face.

"Jason," Mrs. Dawson corrected. "He's going to be family, honey. And don't be so humble. Jason told me all he did was hold pieces in place while you connected them."

"Well, when you're a poor college student, you have to get creative with your gifts." He shrugged. "So what do you need us to do, Mom? We are at your service." Lodan bowed.

"Actually tomorrow I'll need help putting all the chair covers on. Other than that we hired a bunch of kids from the school to set up the reception stuff under the tent. We have caterers and a florist and a photographer. Jason spoils me." She shrugged and teared up.

"You deserve it, Mom," Lodan said and pulled her close for a hug, which sent tears spilling down her face. I looked at Mateo and we threw our arms around both of them in a giant group hug.

"Hey, get off my future wife," Dr. Payne called from his driveway where he'd pulled up. He climbed out of his truck.

We broke up the love fest and Mrs. Dawson wiped at her eyes. "I thought you were busy all day," she said as she walked up to meet him with a kiss.

"Stopped in for a quick lunch and to see if you were okay with all the setting up. But I can see you are in capable hands." He reached out to shake hands with Mateo. "Welcome back." He gave Lizzy's shoulder a squeeze. "It's good to see you guys. But stop making my bride cry." He wrapped a protective arm around Mrs. Dawson's shoulder.

She patted his chest. "It's not their fault. I think I'm a little emotional. Why don't you three head over to Minnie's and catch up over lunch while I fix something for Jason here? He won't have time to dine out."

They headed inside and we piled into the Jeep for the quick drive to the other side of the lake. After we'd caught up with Minnie and one of the bartenders back for the summer, we grabbed a seat, ordered, and Mateo excused himself to use the bathroom.

"Spill," Lodan said as soon as Mateo was out of earshot.

"What?" I asked.

"I know you. What's wrong? Alex? Do I need to send Mateo down to set him straight?"

"I do need to talk, but I don't think it's a bathroom break conversation."

"Is it not for both of us to hear?" Lodan asked. "You've decided not to live with us after all because now that you've been reminded of how hot Mateo is, you're afraid you won't be able to hold yourself back?" Lodan smiled.

When I didn't come back with a teasing retort, I saw his face fall. "Sorry," he said. "I get the feeling it's not a light conversation."

"Not really."

"Why not talk to both of us?"

"Hard to explain without getting into the whole thing." I spotted Mateo heading back and switched topics. "So I think we should plan a huge joint graduation party."

"For who?" Mateo asked, sitting down.

"Well, I'm taking enough credits over the next two summers to graduate in two years with Lodan."

"Perfect. But don't plan on dragging him off to Costa Rica with you straight after. I'll still have a year left in my masters in Boston."

"You could visit us on breaks," I teased, putting an arm around Lodan and pulling him toward me.

Mateo's phone buzzed and he looked down at the screen. His face darkened and he sighed. He reached for his phone, hesitant. "This could be a bit," he said apologetically.

"Your dad?" Lodan asked. Mateo nodded. He answered, got up, and walked toward the empty side of the dock.

"So that's still a struggle?" I asked Lodan.

He nodded, sighed, and took a long sip of his iced tea. "His dad cannot understand how hard he made life for Mateo or why Mateo can't quickly get over the hypocrisy of it all."

One of the strangest and most difficult developments that took place soon after the Truth-Seeking Trip was learning the truth about the Colonel. When Mateo sat down with his parents and came out to his father, his father's reaction floored everyone. The Colonel burst into tears. This man who'd done multiple tours—Mateo had never seen him cry. He apologized, claimed it was his fault. Then he proceeded to confess that he hadn't actually been deployed again the last year and a half. In reality he had retired and had been working as a contractor because it meant he could spend more time with his soul mate. That wasn't the most hurtful part. The heart-piercing part was the fact that his soul mate was a man. In all those years of pushing his son toward girls and shaming him for not having a girlfriend, he'd been in a relationship with a man. He excused it by saying he didn't want his son to struggle as he had struggled with the challenges of being gay. He'd retired because he'd been tired of pretending. He'd been in a relationship with this guy for eight years. Mateo and his mom had since forgiven him for the affair. But the hypocrisy of forcing his own son to feel trapped into being someone he wasn't—Mateo couldn't get over it. He'd gotten up from that talk, gotten into his car, and driven straight to Laketown where he'd fallen apart. Lodan and Lizzy and Mrs. Dawson had comforted him, found safe outlets for his anger like tearing down a barn for a friend of theirs, and sent him back right before Christmas. He'd gone home still devastated, but less angry. It helped that his mom had assured him that his dad had left and wouldn't be welcome to stay there ever again. I had to hand it to his father, he hadn't given up on trying to repair the relationship. The first six or eight months Mateo wouldn't talk to him, but eventually Lodan made a deal with him. He would try with his dad if Mateo tried with the Colonel. We all had that tie that bound us: unusual parental problems.

The waitress placed our food in front of us. She looked familiar, but I couldn't recall her name.

"Could you put his wings back under the heat light for now?" I asked her. "He had to take a call."

She took Mateo's lunch back with her and Lodan and I dug into our burgers, his beef, mine veggie.

"So, here is your shot. Spill it, Wonder Woman."

I rolled my eyes at the old nickname. "I feel like such an idiot even saying this out loud."

"Lizzy, I've seen you drunkenly sing karaoke dressed as an alien, so just speak."

"Can't let that one go." I shook my head, took a long sip from my ice water, took a deep breath, leaned close to him, closed my eyes, and whispered, "I'm fourteen weeks pregnant and Alex and I broke up and I don't know what to do." I opened my eyes.

Lodan had stopped mid-bite and sat staring in shock over his burger. He chewed slowly, swallowed, set down the burger, wiped his mouth, and took a deep, slow breath. He reached for his straw and I couldn't take it anymore.

"Say something. Possible parent panicking over here," I whispered.

"Are you sure we can't tell Mateo?" he whispered and I glared at him.

"Sorry," he said. "I just . . . Wow. That's a lot. Fourteen weeks?" he asked.

"Yes, I have like no time left to make a big-ass decision," I confirmed.

"And don't bite my head off, but again, why not ask Mateo, too?" He wrinkled his brow and squinted his eyes in case I lashed out.

"I don't know if I want to keep it," I whispered, "and I know he's going to be disappointed in me; like I wasn't careful enough or should have planned better."

"He's not going to be that harsh. Give him more credit than that." Lodan defended Mateo and I felt a pang of guilt and then hurt. I wished I had a partner that would defend me like that.

"I know he means well and gives great advice but I wanted to get your opinion first. I knew you'd be less focused on how I got into this position in the first place and more focused on what to do about it."

"But say you do have an abortion. Are you saying we would keep it a secret from him?"

"No, I wouldn't do that to you. I will tell him everything. I simply wanted your input first. Okay?" I put my hand on his arm.

Lodan glanced over at Mateo, pacing on the boat dock, phone to his ear, then back at me.

"What happened with Alex?" he asked.

I sighed and debated whether to get into the whole discussion. "Bottom line, this forced a discussion we'd never had about important life decisions. And it became clear that we differed in our opinions on points too important to ignore. Once it was all out there, we didn't see a path forward that had room for both of us."

"Vague. I need a little something here." Lodan shook his head.

I sighed and tried to zero in on the main deal breaker for me. "Okay, bottom line: he made up his mind too easily."

"About the baby?"

"Yes. He wasn't ready to be a dad. Maybe never would be ready," I explained.

"He felt you should get rid of it?" Lodan confirmed.

"I'd told him I needed to talk and we met by our favorite waterfall. I turned to him and said, 'I'm pregnant' and he let out this big sigh of relief and said, "No worries, kiskadee, I know the safest doctor,' and kissed the top of my head. And I wasn't sure if he meant an abortion doctor or an OB-GYN but couldn't get past his clear sense of relief. Before clarifying about the doctor, I asked what he'd thought I was going to say. He let go of my hands and stared down at his own."

"Did he cheat on you?" Lodan asked, and his protective angry tone made me almost cry with gratefulness.

"No, he hired his ex-girlfriend to work with him this summer since I can't. He thought I'd found out before he could tell me."

"And how did you feel about that?" Lodan asked.

"About her?" I shrugged. "She seemed inconsequential compared to his lack of reaction to our pregnancy."

Lodan nodded. "I'm sorry, Lizzy. He seemed so genuine."

"He is genuine when it comes to the local kids. He's a great teacher and would make an amazing father. But I think he's not ready. And I can't fault him for that." We pulled away from one another when the waitress came to check on us.

"All good? Should I get your friend's stuff to go?" she asked.

"Not yet. Thanks," I said.

"We're good for now. Thanks." Lodan smiled up at her, squinting into the sun.

Once she was out of earshot Lodan leaned closer again. "So you were hoping he'd want to have the baby with you?"

I felt tears surfacing and closed mine to hold them at bay. "Does that sound foolish? Having a child this young?"

Lodan sighed, looked out at the water of the lake for a moment, and then back at me. "Honestly I think it sounds challenging. For some girls, yes, it sounds foolish. But Lizzy, you can tackle anything. You're Wonder Woman and already a second mother to me and Mateo."

I tilted my head and rolled my eyes at him. "Very different," I said.

"Yes and no. You have spent more time in your twenty years rescuing and taking care of people and animals than most do in a lifetime."

"But I have school to finish, and work, and a baby makes traveling to Costa Rica a little challenging."

"There are plenty of women and children here in the US that need education and support, Lizzy. I know you love Costa Rica and its people, but you could make a difference here, too."

"It sounds like you think I should have the baby." I studied his face.

He grabbed both my hands in his. "You know that ultimately it doesn't matter what I think. All that matters is what you think. I will support you either way."

"If I have a baby, I'll be single forever." I pushed away my unfinished lunch and leaned back in my chair.

"No, you won't. And Mateo and I can help. We can be like an updated version of that movie, *Three Men and a Baby*. We'll be *Two Gay Men, a Mom, and a Baby*."

"Wasn't one of the three men gay in the original?" I asked.

"I have no idea. I never actually watched the movie." Lodan smiled and pulled my plate in front of himself.

"Are you done?" He took a bite of my abandoned veggie burger without waiting for an answer.

"My dad is going to be so disappointed," I said, already dreading the conversation.

"At first. Maybe. But when he realizes a baby will keep you stateside, he'll recognize it as the answer to all of our wishes come true."

I dropped my head into my hands. "You really want me to stick around that badly?"

"Somebody has to help me distract Mateo from realizing how hot he is or he'll run off with a dreamy Nascar driver or a Brazilian swimsuit model. He'll be less impulsive if he has me *and* you *and* little you to come home to every night."

"Yeah, 'cause Mateo is SO impulsive," I said.

"Have you done worst-case scenario?" Lodan asked.

"Only every night when the stress of it all keeps me awake," I admitted. "Is it really fair to purposely have a child without a father?"

"We both grew up with only one active parent. Mateo basically did, too. It wasn't ideal, but we all turned out fine. Besides, hello, this kid will have two dads, remember?"

"Did you guys eat my wings?" Mateo stepped up to our table, blocking the sun.

"Lizzy had the kitchen keep them hot for ya," Lodan said while I flagged down the waitress.

"Oh, thanks." I got the full wattage of his crooked smile and deep dimple.

"How did it go with your dad?" I asked.

"Weird. I still have a hard time picturing the guy I grew up fearing, saying the things he says now. It's like I'm talking to an actor playing the role of my father. The irony being the tough, militant, homophobic dad was the actor. I'm only getting to know my real dad now."

"Did he call just to talk?" Lodan asked, starting in on my fries.

"He wants me to meet Karl. They're meeting friends in Nantucket and want to meet us for dinner in Boston."

"Oh, I am so crashing that meal!" I said. "I want to meet the Colonel's soul mate."

"When?" Lodan asked.

"August." Mateo drained the last of his drink as I pictured myself in August at around six months pregnant. Scary little reality check.

The waitress served Mateo a fresh iced tea and his wings.

"Are you okay about it?" Lodan asked.

"I'm glad he gave me a couple months to get used to the idea. It's not that I'm not okay with him being gay, obviously. It's that he chose this guy over all of us, you know? And I still picture him with my mom when I think of him. I don't know how to explain it. It messes with my head."

Lodan dropped a hand on Mateo's knee. "You seem to be handling this better than you did the last few conversations. That's progress."

They exchanged a look and I felt like they needed a moment alone. "I'm going to run to the restroom," I announced.

When I got to the single-occupant restroom there were two young girls waiting in line. They had to be sisters, the elder a magnified carbon copy of the younger girl. They both had a head full of unruly blond curls and big, bright blue eyes. The elder sister bent to tie her sister's shoe and the younger child looked up at me. "My dad said you look like my mom."

"Me?" I asked as her sister cast her a warning look and hissed, "Megan."

"What?" the younger girl asked. "It's nice to say. Mom's pretty."

"Thank you." I smiled down at her. "Are you here on vacation?"

"Visiting my Meema," the younger one said as the bathroom door opened. "My mom's having my brother this weekend so I won't be youngest anymore." She flashed me a proud toothy grin, her lips and teeth tinted blue; no doubt complements of the flavored ice sold at Minnie's.

"Come on, Megan," the older sister said. She smiled up at me. "Sorry if it takes us a bit. We both have to go."

"It's okay." I smiled back. "I have a nice view while I wait." I gestured to the lake behind us.

Surely there couldn't be a clearer sign that keeping this child is the right choice. By the time I got back to the table, my body buzzed with excitement. I felt I might burst.

I sat down, squeezed each of their forearms, and said, "Do you guys want to be part-time dads with me?"

Mateo dropped a wing back onto the plate and looked back and forth from me to Lodan. Lodan looked at me, eyes wide in surprise. Mateo narrowed his eyes at Lodan.

"I said no to a puppy. Did you just spend this whole time convincing Lizzy to vote with you?" Mateo's eyes widened and his jaw flexed as did his arm beneath my hand.

I shook his arm. "No, Mateo, calm down. I'm not talking about a dog. I'm talking about a baby. A human baby."

He turned to me. "What? What do you mean?"

"I'm pregnant," I said and watched different emotions flick across Mateo's face: surprise, concern, and finally confusion. He looked at Lodan.

"Did you know about this?" he asked.

"She just told me while you were on the phone." I could tell that Lodan, like me, was trying to gauge his reaction.

"Are you moving to Costa Rica instead of Boston?" Mateo asked, a hint of anger in his voice.

I shook my head and felt a pang of sadness in my chest for what I'd be giving up for this choice. But just as quickly the happy buzz pushed it aside. "Actually, I'll probably be staying in Boston longer than originally planned."

"What about Alex?" Mateo's jaw tensed again, his eyes a mix of worry and anger.

I shook my head and squeezed his arm. "It's okay. He isn't ready. I'm really okay with that part. I am." I looked him straight in the eye.

Lodan put a hand on Mateo's back. "And the best part is that means we get to be the dads and Lizzy stays in the US. It's a win-win." Lodan flashed me an encouraging smile.

"Aren't you on birth control? Are you sure you're pregnant?" Mateo asked.

I nodded. "Very sure. No doubt. I am going to be a mom come late November." I held my breath as he let this news sink in.

"Isn't this amazing? A baby!" Lodan said. I knew he was worried that Mateo's reaction would make me question my decision. But now that I'd decided, I felt very secure in my decision.

"Mateo, it's not how I would have planned it, obviously, but we all know life rarely follows the intended path."

"But how did you get pregnant to begin with?" Mateo asked and I gave Lodan a loaded look.

"I forgot my pills when I went to see him. We used condoms instead, but we weren't militant about it. I'm sorry. I messed up." I hated when I disappointed people, especially Mateo.

"For the record, it wasn't just you. Alex was responsible as well," Mateo said. He sighed and ran a hand across his face.

His eyes and voice softened. "A baby needs a stable environment, constant care"—he used his knife to punctuate each fact, tapping the tip on the table—"vaccines, lots of equipment. It's expensive and hard."

"You don't think I can handle it?" I asked, a little hurt.

Mateo turned to me, running his hand across his brush cut. "I know you can handle it, Lizzy. Of course you can, but I don't know that we can. I mean you and me and Lodan. That's a lot of pressure to add to our living situation on top of college and jobs. Have you two thought this through at all?"

I looked at Lodan and his face echoed my surprise and worry. Maybe we hadn't or we would have remembered that Mateo doesn't handle surprise changes well.

"I'm sorry," I said. "You're right. I am throwing all of this on you both when I have had a lot more time to sort through my feelings. If you don't want me to still live with you guys, that's totally cool. A baby does change everything. It's okay."

"Lizzy." Lodan looked at me, then pleadingly at Mateo. Mateo remained quiet.

"Lodan, it's okay. I'm good." I put my hand on each of their arms again. "Look, this weekend isn't about me. It's about Mrs. Dawson so let's just table this baby stuff until after the wedding and we can talk about it then, okay?" I looked back and forth from one to the other. Mateo continued rubbing his head and Lodan looked down at his empty glass of iced tea. "Please, guys. Now I feel like I've put a big buzz kill on our reunion."

"Are you all set?" The waitress popped back over to us.

"Just the check, please," Mateo said.

Lodan's phone buzzed and he answered. "Hey, Mom. What's up?"

From his side of the conversation I gathered she needed our help again. Mateo finished up, we paid, and left. Lodan and I kept the conversation going and Mateo eventually loosened up some. But when we went to our separate rooms to get ready for the rehearsal dinner, I was relieved to have a moment to myself. I hoped Mateo could table this so we could all focus on the wedding without a tense energy hanging over everything. I knew Lodan was nervous about seeing Sage and he needed both of us to be strong for him. I couldn't help feeling guilty for possibly creating an issue between Lodan and Mateo. I'd let my relief and excitement at making a difficult decision cloud my thinking. I should have known it wouldn't be easy for Mateo to process an unexpected life-altering event. I pulled my dress over my head, zipped it, and stood sideways in the mirror to see if any bump was visible. It wasn't. I felt a little flutter of excitement. I couldn't wait to be the kind of mom I always dreamed of having.

Fifty

LODAN

LAKETOWN, NY
FRIDAY, JUNE 21, 2019

Thankfully Mateo didn't bring up the pregnancy bomb and neither did I. My fear of him saying something about it helped keep me from completely freaking about seeing Sage again. I wasn't nervous about seeing her, more worried about what she may say or do that could ruin my mom's big weekend. I'd hate that for my mom.

I wiped off the steamed mirror and adjusted my tie. I hated dressing up. I only had this one suit, which I'd purchased for intern interviews this past winter. The material may have been a little heavy for the summer weather. I figured I only had to wear the jacket to *The Kitchen*, but could take it off while we ate and toasted.

A knock at the door had me finishing up quickly. "Be right out." I turned off the light and stepped into the hall where Mateo made my heart stop. He had on a black suit that had been tailored to fit. He wore a black shirt and tie as well. His olive skin had tanned quickly after being outside that afternoon and his sandy eyes sparkled in the dim hall lighting. A rush of desire ran through me and I bit into my lower lip to keep my body in check.

"Look at you." Mateo flashed his magnetic smile and I lost all resolve. I closed the gap between us and pulled his lips to mine. He readily returned my kiss. I ran my hands up into the prickly line of his hair. He groaned and pushed me against the wall. We'd stopped by the house on our way back from the airport and had barely made it to my room with any clothes still on so it wasn't like this was our first chance to connect. Our relationship had always been this way. Neither of us were able to keep our hands off the other. He gripped my head at the base of my neck. His thumbs massaged either side as our kissing intensified. Our chests were thrust together and his leg pushed against the hardness in my pants, making me dizzy with need.

"Boys!" My mom's voice from downstairs shocked us both apart.

We looked at one another for a minute, both of us breathing heavily. Mateo wiped his hand over his mouth and laughed silently. I laughed too. "Be right down." He reached out to fix my tie and I had to fight the urge to lean toward him. He must have sensed it.

"Later." He winked.

My knees felt a little weak as we descended the stairs to find Lizzy and my mom at the bottom. My mom wore a deep purple dress, silver heels, and had her hair down and brushed out. She looked young and happy. I felt a tightness in my chest. We'd had a tough couple of years sorting through the lies and the pain. But as she looked up at me, I felt a sense of peace between us. Lizzy looked pretty in a simple black dress and wedges. She had her arm looped through my mom's. I wondered if my mom ever wished I could just love and marry Lizzy.

I must have been lost in my head a little too long because Mateo leaned down and whispered in my ear, "Time to go." His breath in my ear sent a chill through my body. I headed down the stairs before my arousal reached a level too obvious to hide.

"You both look amazing!" Mateo said to the women. And I agreed.

"Thanks. I think Lizzy will have the two hottest men on her arms all night." My mom squeezed my hand. We posed for a few pictures together, taking turns with our phones. Then we piled into the car and headed to dinner.

Dale, Sage, and Dr. Payne were the first to greet us at the door. I hung back for a minute while Dr. Payne fussed over my mom. I could tell she was pleased by his attention. Sage locked eyes with me, then quickly looked down and grabbed Dale's hand. I watched him squeeze her hand and whisper something to her. In the dim lighting she struck me as much younger than my mother, vulnerable. Not because my mom looked older, just the opposite in reality. It was the difference in the way they each held themselves. I took a deep breath and stepped closer to her and Dale.

"Hi," I said.

"Hi," she replied, smiling shyly. "You look handsome."

"Thanks." I wrinkled my nose. "I don't like suits much."

She laughed and I saw her visibly relax. "Me neither."

I felt Mateo step up behind me and place his hand on my shoulder. I looked up at him and then back at Sage and Dale. "This is Mateo. Mateo, meet Sage and Dale." I left everyone's labels off to avoid any awkwardness. They all knew about one another.

They all shook hands. A round of "Nice to meet yous" were exchanged.

"Did you have any trouble finding the restaurant?" Mateo asked.

"Not with GPS. If only we could apply it to life decisions sometimes," Dale said. We all laughed politely then stalled in a pregnant pause.

"We drove around the lake earlier. It's a beautiful area. And the weather today was perfect," Dale continued.

"Did you grow up boating and water-skiing and stuff?" Sage asked me and the conversation took off. We all fell into an easy exchange of typical getting-to-know-you questions and anecdotes. By the time we'd finished the meal and began the toasts, I felt an enormous sense of relief. This Sage, the one here tonight, reminded me of my mother, her sister. And Dale looked at her as if she were the very center of his world. Maybe it was the romantic candlelight setting, sitting beside Mateo after months apart, or possibly the glass of champagne but I felt a welcome sense of completeness. I had this unusual but remarkable group of family and friends around me. This was my mood when I got handed the microphone to address the party.

I stood, my heart pounding, and Mateo gave me a reassuring smile. It wasn't a huge group. Just over twenty people. My mother's and Dr. Payne's closest friends and family, but I wanted to get this right.

"For those of you who may not know, I'm Lodan." I hesitated. I didn't want to say Heather's son because of Sage. So I skirted around it. "I'll be standing up with the lovely bride tomorrow as her man-of-honor. And it *is* an honor for me, but for you, unfortunately, it means you have to listen to me on this mic." I cleared my throat. My heart slowed down a little. "Thank you all for coming and being here for my mom and Dr. Payne."

"Jason," my mom corrected.

I held my hand up in apology, "Sorry, Jason."

I took another deep breath. "As many of you know, I didn't grow up a typical kid. I've been fascinated by the mechanics of movement, designing, and building. While other kids played baseball and water-skied, I designed a mini town in our spare bedroom. I'm sure you can imagine I didn't have many playdates nor sleepovers. Not because the other kids didn't ask or try. I made the choice. It may sound lonely, life as a design nerd, but I had a happy childhood. A full childhood. I never felt different in any way that made me sad. We were both happy and comfortable in our small corner of the world." I took a sip of water and set the glass back down.

"A few years ago this girl walked into our lives." I shot a look in Lizzy's direction. "Well, a woman actually. I call her Wonder Woman." Lizzy covered her eyes with her hand. "A nickname she loves." I smiled at her but her return grin included dagger eyes. "Lizzy has a special super power which she thankfully used on us. Her super power is drawing the best out of people by encouraging them to view their life from new perspectives. I can't predict what direction our lives would have taken without Lizzy's intervention, but I fear it may have included my mom and me living together until I reached that odd living-with-your-mom age that guaranteed me a life as a bachelor and her a nun." They all chuckled a little and I paused.

"Lizzy must have seen the writing on the wall. She pushed each of us out of our safe, mini bubble and into the chaotic, mysterious, and often messy world at large. She convinced my mom to take a chance on Dr. Pay—Jason," I corrected, flashing him a smile.

"Lizzy encouraged my mom to spend time with Jason. And my mom just blossomed. Turned out he was the sun she needed to coax her out of her protective shell. He helped her to remember she had a life, too." People cooed, Dr. Payne pulled her closer, and my mom wiped a tear, shaking her head at me. I locked eyes on Lizzy. "Thank you, Lizzy, for encouraging us to widen our perspectives." She flashed me an appreciative smile.

"From both of us," Dr. Jason interjected and the group laughed.

"And thank *you*, Jason, for loving my mom like that. For making her a better, happier version of herself; for reminding her she is more than a mother and a nurse. I am lucky to be able to recognize that adoring gaze I've caught in your eyes, because of someone special in my own life." I looked back at Mateo, who winked and gave me a sweet half-smile.

"For as long as I can remember I've had a habit of using a single word to describe people, places, or moments that brought me unexpected pleasure or that feeling I can only describe as warm fuzzies. You know that feeling. We all have our own word for it, I'm sure. My word has always been *vintage*. I'd never looked up the definition until I had to figure out what to say tonight." I made a face and the group laughed.

"And when I did consult *Webster's*, I found the noun version, which read: 'a season's yield of grapes or wine from a vineyard,' but my vintage is more of a feeling than a noun. Farther down I read: 'vintage, the best and most characteristic.' That sounded better. And then: 'of old, recognized, and enduring interest, importance, or quality.' That came closest."

I held up my champagne glass and the guests followed suit. "To you, Mom and Jason, I wish you a marriage that's truly the best, full of quality and importance, and above all enduring. I wish you a marriage that's truly vintage! Cheers!"

The group clapped, hollered, and downed their champagne. I felt my face heat up and sat down with a sigh of relief. Mateo leaned in to my ear and whispered, "That was hot." My ear burned and I squeezed his thigh under the table. "Thanks," I said.

I gladly handed the mic off to Dr. Payne's sister, his maid of honor. When she stood to speak, I happened to catch sight of Lizzy headed away from the celebration, toward the bathroom. It wasn't like her to miss any part of a party. I felt drawn to check on her, but I couldn't walk out during a speech. I glanced at Mateo, but he was politely focused on the speaker. I tried to do the same, vowing as soon as she finished, I'd check on Lizzy.

Fifty-one

LIZZY

LAKETOWN, NY
FRIDAY, JUNE 21, 2019

I felt awful slipping out in the middle of the speeches, especially after Lodan's sweet words, but the Alfredo sauce had been too much for me. For some reason the baby didn't like dairy. This wasn't the first time a creamy delicacy had sent me bolting for the bathroom. I should have known better, but I knew Mrs. Dawson had made the vegetarian choice especially for me. It was my favorite dish on *The Kitchen*'s menu.

Luckily I had the bathroom to myself. As soon as I'd rid my stomach of the offensive creamy culprit, I swished my teeth and mouth clean with one of the free sample-size mouthwashes from the complimentary bathroom basket. Just as I washed my face, another patron came in to use the facilities. I thanked my lucky stars that I hadn't been caught mid-puke or mid-gargle. I stepped through the doorway and right into the back of a tall, muscular blond, wearing khaki shorts, flip-flops, and a navy polo shirt. His broad shoulders reminded me of Mateo's back. He turned to face me.

"Lizzy?" He stepped closer and just as I recognized him, he pulled me right off the ground into a hug. He stood a good foot taller than me. He set me down and asked, "What are you doing in town?"

"Von." I beamed. His real name was Ryan Braun but when I'd first met him I immediately knew he was supposed to be Von. "Lodan's mom is getting married. You here for the summer?" I asked, wondering if the flutter in my stomach was a reaction to him or lingering Alfredo.

"No, back for the weekend to visit my family." He gestured toward the kitchen. His aunt owned and ran *The Kitchen*, though she'd been more like his mom. We'd bonded in the past over not being raised by our own mothers. Ryan's mom had passed while he was still young. "I still have a couple years of school. I'm taking a summer class and I have an internship at my cousin's law office."

"You wanna be a lawyer?" I asked, thinking it didn't fit with his casual approach to academics in high school or his chin-length, wavy blond hair that he kept slipping behind his ears.

"Environmental. I hope. Still a long road ahead. What about you? You've been in Central America for a while, haven't you?"

"I was. I did a gap year there with United Planet, then stayed another to continue some of the work I'd started. But I've been at Boston College for a year now studying sociology and public policy."

"Sounds very Lizzy." His smile went all the way to his eyes so I knew he wasn't making fun.

"Yeah, I loved my work in Costa Rica, but I felt like I needed a better understanding of policy and what methods have or haven't worked in the past."

"Then you heading back down to Costa Rica?" he asked as applause erupted in the other room. The last speech had ended. "You have a boyfriend there, right?"

The mention of Alex reminded me that I shouldn't be flirting with a guy when my near future includes diapers and day care rather than dinners and drinks. "We broke up, but—"

"Great! We should hang out while I'm here." He put a hand on my shoulder and gently squeezed, then looked down at his feet and back up, his face red. "Sorry, that came out wrong. It's not great, I'm sure, for you, necessarily. I just meant . . ."

I laughed and squeezed his arm back. "It's fine. I get it." His skin was softer than I'd expected and I ran my thumb across it a few times before I came to my senses and pulled my hand away.

"Hey, you okay?" Lodan approached, followed by a number of the wedding group who were headed to the restrooms.

I turned to find Lodan's green eyes clouded with concern. I nodded. "I'm fine. I ran into Von."

"Hey, Lodan. Congrats to your mom," Von said.

I watched Lodan take in Von's hand on my arm before answering. "Thanks, Ryan. Dr. Payne's a nice guy." He cast me a questioning look. I flashed him back an eye shrug, alerting him to the fact that I don't know what the hell I'm doing either.

"You still at MIT?" Von asked, dropping his hand from my shoulder.

"Two more years. You finish up at GCC?" Lodan asked.

"Yeah. I finally got my GPA back in line and transferred to the University of Virginia. Charlottesville is a cool town. Everybody is really into the sports teams so the games and tailgating are fun. My family comes down sometimes."

There was an awkward pause. Von must have forgotten Lodan hated traditional sports.

"Von is going to be an environmental lawyer." I broke the pause. "You guys may be able to help each other out someday."

"Thought you were into building cars and stuff?" Von lifted an eyebrow at Lodan.

"I still am but I've shifted my focus a little to more environmentally friendly modes of transport and living." He elbowed me in the side. "This girl is pretty convincing."

I rolled my eyes.

"I believe it." Von turned his attention back to me and my stomach confirmed the flutter had nothing to do with food.

"Hey, you guys move the party and forget to tell me?" Mateo approached and stood protectively close to Lodan as he sized up Von.

"Sorry," Lodan said. "We ran into an old classmate." Lodan must have noticed Mateo's territorial study of Von as well because he quickly added, "Ryan, this is my boyfriend, Mateo. Mateo, Ryan."

The two guys shook hands. They looked like two football captains shaking before the big game. The testosterone hung thick in the air. I doubt Von fully grasped the intensity of the exchange but he still said the perfect thing to diffuse it. "Is the dinner over, because I was just telling Lizzy we should hang out. You two could come, too. It's a nice night. We could take the boat out on the lake, have a few beers. What do you say?"

Mateo noticeably relaxed his shoulders when he realized Lodan was not the focus of Von's interest. But just as quickly he cast me a loaded look. Of course a part of me would love to pretend I had no other concerns in the world than having a few beers with friends, but I'd recently made a decision that ruled that out for a long time.

"That sounds amazing," I said. "But I already made plans with Lodan's mom to have a last single girls' evening together." This wasn't exactly true but I liked the idea as soon as I said it.

Von's face fell and it made me happy and sad at the same time. "Maybe we could have lunch on Sunday?" I suggested and the cheer returned to his face.

"It's supposed to be nice. We could take the boat out and grab something at Minnie's or I could pack us a picnic if you prefer?" His enthusiasm was as unexpected as it was endearing.

Lodan cut his eyes at me in equal surprise.

"A picnic sounds great. I should warn you I'm vegetarian. Do you want me to bring my own food?" I asked.

Von waved his hand in the air. "No worries. I dated a vegan my freshman year. Do you do dairy or no?"

I laughed at the irony. "Actually, if you can skip the dairy that would be good, too." I rubbed my stomach.

"Got it. No dairy." He pushed his hair behind his ears again. And I realized for the first time that he was nervous. I found this both shocking and flattering.

"Well, we should head back. We're my mom's ride. Can't see the groom until the big reveal tomorrow. You know, bad luck and all," Lodan said, then immediately looked uncomfortable.

I stood on my tiptoes and Von leaned down so I could drop a kiss on his cheek. Mateo gave me an odd look. "Is your number the same, Lizzy?" he asked.

"Yep. Just text me Sunday morning and we can decide details. Good to see you, Von." I gave him one final look. He looked adorably vulnerable. I decided I liked the longer hair on him. It balanced out his preppy clothes.

"See ya, Ryan," Lodan said. Mateo casually dropped an arm around his shoulder as they turned to go.

"Nice to meet you, Mateo," Von said and Mateo looked back and responded with a wave.

I overheard Mateo say to Lodan, "Is his name Ryan or Von?"

Fifty-two

LIZZY

LAKETOWN, NY
SATURDAY, JUNE 22, 2019

I woke up to the comforting sound of a light rain hitting the roof of the screened porch, another addition since I'd last visited. I'd opened the window before bed so I could sleep in the fresh country air. But then I'd remembered it was wedding day and immediately felt awful for Lodan's mom. Hopefully the rain would stop soon.

We had stayed up after the party for a bit, just the four of us, entertaining her with stories from our post–high school experiences, and laughing as we shared reminiscent moments from our famous Truth-Seeking Trip. Lodan hadn't shared all of our stops with his mom before last night's chat. Mateo remained a little distant with me, but had honored the request to table discussions for now.

Luckily, by the time we'd both had our hair and makeup (Mrs. Dawson only) done, the rain had stopped, leaving behind gray skies but a fresh, clean, post-rain scent to the air.

"Personally, I'd be fine with the sun keeping a low profile today. This black tux is going to be hot and confining enough without the sun beating down on our backs," Lodan announced as Mateo tied his tie for him. The three of us were standing in the kitchen waiting for Mrs. Dawson. We'd already carefully placed her wedding dress in the car for her to put on after we got to the lake house. She was finishing her packing as they would be leaving from Dr. Payne's the following morning for their honeymoon in St. John.

"Let's take a selfie," I suggested and they both leaned down to my height so we could all fit in the frame. I studied the image after. I looked like a Gap girl bookended by a *Maxim* and *GQ* cover model: one all bronze, beefy muscle and the other pale, angular, waify-hot.

We snuck the bride into Dr. Payne's house up the back stairs and into one of his guest rooms where my mom could stay hidden until the big reveal. My mom had invited Sage to help us get her into her dress. She'd gone all out. Her strapless dress had intricate hand-stitched beading, laced all the way up the back starting just above her butt. It took two of us to cinch her in tight, but the result was incredibly flattering. Combined with the hair and makeup she looked closer to my age than Sage's.

"You look stunning," Sage said as the two stood side by side looking in the long mirror placed in the corner of the guest room for this exact purpose.

"I wish Mom could be here," Heather said.

"She is," Sage said.

I'd slipped out the door to leave them to their family moment and went in search of the guys. When I stepped outside, the gray sky had a cool yellow hue to it and the guests were taking their seats on the covered chairs we'd placed in neat rows, with an aisle down the center. A guitarist and a violinist played acoustic versions of contemporary music. The florist had added fresh white flowers to Lodan's wedding arch. I checked my phone. Sunset was in less than thirty minutes. It was almost go time. I turned to look in the house for the boys and ran into my dad and a petite brunette in a flowy peach sundress. She wore her long hair straight, parted perfectly in the middle, with a thin braid framing her head like a crown. Her lightly freckled face and overall look reminded me of the girls on the cover of the hippie wear I'd seen in Halloween costume shops.

"Look at you." My dad let out a quiet whistle. I rolled my eyes and hugged him hello. "Lizzy, meet Henley."

"Lovely to meet you, Lizzy," she said with a fantastic British accent that made me want to keep her talking. "Sorry I missed you earlier this week." Henley had been working in Atlanta when I'd stayed with my dad on my drive down. She worked as a freelance photographer. "The fresh flowers in your hair are a nice touch."

"Thanks, Henley. My father never told me you were British." I flashed him a questioning look.

"Well, according to my sisters, I'm not anymore. After twelve years living here, my family has reclassified me. What can I say? I enjoy the sun and I'm afraid she didn't book as many appearances on our island."

"And you agreed to move to New York state? Dad, did you neglect to explain the weather?"

"It's been lovely so far." Henley gave my dad a nervous look.

"Don't you need to get back to that wedding party?" my dad asked.

"Actually, I'm looking for the guys. Have you seen either of them?" I turned to look behind me as well.

"No, but we are going to get a seat while there's still room in the back," he said and escorted Henley briskly away. I could not believe my dad had actually found a woman named Henley and asked her out. It made me wonder how they met. I suspected it may have been online. I checked my phone again. Twenty minutes to sunset. I let myself back in through the door off the back deck. The kitchen was full of caterers, the bathroom was empty, as was the living room. I didn't think they'd be in the master with Dr. Payne. I didn't want to wander through his whole house looking. I turned to head back upstairs to Mrs. Dawson when a door down the hall opened and they stepped out one after the other. I watched amused as they quickly adjusted their shirts and ties. Mateo fingered Lodan's hair back into place.

"Did you find Dr. Payne's red room, boys?" I asked, and laughed when they both jumped. They each flashed a guilty grin. Lodan's face burned crimson.

"Now that you got that out of the way, do you think you can keep your hands off one another long enough to get your mom married before the sun sets?"

We hurried up the stairs to get the bride. A few minutes later, the guests in their places and the wedding party in theirs, the sun burst through the clouds. The musicians began playing the Dolly Parton then Whitney Houston favorite, "I Will Always Love You." Mrs. Dawson had told us at the rehearsal that she fell in love with the song after watching the movie *The Bodyguard* with her mother and Sage. She'd announced to them both that it would be the song to which she'd walk down the aisle. It was Sage who had reminded her when they discussed her attending the wedding. The sisters agreed it was a way to keep their mom a part of the special day.

Dr. Payne had been asked to stand facing the lake until Mrs. Dawson reached the first line of chairs. His sister was to let him know when he could look. He began to turn at the crowd's reaction to their first sighting as she floated out the deck door, but Lodan put a hand on his arm and whispered, "Not yet."

When he did turn, friends and family held a collective breath as they watched him. Dr. Payne remained stoic for the bride's first few steps toward him, but then his lips began to tremble and he blinked hard, clearly trying to hold back his tears. When Heather was halfway down the aisle, he shook his head, glanced at his tearful sister, then clasped his hand to his mouth. His sister handed him a kerchief she had at the ready. As he dabbed at his eyes, I took a peek at Mrs. Dawson. Her eyes were clouded with unspilled tears. I squeezed Mateo's hand where he stood beside me in the front row of the bride's side. I glanced at Lodan and caught him rubbing his own eyes. In fact as I skimmed the crowd, a number of tissues and handkerchiefs were eye dabbing the rush of emotion he'd started. When she reached the arch and stood facing him, he reached out and took her hands in his shaking hands. She beamed up at him and he gazed down at her as the sun dipped its first edge into the gray, blue water of the evening lake, lighting the surface on fire with its orange and red reflection. The glowing orb framed their union beneath the arch in a painter's dream sky. The clouds from earlier had lingered to form ever-changing vibrant pink and orange layers of a fairy tale sky.

I caught my dad's eye and he mouthed a "wow" to me from where he stood with Henley. She leaned into his arm, a look of wistful appreciation on her face. Mateo squeezed my hand and I returned my attention to the couple as they exchanged their own vows, then a sweet, gentle kiss followed by a tight squeeze. The solar fairy lights blinked on behind them as the last edge of the sun dipped below the horizon. We all cheered as the wedding party passed down the aisle. Dr. and Mrs. Payne. A nurse and a vet named Payne. I loved it.

Mateo and I were some of the last to make our way over to the reception area. He grabbed himself an iced tea and me an ice water with a loaded look. He glanced around for a bit, then gestured to follow him. He walked back out of the tent, past the chatting groups to the quieter, secluded deck swing. I knew he was ready to speak his mind about the baby and my stomach clenched with nervous anxiety. I realized what he thought was more important to me than what my own father thought and that scared me a little. Was this what it felt like to have a brother?

We sat on the swing, my toes barely touching the deck, his knees bent but firm so that the swing remained still.

"Beautiful ceremony. If I hadn't witnessed it myself I'd have suspected movie magic brought that sunset to life." He looked down at his drink and set it aside on a table.

"I know. I was worried when I woke up to the rain this morning." I cradled my glass in my hands.

"Yes. Me too." He folded his napkin into smaller and smaller squares.

"I know we agreed to wait until after the festivities to talk," Mateo began. "But I have seen the stress and concern in your eyes and I felt sooner rather than later might be healthier for all of us."

"Thanks. I appreciate that," I said.

He turned his intense brown eyes on me and I blinked but held his look. "I'm sorry that I haven't been able to blindly leap onto the baby train with you and Lodan. I know you two think I overprocess my every move and take too long to make decisions, but that is something that is not going to change within me. I sometimes wish I could simply jump into life with both feet like you two have been doing, but can't. And maybe that's why you and I work as friends and Lodan and I work as a couple. We balance one another."

"I hear a 'but' coming."

"But this is a lot for me." He held up his hand. "Not to say it's not a whole hell of a lot more for you."

I raised my eyebrows and nodded.

"Lodan and I spoke at length about this last night and I think he helped me understand my hesitation."

I felt a rush of disappointment but remained focused on his face. "It's okay. It's too much. You shouldn't have to grow up faster because—"

Mateo put a hand on my shoulder. "No, that's not it. I can handle a baby disrupting our sleep and work schedule. I can handle helping care for and teaching and loving this child. I'd be honored to have the opportunity to do so. I'm not afraid of making sacrifices to, as you call it, grow up faster."

"Okaaay?" I tilted my head, searched his eyes.

"Lizzy, you are a beautiful, intelligent, driven, giving woman." He squeezed my bare knee.

"Mateo." I felt a lump form in my throat. "I feel like you're breaking up with me all over again."

"Let me finish." He shot me a look.

"Sorry, continue." I smiled sheepishly at him.

"Some lucky guy like Ryan or Von or whatever his name is, is going to come along and you and he are going to want to marry and get a house and raise your kids and do all that adult stuff that if you do it well, makes life worth living."

"That all sounds great. So what's the problem?"

"Me, I guess. If the three of us spend the next couple of years living together, raising this child, I don't know that I could handle you taking them away from us after I've begun to feel like a father. And how would it impact the child." The earnest concern on his face as he waited for me to catch up, made my chest ache.

"Wow." I leaned back in the seat, causing the swing to buck a little. "You've really thought this through. I haven't even heard the heartbeat yet and I feel like I've already failed my first test as a parent. I should have been the one thinking like this, not you."

He put his arm around me and pulled me close. "You're going to be a great mother. I love how you leap into life without overthinking and make it up as you go along. And I hate to be the voice of reason. I feel like I sometimes take the joy out of things."

I looked up at him and placed my hand on his smooth cheek. "No, you don't, you're just like this big, comforting kite that comes floating in for me to grab and ride back to the safety of the sand before my latest crazy idea takes me off into the wind." I waved into the air with my hand.

"A kite?" Mateo drew his eyebrows tight and squinted his nose.

"Hot-air balloon? Eagle? I don't know." I sighed a disappointed, sad sigh.

"I'm sorry," Mateo said as he rubbed my shoulder.

"I get it. As usual, you make great sense, but I still don't like it. It sounded much easier to do if I didn't have to do it alone."

"I'm not saying we won't be there to help you as much as we can. We can babysit while you date and when your regular care doesn't work out. We can hang out on weekends and go for walks and play on the playground. Lodan and I will spoil this kid like the best uncles ever to be lucky enough to win that role." He gave me a little squeeze. "If after this you still give me the part."

I flashed him a wry smile and squeezed his leg because I couldn't speak over the lump in my throat. I knew he was right.

He pulled me to him for a hug and I lost my battle with the tears. I sobbed as I clung to him and realized I'd let a silly movie about three guys raising a baby carry me down a fanciful rainbow slide of raising a baby with my two best friends. It was a selfish slide. But as I sat there, slobbering all over poor Mateo's tux, he kissed the top of my head and told me what he knew I really needed to hear.

"Telling you all of that was the hard part. Now I need to tell you something else and I want you to just listen."

I didn't move and he took that as an affirmation to continue.

"Although we will be there for you, it's important you understand that you don't need us. Think about it. You take care of everyone around you without giving it a second thought: your father, Lodan, me, the kids and mothers you've worked with in Costa Rica and Boston. You've literally been educating mothers on how to fight for their children, how to better care for, educate, and empower them. Who better than you to raise a baby yourself?" He rubbed my back.

I took a few deep, steadying breaths and felt some of the fear dissipate. He made a lot of sense. I let his words sink in and felt my confidence grow at the truth of what he'd said. I spoke into his chest. "You know you're pretty good at this parenting stuff for a non-homeschooled kid."

I felt his deep laugh against my cheek.

Someone cleared his throat in an unnaturally loud fashion behind us. I sat up and we both turned to find Lodan standing there. His tux jacket was already gone and his tie hung loosely around his neck.

"My mom sent me to find you guys. They are about to start serving the first course."

I wiped my eyes and looked at the big wet mark on Mateo's lapel. "Sorry." I uselessly wiped at it with my hand.

Mateo winked and shot me a smile. "It's okay, I needed an excuse to shed it anyway. I'm sweating my ass off sitting here with you glued to my chest."

I felt Lodan searching my face for a clue as to how I'd taken the news. "I can't believe you refuse to live with a baby!" I couldn't resist messing with him.

"What?" Lodan looked confused until we burst out laughing. Heat crept up his face and he laughed along with us.

"So we're all good here?" he asked, using his finger to make a circle in the air that included all of us.

"Except the fact that your rent just went up and I need to quickly find a studio in a decent neighborhood, tell my dad he's going to be a grandfather, and beg him to help with *my* rent."

"Yeah, so you think we could eat first, 'cause we never had lunch and I'm starving." He reached to pull me out of the swing and the three of us made our way back to the party.

A few delicious courses, speeches, and hair-soaking stretches on the dance floor later, I found the courage to approach my dad with the big news. I located him next to the bar and asked if we could have a chat. Henley excused herself to the restroom and we made our way to the edge of the tent farthest from the dance floor and sat at a high table.

"What's up?" he asked.

I took a deep breath and just blurted it all out from the baby to Alex to Boston to doing it alone.

He listened without comment, without noticeable reaction. After I finished, he took a long swig of his beer, set it down, and said, "I'm moving to Boston."

I'd been gearing up to defend my decision so his response caught me off guard. "What?"

"You're going to need help. It looks like a cool city from what I've seen when I've visited, and I miss having you around." He took another long drink.

"You're not disappointed in me?" I asked.

"Lizzy, you're amazing. How could I be disappointed in you? This Alex is the biggest idiot ever to let you get away, but his loss is my gain. So"—he raised his beer into the air—"thanks, Alex."

I saw Henley lingering nearby, trying to give us space. I motioned her over and hopped off my stool to embrace my dad. "Thank you for not making me feel bad about something I'm really excited about," I whispered in his ear. "Are you sure you want to move in with me and a baby when Henley just moved in with you? What about her?"

"Let's ask her," he said, keeping one arm around me and pulling Henley to his side with the other.

"Henley, how would you like to move with me to Boston, live with

Lizzy, and help her with my grandchild that will be here, when?" He looked at me.

"November," I answered and we both watched Henley process this big news. A huge smile spread across her face. She covered her mouth with her hands and ran to hug me.

"Yes, I'd love to. I miss my sisters and my nieces so much. Yes, it would be so fun." She released me and returned to my father's side. He squeezed her into him.

"And true confession," she said, squinting her freckled ski slope nose, "I could do for a little more excitement. Living by the lake has been peaceful and beautiful, but a little . . ." She searched for the word.

"Dull?" I offered.

"No, I think 'quiet' is the word." She looked at my dad for his reaction.

He lifted his beer into the air. "Perfect. It's a done deal. We'll start looking for a place tomorrow and make a plan." I hugged them both.

"Thank you both so much. You have no idea how much better I feel knowing I'll have you there, too."

"I can't believe I'm going to be a grandpa. I don't even have gray hair yet," he said.

"Mmm." Henley gave him a sly look. "Not too many anyway. " She ran her fingers through his hair.

"Hey, you're not supposed to notice those." He dropped a kiss on her lips. I excused myself to find the boys and tell them that not only did my dad not kill me or lecture me, but would be in Boston, too.

I finally found them sitting on the end of the dock, partially hidden by the wedding arch, their pant legs rolled up and their bare feet dangling in the water. Both had stripped down to white T-shirts and their tux pants. Their jackets, ties, and collared shirts long gone.

"Hey, mind if I join you?" I asked and they slid apart to make space between them. I sat and my toes just broke the surface of the chilly water.

"How did it go?" Lodan asked.

I gave them a quick debriefing and neither was overly surprised.

"Hey, I take back all the crazy things I said about your dad only dating Henley for her name," Lodan said. "I can see now that it's her voice that is magnetic. I could listen to her talk all day."

"Well, now you'll have the chance to," Mateo pointed out. "She'll be helping take care of our niece or nephew."

"Just so that the kid knows we already called the spot of favorite non-blood, but better than blood anyway relatives," Lodan said.

"Did he get into the champagne?" I asked Mateo.

He laughed and held up his thumb and first finger in a mock measurement. "Maybe just a little."

I put my arms around both of them and they threw theirs around me. "Ahh, Lake Cornucopia, tonight it's a whole new set of colors." I sighed. "Life feels pretty good, doesn't it?"

We looked out at the now clear, star-filled sky and the gently swaying purple and blue waves that waltzed across the lake's surface. From back at the tent the DJ announced, "I'd never normally play such a sad song at a wedding but I had a requester that ensured it would make at least four people here very happy. Here you go."

And the first few notes of "Desperado" by The Eagles floated across the air. Lodan and I shared a smile, eyes dancing, and at the same moment declared this selection, "Vintage."

Acknowledgements

This book began as a need to explore the circumstances that would compel a compassionate and kind young woman to take her sister's child and raise him as her own. However, as the characters came to life, it evolved into an exploration of truth and the consequences withholding it or hiding it can provoke. Sometimes we aren't even honest with ourselves. Our fear of being rejected by our friends and families may cause us to push the truth deep within ourselves.

As was the case with many of the characters in this book, that buried truth sometimes festers like a sliver beneath skin. It may work itself out without intervention, but often the irritation spreads like an infection until we are consumed. It begins to eat away at our confidence, our personality, and our decisions. Perhaps when the truth eats at you like an infection, it needs to come out. Making these decisions takes courage and resolve. Hopefully, we all can find that courage when we need it. And if a loved one says they can't love us when we are being our true selves, maybe they should look within themselves and ponder their understanding of love. If you are not loved for your true self, then are you truly loved? On occasion we may have to let people go. It will be their loss.

People I won't "let go" include my four children whom I thank for understanding when I act like I am not "there" its because I am writing in my head and not because I'm purposely ignoring them; my husband for pushing me to make time for writing and for taking the time to read my fiction when he'd rather be reading non-fiction.

A fun piece of non-fiction included in this book is the town of Truth or Consequences, New Mexico. Thanks for being the perfect backdrop for part of my story. I hope you don't mind the fictional liberties taken. The irony is that I chose your town prior to developing most of the plot. Perhaps this was where the truth theme was born. The town, originally named Hot Springs, was selected from a number of applicants to permanently change its name to the title of the show, Truth or Consequences. Ralph Edwards, host of the NBC Radio quiz show aired the show from the renamed town on April Fool's Day in 1950. The change was no joke. In fact, Mr. Edwards returned to the town every year for the next fifty to celebrate their annual "Fiesta." An auditorium and park in the town are named in his honor.

I can't mention honor without noting how honored I am that my readers keep asking for more books. I appreciate your kind words and support. As a writer it can be scary to put your work out there for the masses. I wish I had the time to explore all the ideas in my head. For now I will write when I can and hope that you continue to support my work. I can't thank you enough. I'd also like to extend a special thanks to Ryan Wells for reading and providing honest feedback about the queer relationships depicted in this book. Continue to be the courageous and inspiring role model of what it means to be true to oneself.

Ryan's reaction helped reinforce what I'd hoped to be true. I worried that I would offend members of the queer community by writing in first person as a queer male when I am a straight female. When I began telling this story I had no idea the path it would take. Non-writers probably find this bizarre. As the author am I not in control? Yes and No. I try not to craft a characters' personality because then I fear it would feel crafted. I just start writing from their perspective and let their personality develop. I took this truth trip many times, sometimes driving the car as Lizzy, other times I rode shotgun as Lodan. I took their sexual and emotional journeys with them. I didn't know how they felt until they felt it. Ultimately, I realized the reason I should dare to publish a book written from a queer male perspective is simple. I didn't try to write from a queer male perspective. I wrote how Lodan and Mateo felt when they experienced an undeniable attraction toward one another. I wrote how it felt to fall in love without any guarantees of what will happen. These feelings are universal and not gender specific. Desire, friendship, fear, love, all of our feelings are not driven by gender or sexual preference. They are driven by the fact that we are humans who make connections that can't be denied. When I got that straight in my head, I let go of (most of) that fear of offending readers.

    I hope you all love Lizzy, Lodan and Mateo as much as I do not because of whom they love, but because of how they love. Thank you for taking time to read this book. Please pass it on to friends and family who you think would like it. And if I did offend you in any way, that was not my intent. The truth is, we are all human and therefore as fallible as we are loveable. If you are a member of the LGBTQ community or want to be but are hiding your true self out of fear, please check out The Trevor Project. Be true to you.

Thanks for reading.
RR

About the Author

Rochelle Ransom has been writing books since she was a young girl. She grew up in a small rural town in western New York with little access to TV. This led to an overzealous imagination, a pet chicken named Superchick and a memorable and cherished childhood. Her sister was her first reader and critic. She'd find Rochelle's stories sitting around the house in random notebooks and read them, only to discover they usually had no ending.

After graduating from the S.I. Newhouse School at Syracuse University and obtaining her masters in writing from Emerson College, her characters were more dynamic, persistent and willing to stick around for an ending. However, there was little time for writing once her life became consumed with career, marriage, and four kids. After much support and encouragement from her family she brings you this third book in her collection of stories set in Laketown, NY.

Rochelle lives in Virginia with her family and two dogs, Truffles and Husker.

Other books by Rochelle Ransom:
The Keeping
Fractured Fate

Made in the USA
Middletown, DE
06 September 2023

38028876R00209